The September Girls

The September Girls

Maureen Lee

ORION

First published in Great Britain in 2005 by Orion,
an imprint of the Orion Publishing Group Ltd.

Copyright © Maureen Lee 2005

A CIP catalogue record for this book is
available from the British Library.

ISBN 0 75284 752 X

Typeset by Deltatype Ltd, Birkenhead, Merseyside

Printed in Great Britain by
Clays Ltd, St Ives plc

The Orion Publishing Group Ltd
Orion House
5 Upper Saint Martin's Lane
London, WC2H 9EA

www.orionbooks.co.uk

For Charlotte and Patrick with love

Norman Longmate's book *How We Lived Then*, describing in detail how civilians coped during the Second World War, proved extremely helpful while writing *The September Girls*.

Part One

Chapter 1

September 1920

It was raining. It had been raining when they left Ireland that morning, had rained on the boat and still rained now that they were in Liverpool waiting for Paddy to arrive and take them to the place where they were to live.

Brenna moved impatiently from one foot to the other. Before the night was out, the Caffreys would have a proper house of their own where water would come out of a tap instead of a communal pump outside. And they'd have a lavatory to themselves where all you had to do was pull a chain and everything disappeared – no more emptying buckets in the cart that came around once a week and smelled to high heaven.

Where was Paddy? she fretted. He was desperately late. He'd promised to meet them at Princes Dock. The sky, already full of black clouds, was getting darker and, although it was only September, it was unseasonably cold. The big hand on the clock of the gracious building across the way had moved around twice: two hours. They'd been waiting two hours.

'I'm tired, Mammy.' Fergus pulled at her skirt.

'Your uncle will be here soon, darlin'.' At first, Fergus, six, and Tyrone, two years younger, had been enthralled by the startling sight of the never-ending stream of tramcars that came hurtling around the corner, sparks exploding from the overhead lines, headlights reflected blurrily in the wet road. But now they were bored. Brenna had been impressed enough herself, not just with the tramcars, but the buildings, bigger than any she'd ever seen, bigger even than Our Lady of Lourdes where they'd gone to Mass on Sundays.

And so many people! Hundreds and hundreds of them scurrying about underneath their black umbrellas, but getting fewer now as they climbed on to the trams and were whisked away to God knows where. More people had poured down the big tunnels leading to the ferries that took them to the other side of the River Mersey.

Liverpool must surely be a grand, rich place, she thought, because everybody was terribly well dressed: the men in suits, the women in ankle-length skirts, tailored jackets and big felt hats. One woman wore an astrakhan hat and a matching muff. Like quite a few others, the woman had given Brenna a very odd look. She must look a desperate sight in her black shawl and long skirt spread tight over her swollen belly, Colm's old socks and leaking boots on her aching feet, the toes stuffed with rags. She was worried she'd be told to leave her place at the very end of the tunnel where she and Fergus sheltered from the driving rain. She had a sharp reply ready just in case but, so far, no one had spoken.

According to Colm, the place where they were waiting was called the Pier Head. Every now and then he went for a wander round in case Paddy was standing somewhere else. He returned for the third time.

'Not even a sign of him,' he muttered. He looked worried, as well he might. Paddy had been sent the ten pounds that Colm had won on a sweepstake. It had been a miraculous piece of good fortune. He'd gone into Kildare with the horse and cart carrying vegetables for the market and an American, 'stewed to his eyeballs' according to Colm, had handed him a slip of paper.

'Take this, young feller,' the man had drawled. 'I'll be back in the good old US of A by the time the race is run.'

'What race?' Brenna asked when Colm came back, full of himself, and showed her the paper. He confessed he didn't know.

'What's that written on it?' Brenna could read very little and write even less, but Colm had been taught by the Jesuits in the village where he'd used to live.

'Spion Kop. And at the top it's got the name of the hotel where the American must have been staying: the Green Man.'

None of it made sense, but it turned out that Spion Kop was the name of a horse running in England in the Epsom Derby. The race had been over three days before Colm discovered that Spion Kop had won.

On his next trek to Kildare, he presented himself at the Green Man and produced the slip of paper. The guests had arranged a sweepstake between them, he was told, and according to the list the

4

winner was Mr Thomas Doughty, a rich American, not a common Irish labourer like himself who had no right setting foot inside the door of such a respectable establishment.

After a great deal of argument, and with the aid of a friendly guest who put himself on Colm's side, saying possession was nine-tenths of the law, Colm collected his winnings.

'I near but died,' Colm confessed when he got home, 'when they gave me ten whole pounds.' He spread the notes on the table and he and Brenna stared at them, unable to believe their luck. 'Indeed, that Blessed Virgin o' yours must've been smiling down on me the day I met Mr Thomas Doughty,' Colm said, glowing.

Brenna agreed. She had absolute faith in the Blessed Virgin.

Colm wanted the whole world to know about his good fortune. He wrote and told Paddy in Liverpool, announced it in the pub, boasted about it in the street, until the whole of Lahmera was aware the Caffreys had had a windfall. They'd been deluged with hard luck stories and people wanting to borrow a few bob. Brenna had been terrified, worried someone would break in and steal their precious money while she sat and thought of a million ways of spending it.

Then Colm's brother, Paddy, had written back suggesting he find them a splendid house close to his own in Toxteth. 'Send the whole ten pounds,' Paddy's letter said grandly. 'The landlord will want a deposit and I'll buy beds, chairs and a table so everything will be ready and waiting when you arrive.' In other words, they would buy a new life with their windfall and leave the row of two-roomed, single-storey cottages, more like cattle sheds, for a fine place in Toxteth.

Weeks passed before Paddy wrote and said to come quickly, he had a big surprise waiting. They took for granted the big surprise was a house and left straight away, wanting the new baby to be born in their new home.

Earlier, when Brenna had watched Colm slide the ten notes into an envelope then address it laboriously, his tongue sticking out the corner of his mouth, she'd said, 'D'you not think we should keep a pound back and buy ourselves new clothes for Liverpool?'

'The time to buy clothes is when we're settled. I'll get a good job, like Paddy's, and by Christmas you'll have a fur coat better than Miss Francesca O'Reilly's.' Colm was the most optimistic of men.

Only then, as Brenna sheltered from the pouring rain, did she remember that she'd never truly believed that Paddy had quite as good a job as he claimed. Somehow, she'd never been able to see Paddy Caffrey as a customs officer. He was a bigger braggart than Colm would ever be. Their mother, Magdalena, had been just the same when she was alive, insisting the Caffreys were related to some famous Irish poet that Brenna had never heard of.

Fergus and Brenna had been sick on the boat, and Brenna still hadn't recovered. Her legs felt like jelly and her heart was beating madly in her chest while the baby thumped out a tattoo in her belly. And now there was the missing Paddy and their ten pounds to worry about, making her feel even worse.

The rain streamed off Tyrone's woollen cap. 'We couldn't find Uncle Paddy anywheres, Ma,' he said chirpily.

Fergus began to cry. 'I'm cold, Mammy, and I'm tired.'

Brenna looked at her husband. 'How long are we going to wait, Colm?'

Colm shrugged. 'Let's give it till nine o'clock. If our Paddy hasn't come by then, we'll just have to make our own way to Toxteth. It's on the far side o' where they're building the great Protestant cathedral, so Paddy told me.'

'Did he send the address of our new house?'

'No, Bren. He was going to meet us with the key.'

Brenna bit her lip. 'Then do we know where Paddy lives?'

'I've got his letters in me pocket. It's Stanhope Street, number fourteen.'

'Why d'you think he hasn't come, Colm?'

He didn't meet her eyes. 'P'raps he got the day mixed up, or the time. P'raps he's come down with something.'

'Or p'raps he's drinking himself to death in some pub or other – on *our* money – or he's gambled it all away and there isn't a house for us to move into,' Brenna said bitterly. Paddy was a gambler to his bones. The thought that he could have been so traitorous caused a wave of dizziness to pass over her and she felt even sicker and longed to sit down – a cup of hot tea would have been more than welcome. They'd had nothing to eat and drink since early that morning. She hated feeling weak when she was usually so strong.

'He'd never do that, not our Paddy,' Colm said, not very convincingly.

'We were too trusting, Colm. We should've brought the ten pounds with us and found our own place to live.'

'Don't talk like that, Bren, it scares me. Ten pounds. Ten *pounds*!' His voice was horrified. Never, in all their lives, had they expected to have so much money. 'Our Paddy still might come.'

But by the time nine o'clock came, Paddy hadn't appeared. Colm asked a man in what direction Toxteth lay and he gave them some instructions. 'But you can catch a tram, mate,' he said. 'The number one.'

Colm thanked him, heaved the sack containing all their worldly possessions on to his back, and they set off. Despite the cold, the rain and Brenna's condition, there was no question of spending a penny on tram fares when they had four pairs of perfectly good legs between them.

The rain was lighter now, but just as steady, penetrating their thin, already saturated clothes. A whimpering, snuffling Fergus held his mother's hand, his body limp, so she had to drag him along when she could barely drag herself. There was a terrible ache in the pit of her stomach and her back hurt. Everything hurt, but most of all the strong suspicion – more a feeling of certainty by now – that Paddy Caffrey had betrayed them and the new life would turn out to be worse than the old.

At this time of night, the centre of Liverpool was almost deserted, not that Brenna noticed. She walked with her eyes fixed on the ground, only looking up now and then to make sure Colm was still in sight, striding confidently along, Tyrone running at his heels. She didn't notice the grand office buildings that they passed, the big shops, the rowdy pubs, and was only vaguely conscious of a slight hissing noise coming from the gas lamps, which gave off a dim, yellowish glow.

Suddenly, Colm stopped and waited for her to catch up. 'I've lost me way, Bren, but I think we're nearly there. I'll have to ask someone if they know where Stanhope Street is.'

A few doors ahead, a man had come out of a jeweller's shop and was in the course of locking the door. Colm approached and spoke to him. A minute later, he returned.

'Is it far?' Brenna asked hopefully.

'I dunno. He told me to get back to Ireland and take me filthy family with me.' Colm grinned, but his eyes were hurt. 'Ah, I'll ask this chap on the bike.' He flagged the man down and the bike wobbled precariously as it came to a halt.

'Brakes don't work,' the man announced cheerfully. 'Stanhope Street?' he said in response to Colm's query. 'Cut through Parliament Terrace right behind you, and you'll come to Upper Parliament Street. Turn left, and you'll see Windsor Street on your right. Stanhope Street is the second turning on the left-hand side.'

'Ta, mate. C'mon, Bren.' He and Tyrone went down the passage the man had indicated and disappeared.

The short wait had done Brenna no good at all. Sheer willpower had been keeping her going and she found it nigh-on impossible to get started again. She gritted her teeth and forced her legs to move, but the pain in her gut was sharper now, piercing.

'Mammy,' Fergus whimpered pitifully. 'I can't walk no more.'

'You'll have to, son. Hold on to me hand.' She turned the corner, bent like an old woman, staggering slightly, her breath hoarse in her throat. Colm was standing some distance ahead, the sack on the ground and Tyrone perched on his shoulders. They were in front of a row of magnificent houses set on a slight curve, wide steps leading up to the immense front doors guarded by two white columns.

'Come and see this, girl,' he shouted. 'It's quite a sight.' He hadn't the faintest notion how badly she felt. Somehow, somehow, she managed to catch up.

'There's a party, Ma,' Tyrone giggled. 'A party. See!'

Through blurred eyes, she saw an opulently furnished room with a sparkling chandelier suspended from the fancy ceiling, mirrors and pictures all over the place, and twenty or thirty people, as richly dressed as the room itself, standing around with drinks in their hands, laughing and talking animatedly.

Her tired gaze fell on to the room below: a basement, reached from the road by steep, concrete steps behind black iron railings, in which three women were loading trays with refreshments. Two of the women, dressed in black with frilly white caps and aprons, departed with a tray each.

'I'm hungry, Mammy,' Fergus whispered. He must have noticed the food.

Brenna didn't answer. Never before had she questioned her position in life. She was poor, had always been poor, and almost every person she knew was poor. There were a few well-off folk in Lahmera, the village in which she'd been born and bred: the farmer that Colm had worked for, the doctor, the bank manager, the solicitor and Francesca O'Reilly, who lived in a big house on its own at the edge of the village. Miss O'Reilly had been an actress in her younger days and Brenna had cleaned for her from the age of twelve until the day before she married Colm, but not even her house was half as grand as this one.

She looked again at the big room where the party was being held. Two women about her age were standing by the window laughing gaily over something. Their frocks, what she could see of them, were made of lace and trimmed with beads. One had a black plume in her hair, a silver necklace around her white, slender neck with earrings to match that shimmered and shone and danced madly when she moved her head.

It didn't seem fair. It *wasn't* fair that she should be standing outside in the wet, a new baby lying in her belly, her children starving, their clothes soaked, while these women, so handsomely dressed, fed off the fat of the land. A wave of bitter envy swept over her, so strong that she gasped, clutched the railings and stared at the women, wondering why it was that fate had treated them so differently. Then one, the one with the glittering earrings, noticed her staring and closed the curtains, a look of disgust on her lovely face.

'C'mon, Brenna.' Colm picked up the sack and began to stride away. Tyrone trotted after him.

'I can't.' The railings were supporting her. If she let go, she would collapse. The pain in her stomach had become unbearable and, with a feeling of horror, she realized the baby was on its way. 'Colm,' she called weakly.

He turned, saw her agonized face and came hurrying back. 'What's the matter, Bren?' His own face collapsed. 'Jaysus, Mary and Joseph! It's not the snapper, is it?' Brenna nodded. 'What the hell do we do now?' he asked wildly.

'Find a peeler,' she gasped. A policeman would tell them what to do, where to go for help. 'Hurry, darlin', hurry,' she urged when he stood there, unmoving, his mouth open wide enough to catch a fish. He raced off in the direction of Upper Parliament Street, leaving the sack behind.

9

'Come and sit on the steps, Mammy.' Tyrone put his arms around her waist.

'Not there, lad.' It was the house where the party was being held. 'Next door, and not on the front steps either, the ones at the side where no one can see.' There was a light in the porch, whereas the side steps leading to the basement were in darkness.

'There's a wee roof over the door where you can shelter from the rain.'

Brenna managed to struggle down the steps and seat herself at the bottom, her legs spread wide because it was impossible to hold them any other way. The lads squeezed each side of her: Fergus snuffling and telling her how miserable he felt, Tyrone stroking her neck and murmuring words of comfort.

And now, God help her, didn't she feel the urge to push? She desperately wished she was back in Lahmera where she'd have had a bed to lie on, where the women, her neighbours, would come pouring in to help deliver the baby, just as she'd helped deliver theirs. When it was over and the baby was lying in the wooden box that had served as a crib for Fergus and Tyrone, someone would make a cup of tea. The lads would have already been taken out of the way to another house and Colm would have taken himself to the pub.

She did her utmost to suppress a scream when she felt a pain between her legs, threatening to tear them apart. Her body arched, she uttered a low moan and Tyrone leapt to his feet and hammered on the basement door.

It was opened within seconds by an irritable-looking woman who snapped, 'Here's a farthing, buy yourself some chips. Now, bugger off, you little scally. I've a million things to do tonight.' She was about to slam the door, when Tyrone hurled himself against it.

'Me mammy's sick, missus.' He burst into tears – Tyrone could bring forth tears in profusion when it suited his purpose.

The woman poked her head out of the door and saw Brenna rocking back and forth on the bottom step, her skirt above her knees and about to give birth. 'Lord Almighty!' she shrieked. 'There's babies crawling out of the woodwork in this house tonight. You'd better come in. Mr Allardyce will kill me if he finds out, although I'd sooner be dead than leave a poor, pregnant woman outside in the teeming rain.'

Brenna was hauled to her feet by a pair of strong arms and

virtually dragged inside a warm kitchen full of steam from a kettle and various pans that rattled on the stove.

'You can't stay here,' the woman muttered, and Brenna was dragged again through another door into a cosy sitting room where a fire burnt in a small grate and brasses gleamed on the hearth. A yellow bird in a round cage chirruped a welcome and a ginger cat curled on the couch raised its head and regarded them sleepily. The two boys followed, Tyrone dragging the sack that was bigger than himself.

Brenna was laid gently on the floor and the lads were commanded to hide behind the couch. 'This isn't something for such young eyes to see,' the woman said sternly.

Tyrone said he'd better wait outside for his daddy, who'd gone in search of a peeler.

'There's a young lad with a wise head on his shoulders,' the woman said when Tyrone left. 'How old is he, pet?' She knelt on the floor and began to remove Brenna's shabby underclothes. 'Everything's sopping,' she remarked.

'Four.' Four-going-on-for-forty is what Colm usually said about his younger son, whom he preferred to Fergus, now sobbing quietly behind the couch.

'I thought he was one of the lads who sometimes come begging money for food. I'd give 'em more than a farthing, except they'd only come more often, poor little mites. What's your name, pet? I'm Nancy Gates.'

'Brenna Caffrey. That's Fergus crying and Tyrone who's gone to wait for his da.' She felt much better in the warmth, her heart was beating normally and the urge to push had gone – perhaps it was panic and fear that had brought it on. Nancy Gates seemed very capable. A big, raw-boned woman in her forties with a deep voice, massive arms and an impatient manner, her eyes were kind in her pockmarked face.

'And what were you doing, Brenna Caffrey, wandering along Parliament Terrace at such a late hour on such a wretched night when you were about to drop a baby?' She gave Brenna a look, as if to say she'd been remarkably irresponsible.

'I wasn't expecting the baby for another fortnight, was I? And as to the other thing . . .' She told Nancy about leaving Ireland and waiting for Paddy who'd been sent the ten pounds Colm had won to find them a house. 'We stood by the Pier Head for three hours, but the bugger didn't turn up. We were on our way to look for him when . . .' Brenna shrugged. Nancy knew the rest. 'You're a nice, generous woman,' she said, 'taking us into your house like this. It's not everyone who'd've done it.'

'It's not my house, pet. I'm only the housekeeper-cum-cook, although I live here, too. This is me own little sitting room and me bedroom's behind.' She shoved a cushion under Brenna's head. 'Mr Allardyce won't exactly be pleased if he finds out you're here, not that he's likely to, not tonight. His missus is upstairs doing the same thing as you are, having a baby, and making a great big meal out of it.' A thin scream rent the air and Nancy winced. 'There she goes again, poor lamb. *She* wouldn't mind you being here, not that she has much say about things since she married him.'

'Should you not go up and see to her?'

'She don't need me, Brenna. Doctor Langdon's with her as well as a nurse. All I'm fit for is boiling the water and having a regular supply of rags on hand. Which reminds me, I'd better put something under you 'case the baby pops out when we're not looking, like.' She disappeared into the kitchen and came back with a thin sheet that was in better condition than the ones Brenna had brought with her from Ireland. 'I don't suppose there's a change of clothes in that bag of yours?' she asked. 'It won't do you no good, or the little 'uns, hanging round in them wet things – sounds like Fergus has gone asleep. You're likely to catch pneumonia.'

Brenna didn't answer. She uttered a groan, bared her teeth and managed not to scream when the baby signalled its imminent arrival for the second time that night . . .

'Nancy!' Marcus Allardyce roared from the top of the stairs that led to the kitchen.

'Yes?' After some delay, Nancy appeared at the bottom.

'I'd like some tea, very strong.'

'How about Mrs Allardyce and the others?'

'How about them?' Marcus growled.

'Would they like a drink too?'

'I wouldn't know. You'll have to ask them.' He had no intention of entering the room where his lily-livered wife was in the process of giving birth to their second child – a child he would probably dislike as much as the first. Anthony, five, was a sullen, uncommunicative boy and Marcus had a strong feeling there was something seriously wrong with him.

From her bedroom on the floor above, Eleanor screamed again: she sounded like a cat in pain. 'Don't push, not just yet, Mrs Allardyce,' he heard the doctor say.

'I can't help it,' Eleanor shrieked.

Was there any need for such a commotion? Giving birth seemed such a simple, natural act. Marcus walked along to his study at the back of the house, conscious of his feet sinking into the thick carpet. He trailed his hand over the Victorian desk with its tooled leather top, and stared with pleasure at the crystal inkstand with a silver lid and the other expensive accoutrements on the desk, including a black telephone with an ivory face. He derived much satisfaction from all these things, touching them frequently. All had once belonged to his father-in-law.

He could distinctly remember when he was a small child that his own father had possessed similar things. Peter Allardyce had inherited a thriving shipping company and a large house in Princes Park, but by the time Marcus was ten, everything had gone due to his father's incompetence, an addiction to alcohol and an obsession with fast women. His once pampered, extremely resentful wife had been forced to move with their two children to a small house in Allerton. She never ceased to complain to anyone who would listen, 'This isn't what I'm used to, you know.'

There was just about enough money left in the bank to live on for a few years if they cut out luxuries. Marcus and his elder sister, Georgina, had been removed from their private schools and thrust into local establishments where the education was abysmal and they had to mix with the children of the working classes.

Their father had stuck it out at home for a year but, unable to stand his wife's ceaseless litany of complaints, left and went to live with a woman who owned a millinery shop in Smithdown Road. On the rare occasions his wife and children saw him, he seemed exceedingly happy.

When Georgina was eighteen, she made her own escape and married a purser on the Cunard Line. Marcus and his mother were left with only each other to protest to about the grievous injustice that life had meted out to them.

Obliged to leave school at thirteen, he had gone to work for a firm of local accountants as a messenger and tea boy – at least it meant he had to dress respectably – and studied at night: bookkeeping, accounting, auditing, as well as the branches of maths he hadn't touched at school such as algebra, geometry and calculus. The firm had the *Financial Times* delivered daily and he discovered stocks and shares and read about the vagaries of the stock market.

By the time he was sixteen, he had become a junior clerk, but there was no chance of becoming a fully-fledged accountant without qualifications that he sadly lacked. Apart from which, even with qualifications, if the firm took him on as a trainee, he would have to pay a lump sum that would be returned to him in the form of wages. It was out of the question. His mother was getting frail and even more demanding. His salary was barely enough for them to live on.

Upstairs, Eleanor screamed again and he wondered where the tea was that he'd asked for. He heard footsteps coming down the stairs and a male voice called, 'Mr Allardyce?'

It was Dr Langdon. Marcus went into the hall. The doctor beamed at him. 'You'll be pleased to know that you are now the father of a healthy baby girl. Your wife is as well as can be expected. She's a delicate woman and having babies isn't easy for her. She – and the baby – are waiting for you.'

Eleanor looked as if she'd just given birth to half a dozen babies, not just one. She lay on the bed, her face waxen, hair limp, eyes barely open, as if every single bit of energy had been drained out of her. When she saw her husband approach, she tried to lift her hand, but it fell back on to the coverlet as if it were boneless.

'We have a little girl, Marcus,' she whispered. 'I'd like to call her Sybil. Do you like it?'

'It's a pretty name.' He didn't care what the child was called. Dutifully, he looked down at the cradle beside the bed and saw a small, pale creature fast asleep under the lace covers. He touched the soft chin with what he hoped was a fatherly gesture, then, for appearances' sake, kissed Eleanor's wet, shiny cheek, murmuring, 'Congratulations, darling.'

'Tell Anthony,' she whispered. 'Tell him that he has a little sister. He must have been frightened by the noise.'

Marcus nodded, although he had no intention of telling Anthony anything: the less he saw of his son, the better. He left the room as soon as decently possible – the doctor was muttering something about stitches – and returned to his study. On the wall behind his desk there was a large, framed photograph. He studied it thought-fully. In the gap at the bottom, between the photo and the frame, in perfect copperplate, was written '*H.B. Wallace & Co. 1918*'. Marcus was in the centre of the front row where the senior and office staff were seated: the under-manager and his assistant, two foremen, the accountant, the bookkeeper, the McMahon sisters – both typists – and Marcus's secretary, Robert Curran. The factory workers stood behind, fifty-two of them: the smaller men in the second row, tallest at the back. *His* employees. He rubbed his hands together. *His*.

Marcus was the owner and managing director of H.B. Wallace & Co., something that would never have happened had he not met Eleanor Wallace just after her fiancé had been killed in the first month of the war.

He was thirty, still working as a clerk, having realized to his dismay that, although he was perfectly capable of managing a company, he hadn't the faintest idea how to start one. He lacked any sort of entrepreneurial skills, unlike his great-grandfather who had bought an old fishing boat and ended up with a successful shipping company.

By now, his mother was dead and he had taken in a lodger to provide extra income, much of which went on better clothes, better food and good wine – he was a poor man with a rich man's tastes. He managed to save fifty pounds, although it took a long time, invested it in the stock market, convinced he would double it and make his fortune that way. Instead, within a few weeks, he lost more than half and was too scared to risk his money again.

Eleanor was on the verge of tears when they met. She was in the foyer of the Empire Theatre and grabbed his arm as he passed on his way to the gods where the seats cost only sixpence.

'Would you mind giving a message to my friends in the third row of the stalls?' she asked in a quivery voice. 'Tell them I've lost my ticket and I'm going home.'

'I'm sure the manager would believe you if you explained your ticket was lost,' he said coldly. She was one of those timid, helpless women that he particularly disliked – and far too well dressed for the management to think she would attempt to get in without paying.

'But I don't want to see *The Mikado*,' she wailed. 'I didn't want to in the first place, but my friends insisted. I'm too unhappy to sit through a show. I'd prefer to go home.'

He looked at her again. She was about eighteen, pretty in a pale, wishy-washy sort of way, wore a black silk-satin dress with a heavily embroidered chiffon yoke and hem under a dark-green panne-velvet cloak and carried a jewelled evening bag in her long gloved hands. His mother had bored Marcus silly describing the clothes she'd used to wear compared to those she had to wear now, and he recognized the woman's outfit as having cost a considerable amount of money.

'Why not let me take you home?' he suggested gently. 'You can tell me why you're so unhappy.'

'Thank you, but no. I shall telephone my father and he'll send the car for me.'

She had a telephone, a car and a chauffeur! He couldn't possibly let her go. 'What about dinner?' He smiled his broadest, most appealing smile – if the situation called for it, he could be the most charming of men and women seemed to find him attractive, which rather surprised him as he considered his features to be rather heavy: nose too big, lips too thick, bushy eyebrows too close together. His eyes were a dark, sombre grey, his hair brown and very thick, and he was rather proud of his lustrous moustache. 'I don't like to see a pretty lady so upset,' he said.

She smiled back, unable to resist. 'Oh, all right, but I shall be dreadfully dull company. But what about your own ticket for *The Mikado?*'

'I'm here to buy one for another night,' he lied. 'Will you excuse me a minute while I go to the booking office?' He wasn't prepared to lose sixpence if it could be avoided and was pleased when he got his money back.

From that night on, Marcus showered Eleanor Wallace with flowers and inexpensive, although tasteful gifts. He took her to dinner, the theatre, the Philharmonic Hall, to Southport on Sundays for afternoon tea in an elegant arcade in which a pianist played discreetly in the background. He was using every available penny to make her happy and rid her of the memory of the fiancé who had been killed in the war, to the extent that he sometimes went hungry and had to walk to his office because he didn't have the cost of the tram fare.

Eleanor was an investment and this time he was determined to succeed. An only child, her mother was dead and she would inherit her father's prosperous asbestos company, not to mention all his worldly wealth, including an imposing property in Parliament Terrace and a dark-brown Wolsley saloon with cream leather seats. The fact that she got on his nerves so much she made his teeth ache didn't terribly matter.

To his delight, Eleanor gradually fell for his charms and, six months after they'd met, they got married. The only thing that Marcus regretted was that his mother wasn't alive to attend the extravagant wedding.

He got on well with his father-in-law. Herbert Wallace considered Marcus a man after his own heart, the state of the stock market always at his fingertips, a way with figures, a thorough knowledge of business practice. It was a pity, Marcus had lied, that his own small tools company had come such a cropper due to criminal activity on the part of the chief accountant, causing the bank to call in their loan. By using up his entire capital, he'd added, he'd only just managed to avoid becoming bankrupt.

'I'm not going to let it get me down,' he said stoutly. 'I shall start again as soon as I've enough saved from my present job: I regard it as a temporary position.'

'Good man!' Herbert slapped him on the back. 'That's what I like to see: initiative. Look, why don't you come in with me? After all, once I retire, the firm will be yours. Why not get the hang of things now?'

This was something Marcus had been praying for. He managed to look pleased yet, at the same time, doubtful. 'Are you sure?'

'As sure as I'll ever be about anything.'

He was genuinely upset when, in the winter of 1915, Herbert died unexpectedly in his sleep of a heart attack, missing by two weeks the birth of his first grandchild to which he'd been so much looking forward.

Marcus recalled the night his son had been born. He'd been as unmoved as he'd been tonight when his daughter had arrived. The only person he had ever loved was his mother and he wondered if he was capable of loving another human being. What he loved most were things: expensive things like the house and the car, tailored clothes, handmade furniture, exquisite ornaments . . .

It occurred to him that he still hadn't had the tea he'd asked for at least thirty minutes ago. One thing the study didn't have was a bell rope to summon the servants – he'd been meaning to have one fitted for years.

He went to the top of the stairs and was about to call for Nancy when it occurred to him that the reason for the delay was that she had been helping with the baby's birth. He was about to walk away when, from the kitchen, he heard a woman laugh. It was a tinkling, joyous laugh and didn't belong to Nancy, whose voice was at least an octave lower. Curious, he went downstairs to find the kitchen empty, but the door to Nancy's sitting room partially open. He could hear women's voices inside.

'Two little girls, born within minutes of each other,' Nancy was saying. 'The September girls: Sybil and Cara, both lovely names.'

'Cara means "friend" in old Irish,' the other woman said. She chuckled. 'Ah, if I don't feel like a completely different woman now that's over! I could run around the block with a sack o' taters on me head.'

'You'd better not try,' Nancy advised.

Marcus crept over to the door and peered around. Nancy stood with her back to him and the other woman had eyes only for the baby in her arms. He caught his breath. He didn't think he'd ever seen anyone quite so beautiful before. She was sitting on the floor, her back against the couch, and looked quite radiant: blue eyes like stars in her thin face, a great mane of red-gold hair tumbling untidily on to her shoulders. She wore a nightdress of sorts, undone down the front, exposing her full, white breasts. A wave of dizziness swept over him and he felt a longing to touch them, squeeze the white flesh and kiss the rosy, swollen nipples, bury his head on their softness.

The baby was awake, the little girl: Cara. She waved her arms and made little birdlike noises. A tiny foot emerged from the shawl in which she was wrapped, kicking vigorously.

'Colm will be surprised when he gets here,' the woman said. She had a strong Irish accent. 'He was expecting us to have another wee boy.'

'Is our daddy lost now?' asked a small voice, and it was only then that Marcus noticed the boy sitting at the table munching a sandwich. He looked about the same age as Anthony and was a handsome little fellow.

'He'll be along in a minute, darlin'. Didn't he go running off in search of a peeler? What do you think of your new sister, Fergus?'

Fergus seemed more interested in the sandwich than the baby. 'She's fine, Mammy,' he said without looking up.

'It's time I made us a cup of tea,' Nancy said.

Marcus hurriedly stepped backwards. When Nancy emerged, he was standing in the middle of the room contriving to look extremely angry. 'What's going on?' he demanded. 'Did I hear the sound of a baby in there?'

'Yes.' The woman's voice was blunt and she looked at him defiantly. There was no love lost between them. 'The mother's name's Brenna Caffrey. I found her outside on the steps, so I brought her indoors. The baby came almost straight away. I knew Eleanor wouldn't mind,' she added slyly.

This was undoubtedly true. Nancy had too much influence over his wife. Marcus had long wanted to get rid of her, but she'd been with the family since before Eleanor was born – was virtually a member of it – and it was one of the few things over which Eleanor had put her foot down.

'How long will she be here?'

Nancy shrugged. 'Dunno. Her husband's gone in search of help. He should be back any minute.'

'Well, I want them out of here by morning.'

'All right.' She'd never addressed him as 'sir', as did the other servants.

'I think I requested tea earlier,' he said coldly.

'Sorry, I forgot. I'll make it now. Where would you like me to bring it?'

'To my study.'

'I won't be long.'

Marcus went slowly back upstairs and sat at his desk with a sigh. He thought about his wife, lying like a corpse within the silk sheets, unable even to lift her hand. She probably hadn't yet looked at the baby, let alone touched it, while a glowing Brenna Caffrey actually laughed as she nursed her little daughter. Perhaps he would find it possible to fall in love with a woman if she had a bit more life in her than Eleanor. Someone like the woman downstairs: Brenna Caffrey.

There was a loud banging on the basement door and Brenna said, 'That'll be Colm.'

Nancy went to let him in and a few seconds later he came rushing into the room like a madman, followed by Tyrone who looked as if he'd had a bath with his clothes on, and a tall, haughty nun wearing a black cloak that she removed to reveal a white starched bonnet with wings like a butterfly and capacious robes.

'The peeler sent me to a convent, St Hilda's,' Colm gasped. 'This is Sister Aloysius: she's a midwife. Jaysus, Mary and Joseph!' He collapsed against the wall and burst into tears. 'If the snapper hasn't come already while I was gone!'

'It's a wee girl, Colm,' Brenna said proudly. 'I've called her Cara, like we said we would if we had a girl, although you never believed we would.'

Sister Aloysius knelt beside Brenna and plucked the baby none too gently from her arms. 'Aren't you a clever thing, coming all by yourself,' she cooed, as if Cara's mother had had nothing to do with it. She laid the crucifix attached to a chain around her waist against the baby's forehead and said a little prayer in Latin. 'Is everything there?' she asked Brenna in a completely different tone of voice, quite steely.

'Yes,' Brenna replied in the same steely voice, having taken an instant dislike to Sister Aloysius, nun or no nun. 'Ten fingers, ten toes, two eyes, two ears, a nose and a mouth. And she's got quite a voice on her.'

'And lots of lovely hair, the same colour as Brenna's,' Nancy pointed out. 'Colm, will you get some clothes out of that bag for yourself and Tyrone and take them into the bedroom and put them on, otherwise you'll catch your death of cold. I'll make you both a hot drink in the meantime.' Colm and Tyrone disappeared into the bedroom. 'Would you care for one yourself, Sister?'

'No, thank you. I'll be on me way back, seeing as I'm not needed after all. Would you like me to take your lads with me, Mrs Caffrey?' Her eyes swept disdainfully around the small room. 'It doesn't look as if there's a place for them to sleep this night.'

'I've already told Brenna that she and Colm can have my bed and I'll have the couch,' Nancy said generously. 'The lads were going to sleep on the floor, although I'll be more than a bit short of bedding.'

'Then I'll take them,' Sister Aloysius said autocratically.

'Thank you, Sister.' Brenna felt reluctant to let the lads go, but knew they'd be far better off in the convent. 'I hope they won't be a nuisance.'

'We care for two dozen boys at St Hilda's, Mrs Caffrey, mainly orphans. None is *allowed* to be a nuisance. Where is the other child? I'm afraid there isn't time to wait for tea.'

Fergus and Tyrone were too tired to protest when Colm took them to the door with the nun. He returned minutes later, bleary-eyed, and Nancy disappeared into the kitchen. Brenna expected Colm would take a proper look at their daughter, instead he crouched on the floor beside them and said in a hoarse voice, 'I've news of Paddy, Bren. While the peeler was showing me the way to St Hilda's, he asked me name. When I told him, he wanted to know if I was related to Patrick Caffrey, known as Paddy, and I said he was me brother.'

'Oh, Lord, Colm!' Brenna said tiredly. 'What's Paddy been up to that he's so well known to the peelers?'

Colm bent his head and made the sign of the Cross. 'He's dead, Brenna.'

Brenna snorted. 'He's only twenty-eight and as healthy as a horse. He can't be dead.'

'He is, Bren.' Now the tears ran freely down Colm's gaunt cheeks. 'He was murdered outside some pub. It only happened last Saturday. The peeler said he was throwing his money around like nobody's business, and some bastard followed him outside and stabbed him in the heart. His pockets were empty when he was found.'

'Was it *his* money he was throwing around, or *ours*?' Brenna asked, going cold. She wasn't normally a hard-hearted woman but, at that moment, with a new baby in her arms and her beloved lads just taken to an orphanage, she felt more concern for their ten pounds than the fact Paddy had been murdered.

'I don't know, Bren,' Colm said despairingly. 'I don't know anything any more.'

'Paddy said in his letter he had a surprise for us. We thought he meant a house, but now I don't suppose we'll ever know what it was.' She looked down at Cara's pretty, sleepy face and felt herself go even colder. What on earth was going to happen to them now?

Chapter 2

He didn't know why he did it, why he came every day and waited in the pub across the road to watch and wait and hope that she would appear. The pub was called the Fish out of Water and that was very much how he felt. It was a rough place with sawdust on the floor frequented by the lowest of the low: braggarts and thieves the lot of them, plus a few women of easy virtue who had given up offering to sell him their grotesque bodies.

It was Nancy Gates who had told Marcus where she lived. She'd looked at him curiously when he'd asked what had happened to Brenna Caffrey, pretending merely mild interest in the woman whose daughter had been born five days ago on the same night and under the same roof as his own.

Answering without a trace of her usual insolence, Nancy had told him about the murdered brother-in-law, the mythical house, the fact that the two boys were still living in St Hilda's because the only place the Caffreys could find was a cellar in Upper Clifton Street where damp trickled down the walls and there was no light or heat except from a paraffin stove that stank to high heaven and got on the chests of Brenna and the baby, Cara. The kitchen and lavatory were shared with the whole house.

'And her husband, Colm, can't find a job, but it's not for want of trying,' Nancy went on. 'Oh, he's had the occasional few hours lugging meat around the market and sweeping up afterwards, earning enough to pay the rent, but that's about all. Every morning, he hangs around the docks hoping to be picked for a day's work, but he's a stranger there and the foreman prefers a known quantity, as it were. He's a fine, young fella, Colm Caffrey, as honest as the day is long.' There was a challenge in the glance she gave him.

'I see.' Marcus had nodded stiffly and gone to his study. He sat, staring at the things on his desk, knowing that Nancy had been dropping a heavy hint that he offer Colm Caffrey a job in his factory – she'd clearly taken the family under her wing. There was, in fact, a vacancy at the moment in the Pipe and Sheet section. All he had to do was have a word with the foreman and the man could have a job by tomorrow. It was that easy.

Next day in his lunch hour, Marcus had walked past the three-storey, terraced house where the Caffreys lived, not too far from Parliament Terrace. It was a miserable street of miserable houses all in a state of gradual decay: windows filthy, paintwork peeling, the steps up to the front doors crumbling dangerously. The window of the cellar was barely three feet wide and a foot deep, the thick yellow glass guarded by iron bars. He glimpsed the light from the stove, but could see no sign of the tenants. He noticed the pub across the way and went inside, causing quite a stir in his camel overcoat, dark-brown trilby and highly polished shoes. He ignored the menacing stares, ordered a whiskey and soda, and told the landlord to have one himself – it would help to have the man on his side if any of the ugly-looking customers decided to get unpleasant – and stationed himself at the window.

Nothing happened during the hour he stayed. He went again the next day and the next. On the third day, *she* came out, looking much too thin and pitifully poor in her black shawl, tattered men's boots, her skirt ragged at the hem. He had thought she would look humbled, considering her present circumstances, but she was smiling as she emerged from the house, the baby hidden inside the shawl. He let half a minute lapse and followed. She strode through a series of small streets – she'd obviously gone this way before – and he had trouble keeping up, yet it was only eight days since she'd given birth to a child. Eleanor hadn't moved from her bed. Dr Langdon came twice daily and there was a nurse in constant attendance seeing to her and baby Sybil's needs.

Eventually, the woman he was trailing arrived at the gates of Princes Park. She entered, sat on a bench and loosened the shawl, exposing her lovely hair and the baby's small, white face. It was a crisp, sunny autumn day and the park looked particularly beautiful, the ground scattered with golden leaves, the air fresh and clean and filled with the smells of nature: earth, cut grass and the lingering hint of flowers.

Brenna Caffrey was talking. For a moment, Marcus thought that perhaps she was mad, until he realized she was talking to the baby, pointing things out: a certain tree, the sun, the sky, the children playing who came from two totally different worlds: thin, mean children with scabs on their dirty faces, their clothes in tatters, and their feet bare; and bonny, well-nurtured, well-dressed children who'd been brought to the park by their mothers or a nanny, the smaller ones in expensive baby carriages. They watched their charges vigilantly as if to make sure the two different worlds didn't meet.

He stayed for half an hour, then returned to work, his mind a muddle, wondering why the woman held such a fascination for him. He was attracted to her, there was no doubt about that, and impressed by the way she smilingly faced adversity – it would be interesting to see just how bad things would have to get before she ceased to smile.

Perhaps that was it. He was waiting until the smile turned to despair before he offered to help, when her gratitude would be much more fulsome than it would be now.

There were three bangs on the window and Brenna flew upstairs to let Nancy in.

'It's a lovely day out there, pet,' Nancy panted as she struggled down the narrow cellar steps, a basket over her arm.

'I know, I took Cara for a wee walk to the park again. She loves it there.'

Nancy grinned. 'Did she tell you that?'

'I can tell from her face. I could swear she smiles when the sun shines on it.' Her own face probably did the same when she set foot outside. They'd been in this place a week and it was worse than a prison, what with the lack of daylight and warmth and a proper place to sleep. The furniture comprised two hard chairs, a table, a cupboard and a mattress on the floor where the three of them slept. There was mould on the walls, the shared lavatory was filthy and she only ventured into the kitchen to fetch water; she couldn't imagine preparing food in such a disgusting place.

'I've brought a few odds and ends,' Nancy announced, proceeding to empty the contents of the basket on to the worm-eaten table. 'Milk, some cold beef left over from last night, bread, an apple and an orange. The fruit and milk's for you,' she said in an authoritative voice. 'You're a nursing mother and you need all the goodness you can get.'

'Oh, Nancy!' Brenna cried gratefully. 'Surely the Blessed Virgin must have been watching over me when I sat on the steps outside your kitchen door.' If it hadn't been for Nancy, who'd been every day with food, they wouldn't have had a bite to eat since they'd left Parliament Terrace for a less than grand address.

'Well, the Blessed Virgin might have watched over you a mite longer and harder and made sure you found somewhere more salubrious to live.' Nancy was the first person Brenna had ever met who didn't believe in God. She also knew all sorts of desperately long words that she'd never heard before. What did salubrious mean?

'Now that you're here, and seeing as how you've brought some milk, would you like a cup of tea?' she asked. 'I boiled the kettle on the stove a while ago.'

'No, ta, pet. I can always have tea at home and I'd rather you drank the milk. How's Colm getting along?'

Brenna made a face. 'He's not getting along at all. He spends the whole day going from place to place, factory to factory, asking if they need a strong pair of hands, but even if they do, it's only for an hour or so. He's at his wits' end, Nancy. He's always provided for his family: now he can't and it's killing him.'

'It won't last for ever, pet.'

'I know.' Brenda sighed and her head drooped. 'We miss the lads something awful. Even our Tyrone is desperately miserable at St Hilda's and the other lads tease poor Fergus mercilessly because he's so quiet. The nuns are awful hard and very free with the cane. We're only allowed to see them once a week, on Sunday afternoon. All we could do was take them for a walk.' Her voice faltered. ''Least they're getting three meals a day and have somewhere decent to sleep. It's good of St Hilda's to have them.'

Colm winning the ten pounds had been the opposite of good luck, Brenna thought after Nancy had gone and she was left in the dark, damp room with only Cara for company. Back in Ireland, life had been a struggle – the whole family living in one room and sleeping in another – but at least she'd been able to keep the place clean, do her own cooking, wash the clothes and hang them in the fresh air to dry. Colm had earned a regular wage and was allowed to bring home any fruit and vegetables that were going spare. They'd had meat for their Sunday dinner, even if it was only the cheapest cut. Any spare pennies left over went towards second-hand clothes for the lads. The future held no promise of better times ahead. This was how it would always be: scrimping and saving, struggling to make ends meet. Brenna had wanted better things for Colm and her lads, and Liverpool had promised this and more.

But now she would have given anything to have the certainty and security of their old life back. She recalled the morning she, Cara and Colm had left the big house in Parliament Terrace and made their way to Stanhope Street where poor Paddy had used to live. The rain had stopped, thank the Lord, and a weak sun shone from a pale-blue sky. Her belly still ached from the birth and her legs were a bit shaky, but otherwise, she felt fine.

'The landlord will surely let us have our Paddy's house,' Colm had said, as optimistic as ever. 'Even if he won't, it'll be full of Paddy's stuff that now rightly belongs to us.' He was upset over his brother's violent death, but too concerned about his wife and children to let it bother him right now.

Fourteen Stanhope Street turned out to be a clean, stoutly built house with a big, bay window downstairs and a freshly varnished front door. Colm and Brenna exchanged hopeful looks. 'How will we get in?' Brenna asked. With Paddy gone, there'd be no one to answer the door.

Colm knocked anyway and the door was opened almost immediately by a sharp-faced woman, as thin as a lath, wearing a black frock with a cameo brooch at the neck – Brenna had always yearned for such a brooch. The woman's grey hair was dragged back in a sparse bun at the nape of her scraggy neck.

'I understand this is Paddy Caffrey's house,' Colm said courteously. 'I'm his brother, Colm.'

'Then you understood wrong,' the woman said in a voice as sharp as her face. 'This is *my* house and Paddy Caffrey lodged here, that's the truth of the matter. He shared a room with two other Irishmen. He told everyone he was going to live with his brother who'd be over from Ireland any day now.'

Brenna felt bile rise in her throat. Paddy had been lying to them all the time. 'Can we have Paddy's belongings?' she whispered. The things could be sold and perhaps raise enough to get them back to

Lahmera. Colm's job had already gone to another man: their cottage would have another tenant, but at least they'd be in a familiar place. There were people, friends, who would take them in until they were back on their feet.

'What belongings?' the woman sneered. 'All he owned were the clothes on his back and a few ould books that I got sixpence for in the pawn shop – he owed two weeks' board and lodgings when he got himself killed. Now, if you don't mind, I've got work to do.' She made to close the door, but Colm put his foot in the way.

'But his job,' he said urgently. 'I thought our Paddy had a job with customs.'

'Paddy Caffrey never did a day's work in his life,' the woman replied. Her face softened slightly when, for the first time, she noticed the tiny baby in Brenna's arms. 'He led you on the way he led everyone on. All he had time for was the horses, the dogs and a pack of playing cards. Are you the one who sent him the ten pounds he kept bragging about?'

The glance she gave Colm was so baleful that he took a step back and looked almost ashamed. 'I am indeed,' he stuttered.

'Then you're nothing but a fool,' the woman said cuttingly. 'I heard there was some big card game and I reckon he must've lost the lot 'cos I never seen him again. But the night he died, so I was told, he was in some pub buying round after round, as if he was rich as Croesus. I'm not surprised he was followed outside and murdered for his sins. Wait here just a minute.' She hurried down the long hall that had marble-patterned oilcloth on the floor and flowered paper on the walls. 'I'm sorry about what's happened,' she said when she returned, as if she genuinely meant it. 'You're too trusting the pair a yis. Here's the tanner I got for the books. Your need is obviously greater than mine.' The door closed and Brenna knew it was no use knocking again.

Colm had insisted Brenna take herself and the baby back to Parliament Terrace where Nancy Gates was hanging on to their sack of possessions, to save them lugging it round the streets while they found somewhere to live.

Hours later, Brenna was still in the kitchen waiting for Colm to come back, feeling very much in the way, although the big, kind-hearted woman insisted she was no trouble. 'It's nice to have someone to talk to while I get the dinner ready,' she said. She wasn't the only servant, she explained. There was Phyllis, the maid, who was bad on her feet, never smiled and lived out, and Mrs Snaith who came three mornings a week to do the cleaning. And a lovely China-woman, Mollie Chang, did the washing, collecting it on Monday and bringing it back a week later when she would take away another enormous pile. 'She ties it in a bundle and carries it on her head.' One of the men from the factory doubled up as a chauffeur when one was needed. 'He's called Lennie Beal.'

When Cara fell asleep, Brenna laid her on the couch in the sitting room and gave their saviour a hand. The smell of roasting meat wafted from the oven and a suet pudding filled with dried fruit boiled on the stove that had all of six rings: Nancy said the pudding was called spotted dick. Brenna peeled taters, scraped carrots and shelled peas, as she'd used to do in Lahmera, sitting in the open doorway of her home, the bowl balanced in the droop of her skirt, talking to the women across the narrow street who were doing the same thing. She prepared a tray of tea and biscuits for Nancy to take upstairs to the nurse who was looking after Mrs Allardyce and the new baby, and made tea for themselves.

'How is Mrs Allardyce today?' she asked when Nancy came back, looking sober.

'Poorly. Eleanor's not a strong woman and having babies takes it out of her more than it does most. She hasn't moved from her bed and the baby's hardly stopped crying.' Nancy gave her visitor a shrewd look. 'You probably won't believe this, considering the position you're in right now, but you're very lucky, Brenna. You've got your health and strength, two lovely lads, a perfect baby who hardly cries at all and a tall, handsome husband who thinks the world of you. Eleanor has none of these things. Even her son, Anthony, is a rum sort of child. He sits in his room, hour after hour, refusing to talk to a soul. Saying that, I love the bones of him.' She sighed deeply. 'Lord knows what goes on in that little head of his.'

It was late when Colm arrived, weary and downhearted. 'I've found somewhere,' he said in a despairing voice. 'An underground room, not all that far away, in Upper Clifton Street. It's not big enough for Fergus and Tyrone to live with us, so I've been round to St Hilda's and they said they'll keep 'em until we find somewhere bigger.'

'I'm not going anywhere without me lads!'

'I'm afraid we've no choice, Bren.' Some of Colm's confidence returned. 'It won't be for long, luv. I'll get meself a good job soon, you'll see.'

Now, eight days later, there was no sign of a job, good or bad, and Brenna was stuck in her prison with nothing to do all day except go for walks. There was no food to cook, no house to clean, no one living next door to jangle with, no children to tell stories to, only Cara who couldn't understand. The baby's nappies – an old sheet ripped into squares – were dried on a piece of rope strung across the room, then aired on the back of a chair in front of the evil-smelling stove that made Brenna and Cara cough if it was turned too high.

Nancy had given her a pile of magazines, *Woman's Weekly* they were called, but Brenna was too ashamed to say she could hardly read. She looked at the pictures of mouth-watering pies, smooth sponge cakes, feathered hats, shoes with pointed toes, embroidered linen, tapestry cushion covers, a cottage with a thatched roof, bowls of flowers beautifully arranged and lacy jumpers to knit yourself. The pictures belonged to a life she'd never known and, in her bleak state of mind, wondered if she ever would.

The night they'd arrived, she'd thought Liverpool a grand, rich place to be, but had discovered there were two sides to the city and it wasn't so grand and rich for some as it was for others. Her neighbours, for instance, were dirt poor: their children looked half-starved and their feet were bare, whatever the weather, and some of the little girls wore no underclothes at all. It was the same when she went to the shops for paraffin and saw the longing in the thin, drawn faces of people when they looked at the food they couldn't afford. They bought yesterday's bread, bones to make soup, broken biscuits. Colm said they came into the market where the vegetables were sold and gathered squashed tomatoes, cabbage leaves, rotten potatoes, worm-eaten apples and anything else the stall-holders had discarded as unfit for sale – if he saw anything half decent, he brought it home himself.

Upstairs, a man lived, Ernie something, who only had one leg and walked with crutches. She heard him leave every morning, the crutches tapping, his foot shuffling, taking for ever to reach the door. Nancy said he'd lost his leg in the war and that he caught the tram to

Exchange Station where he sat on the ground outside selling matches.

'Lloyd George – that's the prime minister if you didn't know – promised the veterans they'd return to a land fit for heroes,' she said bitterly, 'but who's going to give a job to a man without a limb? Or two limbs, come to that. Most of the poor buggers end up begging on the streets. Some reward, eh, for risking your life for your country.'

Each day seemed to last a lifetime and she missed Fergus and Tyrone more than she could say, not to mention the sun and the sky, the clouds and the green fields of Ireland. Colm could return home at any time: sometimes with a bob or two in his pocket, sometimes only pennies, and sometimes nothing at all. Brenna always met him with a kiss and a smile because she didn't want him to know how desperately miserable she was.

The monotony was broken in the most unpleasant way when, three weeks later, on a brisk, windy day, with only occasional spurts of sunshine, the peelers released Paddy's body for burial. A tearful Colm had no choice but to let his brother go to a pauper's grave, although he vowed that, if ever he came into money, he'd have him dug up and put in a proper grave with a marble headstone and his name engraved in gold. Brenna pretended to be sympathetic, but couldn't forget that Patrick Caffrey was responsible for the desperate pickle they were now in. She said nothing to Colm, but if she'd had her way, she would have kicked Paddy's body the length and breadth of Liverpool and back again.

They left the sad, dark corner of the cemetery in Toxteth Park where the dead were buried in sacks instead of caskets and walked slowly back to Upper Clifton Street, Cara asleep against Brenna's heart inside the black shawl. She was such a good baby, getting bigger and heavier by the day, full of beans when she was awake and thriving faster than Fergus and Tyrone had ever done due to all the milk her mother drank – Nancy brought round a whole pint a day.

'What's going to happen to us, Colm?' Brenna asked. It was almost November, a whole month since they'd come to Liverpool. Now the weather was getting colder. She dreaded to think what it would be like when winter came.

'I don't know, luv,' Colm sighed. He wasn't normally a sighing man and looked at the end of his tether. No one could have tried harder to find proper work. And no one could have been more patient than Brenna, never complaining when he came home penniless after another fruitless day.

'I've thought of something we can do,' she said. She'd thought of it before, but hadn't mentioned it, knowing it would upset him. 'I can go cleaning. Didn't I clean for Miss Francesca O'Reilly for all of seven years? I can do it again and take our Cara with me, and you can still look for work.'

Colm's face went so red she was worried he was about to have a fit. 'No,' he said angrily. 'I'm not having me wife keeping me and me kids. If I've not found a job by Christmas, I'll just have to think of making money some other way, even if it's only enough to get us back to Ireland.'

'What other way?'

'Never you mind,' he said, so brusquely that her blood ran cold.

'You're never going to do anything underhand, Colm Caffrey?' He'd mentioned more than once that not all the meat in the markets where he sometimes worked reached its rightful destination. The odd side of beef would disappear and be sold on the sly at a knock-down price. Colm, as honest as the day was long, considered it a quite disgraceful practice.

He put his arm around her shoulders and gave them a squeeze. 'I said, never you mind, Bren.'

They made a handsome couple, Marcus thought as he followed half a street behind. The husband was tall and as thin as his wife, with coal-black curly hair under a tweed cap. There was no collar to his shirt and his elbows jutted sharply through the holes in his jacket sleeves – the holes had been patched, but now the patches were hanging off. Unlike Marcus, whose own features he'd always considered rather coarse, this man's were perfectly regular, almost refined. 'He's a fine young fella, Colm Caffrey,' Nancy had said. Had the pair been dressed differently, they could have been a duke and his lady out for an afternoon stroll.

He'd been surprised, while sitting in his usual place by the window in the Fish out of Water, when *she* had come out of the house accompanied by her husband. He had followed as far as the cemetery and saw them disappear behind the hedge to the place where the nameless and the dispossessed were laid to rest. They must have come to see the brother being buried, the one who had gambled away their precious money – Nancy continued to keep him up to date with news of the Caffreys, possibly in the hope he'd come riding to the rescue of her new friends.

Marcus scoured the *Liverpool Echo* every night to see if the murderer had been caught, but there'd been no mention of it: the police probably had more to do with their time than spend it searching for one wastrel who had killed another.

The two people in front were talking animatedly. Then *he* put his arm around *her* shoulders and hugged her affectionately. They stopped and looked down at the baby in her mother's arms, then continued with their walk.

What must it be like to share one's thoughts and most intimate feelings with another human being? Marcus couldn't imagine it, yet there was something awfully appealing about having someone to talk to, someone who would listen while you tried to explain how terribly alone you felt. In his club, he had many friends, all male, who would crease up in embarrassment at the mere mention of such a thing as loneliness.

He turned on his heel and went back to work. He wasn't exactly neglecting the factory, but it no longer occupied his mind day and night. Nowadays, too much of his time was taken up with thinking about Brenna Caffrey.

'I was wondering,' Nancy said to Brenna a few days later when she came to Upper Clifton Street bearing two pork chops, half an apple pie and the usual supply of milk, 'if you'd like to bring the lads around to my place on Sunday?'

'But you always go to see your friends!' Nancy belonged to the Women's Social and Political Union formed by someone called Emmeline Pankhurst. They held meetings every Sunday afternoon. It was all to do with women having the vote – a vote for what, Brenna had no idea.

'This week I'm not.'

'Mr Allardyce might complain.' Brenna had never met Mr Allardyce and imagined him to be about seven feet tall and desperately fierce.

'Sunday's me day off and Parliament Terrace is me home. I can invite whosoever I like: it's got nothing to do with Mr A.'

'Are you sure?'

'Would I ask if I weren't?'

'No.' Yet Brenna had the strongest feeling that Nancy was deliberately missing her meeting just so the Caffreys would have somewhere to take Fergus and Tyrone. It wasn't always fine on Sundays when they went for walks, mainly around Princes Park, usually so pretty but downright miserable in the rain. Only once had they been taken to the room in Upper Clifton Street where their mammy and daddy and Cara lived, and the look of horror on their faces had upset Brenna to the core. Fergus had cried the whole time and said the room reminded him of hell.

'I'll make a nice tea,' Nancy offered. 'What time shall I expect you?'

'Just after two o'clock: the lads have to be back by four.'

A clock somewhere was striking two when the door of the convent opened and the Caffrey boys came out accompanied by Sister Kentigern, an elderly nun who worked in a draughty office just inside. 'I shall expect them to be back at the usual time,' she said curtly.

With three regular meals a day, the lads had put on weight. They had never looked so well – or so desperately unhappy. Fergus made straight for his mammy's arms and Tyrone for his dad's.

'Mind your little sister, me darlin' boy,' Brenna said when it seemed Fergus was intent on hugging them both to death.

Fergus started to cry. 'I wish I was Cara,' he sobbed. 'I wish me and Tyrone could live with you all the time like her, even if it is in hell. I wish we were back in Ireland. I hate Liverpool, Mammy, and I hate Uncle Paddy for not coming to meet us.' The lads didn't know their uncle was dead.

'He couldn't help it, Fergus. He'd have come if he could.' She wondered if that were true. Would Paddy have turned up, despite having lost all their money in a game of cards?

'There's a treat for you today,' Colm was saying. 'We're going to tea with Nancy Gates.'

Tyrone's dull eyes, usually so bright, lit up at the news. Fergus said he wasn't hungry, yet looked pleased. 'Will it be in the room with the yellow bird and the ginger cat?' he asked.

'Indeed it will,' Brenna told him.

The bird began to sing when they went into the warm sitting room, and the cat rubbed itself against everyone's legs. The bird was a canary called Eric, Nancy said, and the cat's name was Laurence. 'They're named after me two little brothers who died when they were only babies, poor little mites.'

'Our Cara won't die, will she?' Fergus asked worriedly.

'A big healthy girl like her? Not likely,' Nancy assured him. 'Now, I've only made ham sarnies with jelly and custard for afters as I expect you've not long had your dinner. It's more a snack than a proper meal. Come on now, tuck in, your mammy and daddy too.'

Fergus discovered an appetite, after all, and the sandwiches had gone when Brenna became aware the lads were being uncommonly quiet. 'Have you lost your tongues?' she asked.

Tyrone looked sideways at Nancy. 'She might cane us if we talk while we're eating,' he said in a small voice.

Nancy screamed that she'd do no such thing. 'Is that what they do in St Hilda's?'

'Yes. Our Fergus gets the cane nearly every morning for wetting the bed. Then he has to wash the sheet and hang it on the line.' Fergus hung his head and refused to meet his mother's eyes.

'He never used to wet the bed,' Brenna exclaimed hotly.

Colm said they shouldn't spoil the two hours by talking about the convent and asked Nancy about the union she belonged to. Nancy explained the members were known as suffragettes. 'They got together in nineteen hundred and three to advance women's rights, particularly the right to vote in elections. Some were sent to prison for their pains, where they were force-fed.' Her big, plain face shone with indignation. 'Two years ago, women over thirty were given the vote, but we shall keep on fighting until it's twenty-one, same as men. Woman form half the population of the country, yet they're treated like second-class citizens – no, not citizens, *subjects*. It's about time we got rid of the royal family and became a republic like America.' She suddenly grinned. 'I suppose it's time I came down off me high horse and made us all another cup of tea.'

It almost broke Brenna's heart to take Fergus and Tyrone back to St Hilda's after what seemed all too short a time. 'It won't be long before we're all back together,' she assured them confidently, although wished she had more faith in her own words. At least

Nancy had invited them back to tea next Sunday. It would give them something to look forward to: her and Colm an' all.

December came and there was ice in the air. The paraffin stove was turned full on and Brenna felt as if the fumes were choking her to death. Cara developed a wracking cough and her breathing was hoarse when she slept.

Christmas was only ten days away and the lads were dreading the idea of spending it in St Hilda's where they were already learning new hymns and special prayers to say at Mass. Nancy was going away for Christmas and Boxing Day. Apparently, she had an elderly father in Rochdale and wanted to keep him company.

It was going to be a really wretched holiday. Colm had lost all faith in getting a regular job and Brenna remembered his threat that he'd have to find some other way of making money if he hadn't found work by Christmas. It made her feel even more despondent. One morning, she felt so low that she sobbed into her pillow as soon as Colm had left, imagining him being sent to jail and she wouldn't see him again for years and years and there'd be even less chance of getting back her lads. It was the first time she'd allowed herself to cry and she felt ashamed.

She sat up, sniffed, wiped away the tears with the back of her hand and told herself sternly that this just wouldn't do. The tears had left streaks in the grime on her hand. Lord Almighty, she was letting herself go on top of everything else. When did she last wash herself all over? She couldn't remember.

There was still hot water in the kettle from the tea she'd made for Colm and she poured some into the metal bowl in which she did the washing, then took off her clothes. Using one of Cara's clean nappies, she washed every inch of her body, shivering mightily in the process. Then she did the same to Cara, although it was pity there weren't some nice, clean clothes to put back on their nice, clean bodies. If ever she had a penny to spare, she'd take herself to the public baths. She fed Cara, made some tea, dipping a chunk of dry bread in it, wrapped herself and the baby tightly with the shawl, and made her way to St Vincent de Paul's where they attended Mass every Sunday.

An arctic gale penetrated her thin clothes like needles. Brenna bent her head against the buffeting wind that kept changing course, whipping up the front of her skirt one minute, and up the back the next. She arrived at the church frozen to her bones, although Cara felt warm and snug against her breast.

The services were over and the church was almost empty: a few elderly women knelt at the front. Brenna dipped her fingers into the Holy Water, made the sign of the Cross and genuflected as she entered the back row where she sat for a while recovering her breath and freeing Cara from the tightness of the shawl. The baby uttered a little cry, stretched her arms and looked around the church with interest. She chuckled and her small body stiffened at the sight of the flickering candles.

After a few minutes, Brenna had recovered enough to kneel. She prayed to the Bessed Virgin as she had never prayed before, pleading with her to cast her gentle gaze over the Caffreys, help them, bless them, lift them out of the darkness into the light. 'We've never done anything wrong, Holy Mother.' Brenna squeezed her hands together until they hurt. 'We only came to Liverpool for a better life, but everything's turned desperately sour. All I want is a job for Colm, a decent roof over our heads and for me wee lads to come home.' As an afterthought, she added, 'Thank you for sending Nancy Gates to help us. I don't know what we'd have done without her. I know she's a non-believer, but you'd be hard put to find a kinder, more Christian woman.'

Brenna left the church feeling calm and serene, convinced the Blessed Virgin had listened to her urgent plea. She had forgotten to point out she wanted her prayers answered before Christmas, but felt sure the Blessed Virgin had probably guessed.

'By George!' Constable Stanley Beal gasped when he read the *Liverpool Echo* that night after a hearty tea. His stomach felt comfortably full.

'What is it, Stan?' enquired his wife.

'Thing here, under Public Notices.' The constable began to read. '"Will Colm Caffrey, brother of Patrick Caffrey (deceased), please contact Messrs Connor, Smith and Harrison, Solicitors, of forty-seven Water Street, Liverpool, where he will learn of something to his advantage." There's a telephone number. What do you think o' that, Irene?'

'I think that this Colm Caffrey is probably a very lucky man, but what's it got to do with us, luv?'

'I met this Colm Caffrey – oh, it must be nearly three months ago now. Wife was on the verge of having a baby late one night in the middle of the street and he was looking for help, a bit wild-eyed like. Took him to St Hilda's, I did, and a nun went back with him. Poor chap, only came over from Ireland that day, looking for his brother, Paddy. It fell to me to tell him that Paddy had been murdered.'

Irene shuddered. 'I hope that poor baby wasn't born in the street. Did you ever find out?'

'No, luv. I meant to, but you know how I am, always too busy.' Stanley walked twice as many miles and did twice as much work as the other men on the beat, at least so he had convinced himself and Irene.

'Is he still in Liverpool, this Caffrey chap?'

Stanley stroked his chin. 'I can find out. I asked him to leave his address at the station in case we wanted to get in touch with him about his brother. Seems we did a few weeks later, when the body was released for burial. Where's the scissors, luv? I'll cut this out and take it with me tomorrow.'

Marcus Allardyce also saw the notice. He looked at it for a long time, then cut it out, tucking it by a corner under the blotter on his desk. Someone else might read it and show it to the Caffreys, but he would keep it to himself. He still followed Brenna if she happened to appear while he was in the pub. He found the whole experience quite exhilarating, although couldn't have said why. The 'something to his advantage' that awaited Colm might change things altogether, and Marcus preferred them to stay the way they were.

Someone was banging hell out of the front door and no one in the house seemed prepared to answer. After a while, Brenna went upstairs, just in case, you never know, it was about a job for Colm. She opened the door and nearly fainted when she found a peeler outside. No wonder the door hadn't been answered: the caller had probably been seen through the various windows and everyone was lying low.

'Mrs Caffrey?' he enquired politely.

Colm must have decided not to wait until after Christmas before deciding to make money a 'different' way and, fool that he was, he'd already been found out.

'No,' she said unsteadily. 'The Caffreys have gone back to Ireland. I'm Mrs . . . Gates.'

The peeler looked disappointed, as well he might, probably hoping to catch a criminal before breakfast and get a medal or something. 'D'you have their address in Ireland?' Brenna shook her head. 'Ah, well, never mind. Thanks, luv.'

Brenna closed the door. When Colm came home tonight, she'd skin him alive. Perhaps he hadn't done anything – yet. But the peeler had had a reason for calling and it can't have been for anything good.

Nancy usually read the day-old paper when she stopped for a morning cuppa after she'd finished with breakfast and before she started lunch. Normally, she wouldn't have dreamt of reading the Public Notices, but her interest was aroused when she saw that one had been cut out. What did Mr A want with it? she wondered. He was the only one apart from her who read the paper. Curious, she was about to go up and look in his study in case he'd left the cutting around when Nurse Hutton came in and said Eleanor only wanted bread and milk for lunch. 'She's feeling very frail this morning.'

'I thought as much. I've just chucked her breakfast in the bin.' It had seemed such a waste: a fried egg, black pudding and two slices of nice lean bacon gone to waste when some poor souls had never eaten such a breakfast in their lives. 'I'll go up and see her in a mo,' she said.

'She's asleep right now, the baby too. Cried all night, she did: the baby, that is. It's probably three-month colic. Maybe she'll be better when the New Year comes.' The nurse sat down and folded her arms, ready for a gossip, although she never had much luck with Nancy who was always very tight-lipped. 'I've never come across such an odd household before. Mr Allardyce only pops in to see his missus when he comes home from work and never stays longer than a few minutes. That boy of theirs can't be normal, sticking to his bedroom twenty-four hours a day, and Mrs Allardyce is the unhappiest woman I've ever come across. It just shows,' she said piously, 'that money can't buy happiness.'

Nancy didn't answer. She didn't say that a blight had fallen over the house the minute Marcus Allardyce had set foot inside and set about courting Eleanor. She had recognized the man for what he was, even if Herbert and Eleanor hadn't. Herbert Wallace had been a generous soul who never believed ill of anyone, and Eleanor, delicate and abnormally sensitive, crazy with grief over the loss of Geoffrey, her fiancé, was easily fooled by Marcus's fake charm. Nancy had dropped a few gentle hints, but although she was regarded as a member of the family, she wasn't close enough to come out and say she was convinced that Marcus Allardyce was a rogue who was using Eleanor as a way of getting his hands on the family fortune.

And she'd been right. Herbert had hardly been in his grave five minutes, when Marcus's attitude to his wife had changed completely. He had no patience with her, spoke to her with the utmost contempt, didn't have a jot of sympathy when she came down with one of her awful headaches – her mother had suffered from the same thing. The worse he got, the worse and more frequent the headaches became, until Eleanor was spending days lying in a darkened room.

'I don't know how you stand it here, Miss Gates,' Nurse Hutton said.

'I'm all right,' Nancy murmured. Sometimes, she longed to leave and get a place in a more cheerful household, but couldn't bring herself to desert Eleanor. To change the subject, she said, 'Seeing as Mrs Allardyce only wants bread and milk, perhaps we could have sausage and mash for lunch.' She preferred a good old-fashioned meal to the fricassées, flans and exotic casseroles she was usually required to make.

'That would be very nice, Miss Gates,' the nurse said sadly when it became obvious a gossip wasn't on the menu, even if sausage and mash was.

That afternoon, Nancy went to see Brenna armed with milk, half a dozen sausages, slightly warm, two bananas, a small, crusty bloomer that she'd made herself and large pat of butter wrapped in greaseproof paper.

'We never used to have butter in Ireland,' Brenna said. 'It was always margarine.'

'You've told me that before. What's the matter, pet? You look a bit shaken.' Brenna had been a long time letting her in, and then had only opened the door a crack as if she were expecting someone different.

'A peeler came this morning. He asked for Colm. Oh, Nancy!' For the first time since she'd known her, Brenna burst into tears. 'Yesterday, I prayed to the Blessed Virgin with all me heart and soul to bring us some good luck for a change, but what does she do but send a peeler round to the house and make things worse.'

'I can't believe the police are being directed from above by the Blessed Virgin,' Nancy said dryly. 'It might be something to do with Colm's brother. Maybe they've found the chap who killed him.'

'I didn't think of that,' Brenna said tearfully. 'Oh, will you listen to Cara now? That cough's getting worse.' She picked up the baby whose face had turned bright red as she struggled for breath and gently rubbed her back. 'I'll give her a feed: it'll soothe her throat.' With a deep sigh, she opened her frock and attached the baby to her breast.

Nancy felt deeply saddened as she walked home. If only there was some way she could help the Caffreys, other than letting them have the Allardyces' leftovers and the milk that she paid for out of her own pocket. Brenna didn't know about that; Nancy had a feeling she wouldn't take it if she did, and so she insisted the milk had been left over from the day before. All Colm's attempts to do an honest day's work had failed miserably. They couldn't go on living in that vile hole in the ground for much longer. It was doing Brenna and Cara no good at all . . .

She still felt sad when she reached Parliament Terrace. What sort of world was it that allowed decent people like the Caffreys to have so little, yet someone like Marcus Allardyce have so much? Liverpool was one of the richest cities in the world, yet half its population lived in abject poverty. It was an absolute disgrace, Nancy fumed. At least there was hope for Russia now that Lenin was in power. In a Communist society, all goods would be publicly owned and be distributed by the state: from each according to his ability, to each according to his means. Such wonderful words! Nancy felt a lump in her throat, confident that one day, perhaps not in her lifetime, Communism would sweep the world and poverty would be a thing of the past.

She spread newspaper on the table and began to peel the spuds for dinner: plain roast lamb with mint sauce, she decided, seeing as she'd been given no orders to the contrary. Eleanor hadn't been much interested in food since she'd had the baby, and Mr Allardyce often forgot to make his wishes known before leaving for work – *he* seemed a bit forgetful lately.

One day she might go and live in Russia, she mused, and began to sing the 'Internationale' in a low, melodic voice. The spuds done, she peeled a parsnip and chopped up a cabbage, then wrapped all the wastage in the paper and took it outside to the dustbin at the bottom of the steps. It was then that she saw the gap where something had been cut out and remembered she'd meant to look for the cutting in his study – she liked to know what was going in. 'I'll look after dinner,' she told herself. But after dinner, Marcus would be there. 'No, I won't, I'll look now. It won't take a mo.'

A scrap of paper was tucked under the blotter on top of the magnificent desk that had once belonged to Herbert Wallace. Nancy wasn't the sort of woman who easily gave way to her emotions, but she felt the urge to jump up and down and shout, 'Hurray' when she read it.

'Will Colm Caffrey, brother of Patrick Caffrey (deceased), please contact Messrs Connor, Smith & Harrison, Solicitors, of 47 Water Street, Liverpool, where he will learn of something to his advantage.' There was a telephone number underneath.

'Well, blow me,' she gasped aloud, picked up the telephone and dialled the number with a shaking hand. 'I'd like to speak to someone about Colm Caffrey,' she said when a male voice answered.

'We have had at least a dozen Colm Caffreys call at the office today, imposters every one. Are you about to claim that you are he, and that Mr Caffrey is in fact a woman?' the voice enquired sarcastically.

'No, but I know him,' Nancy said breathlessly. 'I know where he lives. I know he comes from Lahmera in County Kildare, that his wife is called Brenna and he has two boys, Fergus and Tyrone, and a baby daughter, Cara.'

'Ah! I do believe we have located the *real* Colm Caffrey at last.' The voice sounded relieved. 'When can we expect him in the office?'

'Tomorrow morning, first thing,' Nancy promised.

Well, if anyone needed to learn something to his advantage, it was this young chap, Ambrose Houghton thought as he sat behind his desk opposite Colm Caffrey, his wife and small child. The man was badly in need of a shave, all three were dressed in tatters and the smell they emitted was vile. He wondered if it would look rude if he opened the window a few inches to get rid of it, but decided not to risk it. You could never tell, one of these days the chap might become a valued client. Anyway, the temperature outside was sub-zero and the smell was preferable to the cold.

'Shall we get over the formalities first?' he suggested. After asking the obvious questions, where was he born and when, his mother's maiden name, plus a repeat of the other particulars supplied by the woman who'd rung the day before, and having established that this was indeed Colm Caffrey, brother of Patrick, now sadly deceased, he came to the point.

'It would seem your brother didn't write and tell you about the house he'd won,' he said, and rather enjoyed the startled, unbelieving looks on the faces of Mr Caffrey and his wife. The latter had so far not spoken.

'*Won!*' the wife squeaked now. 'A *house!*'

'A house,' Ambrose Houghton repeated. 'He won it in a card game and wanted the deeds made out to you, Mr Caffrey. He said he would write and tell you that very night.'

'He *did* write and say he had a surprise for us,' Colm Caffrey said, 'but we thought we'd never find out what it was once Paddy had passed away, as it were.'

'It's a pity that the surprise has been so long in coming.' From the look of the pair, it had arrived just in time. 'It's an end-terraced house in Shaw Street, Toxteth,' he continued, 'number one, with two downstairs rooms, a kitchen, two bedrooms, a box room and a small yard housing the lavatory and washhouse.'

'And it's *ours?*' Colm Caffrey said in a strangled voice.

'Indeed it is, sir.' The solicitor considered it rather admirable to address such a ragamuffin as 'sir' but the man was now a property owner, which was more than he was himself.

'It's not like our Paddy to come and see a man of the law.'

'It is when it comes to property, sir. Documents have to be drawn up, stamped and signed, searches instituted, deeds altered. Your brother was very astute. He knew you couldn't just win a house and move in without a piece of paper to prove it's yours.'

'I never knew you could play cards for houses,' the wife said. She had released the baby from her shawl and it stared at Ambrose in a friendly fashion. He smiled and it smiled back.

'You can play for anything on earth,' he explained. 'According to Mr Caffrey, they played all night. There were five of them at the start, but three dropped out when the stakes got too high. At one point, he nearly lost all his money, then, "his luck turned", as he put it, and he won it back. It was early morning when they played one last game and his opponent wagered the house he'd just inherited from his uncle. Your brother must have had nerves of steel, risking all his money on the turn of a card.' He would have loved to be there. The only card game he knew was whist, which he played with his wife for milk bottle tops.

'I'm surprised our Paddy didn't shout the news from the rooftops,' Colm said with a rueful smile. 'It's not every day a person wins a house, but not even his landlady knew about it.'

'That's because the loser is a man well known in the area. He asked Mr Caffrey to keep the matter confidential, not wanting his spectacular loss to be made public and let people know what a fool he'd been. Now, Mr Caffrey,' the solicitor said briskly. 'I'd like you to sign a few papers – do you wish to leave the deeds and other important papers with Connor, Smith and Harrison? We can store them for you in our strong room.'

'Can we get the tram home?' Brenna asked when they were outside. She still felt exhausted after the walk into town in the freezing cold carrying a twelve-week-old baby who had felt more like a ton of bricks by the time they'd got there. 'Surely we can spare the tuppence. We won't need to pay rent next week.' She still couldn't believe they had a *house*.

Colm seemed amenable to the extravagance. They sat on the tram, hardly speaking throughout the journey, too stunned to believe their good luck.

'Our Paddy turned up trumps, after all,' Colm said at one point.

'Indeed he did.' Brenna felt ashamed of all the names she'd called her brother-in-law. She resolved to say a prayer for Paddy's soul every night for the rest of her life.

Shaw Street was only a short walk from Upper Clifton Street, and *their* house was the first in a neat terrace of eight, the front doors separated from the pavement by a single step. Colm produced the keys on a ring – two for the front and two for the back – and opened the door. They looked at each other, took a deep breath and stepped inside, Brenna and Cara first, into a narrow hall with stairs at the end and two doors on the left leading off: the first to a parlour in which there was a worn, but comfortable leatherette three-piece, the next to a sitting room that had a table and four chairs and a door leading to the kitchen. Brenda was surprised: she hadn't been expecting furniture.

Wordlessly, they examined the grubby wallpaper, the cracked oilcloth on the floor, the kitchen with a deep brown sink and wooden draining board and a cupboard to store food. One of the walls had been painted white and there was a tin of distemper on the draining board and a clean brush. They looked in the tiny yard, the stinking lavatory with squares of ancient newspaper jammed on a nail and two large spiders that raced up invisible threads and disappeared through a crack in the ceiling, the washhouse with its rusty boiler and lumps of coal left on the floor, then went upstairs to where there was more grubby wallpaper, a cracked window in the box room, the fireplaces in the bedrooms, like those downstairs, piled high with ash and rubbish. There were beds in every room: a double at the front, two singles in the back, and another single in the box room with two blankets folded on top. They were old beds, but perfectly respectable: the mattresses without a mark on them. After a while, they finished up where they'd started, in the hall.

'What d'you think, luv?' Colm asked.

'It's like a palace,' Brenna breathed, starry-eyed. 'Your Paddy must have bought the furniture and started to distemper the kitchen. The little bed in the box room was probably for him. Remember that woman, the one who gave us the sixpence, saying he was going to live with his brother? It looks as if he might've already been sleeping there. Poor Paddy,' she sniffed.

Colm put his hands on his hips and looked the walls up and down. 'The place wants scrubbing all over, Bren,' he said practically.

'I know. Let's go back to Upper Clifton Street and fetch our things. I brought a scrubbing brush and some floor cloths from

Ireland. We'll sleep in our house this night, Colm, and as soon as it's cleaned up a bit, I'll fetch our Fergus and Tyrone from St Hilda's. On the way, I'll call in Parliament Terrace and tell Nancy the news and ask her to thank Mr Allardyce: it was him who saw the notice in the paper and cut it out.'

'Do you think it's wise to take the lads away, Brenna?' Colm frowned. 'I haven't got a job. Even if this was the biggest and best house in the world, we still need to eat.'

'The Blessed Virgin's looking after us, I can feel it in me bones. You'll find a job any minute, by Christmas I expect. If necessary, I'll pawn me wedding ring to see us through.' She would have done it before, but had been worried she might never get it back. Now she felt sure it would be no problem.

Three hours later, when it was almost dark, and a mist had descended on the city like a thick, grey veil, Brenna banged on the door of St Hilda's. Cara had been left at home with her father for a change. The door was opened almost immediately by Sister Kentigern.

'I've come for our Fergus and Tyrone,' Brenna announced in a loud voice. By now, she felt delirious with excitement. There'd never been a day like this in her life before.

'But it's not Sunday, Mrs Caffrey,' the nun protested.

'I know that, Sister. I've come to take them away for good. We've got a house of our own now, with plenty of room for them to sleep.'

Sister Kentigern sniffed disapprovingly. 'You can't expect to take them at a moment's notice, Mrs Caffrey. Your request needs to be processed.'

'I can do it whenever I like, Sister.' Brenna brushed the nun aside and strode into the convent, shouting, 'Fergus, Tyrone, where are you? Fergus and Tyrone Caffrey, your mammy's come to take you home.' Sister Kentigern scuttled after her, having trouble keeping up on her old, stiff legs.

Brenna stopped and said kindly, 'I'm sorry, Sister, but I want me lads back and I want them now. It's been good of you to keep them all this time, but I can't wait another minute to have them under the same roof as their mammy and daddy.'

The nun looked at her shining face, then turned away. 'They'll just be finishing their tea, Mrs Caffrey,' she muttered.

'And where would that be, Sister?'

'In the dining room – go down the corridor to your right and through the door at the end.'

'Thank you, Sister Kentigern, the Blessed Virgin will smile on you for that.' Brenna strode along the corridor, Colm's boots slithering on the stone floor, and threw open the dining-room door with such force that it bounced off the wall and nearly came back and hit her. 'Fergus, Tyrone,' she shouted, her eyes raking the rows of white-faced boys for her own dear two.

'Mammy!' they shouted together. There was a clatter as they dropped their spoons, then came racing towards her. Brenna held out her arms. 'Come along, me darlin' lads. We're going home.'

They went to bed, Fergus and Tyrone, completely exhausted, having raced around the house, up and down the stairs, in and out of the rooms, at least a dozen times. Brenna felt obliged to go next door and apologize to her neighbour, who turned out to be a tough Scotswoman called Katie MacBride, for the unaccustomed noise.

'Och, it don't matter,' Katie assured her. 'It's nice to have bairns next door for a change. The man who used to live there was a miserable ould git. If you've a minute to spare tomorrer, girl, come round and have a cup of tea with us.'

Colm had lit a fire in the living room, using the bits of coal from the washhouse and all the wood he could find. He and Brenna sat and watched the flames die down. Tomorrow, he would look for work again and she planned to take the boys on a hunt for firewood. But that was tomorrow and tonight was tonight and they were happier than they'd been in a long time.

Eventually, after the fire had lost virtually all its warmth, Colm turned off the gas mantle and they went to bed: not in the big bed in the front room where Cara lay sleeping, but the little one that Paddy would have occupied had he been living with them. There, they made love, something they hadn't done once since they'd come to Liverpool because they'd felt too desperately miserable, and the dark, dank cellar hadn't seemed the right place.

Afterwards, they crept, hand in hand, to their own bed, glancing in on the lads on the way. They were dead to the world, one at each end of a single bed, because Brenna didn't have enough bedding for two.

'It seems so *big*, our house,' she whispered. 'We've got a landing, Colm. I never dreamt one day we'd have a landing.'

Earlier that night, Marcus had entered the house in Parliament Terrace and was just divesting himself of his hat and overcoat, when Nancy came running up from the kitchen. She actually smiled, took the clothes off him and put them on a hook on the wall. He wondered what on earth he'd done to earn such a friendly reception.

'Oh, Mr Allardyce,' she said in a voice throbbing with warmth, 'thank you for cutting that notice out the *Echo*. I found it on your desk. You must've meant to show it me, but forgot. I rang the solicitors, I hope you don't mind, and it turns out the Caffreys had a house all this time. I'm going to see it tomorrer. Brenna and Colm are ever so grateful. If it weren't for you, they'd never have known.'

Christmas was only three days away and still Colm hadn't found a job. He managed to earn a few extra bob delivering Christmas trees and fowl by horse and cart to rich houses in Princes Avenue and other fine addresses in the area, as well as packing boxes of fruit for those who could afford such luxuries. He brought home a bunch of purple grapes for Brenna.

'Are these pinched?' she asked sternly.

'No, luv, it's just a bunch that was over,' he answered with a straight face.

The house was warm: a fire burnt from early morning until late at night in the living room. With the extra money Colm was earning, Brenna had ordered a sack of coal and each day bought a penny bundle of firewood. She would lay the fire before she went to bed so it was ready to light as soon as she got up next morning. Katie MacBride from next door had unearthed two pairs of curtains, so thin and faded that the patterns were barely visible, but Brenna didn't care. They would do for downstairs until she could afford better. She tacked newspaper over the bedroom windows, bought a second-hand mat for in front of the fire, more blankets so the lads could have separate beds, and a clothesline for the yard. Spending so much money made her feel like the Queen of England.

Colm said one night that he was worried about her. The children were in bed and they were enjoying a few peaceful hours in the fading firelight, so saving on the gas.

'Why?' Brenna asked.

'You're too happy, luv.'

'Don't be an eejit, Colm. How can anyone be too happy?'

'You're acting like everything's perfect, but it's not.'

'It will be soon,' Brenna said serenely. 'The Blessed Virgin's answered two of my prayers by sending us this house and letting us have our lads back. She's bound to answer the third and find you a job.'

'I wouldn't bank on it, Bren. Anyway, I thought it was our Paddy responsible for getting us the house, not you know who.'

'It was her who prompted Mr Allardyce to cut the notice out the paper.'

Colm looked confused, but didn't bother to argue, just as Nancy had given up pointing out that if the Blessed Virgin was all she was cracked up to be, she wouldn't have allowed Paddy to be killed and let the Caffreys spend nearly three months in a disgusting cellar. 'I don't want you coming down to earth with a bump one of these days,' Colm said fondly. 'It might hurt.'

She sat on his knee and put her arms around his neck. They'd never had a honeymoon, but it was how the last few days had felt, as if they'd only just got married and everything was new and fresh. 'Don't be such an old misery, Colm Caffrey,' she whispered in his ear. 'Everything's going to be fine. Come on, darlin'. Let's go to bed.'

'In our Paddy's room?' Colm wiggled his dark eyebrows.

'We'll stop off in your Paddy's room on the way.'

'Our Cara can sleep here when she's bigger,' Brenna said as she stretched out on the narrow bed, 'and we can have our own big bed to ourselves. This is awful cramped.'

'I can't wait.' Colm lay beside her and put his arms around her waist. Brenna's head fell back and became painfully lodged between the mattress and the wall.

'Me head hurts,' she complained.

Colm slid his hand beneath her neck and pulled her towards him. 'What's that?' he muttered.

'Me head, you eejit.'

'No, under your head. There's something inside the mattress.'

'Let's feel.' Brenna smoothed her hand over the place where her head had been. It felt hard and lumpy. 'It makes a noise,' she said, 'a jingling sound.' She leapt out of the bed, sending Colm crashing to the floor, and pulled the mattress off. 'Will you light the mantle, luv? Did you leave the matches downstairs?'

'No, they're in me pocket.' Colm got painfully to his feet, rubbing his elbow.

For a few impatient minutes, she waited for him to find the matches, strike one and hold it to the gas mantle. A pale light flickered, revealing his mystified features, turning brighter until the room was fully lit. She sat on the bedsprings and examined the striped mattress, and saw that the seam was undone leaving a gap wide enough for a hand to go inside.

She reached and pulled out a small package wrapped in brown paper and tied with string. 'You undo it, luv.' She shoved the package at a still mystified Colm. 'It's likely to be your Paddy who put it there.'

Colm took ages untying the string. He removed the paper. The package had been wrapped again in a dirty piece of rag that he unfolded and lay on the floor so they could see the contents.

Money! A pile of coins and quite a few notes. After a long silence, Brenna asked in an awed voice, 'How much is there?' She didn't speak again until Colm had finished counting.

'Eight pounds, five shillings and threepence,' he said.

There was another long silence. This time it was Colm who spoke first. 'It's the stake money,' he said.

'The what?'

'The stake money. This'll be part of our ten pounds. I didn't think of it before, but if our Paddy won the card game, he'd have got his own money back an' all – *our* money. The thirty-five bob or so that's missing is probably what he was throwing around in the pub the night he died.'

'Jaysus, Mary and Joseph, Colm, are we not the luckiest family alive!'

'Our Paddy had to die to make us lucky, Bren.' He spoke bitterly. 'Don't ever forget that.'

'You know I never will,' she said quickly, although she had, if only for a second or two. 'We'll ask the fathers at St Vincent de Paul's to say a Mass for him on Christmas Day.' She stroked his lean neck. 'Come back to bed, darlin'. Let's go back to where we were before we found that package in the mattress.'

Later, when she was back in her own bed listening to Cara's easy breathing – her cough had disappeared since leaving the cellar – Brenna began to make a list of the things she would buy. The whole family would be kitted out with new clothes – Nancy had told her about a place called Paddy's Market where decent clobber could be had for next to nothing. She'd get a piece of ham for Christmas dinner and make a proper pudding for afterwards, buy Fergus and Tyrone a toy each: one of those cars that you wound up with a key and went by themselves, a rattle for Cara, a nice warm muffler for Colm, something for Nancy – a book, perhaps, one with big, long words that she'd love. And a little gift for Mr Allardyce, whom she'd never met, but couldn't be nearly as horrid as Nancy had painted him.

Thanks to Mr Allardyce, Paddy and especially the Blessed Virgin, the Caffreys would have the merriest Christmas that anyone in Liverpool had ever known. Not only that, when it was over, they'd give Paddy the proper burial he truly deserved.

Smiling, Brenna fell asleep.

Chapter 3

A cloud shaped like an old, creased dog crawled across the sky, slithering awkwardly in and out of the window frame. Eleanor Allardyce craned her head and watched the fluffy white tail disappear, wondering why church bells were ringing and why no sound came of the builders working on the site of the big cathedral that was being erected less than a hundred yards away, the thick walls looming over the yard at the back of the house. She remembered then that it was Christmas Day and a knot of something unpleasant formed in her throat when she realized Marcus would be home.

Since last week, she'd felt well enough to leave her bed for a few hours each day, but always went back before Marcus returned. 'I've done too much,' she would claim to Nurse Hutton. It meant she would see him for just a few minutes when he poked his head around the door to ask how she was. He only did it for propriety's sake, knowing Nurse Hutton would be there, fussing around. The same reason forced him to be polite, although she was aware of the disdain in his eyes.

Her bed had become a sanctuary of sorts since she'd had Sybil – three months ago tomorrow, she recalled with a sigh – but she couldn't stay for ever. The time had come to resume control of the household – and subject herself to the lash of her husband's cruel tongue. Anyway, Marcus aside, she was bored beyond belief and sick to death of the company of Nurse Hutton and the various night nurses who spoke to her in the same tone as they did to Sybil, as if she were a baby.

Oh, for a walk into town, a stroll around the shops, to look at clothes and treat herself to a leisurely coffee in Frederick & Hughes, her favourite store. She closed her eyes and visualized the gracious restaurant with its sparkling chandeliers and stained-glass windows, the clink of china, the scrape of cutlery and, best of all, the pianist attired in evening dress playing tunes from the latest shows on the white grand piano.

For years now, it was the only thing she enjoyed: shopping, getting away from the house. Marcus told her she was extravagant: he resented the fact that she had her own money, that *that* part of her life wasn't under his control, but Mummy had left her a huge sum when she died and it was kept in her own, private account. A few times Marcus had insisted it be transferred to his, but she'd adamantly refused. She shuddered, recalling how cross he'd been.

There were noises outside and she swung her legs out of bed and went over to the window. It had snowed a little during the night and a crowd of people were walking past: a man and woman and half a dozen children carrying brightly wrapped parcels, all looking incredibly happy and singing as they went: 'Away in a manger, no crib for a bed, the little Lord Jesus laid down his sweet head . . .'

'. . . The stars in the bright sky, looked down where he lay,' Eleanor sang softly, her face resting against the velvet curtains, 'the little lord Jesus, asleep in the hay.'

'Ah! You're awake, I see,' a voice said from the door, '*and* on your feet. There's a turn-up for the books.'

'Marcus!' She turned swiftly, stumbling in her haste. 'You didn't knock,' she said accusingly.

'You're my wife, Eleanor. I didn't see the need to knock.'

'Where's Nurse Hutton?'

'Looking after our daughter, perhaps, seeing as her mother has no idea how to do it.' His lip curled like an actor in a film. She half expected him to caress the points of his moustache and leer. He was immaculately dressed in a dark-grey suit with a faint stripe, grey silk waistcoat and snow-white shirt. Ruby cufflinks glinted on his wrists and his tie was secured with a matching pin – they'd been her mother's gift to her father on their wedding day. The recollection made her want to weep.

'I've been unwell, Marcus,' she stammered.

'But now you seem much better. I think I could hear you singing when I came in. I take it we can expect you down to dinner? The Manns and a chap called Thomas Percival are coming.'

'Thomas Percival? You mean Uncle Thomas.' She felt both delighted and surprised. 'I thought he was in India?'

'Well, now it would appear he's back,' Marcus said shortly. 'He rang the other day and virtually invited himself, said he was an old friend of the family.'

'He and Daddy were best men at each other's weddings. We always used to have Christmas dinner together until he lost wife and daughter on the *Titanic* and went to live abroad.'

Marcus shrugged, disinterested. 'Perhaps you might care to go down to the kitchen and see how the meal is progressing?'

'I will when I'm dressed.'

He left and her shoulders sagged with relief. She went over to the wardrobe and took out a plain morning dress — she'd change into something grander for dinner. In the small bathroom that adjoined her room, she washed and examined her face in the mirror: skin like wax and completely colourless due to the lack of fresh air and sunshine. And her thick, pale-brown hair was limp and lifeless, yet there'd been a time when everyone used to tell her how pretty she was.

She exhausted herself by giving her hair a good brushing and had to sit on the edge of the bath, breathless from the effort. As soon as Christmas was over, she'd go to Frederick & Hughes and get her hair cut, one of those new, short styles that were all the rage, and buy a frock, the very latest fashion, with a daring calf-length skirt.

But what was the point? What was the point of *anything* when she was married to Marcus who made her so unhappy all the time? It didn't matter in the slightest how she looked or even if she was the prettiest woman alive. She might as well take to her bed and stay there for the rest of her life.

Nancy had gone to Rochdale to stay with her father and wouldn't be back until the day after Boxing Day. Eleanor hadn't seen much of Nancy since Sybil was born. Nurse Hutton would frown and sniff disapprovingly whenever the housekeeper came into the bedroom and sat on the edge of the patient's bed 'ready for a natter', as Nancy called it.

'Mrs Allardyce isn't very well today, Miss Gates' or 'Mrs Allardyce has just taken a pill and needs her sleep,' the nurse would say, and Nancy would make a face that only Eleanor could see, and leave. Some nights, she'd slip upstairs while Sybil was being bathed and they'd have a little chat. Nancy had told her all about Brenna Caffrey whom she'd befriended.

Phyllis's sister, Gladys, filled in when Nancy was away. When Eleanor went into the kitchen, the smell of roasting turkey made her feel slightly nauseous – in her younger days she'd used to love Christmas smells, particularly mince pies. Today, she wasn't sure if she could face one, or even the dinner itself, with memories surfacing of old festive dinners when her father was alive and had invited loads of guests, not just the Percivals. She could only faintly recall her mother who had died when she was four and Nancy had taken her place.

'Good morning, Mrs Allardyce,' Gladys said sourly. She was a tall woman with an unnaturally long face and iron-grey hair, the stiff waves kept in place under a hairnet. Like her sister, she rarely smiled.

'Good morning, Gladys. How are you getting on?' Oh, she was useless with servants, didn't know how to be firm. Marcus accused her of treating them as equals. 'There's no need to say "please" or "thank you" to someone whose wages I pay,' he'd thundered once, and had told her not to be stupid when she'd replied it didn't hurt to be polite. Daddy, a self-made man who had known what it was like to be poor, had always made friends with the servants. He didn't care if his daughter spent time in the kitchen helping Nancy prepare the food.

'Well, Miss Gates left everything ready,' Gladys admitted reluctantly, as though she'd sooner claim all the credit for herself. 'The turkey was already stuffed and the pudding made. There hasn't been much more to do than prepare the veg. Our Phyllis is giving the dining room a last dust over before she sets the table. She'll be back in a minute to give us a hand.'

'Good,' Eleanor said awkwardly. It would seem the household could run smoothly without her.

She wandered back upstairs. The house seemed smaller than it used to be, and darker, the shadowy corners hinting at menaces unknown. It was also far too warm: Marcus badly felt the cold and insisted on huge fires in his bedroom and all the downstairs rooms. Dare she escape and go for a walk? She longed for the feeling of cold air on her cheeks, but Marcus was bound to find something wrong: she was neglecting her duties, neglecting her children, neglecting *him*, as if he were keen on having her company.

Talking of children! Eleanor steeled herself and opened the door of Anthony's room. He looked up immediately, his face, as usual, vacant of expression. His lovely golden eyes were always the first things that met her whenever she went in. He was sitting at the desk that he himself had turned to face the door – originally, it had been placed against the wall. He was the most beautiful child, rosy-cheeked with butter-blond hair and skin as smooth as an angel. In the summer, when he'd turned five, Marcus had insisted he go to school and had carried the child, screaming, out of the house that he was terrified of leaving, into the Wolsley, and taken him to see the headmaster of the small, private establishment that Marcus had attended himself. An hour later, they were back.

'They won't have him,' Marcus snarled when Eleanor asked what had happened. Anthony had scampered like an animal upstairs. 'The head didn't put it into words, but he obviously thinks the boy isn't right in the head.'

'We've always known he was – different, Marcus,' Eleanor said carefully.

'Different's one thing, being a bloody lunatic's something else. What's going to happen now? Will the boy stay in his room for the rest of his life?' He stamped into his study and was in a filthy mood for the rest of the day.

'Happy Christmas, darling,' she said now when she encountered Anthony's golden eyes. 'Would you like to come downstairs later? We have some lovely presents for you.'

The child just grunted something unintelligible and bent over the desk. Eleanor approached and gasped. 'Oh, what a beautiful painting!'

It was the scene from his window at dusk. The dark sky slashed with brilliant dashes of orange and purple, and houses opposite barely visible in the shadows, a smudge of yellow indicating the position of the windows. Gas lamps shone hazily in the passage below. The perspective, difficult from such an awkward angle, was perfect. She'd always found it hard to believe there could be something wrong with a child who was such a brilliant artist. Even when he was younger, he had impressed people with his crayon drawings. He could walk at twelve months, was physically strong, ate well and adored his picture books. Once shown, he could do anything: wash and dress himself, ride his little three-wheeler bike in the hall downstairs, play with his train set, even tie his laces, which

Nancy said was remarkable for someone so young. So how could he possibly be a 'bloody lunatic', as Marcus claimed?

She stroked his head, but he didn't move, just continued painting, adding dashes of grey to the sky that had looked perfect before, but now looked even more so. He never responded to her, to anyone's, touch. He'd never kissed her, put his chubby little arms around her neck, said mummy or daddy. Indeed, he'd never spoken a word that could be understood: just made funny, strangled noises that didn't make sense. He was remarkably self-reliant and never seemed to need company, just wanted to be left alone with his paints and books and toys. He even ate in his room: tasty little meals prepared by Nancy who thought the world of him. Eleanor always sensed her presence was unwelcome and he was wishing she would leave.

Dr Langdon had examined him several times and judged him a slow learner, but could offer no explanation as to why Anthony was good at so many things. 'It'll all come right eventually,' he usually said, rather patronizingly, Eleanor thought.

She came out of Anthony's room and stood at the top of the stairs. All of a sudden, her head felt as light as air and there was buzzing between her ears. Somewhere in the house was her husband: unapproachable, unfriendly, hating her. Her son was unlike other children, an oddity, and she had no idea what would become of him. Another woman was looking after the daughter she'd been too ill to look after herself. Eleanor's feet edged forward until only the heels were touching the top stair. It was Christmas Day, but there was no gaiety, no merriment in the house and, visualising the long years ahead, she couldn't imagine any change. This was how it would always be and she couldn't stand it any more. She swayed and the stairs, magnified and threatening, loomed up to meet her. She imagined tumbling down, head cracking, limbs snapping, and lying in a broken heap at the bottom, hopefully dead or, if not, terribly injured.

Somewhere, a door opened, and a horrified voice, Nurse Hutton's, gasped, '*Mrs Allardyce!*'

Eleanor grabbed the banisters, just in time. There must be a better way out.

Nancy was back when Eleanor went down to the kitchen the day after Boxing Day. A fire roared in the grate, the kettle was on the stove and she was standing in the middle of the room, arms akimbo, looking annoyed. 'That Gladys,' she complained, 'always leaves things in the wrong place. Where's the roasting tin, I'd like to know?'

'Why do you want the roasting tin now?' Eleanor enquired.

'I don't. I just want to know where it *is*.' She opened the oven door. 'Here it is! Silly woman, it should go under the sink.' She put the tin in its proper place. 'You look well,' she remarked, glancing at Eleanor's smiling face. 'It's nice to see you up and about again. How did Christmas go? Sit down, pet. I was just about to make a cuppa.'

Eleanor seated herself at the table on the same chair in the same spot – at the end nearest the fire – where she'd sat for as long as she could remember. She felt a glow of familiarity: she'd badly missed her little chats with Nancy. 'Dinner was nice – but not as nice as it would have been if you'd made it,' she added hastily. 'Uncle Thomas came and brought me the most beautiful shawl – do you remember him?'

'Of course I remember Uncle Thomas. He was your dad's best friend. I thought he lived in India.'

'He does, but he's back in England for a month, mixing business with pleasure. He's staying at the Adelphi for a few days before going to London, and has invited us to tea this afternoon at three o'clock.'

'Us?' Nancy raised her thick eyebrows.

'Us,' Eleanor said firmly. 'You and me. He was upset you weren't here. He looks upon you as part of the family. Oh, and he brought Anthony a lovely clockwork toy that he's played with ever since. And Marcus had invited an American couple, the Manns, to dinner. They're on a three-month tour of Europe and Marcus is hoping Mr Mann will buy brake and clutch linings from the factory for his car plant in Pennsylvania. They have three children, all grown up, and Mrs Mann said that she was in bed for six months after the first: twice as long as me. She was anaemic, whatever that means.' Eleanor had felt quite smug at the time. It would seem she wasn't the only woman in the world who took to her bed after having a baby. 'Anyway, the meal went very well, much better than I'd expected.'

'What did you do yesterday?' Nancy sat down and shoved a cup of tea and the sugar bowl in her direction.

'Marcus spent all afternoon in his club. There was a chess tournament or something followed by a dinner – men only – so

Nurse Hutton and I took Sybil for a walk. Anthony wouldn't come with us. When we got home Gladys and Phyllis had gone, so we made ourselves tea and ate down here. I quite enjoyed myself.' She could tell by Nancy's face that the inference she had enjoyed herself because Marcus wasn't there hadn't gone unrecognized. They never discussed him. Eleanor never complained and Nancy never criticized, although it was obvious she disliked him. 'I missed you, Nancy,' she said warmly.

'And I missed you, pet. I kept thinking about you all the time.'

'How's your father?' she asked politely.

'Old and curmudgeonly.' Nancy grimaced. 'The neighbours came on Christmas Day and we had a singsong. Yesterday, we went to a whist drive and he won a basket of fruit. Soon as we got home, he ate the whole damn lot and spent the night in the lavvy at the bottom of the yard. He was still there when I left, silly old sod.' She smiled affectionately all the same. 'Do you mind if I do something light for lunch, like cold turkey, pickle and bread and butter? I'd like to pop round and see how Brenna's getting on before we set off for the Adelphi. I didn't have a chance to tell you before, but she's got a house, a lovely little end terrace in Shaw Street and her husband's got a job at last. I bet they had a real, rip-roaring Christmas over there.'

'Cold turkey will do fine,' Eleanor said, doing her utmost not to sound as resentful as she felt. She didn't want Nancy knowing how jealous she was of the woman her housekeeper went to see every single day. She knew she was being horribly unreasonable. Brenna Caffrey had been leading a perfectly awful life, living in a cellar with a new baby born the same night as Sybil, her husband unable to find work, her sons in an orphanage. She'd kept hoping the family would give up and go back to Ireland. She wanted Nancy to herself, not sharing her with Brenna, no matter how badly off she was. And now Brenna had got a house and her husband a job and they'd probably stay in Liverpool for ever.

'What are you thinking?' Marcus asked loudly as he stared into his son's round eyes. The boy was sitting on the floor playing with the toy that Thomas Percival had brought. It was most unusual: a miniature carousel that turned when wound with a key and played a tune: 'Greensleeves'.

'Do you know I'm your father?' he asked in the same, loud voice. 'Do you know your name? Do you know *anything*?' He was beginning to lose his temper – five minutes with Anthony and he could easily kill the child. 'If you don't buck up your ideas soon, boy, you'll be put in a home.'

Christmas had been very embarrassing. Thomas Percival had asked to see his old friend's first grandchild so he could give him the toy.

'He has a very bad cold,' Marcus lied. 'The doctor has ordered him not to leave his room.' This Percival chap would probably expect the boy to shake hands, engage in conversation, even if it was limited, but Anthony was incapable of normal behaviour. He was deeply ashamed of his son. The situation reminded him of *Jane Eyre*, except it was a crazy child instead of a crazy woman hidden in a bedroom rather than an attic.

'A little peek wouldn't hurt, surely, so I can give him his present,' Thomas Percival persisted.

'We'll just have to see. He's not feeling very well. Last time I looked, he had a roaring temperature.'

Sybil had been brought down for the visitors to admire. 'She's just woken up,' Nurse Hutton said when she came in with the baby.

'Isn't she beautiful,' Mrs Mann had gasped.

Marcus had assumed she was just being polite. Whenever he looked at his daughter she was either asleep or bawling her head off and he thought her a scrawny little thing. He glanced at her now and, to his amazement, saw that Mrs Mann was right. He hadn't seen the child with her eyes open before, hadn't known they were a warm nut-brown. And her hair must have grown overnight because her head was covered with feathery curls the colour of the sun, making a shining frame for her tiny, heart-shaped face. She'd grown too, inevitably, filling out so that the scrawny look had gone. He felt a moment of terror: Anthony had been just as beautiful, but look at the way he had developed.

'Can I hold her?' He held out his arms, ignoring the look of amazement on the faces of Nurse Hutton and his wife.

The baby was placed in his arms and he stared down at her, willing her to acknowledge him in some way, as Anthony had never done. Suddenly, she chuckled and a hand reached up, as if to touch his face, but not quite reaching.

'She knows who I am,' he said, the words thick in his throat. This was his *daughter* he was holding, his own flesh and blood, the result of an unsatisfactory few minutes spent with Eleanor in her bed.

'Can I have her, Mr Allardyce? It's time for her four o'clock bottle.'

Had they not had company, Marcus would have given the nurse the sharp edge of his tongue. His daughter seemed perfectly content in his arms, chuckling away, waving her fists in the air. He could feel the slight movement of her legs against his midriff and wanted to keep her there, close to him.

'Mr *All*ardyce!' the nurse said sharply.

Reluctantly, he handed the child over. Tomorrow, he'd have a word with Nurse Hutton, impress upon her that *he* was in charge, and if he wanted to hold his baby, then he would. Another scene like this and she would be dismissed and a replacement engaged who would be told where she stood from the start. It was Eleanor's fault for letting the servants walk all over her, allowing Nurse Hutton to become far too possessive.

'You're an embarrassment,' he snapped at Anthony two days later as he stood at the door of his son's room and looked into the nothing eyes. 'An embarrassment. I'm ashamed of you.' It mightn't be a bad idea if he carried out the threat he'd just made and put the child in a home. In fact, the more he thought about it, the more he warmed to it. He'd tell everyone that he'd gone to boarding school. Some people, the really rich, sent their children away at the age of five. It was a shame because he was a handsome little chap and Marcus would have liked to show him off to the Manns and Thomas Percival – Eleanor had brought down some of his paintings and they'd been deeply impressed, had even asked if they could have one.

'A home, that's it. I'm putting you in a home, my boy.' What *use* was the child? None at all, so far as he could see.

The carousel stopped, but Anthony didn't notice. Was he having them all on? What went on in that head of his?

Marcus closed the door and returned to his study. Finding a home for Anthony was something he couldn't delegate to his secretary. The matter would have to be kept secret between him and Eleanor. She was bound to object, but Marcus was the head of the house and his will prevailed. Leaning back in the chair, he wondered how

Brenna Caffrey would react if she were his wife and Anthony their child. He felt sure she would fight him all the way and, in the end, it would be *her* who would win. It gave him a curious little thrill, the idea of having fuming arguments with Brenna, then carrying her struggling body to his bed.

He opened the top right-hand drawer of the desk and took out a white, Irish linen handkerchief with M embroidered on a corner in blue. It had been under the tree on Christmas Day, a present from her for bringing Nancy's attention to the notice in the *Liverpool Echo* that led to the husband discovering that he owned a house. It was rather ironic that he should turn out to be her saviour when he would have preferred Brenna stay in the cellar in Upper Clifton Street, watch her sink lower and lower, get paler and paler, the baby sicker. Only *then* would he have offered to help and would have expected rather more than a handkerchief in return. He had thought of offering the husband a good job in his factory, having a hold over her that way, but Nancy had told him he'd found one for himself. Marcus grimaced. His plans to capture the woman with whom he was obsessed had twice been thwarted but, one day, he was determined to get his hands on Brenna Caffrey.

'You can't send him away,' Eleanor wept. 'You can't.'

'I can, and I will,' Marcus said impatiently. 'I've found a place near Chester that will take him.'

'But a *home*, Marcus, a *home*! Only poor children go in homes, orphans.' She looked at him frantically. 'Is it a lunatic asylum?'

'It's called the Baldwin Home for Backward Boys. It was started by a Dr Richard Baldwin half a century ago. It costs twenty-five pounds a year: hardly a place for the poor.'

'Are the other children idiots? Are they *taught* things?'

'Here's the brochure.' Marcus tossed a well-presented booklet with a stiff cover across the desk. 'It doesn't mention classes, but there are outings, games.'

'Anthony needs to be taught,' Eleanor said stubbornly.

'What, and by whom?' Marcus demanded.

'I don't know.' She subsided into the chair in front of the desk. It was the last thing she'd expected when Marcus had called her into his study after dinner – last week, he'd summoned Nurse Hutton and given her a good dressing down. She wouldn't tell Eleanor what for, but had been very subdued and tearful ever since – and Marcus had been spending a surprising amount of time in the nursery with Sybil. Eleanor had supposed she was in for a similar telling off and was shocked beyond belief to discover he was intent on sending Anthony away. She had no idea what to do with Anthony, but wanted him protected from the outside world, not thrust into it all on his own, unsure what was happening. 'Perhaps we should get him a private tutor?' she suggested. 'It's worth a try.'

'It would be a complete waste of time and you know it,' he snapped.

'I don't think I can live without Anthony.' Her voice broke into a sob.

'Eleanor, that's nonsense and you know it.' He clasped his hands together on the desk, so tightly that the knuckles showed white. It was a sign she was getting on his nerves. 'How many times a day do you see the boy? Twice, three times?'

'More than that,' she argued. 'At least half a dozen.'

'And how long do you stay? No more than a few minutes, I bet. The boy is a burden. He – we – would be far better off if he were in a home where trained people would look after him.'

'I don't want him to go away,' she said stubbornly. 'He's not perfect, but he's my son and I love him.'

He turned away and made a dismissive gesture with his hand. 'He's going, Eleanor. I've made up my mind.'

She went straight to Anthony's room. He was sitting on the bed, idle for once, wearing the pyjamas he'd put on himself, and staring into space.

Eleanor sat at the bottom of the bed. 'Hello, darling.' His face didn't change, not that she had expected it to. 'Your father is going to send you away. I . . .' She dissolved into tears. She'd been feeling so much better since Christmas, almost her old self, although she'd never been a level-headed, rational person. She was much too highly strung, cried over nothing, lived in a state of continual anxiety over things that common sense should have told her didn't matter a jot. Christmas Day wasn't the first time she'd seriously considered ending her life. When Geoffrey, her fiancé, had been killed, she'd lain on the bed with a pillow pressed against her face, and it was only when she began to lose consciousness and she'd thought of how Daddy would feel if she died by her own hand, that she'd let the pillow go.

Now she was sitting on Anthony's bed and the tears wouldn't stop. She put her hands to her face and rocked back and forth, the pain of her misery impossible to contain. The tears trickled through her fingers and fell on her blue silk skirt.

But this wasn't the way to behave in front of a vulnerable child. She sniffed and wiped her eyes with the back of her hand, looked up and felt herself go cold. A silent Anthony was rocking back and forth, his hands over his face, aping her movements, except that there were no tears. She'd never known him cry.

'Anthony!' She pulled him into her arms and held him close until his heaving body was still. 'You're not leaving,' she swore. 'You're *my* son, and you shall stay.' She'd go back and tell Marcus this very minute.

But Marcus was adamant: he'd made a decision and refused to be deterred. He was about to write to the home and ask them to take him as soon as possible. 'Imagine,' he said softly, 'just imagine if someone waved a magic wand and Anthony was completely obliterated from your mind. Wouldn't you feel better without him?'

'Perhaps,' Eleanor had to concede, remembering how she had to steel herself to go into his room and how despairing she felt when she came out, 'but no one's going to wave a magic wand. Anthony's here, he's part of our lives and I'll feel worse without him.'

'Then you'll just have to get used to it, Eleanor.'

'I won't let you take him.'

'How will you stop me?' He looked amused.

It was a question she couldn't answer. He was twice as strong as her. She could scream and kick and protest as much as she liked, but it would do no good. Her child was to be taken from her and there was nothing she could do about it.

She was on the verge of hysteria when she went down to the kitchen. Nancy's duties were over for the day and the room looked unnaturally bare, everything put away ready to be taken out again next morning.

'Nancy,' she called. 'Nancy, where are you?'

The sitting-room door opened and Nancy poked her head out.

'Where you'd expect me to be, pet? In here. What's up?' she asked when she saw her distraught face.

'It's Marcus, he's putting Anthony into a home for backward boys. Oh, Nancy,' she sobbed, 'what on earth am I to do?'

'I'd best get going,' said a voice, and a woman with red-gold hair and pink cheeks came out of Nancy's sitting room. She pulled a black shawl over her head and nodded at Eleanor. 'If someone wanted to take one of my lads away, they'd have to do it over my dead body,' she said curtly.

Eleanor felt a rush of blood to her head. How dare this low-class, ill-dressed person make such a derogatory remark? 'Were your sons carried over your dead body into the orphanage?' She took it for granted the woman was Brenna Caffrey.

Brenna tossed her head. 'It was a choice between St Hilda's and a filthy cellar. I did what was best for me lads and took them away the minute I had the chance.'

'You don't know my husband. If he makes up his mind to do something, nothing will stop him,' Eleanor said hotly, wondering why she was bothering to argue with someone whose opinion she didn't give two hoots for.

'Then take the lad away yourself and put him somewhere safe. It'd show your husband he can't push you around.'

'There's nowhere she can take him, Brenna,' Nancy put in. 'Eleanor hasn't a single relative in the world.'

'Then he can come to mine,' said Brenna Caffrey.

It was the most stupid idea she'd ever heard. Move her dear little boy from Parliament Terrace, where he was used to every luxury under the sun, to a slum where he would be looked after by an ignorant Irish woman! It was out of the question.

But as the days passed and Marcus showed her the reply he'd had to his letter saying Anthony had been accepted by the Baldwin Home for Backward Boys and they would expect him the following Monday, her panic rose.

'What's the Caffreys' house like?' she asked Nancy.

'It's only half furnished: there's no carpet on the floor, not like here. Brenna hasn't got enough bedding, enough crockery, enough of anything, come to that. But it's clean and welcoming and full of love,' Nancy said gently.

'Anthony would hate it.'

'He'd hate that home even more. And you could go and see him every day.'

'You know how difficult it is to get him to leave the house,' Eleanor sighed.

'Marcus will have the same difficulty on Monday.'

Eleanor looked at her friend beseechingly. 'What would you do, Nancy?'

'Me? I'd take him to Brenna's. It wouldn't be for ever. Once Mr Allardyce realizes he can't get his own way, you can bring Anthony back. You'll have made your point. He'll understand the same thing will happen if he tries to send him away again.'

Eleanor shuddered, visualizing Marcus's reaction when he discovered Anthony had gone. 'Maybe he'd be better off in a home,' she said lamely. 'They might find out what's wrong with him. One day, we'll have to find out what's wrong, Nancy.'

'They won't find out in that place, pet. I read the brochure. It's where rich folk put their unwanted kids when they want them kept out of sight and out of mind.'

'I see.' Eleanor bit her lip. 'Then he won't go there. I don't care what Marcus says. He's *my* child every bit as much as his.' She squared her shoulders. 'Let's take him to Brenna's on Friday before Marcus comes home. If he rants and raves, I'll just have to put up with it.' She might even raise the courage to rant and rave back.

On Friday, they waited until it was dark when Phyllis had left and Nurse Hutton was busy with Sybil; she had hardly anything to do with Anthony and wouldn't notice he had gone. Marcus wasn't due home for another hour. Nancy carried a warmly wrapped Anthony in her strong arms and Eleanor a few clothes and bedding in a suitcase and a box of painting materials. They walked quickly through the narrow streets that were virtually on her doorstep, but where Eleanor had never walked before.

They didn't stay long in the Caffreys' mean, barely furnished house in Shaw Street: Marcus would expect his dinner the minute he got home and Eleanor to be seated at the table with him. She hardly spoke on the short journey home, thinking of the son she'd left behind in a house full of strangers.

★

'Can't he talk?' Tyrone asked.

'No, darlin',' Brenna replied.

'Is he a loony, then?' enquired Fergus. The lads had just arrived home from their new school.

'He might be, he might not.' Brenna shrugged. 'No one knows. Don't stare at him. You'll make him uncomfortable.'

Anthony was curled up in a chair, not looking at anyone, clutching the box of paints to his chest. From his face, it was hard to tell how he felt about anything. 'He's a rum child,' Nancy had said once. Brenna bent and tried to embrace the little boy, but although Anthony didn't exactly recoil from her touch, he stiffened, as if he'd drawn into himself.

'He's a fine-looking little fella,' Colm commented later when he came home from work: Anthony hadn't moved from the chair. Another miracle had occurred just after Christmas when Ambrose Houghton, the solicitor, had called to say a client of his, Cyril Phelan, was badly in need of a strong man in the yard where he sold building materials and was Colm interested? Colm had accepted like a shot and was now in receipt of the princely sum of twenty-five shillings a week.

'He's as handsome as a prince,' Brenna agreed, 'but aren't our two every bit as bonny?'

'They are indeed. Are you not giving him a meal, Bren?'

'According to her ladyship, he's already eaten.'

'She's not a titled lady, is she?'

'No, but she acts like one.' Brenna wrinkled her nose. 'She looks down on me as if I were a piece of muck.'

'She can't look down on you too far, Bren, if she's willing to leave her lad with you.'

'Ah, poor thing.' Brenna's face softened. 'For all her money, I feel desperately sorry for her. Fancy being terrified of your very own husband!'

'They're not all angels like me,' Colm bragged, and she punched him playfully.

Eleanor was hardly able to believe her luck. That night, Marcus ate only half his meal, then announced he was going to bed: he could feel a cold coming on. It didn't happen often that he was ill, but he usually made a huge fuss, disrupting the entire household. Nurse

Hutton was commanded to prepare a hot water bottle, Eleanor to look for Aspro and any other cold remedies in the house, and Nancy to fetch a dish of boiling water so he could breathe in the steam.

The three women exchanged relieved looks when Marcus's bedroom door finally closed. Nurse Hutton announced it was her night off and she was going to the Century picture house in Mount Pleasant to see *Broken Blossoms* with Lillian Gish and Richard Barthelmess and would Eleanor and Nancy please listen in case Sybil woke? The night nurses had been dispensed with after Christmas.

'But I doubt if she will. She's been as good as gold these last few weeks. I just knew it was that nasty three-month colic that made her cry so much.'

Eleanor went to Shaw Street to see Anthony the next morning. Nancy promised she'd go that afternoon and leave Eleanor free to do some longed-for shopping. He had settled in well, Brenna told her. 'He and our Fergus have taken a fancy to each other. They're in the back yard playing on the swing. Fergus is a nice, gentle lad, not like Tyrone who's a bit of a monkey.'

The swing was merely a length of rope suspended from hooks on each side of the door that led to a passage behind the house. Fergus was pushing and Anthony's eyes were tightly closed and his face, usually empty of expression, bore a look of dreamy bliss. She said, 'Anthony,' but he didn't open his eyes, so she went back indoors, terrified at the sight of her cosseted child playing on such a roughly made contraption.

'Is the swing safe?' she asked Brenna in the paltry little kitchen where she was drying dishes.

'Colm put it up. He wouldn't let our lads use it if it weren't,' Brenna answered crisply. 'Would you like a cup of tea?'

'Yes, please.' Seeing the collection of cracked cups and saucers presently being dried, she would have preferred to refuse, but reckoned Brenna, with her sharp eyes and sharp senses, would probably guess the reason why.

Brenna fitted very well into her new house, Eleanor thought as she daintily sipped tea in front of the fire and watched Anthony through the window. In her long black cotton frock with a frayed hem, her laughing little girl, Cara, tucked firmly against her hip, she flitted from room to room, dusting and tidying with her free hand, adjusting a row of holy statues on the sideboard an inch one way, half an inch the other, issuing orders. 'Don't push Anthony too high now, Fergus,' she admonished from the kitchen door. 'Tyrone, will you stop that racket,' she shouted when there was loud banging from upstairs. 'Colm brought home some old wood and nails and he's making a fort,' she explained to Eleanor. 'He'll be home for his dinner in a minute, Colm. He only works till midday on Saturday.'

'I'd better leave.' Eleanor jumped to her feet.

'Stay where you are,' Brenna ordered. 'You can eat with us. I've got onion soup ready in the pan.'

Eleanor obediently sat down again, wishing she'd had the courage to bring a supply of food, but had been worried Brenna would take umbrage. The subject of paying for Anthony's keep hadn't come up. Nancy said she'd discuss it that afternoon.

A neighbour came, a brawny, red-faced woman with black hair screwed tightly in metal curlers and a cigarette hanging from her bottom lip, as if it were permanently stuck there. Her voice was like a rusty saw. 'I've brought ye that toasting fork I mentioned, Brenna. It's forty years old, yet as good as new. I was given to when me and me ould feller got married.'

'Thank you, Katie,' Brenna cried. 'Oh, see! Now I can toast two pieces of bread with one hand!'

The woman gave the visitor a strange look that took Eleanor some seconds to realize was a smile. She smiled nervously back, wishing she hadn't worn her crushed strawberry velvet coat with the sable collar and cuffs and hat to match, but something plainer. She felt hideously over-dressed.

'If you ever want your fortune told, Katie's the one to ask,' Brenna told her when the woman had gone. 'She reads tea leaves for sixpence a time.'

'I'll remember that,' Eleanor promised politely.

Not long afterwards, Colm arrived, smelling of sawdust. He removed his tweed cap and muffler, and his black curly hair and flannel shirt were full of it. He was a fine-looking man: at least six feet tall, slimly built with dark, laughing eyes. The boys took after him, and Cara was a miniature Brenna, with the same golden curly hair. He gave Eleanor a friendly nod. Tyrone came running downstairs to greet him, Brenna kissed him on the lips and he took the cooing baby from her and held her with both hands above his head until she almost reached the ceiling. Cara shrieked with delight and he let her down and tucked her under his arm like a parcel. 'Where's our Fergus and Anthony?' he asked.

'They're in the yard,' Brenna replied. 'Dinner's ready, darlin',' she added as she went into the kitchen.

Eleanor thought enviously that the family were like a daisy chain, visibly connected to each other. The little house was warm and full of love, as Nancy had said. In this one important aspect it was far superior to the much grander house in Parliament Terrace.

'I'll be having a word with them.' Colm left the room with Cara still under his arm and she heard him say, 'Hello there, lads. Ah, I see you're liking the swing, Anthony.'

And Fergus replied — Eleanor would retain the memory of the exact words said in the same childish voice for the rest of her life — 'It's no good talking to him, Daddy. He can't hear.'

She got to her feet and put the half-drunk tea on the table with a crash. For quite a while, she stood as still as the statues on the sideboard while the meaning of Fergus's words gradually sank in and her heart began to thump crazily in her chest. She heard Fergus speak again.

'He's like old Mr Flanaghan who lived by us in Lahmera. Everybody used to say he was as deaf as a post.'

'And so he was,' Colm agreed. 'Do you remember Freddie Flanaghan, Bren?'

'I do indeed,' Brenna replied through the open door.

Eleanor pressed her hands against her cheeks. Slowly, very slowly, everything fell into place. Anthony had lived in a silent world since the day he was born. He didn't know she was his mother, Marcus his father. He'd never heard a word anyone had spoken to him, but had learned by imitation, by doing what he was shown, not what he was told. 'He doesn't know who I am,' she whispered when Brenna came in and began to set the table. 'Why didn't we realize? Even the doctor didn't guess that he was deaf.'

'I didn't realize and neither did Nancy,' Brenna said practically, 'but now you can do something about it.'

'Of course!' Excitement flowed through Eleanor's veins, making her body tremble. 'There are schools for deaf children. They can be taught sign language and how to speak — Anthony has a voice. He's not mute.'

'That's right, darlin'.' Her excitement was reflected in Brenna's blue eyes.

'He's terribly intelligent. He paints the most beautiful pictures.'

'He drew our Cara last night and Colm is going to make a frame and put it on the wall.'

'Your little boy, Fergus, is a marvel. Five minutes with Anthony and he just knew what was wrong. I'll always be grateful to him. Oh!' Eleanor badly wanted to weep. She had wept many times in her life, but never before with happiness.

Marcus replaced the telephone in its cradle. It responded with a curt click and he released the sneeze he'd been holding in during the latter part of the conversation, then loudly blew his nose. His cold, he suspected, was getting worse. He had just called the Baldwin School for Backward Boys and told them not to expect his son on Monday. He felt slightly numb from the news that Anthony was deaf, yet was just as glad as Eleanor. He no longer had to be ashamed of having an idiot child. And it was Fergus Caffrey, only six years old, who had understood the nature of his son's problem. Fergus had come back with him to the house, Anthony unwilling to be parted from his new – first – friend.

He still couldn't get over what Eleanor had done: removing the boy from the house, not caring about his reaction and raising him from his sick bed to tell him the news. He'd never seen her so excited, but it was no excuse for going against his wishes – and to take him to the Caffreys' of all places. The lives of the two families were becoming entwined in ways he'd never remotely envisaged.

Brenna felt very much out of sorts, although this should have been a good day, one of the best. For the first time in her life, she was actually pushing one of her children in a baby carriage! It was a giant Marmet model, a brilliant, shining black, and Cara, almost six months old, was fast asleep under the hood looking deceptively tiny. Brenna's shopping was stacked at the foot: a pound of mince, two pounds of 'taters, a bag of flour and half a pound of lard. She planned to make a meat pie for that night's tea.

The carriage had been acquired yesterday from Oliphant's pawnshop in Upper Parliament Street. Faily Oliphant had been asking ten bob, but Brenna had flirted with him madly and he'd let it go for seven and sixpence, the pillow and little quilted coverlet included. It had seemed a terrible extravagance, but Brenna had been finding it increasingly difficult to carry a baby *and* the shopping and it would be ages before Cara could walk properly and she and Colm might have more children and the carriage would be used again and again – or so she reasoned while she flirted with Faily Oliphant and considered parting with such a monstrous sum. The stake money was still kept hidden in the mattress in the spare room, very much reduced since the day they'd found it. And if they didn't have more children, why the carriage could always be sold, possibly at a profit, she'd thought that night, after she'd polished it all over and Colm had rubbed the rusting spokes with emery paper and they'd come up sparkling.

So, as she proudly pushed Cara through Princes Park on a sunny March afternoon with a brisk wind blowing that was neither warm nor cold, and with St Patrick's Day only forty-eight hours away and Katie MacBride willing to look after the children so she and Colm could go to a ceilidh at the Irish Club to which Brenna was greatly looking forward, she felt cross with herself for feeling so out of sorts, so sour, when almost everything was going so well. Only *almost*. If it hadn't been for Eleanor Allardyce, life would have been perfect.

Brenna felt she was losing Fergus. Since the night Anthony had stayed in Shaw Street, the two boys had become inseparable. Fergus spent every weekend in the house in Parliament Terrace – he would have gone every day if she hadn't put her foot down. He slept between the finest sheets, ate the finest food and Eleanor had actually bought him a *suit*!

'I thought he'd feel more comfortable when we all went out together,' she'd said.

'Out where?' Brenna gritted her teeth at the implication that her son wasn't fit to be seen in Anthony's company in the clothes *she* provided.

'Shopping, to see a film,' Eleanor said airily. 'We went to Blackpool in the car on Saturday. I took them in the lift to the top of the tower.'

Brenna already knew this and wondered why she'd bothered to ask. She insisted the suit be kept at the Allardyces' otherwise Tyrone might feel jealous and want one.

She would have put her foot down even harder and stopped the relationship altogether, but it would have hurt Anthony and he was a sweet little boy. It wasn't his fault that his mother was a selfish bitch intent on stealing another woman's child.

Colm and Nancy thought she was unreasonable to complain. 'You sound awfully bitter, Bren,' Colm said reprovingly when she'd said she couldn't see why the lads didn't spend every other weekend in Shaw Street. It would be fairer. 'Fairness doesn't come into it. We couldn't take them to Blackpool in a dead posh car, could we? Eleanor's even got a chauffeur.'

Brenna didn't say they could walk down to the Pier Head: him, Tyrone and Cara included, and watch the ferries sail to and fro across the Mersey and the big liners leave for foreign shores, or play football in the park. Eleanor hadn't suggested they take turns in each other's houses, taking for granted that Fergus would far prefer Anthony's to his.

'Anthony's never had a friend before,' Nancy told her. It was Nancy, the non-believer, who took Fergus to Mass on Sunday mornings. 'Fergus has really brought him out of himself – and it's doing Fergus good an' all. He's not nearly so quiet and shy as he used to be.'

Perhaps she *was* being unreasonable, Brenna thought miserably, but would Eleanor be so accommodating if it was Fergus who was so much in need of Anthony's company? She somehow doubted it.

She manoeuvred the pram down steps, ducking her head to avoid the branches of a tree that bore a covering of tiny green buds. The sight made her heart lift. During the months ahead, the buds would turn into leaves, blossom would appear, by which time she would be pushing the pram along the same path in the summer sunshine and thinking about autumn when the leaves would turn gold.

Brenna smiled. Life was too short and too precious to let her personal feelings get in the way of her son's happiness. Just because she loathed Eleanor Allardyce, it was no reason to stop Fergus and Anthony from seeing each other. She vowed never to complain about it again, at least, not out loud. From now on, she'd keep her feelings to herself.

She felt in a much better mood and was singing under her breath when she left the park by Devonshire Road and walked past Our Lady of Mount Carmel, the school that the lads attended. She was about to turn right and make her way back to Shaw Street, but turned left instead and into Toxteth Street where Colm worked for Cyril Phelan in his builders' yard. Cyril was a hard taskmaster, but surely wouldn't object to Brenna exchanging a few words with her husband. She'd never done it before, but wanted Colm to see her smiling again before she went home. Even if they just waved to each other, it would be enough.

The yard was situated behind a thick wooden fence and she stopped by the open gates and peered inside at the heaps of gravel and sand, neat piles of bricks, lengths of pipe of all different sizes, ladders, blue-grey slates stacked carefully against the wall at the back of the Phelans' end-terrace house — it was no bigger than their own house, Brenna noted with a sense of satisfaction. A man was shovelling sand into a wheelbarrow, but there was no sign of Colm. She edged the pram a few feet inside and glanced down a path between the stacks of timber, but he was nowhere to be seen. Perhaps he'd taken the handcart to deliver something, in which case she was wasting her time.

She was in the course of turning the pram around, when the Phelans' back door opened and Colm emerged, accompanied by a desperately smart young woman a few years younger than herself. Her black hair was short and glossy and framed her neat little face like one of those hats Eleanor sometimes wore — a cloche, Brenna remembered it was called. She wore a grey suit with a bloused top, a straight skirt that finished at her calves and black shoes with incredibly high heels and pompoms on the toes. Brenna, in her shawl and old frock and still wearing Colm's worn-down boots — new shoes seemed even more an extravagance than a baby carriage — felt horribly drab in comparison.

She became aware that Colm and this fashionable young woman seemed very friendly. She actually had her hand on his arm and they were laughing over something. What? she wondered. The woman stepped back into the house, closed the door and Colm came whistling into the yard, stopping abruptly when he saw Brenna. Was it just her imagination that he looked slightly annoyed?

'Who was that?' she asked coldly, forgetting that she'd only come so that he could see her smiling again.

'Elizabeth Phelan, Cyril's daughter,' he replied, just as coldly. 'She made me a cup of tea.'

'I didn't think either of the daughters lived at home.'

'They don't. Lizzie only came to see how her mother is.' Mrs Phelan had recently had an operation to remove gallstones.

'Is she married?' Brenna prayed that the answer would be 'yes'. There was something about the way Elizabeth Phelan had put her hand on Colm's arm that had made her feel uneasy. She told herself she was being daft. Colm was the most faithful of husbands and hadn't given her an ounce of worry in all the years they'd been married, despite all the tempting looks that came his way when they were in female company.

'No, Bren, she's single,' he replied. 'She belongs to the same organization as Nancy, the Women's Social and Political Union. Look, luv, Cyril will be back any minute and I'd sooner he didn't find you here. I'll see you tonight.' He put his arm around her waist and ushered Brenna and the baby carriage outside.

'Hello, pet,' Nancy said, surprised. It wasn't often Brenna visited during working hours.

'Are you in the middle of something?'

'Only me afternoon cuppa. I'll be starting on the dinner soon. Come in.' Cara had woken the minute she'd been lifted up and Nancy tickled her under the chin, as if she were a cat. 'I'd swear this child gets bigger and bonnier every time I see her.'

Brenna didn't waste time beating about the bush. As soon as they were seated, she said, 'What do you know about a woman called Elizabeth Phelan?'

Nancy blinked. 'How on earth do you know her?'

'I don't, but Colm does. I've only seen her. She's Cyril Phelan's daughter.'

'Is she now? I never knew that. I've met Lizzie loads of times, but she's more an acquaintance than a friend.' She looked at Brenna curiously. 'What's this all about, pet?'

Brenna was beginning to wish she'd never gone near the yard, never set eyes on Elizabeth Phelan. She'd decided to stop worrying about Fergus, but now had Colm to worry about instead. 'She looked so interesting,' she said casually. 'I wondered what she did for a living, that's all.'

'She's a secretary,' Nancy replied.

Brenna had never heard the word before. 'What's a secretary?'

'The sort of job that's usually been done by men. It's only recently that women have been taken on. Lizzie works in a bank. She's ever such a clever girl and can type and do shorthand and is studying for some accountancy qualification. During the war, when she was barely sixteen, she went to France with the Red Cross, spent two whole years there. If I tell you something,' Nancy said in a low voice, as if people were outside, ears pressed against the door, 'will you promise not to breathe a word to a soul?'

'Cross me heart,' Brenna promised. Nancy's description of what a secretary did had left her no wiser. She had no idea what shorthand was or accountancy.

'When she came back from France, Lizzie didn't go back home, but moved into a flat of her own in Mount Pleasant where she lives quite openly with some fella. They're not married.'

'Never!' Brenna pursed her lips primly, shocked to the core. 'That's disgusting.'

Nancy chuckled. 'I admire her, although I wouldn't have the nerve to do it meself. Not everyone finds a scrap of official paper necessary before they settle down with a chap. Mind you, the last I heard, she'd chucked him out. Didn't come up to expectations maybe.' She chuckled again. 'She's probably on the lookout for a replacement. A very liberated young woman is Miss Elizabeth Phelan.'

'Eleanor! Eleanor Allardyce! How lovely to see you! It's ages and ages since we met: years, in fact. How are you, darling? Do you mind if I sit down a minute?'

'Please do.' Eleanor removed her bag from the chair to make way for Lily Mayer with whom she'd been at the Gladstone Academy for Young Ladies in Rodney Street and had met occasionally since at parties and in places like the Philharmonic Hall or Frederick & Hughes, where she was now having afternoon tea with Anthony and Fergus on a beautiful afternoon in June. She felt as if she had been trapped inside a cloud of expensive scent as Lily slid on to the chair in her wide-brimmed straw hat and cream silk frock with fringes of amber beads at the neck and cuffs. 'I love your frock,' she said.

'Chanel!' Lily cried. 'Bought in this very shop only last week, although it's much more fun popping over to Paris. We live mostly in London nowadays and Paris is easily reached on the night train. Liverpool is so deadly dull.' The Mayer fortune had been made from the slave trade then, once this was abolished, from importing alcohol from the West Indies. 'Now, who are these dear little boys? They can't both be yours, surely.'

The boys were staring at Lily, round-eyed. Eleanor introduced them. 'The fair-haired one is Anthony and he's mine. The other is Fergus. He's the son of a – a friend,' she lied. She felt the same dislike for Brenna as Brenna obviously felt for her. 'I have a little girl too, Sybil, nine months old. She's at home with the nurse. Darlings, this is Lily Mayer. She and I were at school together.'

'What on earth are they doing?' Lily asked in astonishment as the two boys began to make signs at each other with their hands.

'Anthony is deaf and Fergus is translating what I just said into sign language.'

'How charming, how *touching*,' Lily gasped.

'Isn't it?' Eleanor said drily. Although she couldn't be more pleased that Anthony was able to communicate at last, she wished it was with her and other members of the household, not just Fergus, who seemed able to pick up sign language far quicker than anyone else. She was trying valiantly to remember how to form words, but it was taking an awfully long time. Daniel Vaizey, Anthony's tutor, said the boys were constructing a language of their own, but it didn't matter terribly.

'Anthony has a quick brain. He'll soon pick up the right signs once the boys are separated,' he'd said.

'Should they be separated now?' Eleanor had asked, alarmed.

'Not for a while yet. Just now, Fergus is important to Anthony's well-being. He'd be lost without him,' Daniel assured her.

'Well, darling, I must go.' Lily got to her feet. 'Oh, I forgot to ask: how is that incredibly handsome husband of yours? I was at your wedding, remember?'

'He's very well, thank you. I see you're not married yet.' The third finger of Lily's left hand was bare.

'I'm having far too good a time to settle down and burden myself with a husband and children. I have loads of men friends and shall marry when I'm thirty. Bye, darling. Bye, boys.' With a wave, Lily was gone.

Eleanor asked the children if they would like another cream cake. Fergus nodded furiously and Anthony, watching, did the same. She signalled to the waitress and ordered the cakes, more lemonade and another pot of tea for one.

'Anthony wants to pee,' Fergus said.

Eleanor glanced at the neighbouring tables to see if anyone had heard, but it seemed not. 'Say "use the lavatory", darling. It sounds so much better.' Fergus looked at her blankly. At least he had an attractive Irish accent, so much nicer than the nasal Liverpool brogue. 'Perhaps you could take him. You'll be quite all right by yourselves.'

When did I ever have a good time like Lily Mayer? she asked herself as she watched the boys disappear into the Gentlemen's toilet. During the few months when she and Geoffrey were courting, that's all. They'd met in this very restaurant where he'd been lunching with his mother. The friend Eleanor was with knew him slightly as he went to football matches with her brother and it seemed only natural for all four to sit together. She was introduced to Geoffrey, barely eighteen years old, as she was herself. It was love at first sight and the time that followed was magic and all too short. Within six months the war had started and Geoffrey was dead.

Since then, the restaurant in Frederick & Hughes had become her favourite place in the world, although if she came alone she found it hard to suppress the tears when she thought about the way things might have been and the way they actually were.

'I thought I might take Anthony out today,' Daniel Vaizey said on Monday morning. 'There's an art exhibition over Crumbs in Bold Street: you know, the shop where they sell artists' materials? I thought he would find it interesting. I went on Saturday and some of the work isn't nearly as good as his.'

'I'd love to come with you,' Eleanor said impulsively and immediately blushed, regretting the words. They sounded terribly forward.

'Well, in that case, we can all go together.' Daniel appeared not to notice her blush. Either that, or he was just being his courteous self. Like Anthony, his younger sister had been born deaf and he'd taught himself sign language so they could converse. When Marcus had decided that his son must have his own tutor, Daniel had been the only person to reply to the advert in the *Echo*. Teaching wasn't his profession, he explained, but a way of supporting himself while he studied languages, his ambition being to travel extensively abroad. 'But not as a tourist, I couldn't afford to. I shall have to find work.'

He and Eleanor got on well. He was a tall, athletically built young man, strong-featured with a lovely smile. She wished she hadn't blushed earlier when she'd said she'd love to go to the art exhibition because she found him enormously attractive and it was something she'd sooner he didn't know.

Chapter 4

The jelly hadn't set! Brenna had put it on the back step the night before, but next morning when she looked it was hardly any thicker. She made a face at it.

'What's the matter?' Colm came into the kitchen, struggling into his flannel shirt.

'The jelly for Cara's tea hasn't set − I left it on the step all night long.'

'Well, it's too warm, isn't it? It'd have been better to put the bowl in cold water in the sink. And the sun's shining directly on the step − see!' He pointed outside, to where the small yard was filled with sunshine. It was a lovely day for Cara's first birthday. 'It might even have set a bit and now it's melted again.'

'P'raps I should've asked you to make it,' she said sarcastically.

'I'm only pointing out the obvious, Brenna.'

'Ta.' She turned her back on him, cut two thick slices of bread and took them into the living room to toast by the fire. On the same day last year, the day they had arrived in Liverpool, the weather had been unseasonably cold. This year, they were experiencing a beautiful Indian summer and it was unseasonably warm.

'Is there any tea going?' Colm called from the kitchen where he was having a shave.

'It's on the hob.'

'Bring us a cup, there's a good girl.'

'I'm making the toast,' she snapped. 'I can't do two things at once.'

Colm poked his head around the door, his chin fluffy with shaving soap. 'Have you got a cob on?'

'No, I'm just pointing out the obvious.'

He shrugged. 'Trouble with you, Brenna, is that you can't stand being told you're in the wrong.'

'Trouble with you, Colm,' she snapped, 'is that these days, I'm in the wrong all the bloody time.' The other night, he'd been on at her for not being able to read properly, forgetting entirely that she'd left school at twelve and hadn't been there half the time any road, but at home helping to raise her two little sisters because her da was dead and Ma couldn't cope. Since then, Ma had died and she'd lost touch with Sheila and Colette.

'Can't you bring yourself to look a bit smarter?' he'd had the nerve to ask yesterday, as if they were made of money and all she had to do was take herself to some posh shop and buy an entire new outfit, including shoes with pompoms on the toes like Lizzie Phelan. Either that or pay through the nose and get something off the tallyman who'd come knocking on the door once a week until every penny was paid back with a huge borrowing fee on top. When it came to clothes, the children's needs came first, then Colm's and Brenna's last. She'd got a few things from Paddy's Market: flat, lace-up shoes, already well worn, but very comfortable, that had only cost a penny-ha'penny – it was with a feeling of jubilation that she chucked Colm's old boots in the bin – and two frocks for a tanner each, neither exactly the latest fashion. She'd considered taking up the hems, making them calf-length like those Eleanor Allardyce wore, but the skirts were full and would probably look ridiculous – they'd look even more ridiculous with the shoes. She still hadn't been able to afford a coat and was stuck with her shawl. As most women in the area wore shawls, she hadn't seen anything wrong with them until Colm suggested she smarten herself up.

'You're a daft lad, Colm Caffrey,' she muttered, turning the toast over when one side was done – *too* well, she noticed with a grimace. She'd been so wrapped up in angry thoughts that she'd let it burn.

'What did you just say?' Colm appeared again, clean-shaven, mopping his chin with a ragged towel – she needed new towels more than new clothes.

'I was talking to meself.'

'You've let the toast burn.'

'I'll scrape it off in a minute, when I've done the other side.'

'You said I was a daft lad,' he said indignantly. 'I heard you quite clearly.'

'Well, if the cap fits, wear it.' She scraped the burnt side of the toast into the fire, put it on a plate and spread the margarine – the other side was hardly done. 'Are you ready for your tea now?'

'Yes.' He sat down and frowned at her. 'So, why am I daft?'

Brenna took a deep breath. She'd been wanting this conversation for a long time. 'For expecting me to dress like Lizzie Phelan, think the way she does, know the things she knows. You married an ignorant Irishwoman, Colm, not a smart young lady who went to some posh school and passed examinations in things I've never heard of.'

'Lizzie passed the scholarship and went to secondary school. Anyone can do that.'

'*I* couldn't. I was working when I was twelve.'

His brow darkened. 'What's Lizzie Phelan got to do with things, any road?'

'You're always on about "Lizzie said this" and "Lizzie said that". She's filling your thick head with all sorts of mad ideas. For instance, since when have you cared about Irish politics?' He'd been lecturing the lads on something or other when she'd last done the ironing and she'd been too tired to take it in.

'For a long time,' he said hotly. 'We used to talk about it in the pub in Lahmera, but I never saw much point in discussing it with you. You just said yourself you're ignorant.'

'I might be ignorant, but I'm not stupid,' Brenna reasoned. 'There's been nothing stopping you from *talking* about things like politics.' She didn't believe for a moment it had been discussed in the Shamrock, where the sound of drunken singing and raucous laughter could be heard until closing time when Bernie Murphy, the landlord, threw the lot of them out.

'Did you know that Lloyd George has brought in the Home Rule Bill and it looks like Ireland will be partitioned and never united again: there'll be two separate parliaments, one for the north and one for the south.' While he spoke, Colm's face had got redder and redder and his voice angrier.

'No, I didn't know,' Brenna confessed, 'but now I do and I think it's a desperately bad idea.'

'Do you?' He looked surprised.

'Indeed I do. Did you think I was without a brain in me head, Colm?'

'Of course not.'

They sat in cold silence for a while. Colm finished the toast, washed it down with tea then said, 'It's your own fault I go on about Lizzie. You've got a bee in your bonnet and you ask about her the minute I get in from work. What am I supposed to do, refuse to answer?'

'Oh, so you'd prefer to have kept her a secret?' If she hadn't seen Lizzie that day, he'd probably have never mentioned her.

'Who's being daft now, Brenna?'

The conversation might have continued if Tyrone hadn't come down demanding his breakfast. Brenna told him sternly to wait until Fergus appeared and she'd brought Cara down so she could make porridge for them all rather than in dribs and drabs. 'You can make yourself a piece of toast if you're hungry,' she offered generously, 'but stay well back from the fire.'

'Why do we have always have a fire when it's so hot, Ma?' Tyrone enquired.

'Because it's the only way we have to heat the water, darlin'. And make toast.'

'I'm off now, Bren,' Colm called, and the front door slammed without him waiting for a reply – or a goodbye kiss.

Brenna's lips tightened as she sat and watched Tyrone hold the bread in front of the fire, his face all screwed up as if it were a terrible effort. It was nice to have bread to spare and a warm fire – not that one was needed today. She was enjoying getting things for the house: the occasional picture for the walls, pretty lace curtains in the parlour, new dishes – *really* new, with only the tiniest of cracks and chips; they were called 'seconds'. Every day, she walked for miles with Cara in the pram, searching the second-hand shops for bargains like the lovely lacquered tea caddy she'd got for a penny with a teaspoon inside that was a 'Gift from Morecambe', or so it said on the handle; patchwork quilts for the lads' beds; a statue of a lady in a frilly frock with a parasol over her shoulder that stood in pride of place on the mantelpiece in the parlour; a mirror with a brass frame that she could never quite get clean. She'd never imagined one day having a house of their own and wanted to make it comfortable and welcoming for Colm and the children.

But Colm no longer seemed interested in her acquisitions. He was too taken up with Lizzie Phelan who came to the builders' yard every day in her dinner hour to visit her ma, although Mrs Phelan had long ago recovered from the operation to remove her gallstones. Brenna knew because, most days, she made a point of being in the vicinity of the yard when Lizzie arrived, lurking around a corner where she couldn't be seen. Soon afterwards, Colm would disappear into the house. What Cyril Phelan and his missus thought of this, Brenna had no idea, but *their* daughter was after *her* husband, of that she was convinced. If what Nancy had to say about Miss Elizabeth Phelan were true, she wouldn't care if he were married or not.

Colm was halfway to work before he remembered he hadn't given Brenna a kiss. Still, she probably hadn't noticed, and if she had, she probably wouldn't care. He loved his wife with all his heart, but lately he'd become aware of her limitations. Brenna didn't *think*, least not about anything important. She wasn't interested in anything that didn't concern him, the children, or the house. He was fed up with discussing what sort of wallpaper they'd have in the parlour – when they could afford it, that is – admiring the tea cosy she was knitting, not just once, but every day after she'd knitted another inch. There were so many more important things than tea cosies to think about, and he couldn't see Lizzie Phelan giving a fig about an unset jelly.

She was trying to persuade him to join the Labour Party and he was giving the idea serious consideration. 'The country badly needs a government that will look after the poor,' she cried, her brown eyes glowing with passion. 'Labour will get rid of poverty and there'll be jobs for everyone who wants one, women as well as men. The Tories and Liberals only represent the rich.'

She was the cleverest person he'd ever met, despite only being a woman. Talking to her, he would become fired up with enthusiasm or anger. Every day, she read a newspaper – *The Times* – from cover to cover and seemed to know everything there was to know about every subject under the sun, whether it be the revolution in Russia – 'The best thing ever to have happened in that benighted country,' she said joyfully when Lenin recently announced a new economic policy – or the national miners' strike in Britain earlier in the year, which she'd supported fully. 'The miners work under the most appalling conditions,' she claimed, her shapely little body quivering with indignation. 'Their pay is atrocious.' She'd actually been in tears when the strikers were forced to return to work for reduced wages after a few months. 'It's so humiliating,' she wept. Colm had patted her shoulder awkwardly and she'd turned to him, saying, 'Oh, I'm so glad to have you to talk to, Colm. You're one of the few people who under*stands*. Most don't give a damn what goes on in the rest of the world, no matter how dreadful it might be, so long as it doesn't concern *them*.'

'That doesn't bode well for the future, Colm,' she said when the Fascists won thirty-five seats in the Italian government. 'There's this chap, Adolf Hitler, another damn Fascist, who's just become president of the National Socialist Party in Germany and is stirring things up over there.'

He was flattered that Lizzie spoke to him as if he were an equal, was actually interested in his opinion. She made him feel very important. When he compared her with his wife, Brenna definitely came off the worse.

The lads had gone to school and Brenna was teaching Cara to sing 'Happy Birthday'. She could already say Mammy and Daddy, Ty for Tyrone, but hadn't yet managed Fergus. Although Nancy hadn't said anything, Brenna got the distinct impression that she was more advanced than Eleanor's Sybil, whose first birthday was also today. The girls had been born within minutes of each other and even Nancy wasn't sure who'd arrived first. The September Girls, she'd called them.

'Come on, darlin',' Brenna urged. 'Happy birthday to you, happy birthday . . .' But Cara merely giggled and cried, 'Mammy, Mammy, Mammy' in her shrill little voice. She lurched around the room like a drunken sailor and appeared more surprised than hurt when she fell over, but quickly got back to her feet with the help of a table leg.

'Whose Mammy's brave little girl?' Brenna cooed. Most children would have screamed blue murder.

Nancy was coming to tea at five o'clock, but couldn't stay long because Sybil was also having a party that wouldn't start until six when Mr Allardyce would be home. He adored his daughter and wouldn't have missed it for the world. One time when Brenna had been in Parliament Terrace, she'd heard him singing Sybil a lullaby before she went asleep and it was him, not Eleanor or Nurse Hutton, who was teaching her to walk.

'We're eating in the kitchen,' Nancy explained, 'so me, Daniel Vaizey and Nurse Hutton can be there.' She grinned. 'The lord and master would never let us in the dining room in case we contaminated it. I'll set the table so it'll be ready when I get back from yours – I can take Fergus with me, save you the journey. Tomorrow, Eleanor's taking him and Anthony to see *The Kid* with Charlie Chaplin. I wouldn't mind seeing it meself. I read in the paper it's a scream.'

'Is she now?' Brenna said evenly.

Nancy looked at her searchingly. 'You don't mind, do you?'

'Not a bit,' she lied, and tried to look pleased about it.

Yesterday, she'd made two-dozen fairy cakes and a raspberry jam sponge that had a little white candle in the centre. This morning, Tyrone had suggested the jelly be poured into separate bowls on the assumption seven small amounts would set quicker than one big one. She went into the kitchen and gave one of the bowls a shake. To her relief, it was less wobbly than the last time she'd checked.

'Thank goodness,' she breathed. She'd already made custard to go over the jelly and bought an ounce of hundreds and thousands to sprinkle on top. All she had to do was make the sarnies. She'd leave them till later.

'Mammy, Mammy, Mammy!' Cara came staggering into the kitchen.

Brenna picked her up. 'Cara, Cara, Cara!' She stroked her little girl's soft, dimpled cheek. 'That's your very first birthday cake,' she told her. 'Let's hope by the time you're twenty-one we can afford a great big one with your name on and icing an inch thick. I wonder where we'll be in another twenty years.' She sighed. 'Let's hope your daddy remembers to ask Cyril Phelan if he can work through his dinnertime and come home early.' Colm didn't normally finish until six o'clock. 'If he doesn't, I'll . . .' She paused and sighed again. 'I don't know what I'll do.' She would have reminded him had he not left the house so abruptly that he'd forgotten to kiss her. She buried her head in Cara's shoulder and whispered, 'Your daddy's making me awful miserable, darlin'.' Cara responded with a giggle and pulled her hair. 'That didn't help a bit,' Brenna sniffed.

'Is your daddy in love with Lizzie Phelan?' she asked aloud as she carried Cara into the living room, sat at the table and drained the pot of the last of the tea: it was stone cold, but she drank it all the same. 'Has he kissed her? There's no way of finding out other than asking him straight out, not that your daddy would admit it if he had, but I could tell by his face if he was lying. He's a hopeless liar, your da.'

Anyway, did she really want to know? Colm was right: it was her own fault he went on about Lizzie. She encouraged him, asking question after question, yet it didn't follow that, because he spoke to the boss's daughter for half an hour or so a day, that they were attracted to each other. Perhaps it was time she shut up about it, forgot she'd seen them together that day, Lizzie with her hand laid possessively on Colm's arm – the hand seemed more and more possessive the more she thought about it. Yes, that's what she'd do: forget about it. What the head didn't know, the heart didn't grieve over. But before she forgot about it, she'd like to know where she stood.

'Don't do that, darlin',' she said when Cara picked up the cup and began to bang it against the saucer. Brenna stared at the mess of tea leaves that were left. Well, there was one sure way of finding out what was really going on. 'I'll ask Katie next door if she'll read the leaves for me.'

It was a heathen practice, sternly frowned on by the Catholic Church, but women from many faiths came from far and wide so Katie could predict their future from the leaves, paying sixpence a time. Men, it seemed, weren't interested in knowing how their lives would turn out.

During the day, Katie MacBride was just an ordinary housewife, rarely seen without her hair full of curlers, a ciggie stuck in the corner of her mouth, and wearing an old frock that had seen better days. But by six o'clock, the curlers had been removed, the dyed black hair combed into a halo of frizz and she had turned into a mysterious creature clad in dense, black velvet, cheeks heavily rouged, lips heavily painted, only the ciggie, parked at an acute angle between the unnaturally red lips, reminding everyone that this was the same old Katie.

Sometimes, Katie's living room held as many as half a dozen women, all sitting around the table waiting anxiously for it to be their turn to go in the parlour and have their fortunes told.

Brenna waited until midday when Cara, who'd been a little divil all morning, began to look sleepy. She took her upstairs for a nap, then went next door.

Katie was sitting on her front doorstep, smoking the inevitable ciggie and enjoying a glass of gin. She swigged neat gin by the gallon, but Brenna had never seen her drunk. The sun had drifted over the rooftops and now caressed the front of the houses on their side of the little street.

'I'd like me leaves read,' Brenna said shyly. She'd never asked before, not seeing the need, imagining her own future stretching ahead without a hitch.

'Now?' Katie enquired.

'If you don't mind. I'll give you the sixpence as soon as Colm gets his wages.' Being Friday, he'd be paid that night.

'Bugger the sixpence,' Katie said dismissively. 'Aren't you me next-door neighbour? Aren't I coming to your Cara's party tonight?'

'You are indeed, but I'd sooner pay.'

'And I'd sooner you didn't, luv. Come and sit in the parlour while I make the tea.'

It was a room Brenna had never been in before. Katie closed the curtains, lit a nightlight in a glass bowl, put it on a small round table in front of the fireplace and told her to sit down. She left and Brenna took in the heavy black furniture with a glassy sheen, the sequinned runner on the sideboard where an ornate clock with gold figures ticked away a few more seconds of her life, and the tapestry hanging above the mantelpiece depicting the signs of the zodiac. She would never have guessed from outside that the scruffy piece of lace covering the window hid such rich curtains: bronze silk that shimmered slightly in the glow from the flickering nightlight, which issued a strange smell and made her want to sneeze.

Katie came in with the tea and a large glass of water, although it might have been gin. She had removed her shabby apron and now wore a fine black shawl. A bright red scarf was tied like a turban over her curlers – it must be too early to take them out. Jet earrings dangled from her ears and a ciggie from her mouth.

'Drink this.' She placed the tea on the table and the cup gave a little musical 'ping' as it scraped against the saucer. It must be the very best china.

'It's got no milk in.'

'Milk sullies the leaves: they're best left pure. Don't drink every drop now, leave enough to let the leaves move round a bit.'

Katie the fortune-teller seemed different from Katie her jolly neighbour: her eyes were strange and misty, her voice deeper and her normally cheerful face desperately serious. Brenna was beginning to wish she hadn't come. It was crazy to believe the future could be told from a few tea leaves, apart from which the tea tasted horrible without milk. She sipped it as fast as she could, hoping Cara would wake up and yell for her mammy and she'd be obliged to go home. The tea almost gone, she showed Katie the cup.

'Now put it upside down on the saucer and turn it five times to the left and five to the right, then give it to me.'

Brenna did as she was told and Katie stared intently at the contents. 'I thought you only had three children,' she said in her new, strange voice.

'I do – you know that as well as me.'

'There's four here. I can see them quite clearly.'

'Then the leaves must be wrong, I've only three.'

'The leaves are never wrong, madam.'

'Well, they're wrong now.' Brenna wriggled in the chair. Being addressed as 'madam' made her feel uncomfortable, as if Katie had forgotten who she was.

'There's a flower here, a rose without thorns, which means you will lead a long and healthy life, madam, but there's a cross beside the rose that indicates a great tragedy will intervene.'

'What sort of tragedy?' Brenna's stomach gave an unpleasant turn.

'The leaves don't say, but you will lose something very precious.'

'It's not Colm or one of the children, is it?'

'The leaves don't say, madam,' Katie repeated tonelessly. She took a long swallow of the water that might have been gin. 'I see a dagger dripping blood meaning a cruel betrayal, and what's this?' She peered into the cup. 'I can't quite make it out . . .' She closed her eyes and opened them so suddenly that Brenna backed away, startled. 'It's a woman, a woman crying because she has lost her loved one.'

'Who is it?' Brenna asked, but didn't wait for an answer, because an unearthly scream came from next door: Cara, alerting her mother to the fact that she'd woken up and urgently required attention. Brenna jumped to her feet. 'I've got to go,' she said urgently. 'Thank you, Katie, I think I've heard enough.'

'But I haven't finished, madam.' Katie's misty eyes regarded her as if she were a stranger. 'One day the loved one will return.'

'As I said, I've heard enough.'

'Brenna!' Nancy gasped. 'Lord Almighty, pet, what's the matter? You've actually walked through the streets wearing your pinnie. That's not like you. Where's Cara?'

'In the pram outside.' Brenna burst into tears. 'I've just had me tea leaves read. Oh, Nancy! You wouldn't believe the awful things that's going to happen to us.'

'You're right there, Brenna,' Nancy said grimly. 'I wouldn't believe that sort of codswallop for a minute and I'm surprised at you for believing it too. Sit down, girl, and I'll fetch you a sup of sherry, calm your nerves, like.'

'I'm going to suffer a great tragedy, a betrayal and some woman, I don't know whether it's me or not, is going to lose a loved one.' She had a feeling Katie had said the loved one would return, but couldn't be sure.

'Oh, yeah! And the cow's going to jump over the moon. Who was it told you this load of baloney: Katie MacBride?' Brenna nodded and Nancy plonked a glass on the table in front of her. 'That's cooking sherry, but it tastes all right. I take a sup meself now and then.'

'Katie seemed desperately serious. I couldn't help but believe her.'

'Huh!' sneered Nancy. 'I've heard she pretends to go in a trance or something. She's a sham, pet, *and* she's permanently pissed.' She slammed her big fist on the table. 'Ask her to read your leaves tomorrow, and she'll come up with an entirely different story, and a different one the day after that. You're not to believe a word she said, Brenna, do you hear?'

'Yes,' Brenna said meekly. Nancy was so down-to-earth and full of common sense that it was easy to believe that Katie was talking a load of baloney. For the first time, she noticed the big, elaborately decorated cake on the table. 'Is that for Sybil's party?'

'Yes. I made it and Eleanor did the icing. I'll keep you a piece if you like.'

'That'd be nice, and I'll keep a piece of Cara's sponge for Eleanor.'

Nancy laughed. 'You don't like her, do you?'

'She's all right. I'd better get going, you'll be in the middle of making the midday meal and I'm holding you up. Anyway, I feel desperately tired. I might have a little lie down this avvy if Cara will let me.' She stood, so quickly that her head swam. 'Oh, Lord!' She put a hand to her forehead. 'It must be that sherry,' she said before fainting dead away.

When she came to, Nancy was holding a little bottle under her nose that smelled so foul it made her want to be sick. 'What's that?' She pushed the bottle away.

'Smelling salts.' Nancy helped her into a sitting position on the floor. 'You've never struck me as the sort of woman who faints, Brenna.'

'I've only done it once in me life before,' she said shakily, 'when I was expecting our Fergus.'

'Ah, well that explains it. Here was me thinking it might be something serious.' Nancy's face creased into a smile of relief. 'You're in the club, Brenna. Congratulations. I bet you're dead pleased.'

But Brenna didn't smile back. 'Katie insisted I had four children,' she whispered. 'Oh, Nancy! She actually *knew* there was a fourth lying in me belly.' The first of Katie's predictions had already come true, and she refused to accept Nancy's insistence that it was nothing but a coincidence.

Colm didn't come home early for Cara's party. It had completely slipped his mind, he confessed when he arrived to find everything over. Nancy had taken Fergus to Parliament Terrace, Katie MacBride had gone, Tyrone was playing outside and Cara was asleep.

It hadn't been a very happy meal. The custard had tasted burnt, Brenna felt too distressed to enjoy herself and it was clear that Nancy was finding it hard to be civilized to Katie who arrived in all her finery so she'd be ready for the clients who would arrive in an hour's time. She didn't mention Brenna's visit that morning, not even after Nancy had gone. It was as if she'd forgotten all about it.

'I'm sorry, Bren,' Colm said, apologizing for the third or fourth time.

'It doesn't matter,' Brenna said dully. 'It really doesn't matter.' She wondered if another of Katie's prophecies been taken care of, leaving only the great tragedy and the crying woman to look forward to. She doubted it. Just missing your daughter's birthday tea couldn't possibly be counted as a betrayal.

In the kitchen of Parliament Terrace, different tensions hung in the air. Anthony and Fergus were happily stuffing themselves, despite Fergus having eaten less than half an hour ago, although the food in Shaw Street hadn't been nearly so rich. In her high chair, Sybil was being fed shreds of chicken breast mixed with mashed potato and grated carrot by Nurse Hutton: not exactly party food, but there was trifle and apple pie for afters, followed by birthday cake. Eleanor and Daniel Vaizey were tucking into the crab vol-au-vents and slices of ham and egg pie that Nancy had made that morning. Marcus had brought up two bottles of white wine from the cellar.

Marcus was pretending to watch his adored daughter eat, but the smile on his face was forced and his body was stiff. Nancy picked at her food. Despite her size, she had only a small appetite and had had enough to eat at Brenna's. Her smile was also forced and her body as stiff as that of her employer. She couldn't remember ever having felt so fearful, the reason being that it was evident to anyone with eyes that Eleanor and Daniel were head over heels in love.

Why hadn't she noticed before? Nancy wondered. Perhaps it was because she'd never seen them together, not at such close quarters, not sitting next to each other, shoulders touching, hands touching occasionally, knees almost certainly touching under the table. Or perhaps they'd only just realized they were in love. What they didn't realize was that the sheer rapture on their faces, the way their eyes smiled when they met, the air of excitement and joy that surrounded them, almost visible in its intensity, gave the game away completely. They may as well have held up a notice announcing, 'WE ARE IN LOVE.' It was *that* obvious.

What's going to happen now? Nancy asked herself. It was the same question she'd asked when she'd left Shaw Street and Colm hadn't turned up for Cara's tea. She'd never seen Brenna looking so down: not just because of Colm, but the twaddle she'd been fed by that bitch, Katie MacBride. Then, as now, she couldn't think of an answer.

Sybil tried to snatch the candle off the birthday cake, unable to understand she was supposed to blow it out.

'She'll know what to do next year,' Nurse Hutton said. 'Won't you, darling?'

Sybil replied by thumping her hands on the tray of her high chair.

'Let Anthony do it,' Marcus said when it looked as if the nurse was about to do it herself.

Fergus gave Anthony a nudge that must have conveyed what was expected of him and he blew out the tiny, flickering flame. Fergus gave him another nudge and they grinned at each other. It was as if the two boys shared a brain, Eleanor thought.

This was quite the nicest meal she'd ever had in Parliament Terrace. Everyone appeared to be enjoying the party hugely, even Marcus. He could scarcely take his eyes off Sybil, who was growing into such a pretty little girl with a lively personality. It upset Eleanor that she didn't feel all that close to her daughter – those first three months in bed had done enormous harm – but she was pleased that Marcus had built up such a wonderful rapport with his little girl. It often happened in families that the parents favoured different children – Daddy's girl' or 'Mummy's boy'. The equilibrium was unlikely to be spoilt by them having another child, as Marcus hadn't visited her room at night since Sybil was conceived, greatly to Eleanor's relief. She found his visits something of an ordeal.

It had been so different with Daniel: miraculously and stupendously different, a truly magical experience.

'Thank you,' she murmured when Nancy gave her a slice of birthday cake. Daniel accepted a piece and she felt his shoulder press against her own. Beneath the table, their knees touched.

'Is this the cake you iced?' he asked. 'It's very artistic. Now I know where Anthony gets his talent from.'

Eleanor lowered her eyes and didn't respond to the compliment. It was important – not just important, but absolutely vital – that Marcus didn't guess they were in love. Nothing would come of it, they both realized that, but were happy to leave things as they were and just enjoy themselves.

It was at the art exhibition in Bold Street they'd attended three months ago that she'd realized he was attracted to her as much as she was to him. Afterwards, they'd had coffee in the Adelphi where the conversation was entirely innocent, but she'd felt an awareness developing, a feeling she couldn't describe, as if she and Daniel were about to embark on a long, exhilarating journey.

For weeks, they had been content with merely knowing how the other felt, exchanging delicious little glances, experiencing the thrill of just being in the same room as each other.

Two months ago, when he was about to leave and she accompanied him to the door, he'd whispered, 'I can't stand this much longer, it's driving me insane. I want you, Eleanor. I want you so much that I can't sleep at night, I can't *think* straight any more.' He ran his finger around the collar of his sparkling white shirt, as if it were too tight, preventing him from breathing. 'Is there a chance that we can . . .'

He left the rest of the sentence unsaid, but she knew exactly what he meant, feeling a similar tightness in her breast. 'Shall I come to your rooms one day?' she whispered back.

His blue eyes brightened. 'When?'

'Now! Leave and wait for me outside the Adelphi. I'll follow in about half an hour.'

She didn't know how she got through the next thirty minutes. She changed her clothes, right down to her underwear, and slipped into the pink crêpe-de-chine step-in cami-knickers trimmed with cream lace that she'd only recently bought. Had she had Daniel in mind when she bought them? she wondered, as she stared at her slim, girlish body in the mirror. She looked more like eighteen than twenty-five – and felt it. She was about to put on her new white crêpe-georgette frock with a stand-up collar and bishop sleeves that had cost the earth, when she recalled that they would have to catch a tram to Spellow Lane and it would be wise to wear something less obviously expensive. She chose a demure blue voile afternoon frock and a straw boater with a blue ribbon band that shouldn't cause anyone to stare.

Nancy was asked to keep an eye on Anthony who was immersed in his homework – Daniel was tutoring him in maths and English too. 'I'm just popping into town,' Eleanor told her. She was surprised that her voice sounded so normal.

Another half an hour later, and she was in Daniel's over-furnished rooms, lying on the big, bouncy bed, while he tenderly removed the clothes she'd only recently put on until she was completely naked and shivering with delight and trepidation at what was to follow.

But Daniel was as gentle as could be, entering her very slowly, moving leisurely while she adjusted to his rhythm and felt herself respond. The movements became faster and faster and she cried aloud because something was happening that had never happened before: a feeling of happiness, greater than she had ever known, was surging through her, flooding every vein and touching every bone, making her dry body come alive. The feeling grew and grew, becoming almost unbearable, until it ended quite suddenly. The ending was the best bit of all and she lay on the bed, completely exhausted. It was over and it had been a truly wonderful experience.

Daniel bent and kissed her on the lips. 'I love you, Eleanor,' he murmured.

'And I love you,' she cried.

'Can you come again tomorrow?'

'I couldn't possibly. Once, possibly twice a week, is all I could get away with, or people will suspect something's going on.'

Daniel pulled a face. 'Oh, well, I suppose one or twice a week is better than nothing at all.'

Now here they were at Sybil's party and Daniel was her son's tutor and she was Marcus's wife. She was perfectly satisfied with the first arrangement, but not terribly pleased with the second.

'I'm going to learn to read proper,' Brenna said. She was looking through a book that Cara had been given for her birthday: a child's ABC with a picture beside each letter.

'That's a good idea, Bren,' Colm said encouragingly. He'd never known her so quiet and it worried him. He was genuinely sorry he'd missed Cara's party, yet Brenna didn't seem to care. Any other time, he'd have expected an ear-bashing that would have gone on all night, although she would have forgiven him by the time they went to bed.

'I know all these words. A is for Apple, B for Bed, C for Cat.' She let the book drop on to her knee with a sigh.

'Are you all right, Bren? You don't seem yourself tonight.' He regarded her with concern.

'I've had a busy day and I'm tired, that's all.'

He felt even more worried: Brenna was never tired. 'Would you like me to make you a cuppa, luv?'

'That'd be nice, Colm. Ta.'

He fetched the water and put it on the hob. 'The fire's low, it'll take ages to boil.'

'It doesn't matter,' she said listlessly, adding, 'the Allardyces have bought an electric kettle. You just have to plug it in and the water boils.'

Was *that* was what bothering her? Was she jealous, wanting electricity in their own house so they could have a similar kettle? No, Colm decided. She wasn't the sort to go into a decline all because of a kettle. Brenna was never discontented with her lot, although she moved mountains to improve it. If he hadn't thought it downright impossible, he might have believed she'd overheard Lizzie Phelan invite him to a party at her flat tomorrow night and, what's more, heard him accept.

'There's just a few friends coming,' Lizzie had said. 'I thought you'd like to come, too.'

He felt privileged to be regarded as her friend. 'I'll be there,' he promised. It was only a party and he wouldn't be doing anyone any harm. He'd say to Brenna he was going to his first Labour Party meeting and, if he was late home, that they'd all gone for a drink afterwards. If he thought for a moment that she'd have stood for it, he'd've told her the truth, but Brenna would never comprehend his relationship with Lizzie was merely a meeting of minds.

But now Colm was wondering if he could possibly lie to Brenna when she was in such a low mood? If there were no improvement by tomorrow, then he wouldn't go to Lizzie's party.

Next morning Brenna appeared much better, if not exactly her usual good-humoured self. She snapped at the children, snapped at Colm and, by the time evening came, he was glad to have the excuse of the meeting to get him out of the house, even though it was a lie.

'Do you need to wear a collar and tie to the Labour Party?' she asked sharply.

At first he thought his attempt to look respectable had made her suspicious, but it was merely a continuation of the bad temper the family had suffered from all day. He mumbled something about it not hurting to turn up looking decent. She didn't reply.

Lizzie's flat was on the top floor of a tall house in Mount Pleasant, not far from where it had been planned to build the Catholic cathedral: the work had been abandoned when they got as far as the crypt. The front door of the house was open and, as Colm climbed the stairs, he could hear dance music. He hoped he wouldn't be expected to dance: after a few drinks, he could manage an Irish jig, but that was all.

'Colm! There you are!' Lizzie cried when he went inside. She wore a pretty, frilly frock – he'd never seen her in anything so feminine before. 'Folks, this is Colm Caffrey. I won't introduce you, Colm, you'll never remember the names. What would like to drink?'

'Beer,' he muttered. The flat appeared to consist of one large room with a kitchen off and a door that no doubt led to the bedroom. There were about twenty people there and a few had turned to look when Lizzie had introduced him, but were now re-engaged in furious conversations. Two couples were dancing. Colm attached himself to the edge of a group discussing world hunger while clutching plates piled high with sandwiches. Lizzie brought the beer and told him there was plenty of food in the kitchen and to help himself. Before he could say, 'Ta,' she was whisked away to dance by a chap wearing a cravat and a velvet waistcoat.

The conversation turned to the subject of D.W. Griffith, of whom Colm had never heard, but it turned out he directed films and one, *The Birth of a Nation*, was an all-time classic. He appeared to be the only one who hadn't seen it, which wasn't surprising as he'd never been inside a picture house. The turmoil in Russia following the revolution was next, and for the first time Colm ventured an opinion, 'It's the best thing that's ever happened to that benighted country,' he opined, using exactly the same words that Lizzie had used to him.

'The Tsar was undoubtedly a shit,' proclaimed a man with a straggly beard that came down to his chest, 'but the Bolsheviks are no better. The country is in a worse state now than it was before.'

'Yes, but Victor,' a woman argued, 'they're not being given much chance to make things better, are they? They have the French, the British, and the Americans against them, not to mention the Japanese who have seventy thousand troops in Vladivostok. How can they feed the people when they're continually at war?'

Colm melted away, wishing he hadn't spoken and scared someone would ask for his opinion and he wouldn't have one to offer. He was relieved when, after about three hours of torture, two of the guests announced they were going home and it meant he could go, too.

'Stay a little while longer, Colm,' Lizzie pleaded when he

approached to say he was leaving. 'There's something I wanted to ask you.'

He had to hang around for at least another half an hour before everyone had gone, although didn't mind. Out of all these highly intellectual people, Lizzie didn't want *him* to leave.

'What was it you wanted to ask me?' he enquired when the door closed on the last of the guests. She leaned against it, smiling. The frills on the frock had slipped off her shoulders and he could see the white slope of her breasts, the nipples prominent through the thin material.

'This!' She came towards him, still smiling, laid her small hands on his cheeks then, raising herself slightly on her high heels, pressed her lips against his. He was about to push her away, when he felt her tongue force its way between his teeth and begin to probe his mouth.

Colm's knees buckled. It was a practice he'd heard of, but never experienced. Her perfume was making him dizzy. He blinked, still in enough control of himself to have another attempt at pushing her tempting little body away, when she rubbed herself against him and murmured, 'I've wanted us to do this ever since we met,' and he was lost.

He walked like a maniac through the bright, moonlit streets, back to Brenna, back to the love of his life, the only woman he had ever wanted, the only woman he had ever touched – until tonight.

Lizzie had seduced him! And he, weak, shameful person that he was, had succumbed. Until tonight, the only part of Lizzie that interested him was her brain. Until tonight, all he'd wanted them to do was talk. Now he never wanted to see her again. He'd leave the builders' yard, find another job – easier said than done, but he'd manage it somehow.

All the lights were out in the house in Shaw Street: Brenna must have gone to bed. He went in the back way and crept up the stairs so he wouldn't disturb her or the children. Moonlight flooded through the window of the room where she lay, fast asleep, her red-gold hair spread over the pillow, and he thought how beautiful she was. He took off his clothes as quietly as he could, but couldn't remove the studs from his stiff collar – he should have taken it off downstairs.

Eventually, the front stud shot out and landed on the oilcloth with a tiny clatter. The slight noise was enough to wake Brenna.

'Hello, darlin',' she said sleepily. 'How did the meeting go?'

'It was all right.'

'Colm, I'm sorry I was in such an awful twist with meself earlier,' she contritely, 'but I did something desperately stupid yesterday – I let Katie tell me fortune from the tea leaves and she came up with some terrible things.'

'That was a daft thing to do, Bren.' He dragged off his vest, longing to get into bed and hold her.

'I know that now. Colm,' she said in small voice, 'I'm expecting another baby.'

Colm struggled out of his trousers, threw them on the floor, slid into bed and reached for her. 'That's great news, luv. Jaysus! I missed you tonight. I don't think I'll go to another Labour Party meeting.'

She nestled against him. 'I'm glad, darlin'. Me and Tyrone played Snap with those cards I bought the other day. You'd've enjoyed it.'

'I would indeed.' Playing cards with his wife and son would have been far more enjoyable than the party, including the aftermath with Lizzie.

'What's that smell?' Brenna raised her head and sniffed. 'It's scent, that expensive stuff Eleanor Allardyce uses.' Her voice rose. 'Where the hell have you been, Colm, to come home stinking of scent?'

'Lizzie Phelan was at the meeting,' he said easily, his heart beginning an ugly thump in his chest, as a feeling of sheer terror possessed him. 'She was sitting next to me. It must have just drifted across or something.'

'Drifted across!' Brenna was sitting up now. 'It's all over you: on your face and on your neck. I bet it's on your shirt and jacket too, or did you have nothing on when the scent just drifted across?'

'No, luv.' He was stuck to the bed, too weak to move.

'Did you sleep with Lizzie Phelan tonight, Colm?' Brenda asked quietly.

'No, luv.' He began to cry. 'Yes, luv, but only because she egged me on, pressed herself against me. I hardly knew what I was doing.' He rolled over and tried to take her in his arms, but she shoved him roughly away.

'Get off me!' she hissed. 'I don't want you touching me ever again, Colm Caffrey. I'll never forgive you for what you did tonight.'

'I didn't mean it, Bren. As I said, she egged me on . . .' His voice trailed away. It was no excuse, and he knew it. If only he could have the last few hours back and live them again. If only he'd thought to get washed before he came upstairs. 'Where are you going?' he asked when Brenna got out of bed.

'I'm going to sleep in Cara's room, in Paddy's bed. I'll sleep there permanent from now on and you can have this room to yourself.'

'There's no need for that, luv.'

'Oh, yes, there is. We've spent our last night together in this bed, Colm. It'll never happen again. From now on, you can sleep on your bloody own.'

She lay in Paddy's bed and stared through the bars of Cara's cot at the dark-blue sky scattered with stars. She knew she would never sleep that night. Her head felt as if it were on fire and there was another fire in her gut at the thought of Colm with another woman, doing the things that were special to him and Brenna. Had he held her in his arms afterwards and told her he loved her? It hurt so much that she wanted to scream and scream and never stop so there'd be no room in her head to think about Lizzie Phelan and her husband.

Cara whimpered in her sleep and Brenna put her hand through the bars of the cot and gently patted the warm little body. 'There, there, darlin',' she murmured. 'Your mammy's here.' She left her hand where it was, getting some sort of comfort from the rise and fall of Cara's breathing. At least she had the children to love and love her back. She wasn't sure if she still loved Colm, but supposed she must or the hurt wouldn't be this agonizingly painful.

She withdrew her hand and curled up under the covers. She'd never get comfortable – the pillow felt as if it had been filled with concrete. At some time during the day, she'd managed to convince herself it was just a coincidence that Katie had insisted she had four children when she only had three, little knowing there was another on the way. The other things were nonsense, 'a load of baloney,' as Nancy had said: the cross beside the rose that indicated a great tragedy, the dagger that meant betrayal, the weeping woman.

But that night, Colm had slept with Lizzie Phelan. What greater betrayal could there be than that?

Chapter 5

I can't be!

Eleanor stood sideways and looked again at her full-length reflection in the wardrobe mirror. 'I can't be,' she repeated aloud, yet there was no denying that her stomach was swollen and some of her frocks – the fitted ones – felt too tight, not just on her hips, but on her waist.

'I'm pregnant!' She was quite sure of it, yet hadn't been sick or breathless or off her food. She felt particularly well, had done for weeks. Her periods had never been regular and there was nothing unusual about missing a few. 'Perhaps I haven't felt ill because it's Daniel's child.' She remembered Daniel had promised she wouldn't conceive and had been taking some sort of precautions.

'I don't mind,' she told herself. 'In fact, I'm glad: really, really glad.'

The situation was becoming impossible. They were so much in love and it was torture being apart. But now she was having their baby and she would have to leave Marcus and live with Daniel instead. She couldn't wait to tell him the news: it was such a pity it was Sunday and she wouldn't see him until tomorrow. He would give up his rooms and they would rent a little house not too far from Parliament Terrace so she could come and see Sybil – Marcus would never let her have his precious little girl, but would almost certainly let Anthony go with her.

Excitement mounting, she sat on the bed and began to plan her life with Daniel. She would still pay his fees for tutoring Anthony because it was all he had to live on and she hoped he wouldn't find it too degrading. A woman would be engaged to clean and do the washing, but she would do the cooking herself – she was already looking forward to it. There was discarded furniture in the cellar, very old-fashioned, but would do until she bought new, more modern designs suitable for a much smaller house. Nancy was good at using the Singer sewing machine that was kept in the laundry room and would make some pretty curtains. It was all going to be quite wonderful.

The gong went for lunch and she went down to the dining room and found Marcus his usual grumpy self. They hardly spoke over the meal and she thought what heaven it would be never to eat with him again. As it was Sunday, Fergus was there, but Marcus insisted he and Anthony ate in the kitchen. 'The pair of them get on my nerves,' he'd complained months ago.

He finished eating and announced he was going to his club. Eleanor stayed at the table and wondered what to do with the afternoon. She would be quite happy just to sit and think about the life she would have with Daniel, but she usually took the boys out to Chester or Southport where they would have tea. Southport was the favourite, as they enjoyed playing football or cricket on the golden sands that seemed to go on for ever before they reached the sea. Lennie Beal, who worked in the factory and acted as their chauffeur, would arrive any minute to take them in the car. She could send him away if she cared to but, apart from seeing Daniel, Eleanor wasn't sure what she wanted on the day she had discovered she was expecting his child.

Then she had a brilliant idea: she would ask Lennie to take them to Southport, but to go via Spellow Lane, where they could stop and she'd tell Daniel the marvellous news.

The November day was crisply cold, but the sky was clear and the sun shone through the windows of the Wolsley making the leather seats feel quite hot. Liverpool had never looked so beautiful, Eleanor thought as they drove through the near-empty streets. All the shops were closed and there were few pedestrians about and hardly any traffic.

'Tell me where to stop, Mrs Allardyce,' Lennie said when they approached Spellow Lane.

'In about another hundred yards, outside a little tailor's shop called Myersons. The person I want to see lives over it.'

'Anthony wants to know who the person is you're going to see.' Fergus said when the car stopped. The boys had been conducting an animated conversation using sign language ever since they'd left Parliament Terrace. Fergus had obviously passed on this little piece of information.

'Tell him it's no one he knows.' If he knew it was Daniel, he would insist on coming in.

She knocked on the door at the side of the shop and thought she could live with him in his rooms while looking round for a house. They were quite comfortable, if a bit too crammed with furniture. He opened the door and his eyes widened in surprise. Eleanor pushed her way in and quickly closed the door. 'The boys are outside in the car. I don't want them to see you.'

'Why not?' His hair was tousled and his shirt without a collar. He wore black and white striped braces. She thought he looked utterly adorable. 'Kiss me,' she demanded.

He laughed. 'With pleasure.' He took her in his arms and kissed her soundly. 'Why the visit? I assume it's not for the usual reason, not if you've brought Anthony and Fergus with you?'

'We're on our way to Southport, but I've got something to tell you. Can we go upstairs?'

'Of course.' He stood aside to let her go in front. In his sitting room, a small fire burnt, tea stood on the hearth and maps were spread over the table. It looked warm and snug. 'I was just studying the world,' he said.

He would just have to delay his travelling plans until their child had grown. She smiled, and was actually able to feel the radiance shining from her face. 'Daniel, darling, I'm expecting a baby – *our* baby.'

His jaw dropped. 'You can't be!'

'But I am.' Her voice faltered. His reaction was not what she had expected.

'But I always made sure that you wouldn't.' He picked up a map and began to fold it neatly along the creases. His hands were shaking and there was perspiration on his upper lip.

Eleanor sat inelegantly on a chair with a thump. Her head was spinning and she badly wanted to be sick. 'Then you failed, because I'm pregnant, quite visibly so underneath my frock. Would you like me to show you?' she asked in a hard voice that didn't sound at all like her own.

'It could be your husband's.' He reached for another map to fold, but she tore it from his hands.

'It can't be my husband's. It can only be yours.'

'Perhaps the first time we . . .' he waved his hand towards the bedroom door, '. . . the first time, I may not have withdrawn quickly enough.'

'Then that, Daniel, is the reason why I'm expecting *our* baby,' Eleanor said in the same hard voice.

'What do you want me to do?' he asked helplessly.

'For a start, you could take some responsibility for your actions.'

'In what way?'

'I thought you would want us to set up home together. I thought you loved me, you said so often enough. I love *you*.' She was doing her utmost not to cry and was angry with herself when she felt two tears trickle down her cheeks. She wiped them away with her sleeve and willed no more to come.

'I love you! Oh, darling, I love you with all my heart.' He knelt at her feet and put his arms around her waist. 'But . . .' he sighed.

'But what?'

'We agreed, didn't we, right from the start, that this was just an affair? We were just having a wonderful time and it would lead nowhere.' He looked at her pleadingly, as if expecting she would agree, go home and not bother him again.

'We did indeed, Daniel, but it's no longer just an affair: it has led to me becoming pregnant with your child.'

He shrugged. 'I have so little money to take on you and a baby.'

'I thought you had been saving all these years to travel around the world?'

'There's about thirty-five pounds saved.' He got to his feet and backed away across the room, as if she was about to snatch the money off his person.

She had more than a hundred times that much, but had no intention of telling him. The money might persuade him to take her on: money was the only reason Marcus had wanted her and she wasn't going to let it happen again.

'Perhaps your husband will accept the child as his own?' he suggested.

'You really think so?' She was tempted to laugh.

'Eleanor, ever since I was sixteen I have longed to travel. It's what

I want to do more than anything in the world.' There was that pleading look on his face again.

Eleanor stood. 'Oh, well, don't let me stop you.'

'Under different circumstances,' he said piously, 'I wouldn't dream of letting you down, but you have a wealthy husband, a beautiful home. You won't exactly be destitute.'

'No, I won't, will I? Well, goodbye, Daniel. The boys will be wondering where I am.'

He followed her to the door. 'Do you want me to come to tomorrow?'

'Of course. Anthony needs you, but that's the only reason. I would prefer it if I never saw you again.'

'Nancy?'

'Yes, pet?' It was Nancy's day off, but she was in the kitchen making an evening meal.

'I've got a frightful headache and I'm going to lie down. Tell Nurse Hutton to leave me alone, will you? I don't want her fussing around.'

Nancy looked at her searchingly. 'You look awful pale. Would you like some Aspro? It seems ages since you last had one of your heads.'

'I think it was the wind in Southport. It was quite penetrating on the beach, actually brought tears to my eyes.' She'd cried herself silly on the beach. The boys were too far away to see and Lennie Beal was waiting in the car.

'Look, pet, sit down and I'll make you a nice, strong cuppa – I love using this new kettle. I'll get the Aspro and you can take a couple, *then* lie down. What d'you say, eh?'

'All right.' Eleanor sat in her usual place at the table, a far nicer place to be than her cold bedroom where she would just cry and cry and only feel worse. But sitting in her old place by the kitchen fire, the place where she'd sat ever since she was a little girl and her father was alive and life had seemed so uncomplicated and happy, made a lump come to her throat and she burst into tears.

'Eleanor!' Nancy was beside her in an instant, stroking her hair. 'Oh, my poor girl. What's the matter?'

'I'm having a baby, but it's not Marcus's, it's Daniel's, and he doesn't want any more to do with me.' It was such a relief to let it all pour out.

'Holy Mary, mother of God,' Nancy gasped. 'What are you going to do now, pet?'

'I've no idea. I couldn't possibly tell Marcus. He'd kill me.' Eleanor shuddered at the idea of telling her husband the truth.

'I think you'll find Marcus already knows about you and Daniel,' Nancy said, and Eleanor's blood turned to ice in her veins.

'How could he possibly know?' she asked shakily. 'I thought we'd kept it a secret.'

'It was obvious weeks ago at Sybil's party – that's when I guessed meself. I never said anything. I expected you'd tell me in your own good time.'

'Obvious?' She felt utterly stunned.

'It was written all over your faces, pet.' Nancy groaned. 'Oh, Eleanor, and now you're expecting a baby. You've got yourself into a dreadful pickle.'

Eleanor laughed a touch hysterically. 'I don't suppose you can think of a way out of it?'

'Not at the minute, girl.' They both sat silently staring into the fire. 'You could always throw yourself on Marcus's mercy,' Nancy said after a while, although her expression was doubtful.

Eleanor raised her eyebrows. 'Do you really think that would work?'

'Nah.' Nancy shook her head. 'It was a soft idea. I doubt if he's got an ounce of mercy in him.'

'There's nothing else for it, I'll just have to leave – I'd already planned to. I had expected to be living with Daniel, but that's not on, I'm afraid.' The thought of Daniel made her want to cry again.

'But it wouldn't be right, you leaving,' Nancy said angrily. 'This house belonged to your father and he left it to the both of you: you and Marcus. Why should you have to leave? No matter what you've done, Eleanor, you've every right to stay.'

'Oh, Nancy! He'd make my life even more of a misery than he does now. You know he would. I couldn't stand it.' She had another thought. 'He might even have the right to throw me out: after all, I've committed adultery.' Making love with Daniel hadn't seemed like anything so gross as adultery, such an awful word.

'It still doesn't seem right,' Nancy muttered.

★

Over the next few days, her mind was in turmoil and she was plagued by headaches. Daniel came, but she made sure they didn't meet, although half hoped he would come and say he'd changed his mind: that he loved her too much to let her down, that he wanted them to spend the rest of their lives together. It was what she'd thought he'd wanted, the impression that he'd given. How could she have been so naive as to believe him?

Her tortured brain relived their last conversation, word for word, every inflection in his voice, the varying expressions on his face. Perhaps, as he'd claimed, he really did love her, but there was something – travelling – that he loved more. He may not have even realized it himself until faced with the choice.

But she wasn't too sure that, if he changed his mind, she still wanted him. His initial reaction was the only one that really mattered and she wanted his total commitment, not some half-hearted promise to look after her and their child because his conscience pricked.

But Daniel's conscience mustn't have pricked because he didn't come, clearly as anxious to avoid her as she was him. And, while Eleanor struggled to come to terms with being so cruelly let down, she also had to contend with her terror of Marcus. He knew! He'd known for weeks. Why hadn't he said anything? What was he waiting for?

Eleanor didn't think she would ever raise the courage to face him. The best thing would be to find a house – *quickly* find one before her pregnancy became obvious – and then just go when he was at the factory or his club, taking only her clothes, and leaving both her children behind. Any minute now, Daniel would be dismissed – she was surprised Marcus hadn't done it before – and it didn't seem fair for Anthony both to lose his tutor and be taken away from the only home he'd ever known. It would break her heart more than it already was, but she was prepared to make the sacrifice in order to do what was best for her child. Anyway, she was hopeless at communicating with him, just couldn't remember the signs. Nancy was better at it than she was and Fergus would be there to act as Anthony's ears.

She'd start looking for a house tomorrow, Eleanor resolved with a sigh.

★

Brenna and Colm had swapped rooms. Now Colm occupied the box room and Brenna and Cara slept in the big double bed, the empty cot in the corner waiting for the new baby who should arrive next May: Rory if it was a boy, Maire for a girl.

Fergus and Tyrone had noticed the new arrangements, but hadn't said anything: the significance of their mammy and daddy sleeping apart no doubt escaped them.

The baby was like a lump of lead in her stomach. Brenna dreaded to think what it would be like in another four or five months. She felt lethargic and slightly sick most of the time and kept stumbling clumsily all over the place, banging into the furniture and tripping over the mats. She climbed stairs like a ninety-year-old.

'I never felt like this with the other three,' she told Colm. It was impossible to ignore someone in such a small house and, after a few days of coldness on her part, she'd started speaking to him again.

'I know, luv.' He couldn't have been more sympathetic and understanding, refusing to let her lift a finger once he was home from work, washing dishes and putting the children to bed. He insisted she did the laundry on Sundays, supposedly a day of rest, so he could do the mangling and put the heavy things on the rack and hoist it up to the ceiling, a task that required a very strong hand. Brenna didn't seem to have a strong anything these days.

She appreciated all he did. He wasn't helping in the hope that she would forgive him for sleeping with Lizzie Phelan: he'd have done it anyway, because he was that sort of man and she still loved him desperately. What she wanted more than anything was for them to lie in bed and for him to stroke the heavy lump and make it lighter, make her stronger, make her smile, because she didn't feel much like smiling any more.

He'd lit the fire before he went to work, and made tea and porridge for the children, and now the house was empty except for her and Cara, who was playing under the table with the little building blocks her daddy had made. Brenna forced herself out of the chair on to her feet. The house needed tidying, there was dusting to be done. She might feel as weak as a puppy, but she was determined her house would stay clean.

Upstairs, she made the beds: there were little sticky bits on the lads' pillowslips from the rock that Fergus had brought back from

Southport. 'Mrs Allardyce bought it for us, Mam. She got a stick for our Tyrone, too.'

'That's very kind of her, I must say,' Brenna had said, tight-lipped.

'She was dead miserable today, Mrs Allardyce. She kept crying all the time. Her eyes were all red.'

'Huh! What's *she* got to cry about?'

'I dunno, Mam. I didn't ask. She only cried when she thought me and Anthony weren't looking.'

'Probably upset her hair doesn't look right or she doesn't like her latest frock,' Brenna muttered.

She opened the window and gave the pillows a shake, then put them back on the beds – another time she would have changed the slips, but the days of changing pillowslips before they'd seen the week out were over for the time being.

Colm had already made his bed. She wanted to weep when she saw how neatly it was done: the sheets tucked firmly under the mattress, the pillow plumped up. The books he'd taken to reading were in a tidy heap on the pine chair she'd bought for threepence in a second-hand shop, carrying it home triumphantly on the pram.

The top book was called *The Levellers: A History* – she had to divide the words into syllables and pronounce them slowly, but they still didn't make sense. The other books had equally difficult titles that she didn't bother trying to read – her own efforts to improve her reading were proceeding very slowly. Colm's books were all about politics, that much she knew. He read them after she'd gone to bed. 'I want to better meself,' he'd told her. 'I don't want to work in a builders' yard me whole life.'

Brenna had no idea if he still saw Lizzie Phelan. The last time her name had been mentioned in the house in Shaw Street was the night he'd confessed they'd made love.

It had come as a relief to Colm to find he didn't have to leave his job. When it was time to have his dinner on the Monday after the fateful party, he hid himself at the end of a stack of timber and sat on an upturned bucket to eat his sarnies. It was one thing, in the heat of the moment, to vow he'd find another job, but easier said than done in the cold light of day. He hoped Lizzie wouldn't come looking for him when he failed to turn up in the kitchen for a drink.

A few minutes later, she called him. 'Colm? Colm? Tea's made.'

He huddled down on the bucket in an attempt to make himself invisible, but minutes later she appeared, dressed in one of her smart outfits and looking extremely pretty and highly amused.

'Colm!' she laughed. 'Oh, poor Colm! You're embarrassed, aren't you, after what happened on Saturday?'

'Yes,' he admitted.

'There's no need to be. We didn't do anything to be ashamed of.'

'*I* did.' Colm scowled. 'I happen to be a married man.'

'We made love, Colm, that's all. What difference can that make to your marriage?'

'Me wife's found out, for one thing and, for another, it's just not right. I've broken one of the Ten Commandments.' He hadn't exactly coveted another man's wife because Lizzie wasn't married, but it felt like a sin all the same.

'Oh, dear!' She fetched another bucket and sat beside him, not appearing the least concerned. Her legs, glistening in their fine silk stockings, were almost touching his. 'Is your wife cross?'

'You could say that,' he replied sardonically, edging his legs away.

She put her head on one side and looked at him curiously. 'I'm a believer in free love. I can never understand why people make such a fuss if their partner sleeps with someone else. What we did didn't mean anything, it was just nice while it lasted and shouldn't make any difference to your marriage.'

'Well, it has,' he growled.

'Would you like me to see your wife and explain things?' she offered.

He managed a grin. 'I don't think that's such a good idea.' He didn't even try to imagine what Brenna's reaction would be if Lizzie turned up on the doorstep.

'Oh, well.' She stood. 'I'd better get back to work. There's tea made in the kitchen if you want it. I expect you'd prefer it if I never came again.'

'It's *your* house. I'm not the one to say whether you should come or go.'

'I was only coming for you. I fancied you, Colm, the minute I set eyes on you, but I don't want you eating your sandwiches outside in the depths of winter because you're too embarrassed to face me.'

By God, she was a forward woman! To actually tell him that she fancied him! In other words, she'd set out to seduce him right from the start. He grudgingly admired her nerve, but wished it had been some other unlucky chap she'd fancied and not him.

'Tara, Colm.' She tripped away, but seconds later was back. 'You know,' she said seriously, 'you should do something with that brain of yours. It's wasted working for me dad. Read more books, study, broaden your mind. It's said that knowledge is a dangerous thing, but only by those with power and money because they don't want people like you and me to understand what's going on in the world in case we try to do something about it. I hope you join the Labour Party: you'll be an asset, and you won't find me there. I've decided to join the Communists instead.' And with that, Lizzie Phelan disappeared. It would be twenty years before they met again.

Eleanor approached a letting agency and found a house with relative ease, although it was rather larger than she'd wanted. The smaller houses were in poor areas where she wouldn't dream of living – she had no intention of walking down the yard to the lavatory and couldn't survive without a bathroom. She settled on a four-bedroom semi-detached house in Tigh Street, a small cul-de-sac off Princes Drive. It had a greenhouse at the back that was full of mysterious-looking plants and had been occupied by an accountant who had recently retired to the countryside. The property company had had the place decorated from top to bottom before reletting. They weren't the colours Eleanor would have chosen, but would do.

After signing the five-year rental agreement, she went to Frederick & Hughes for coffee and to think about the enormous thing she'd just done. Very soon – and it would have to be soon because the bump in her stomach was becoming more apparent by the day – she would be living alone for the first time in her life, a terrifying thought, but it would only be until the baby came along. It reminded her that she must see a doctor – not Dr Langdon – and make arrangements to go into a nursing home when her time came.

The coffee finished, she signalled for the bill and the waitress brought it over. To her consternation, she discovered she had just enough money in her purse to pay and she'd intended purchasing a supply of headache tablets and witch hazel and cotton wool to make pads for her eyes when the headaches were at their worst – one was thumping away behind her eyes at this very minute. She had an account with Frederick & Hughes, but they didn't have a chemist's department. It meant money would have to be drawn out of the bank, something she hadn't done in ages. There was always enough left to buy odds and ends from the allowance Marcus gave her to settle the less important household bills.

She entered the dark interior of the bank and presented a withdrawal cheque for the sum of twenty pounds, having realized she would need money to buy things for the house – not every shop accepted cheques and she would need cash for the smaller items.

The man behind the counter smiled. 'Please take a seat, Mrs Allardyce. I'll be with you in a moment.' It was a good five minutes before he returned and counted out the money twice before putting it in an envelope and pushing it under the grill. 'Be careful with that, won't you, Mrs Allardyce? It's a lot of money for a lady to be carrying round.'

'I'm sure I shall manage,' she replied coolly, thinking him rather patronizing.

Home again, she saw Daniel's coat on the hallstand and could hear Nancy in the kitchen preparing dinner. The pram was in the hall: earlier, Nurse Hutton must have taken Sybil for a walk. It would seem the house could run quite well without her in every respect. Other people looked after her children, another woman made the meals, yet more women cleaned and washed on her behalf. There was very little that Eleanor actually *did*.

She went up to her room, undressed down to her petticoat, made the pads for her eyes and lay on the bed, feeling that at least she'd done something terribly brave in renting a house and taking care of her own destiny for a change. Half asleep, she heard Daniel leave and Nancy shout from the kitchen, 'Is Eleanor back?'

'I think I heard her go into her room earlier,' Nurse Hutton replied.

'Me want milk,' Sybil yelled.

'Milk, *please*,' the nurse admonished.

'Me want milk, *pleath*.'

'That's a good girl. Shall we go downstairs and ask Nancy for some?'

'Yeth, *pleath*.'

Marcus came home and shortly afterwards the gong went for dinner. Eleanor couldn't have eaten a thing. Despite the pads on her eyes, her headache felt worse than ever. She blamed Daniel. Until the fateful conversation in his rooms, she'd been free from headaches for months. She ignored the gong, knowing that Nancy would come to investigate her non-appearance at the dinner table. A minute later, Nancy did, knocking softly on the door before she opened it.

'What's the matter, pet?'

'I've got one of my heads. I don't feel like eating.'

'Do you want some tablets?'

'I've already taken some, but they haven't worked.' She suspected she'd taken too many and it was why she felt so sleepy.

'You poor lamb!' Nancy clucked. 'I'll just close the curtains. It's turned dead horrible outside. Can you hear that wind? It's just started to rain and I've got a meeting tonight. I'll be leaving straight after dinner. Oh, and Fergus is late. Colm's taken him and Tyrone to see a bonfire somewhere, although it's not exactly the weather for it. He'll be round later.'

'Is it Friday?' It must be if Fergus was coming.

'Yes, and Guy Fawkes' Night an' all. We should have got some sparklers for Anthony and Sybil. They'd have loved them.'

'Maybe we could get some tomorrow?' She'd wondered what the strange banging and whistling noises were, had thought they belonged to the dreams she seemed to be drifting in and out of.

'Maybe. Look, pet, I'll have to go. Himself will have finished the soup by now and be wondering what's to follow.'

'Bye, Nancy,' Eleanor said lazily. Despite the pain in her head, she was faintly enjoying the sensation of being suspended between dreams and reality. More time passed, but it could have been minutes or hours, she had no idea. She was asleep again when the door of her room swung up. Before she could move, it was slammed shut and the sound almost made her skull split in two. The light went on. Marcus was standing at the foot of the bed. Eleanor had never seen him look so angry. She sat up and backed away until she was pressed against the headboard and could go no further.

'Why did you draw twenty pounds out of the bank today?' he demanded.

'How on earth do you know that?'

'A cashier rang to advise me that my wife was about to withdraw a large sum of money. There was nothing he could do to stop you, but he thought I should know.'

Her fear gave way to indignation. 'That's my own private

account. It has nothing to do with you, or the cashier, how I make use of it.'

'I'm your husband, Eleanor. I'm entitled to know what you're up to. What was the money for?' He came close, bending over her, his eyes glittering with rage. 'What's it for, Eleanor?'

'It's none of your business,' she stammered.

'Oh, yes it is. Is it for your paramour, for Daniel? Are you paying him to sleep with you?'

'Don't be silly, Marcus.' She shivered – he'd brought a waft of cold air in with him – and got off the bed the other side. She pushed her feet into slippers and went to fetch a dressing gown from behind the door. She was halfway there when Marcus hissed, 'You slut! You're expecting his child,' and she realized her thin petticoat emphasized the swell of her stomach where Daniel's baby lay.

'Yes, I am,' she said. It was all she could think of.

With two bounds, he was across the room and had slapped her face, hard. She screamed and he slapped her again. 'You slut!' he repeated. He shook his head and looked at her, perplexed, as if she'd been an exceptionally naughty child. 'What am I to do with you?'

Her head was ringing from the blows. She forgot about the dressing gown and made her way towards a chair and gingerly sat down. She'd been there for no more than a second, when Marcus dragged her to her feet, his hand an iron band around her arm, hurting badly. 'Is the money to get rid of it?' he rasped, his face only inches from hers.

'*No.*' It hadn't crossed her mind to get rid of her baby. She plucked up every bit of courage she possessed. 'I'm going to leave you, Marcus,' she said unsteadily. 'I already have a house and the money is to buy things for it.'

'You're going to live with *him*?' His face went livid and the hand on her arm tightened. 'What will people think? You'll be exposing me to the world as a cuckold.'

'I shan't be living with Daniel,' she said weakly. 'I intend to live alone.'

His eyes popped. 'Alone?'

'I think I will be happier alone than with you.'

'You're not taking the children.' He was blustering now and seemed to have lost some of his composure.

'I hadn't planned on taking the children. They'll be better off with Nurse Hutton and Nancy – and you.'

He released her arm and began to walk around the room, lips working, as if he was about to speak, yet nothing came. He was rattled. She was wondering why when the awareness came that he didn't want her to leave. She'd come with the house, one of the contents that he prized so much, like the gold watch that had belonged to her father, its thick chain draped across his chest, and the signet ring with a single diamond that had once gleamed on her father's finger but now gleamed on his. All these things, Eleanor included, went towards the image he liked to present to the world. Five minutes ago, he had come storming in, prompted by the cashier in the bank, to have a flaming row, forbid her to see Daniel again and reduce her to a pathetic wreck as he had done so many times in the past, not for a moment expecting her to say she was leaving him.

'Look, Eleanor,' he ran his fingers through his hair, suddenly reasonable, 'look, I'll accept the baby as my own, but Daniel will have to go, naturally, and I'll engage another tutor. Then I shall forget this ever happened and we'll return to the way we were before.'

'I never cared for the way things were before, Marcus,' she said coolly, although she felt anything but cool. Earlier that day, when she'd signed the rental agreement, she had tasted freedom and the taste was still in her mouth. What's more, she knew his reasonable manner would be gone within a week, it was inevitable, and then she'd have to be punished for the sin of sleeping with another man and carrying his child. Knowing Marcus as she did, the punishment could continue for the rest of her life and her child might be punished most of all.

'What do you want from me, Eleanor?' he demanded. She could tell that his anger was mounting again.

'Nothing.' She shrugged. 'Absolutely nothing.' She was leaving and he couldn't do anything to stop her.

It might have been the 'nothing', or it might have been the shrug that made him completely lose control. Unexpectedly, he grabbed her and propelled her towards the door, 'In that case, if you're going to leave, you can do it now!'

'But Marcus . . .' She was still in her petticoat and tried to grab the door as he pushed her through, but her hands just slipped away. 'Nancy! Nancy!' she screamed, as he dragged her downstairs.

'You won't get any help from that quarter,' Marcus laughed. 'She's out.'

'What's going on?' Nurse Hutton had come out of Sybil's room.

'Mind your own business, Nurse. It has nothing to do with you.'

'But Mr Allardyce!'

Marcus ignored her. By then, they were at the foot of the stairs, Eleanor struggling all the way, but her strength was barely half his. He opened the front door and flung her outside. Fireworks lit up the sky, and the rain was pouring down. She stumbled down the steps, sat at the bottom and began to cry.

Brenna found her there, still crying, when she arrived with Fergus.

Fergus raced down the basement steps, entering the house through the kitchen, and Brenna gasped, 'Jaysus, girl. You'll freeze to death out here. Here, put this on.' She transferred the shawl from her own shoulders on to Eleanor's, who immediately felt colder as the shawl was very wet. 'What's happened?'

'Marcus has thrown me out,' Eleanor wept. Oh, to be found in such a position by Brenna Caffrey, of all people.

'Holy Mary, mother of God! In this weather? I'll be having a wee word with that gentleman, and you'll be back inside in a jiffy.' She made to mount the steps, but Eleanor grabbed her skirt.

'I'd sooner you didn't. I don't want to go back inside.'

Brenna rolled her eyes. 'So you'd rather sit here in your underclothes and die of pneumonia?'

'I'm waiting for Nancy to come home and I'll stay with her tonight.' Nancy wouldn't take any notice of Marcus, no matter what he said or did – he wouldn't have dared do this to her had Nancy been home, ready to defend her with her life.

'Why not go and wait in Nancy's now?' Brenna suggested.

'Because Marcus knows that's exactly what I'll do and he'll only throw me out again.' Eleanor sniffed and wiped her nose with the hem of her petticoat, imagining him waiting in the kitchen to do that very thing.

'Here's a rag. It's not been used, so it's quite clean.'

'Thank you.' She reluctantly accepted the rag. 'Look, I know you're only being kind, but I wish you'd go away. I don't like being seen in this state.' She felt mortified by the indignity of it. Brenna was probably smugly thinking that Colm would never do such a thing to her.

'I bet you don't. I wouldn't either,' Brenna snorted. 'Why don't I fetch you a blanket or something from Nancy's? Your husband won't dare throw *me* out: if he tries, I'll give him what for. And he'd have a black eye by tomorrer once our Colm finds out.'

'That doesn't sound a bad idea.' Her body had become a giant goose pimple and she couldn't stop shivering.

Brenna returned with a blanket and reported there was no one about. 'Perhaps he hid, your husband, when he realized it was me and not you. Here, tuck this round you, although it'll be soaked through in no time in this rain. Come back to mine for a cuppa and a warm by the fire,' she coaxed. 'Colm's out and our Tyrone's looking after Cara, so I can't very well hang round here for long. Fergus is big enough to come on his own, but I can't get out of me head that Paddy, me brother-in-law, was murdered not far from here.'

By now, Eleanor didn't need much coaxing. She was having a baby and it wouldn't do to get a chill, and Brenna was in the same condition and hadn't been very well, according to Nancy. It could be hours before Nancy came home, Brenna was being so kind and nice, and she badly needed someone kind and nice at that moment. What's more, she felt in urgent need of a cuppa and a warm by the fire.

She never forgot, even when she was a very old woman, the walk back to Shaw Street in her petticoat with a blanket over her head, Brenna linking her arm. It was the night a friendship was forged that would last a lifetime.

They didn't talk much. Brenna remarked she must have done something desperately awful to annoy her husband, and Eleanor snorted and said 'inflame' would be a better word. 'I'll tell you about it sometime.'

When the rain became heavier, they shrieked and began to run, and Eleanor gave Brenna half the blanket to shelter under and actually found herself laughing.

★

When Daniel Vaizey arrived at Parliament Terrace on Monday, Marcus opened the door and sacked him on the spot.

'But I'm entitled to a month's notice or money in lieu of,' Daniel protested, not very forcefully, having guessed the reason for his sacking. 'And what about Anthony? He needs me.'

His answer was to have the door slammed in his face. He wandered away, feeling unbearably sad. In a few months, Eleanor would give birth to his child: a child he would never see, never touch. He wouldn't even know if it was a boy or a girl. Was it worth giving up something as dear as a son or daughter just to go travelling? The question would haunt Daniel Vaizey for the rest of his life.

Marcus knew he'd made an error of mammoth proportions by despatching Eleanor from the house in such a brutal way. He had lost his temper and, although he considered himself justified in doing so and that Eleanor had deserved everything she'd got, he should have behaved more like the gentleman he was. Nancy wasn't speaking to him, Nurse Hutton was being very cold. Only Sybil was pleased to see him. He had been sent to Coventry in his own home. Being cold-shouldered by the servants didn't particularly bother him: what vexed him was that Brenna Caffrey had become involved.

On Friday night, he'd watched through the window as Eleanor sat weeping on the step, at first with a feeling of triumph in his heart but, as his anger diminished, he realized he'd gone too far. He had forgotten it was raining and hadn't noticed that she wasn't wearing proper clothes. He hadn't been aware of anything except his own blind rage at what she'd done and was about to do. He had actually moved in the direction of the front door to let Eleanor in, when he heard voices and returned to the window just in time to see Brenna Caffrey drape her shawl around his wife's shoulders.

He groaned. She still haunted him, Brenna, although he no longer followed her in the street. They'd come face to face a few times over the last year and he'd been in receipt of her glowing, dimpled smiles. She thought very highly of him, under the impression that he was responsible for finding the cutting in the *Echo* that led to Colm discovering he owned a house.

But what would she think of him now she knew he'd thrown his pregnant wife on to the street? She'd hate him. She'd call him every name under the sun. Marcus put his face in his hands and groaned again.

'This is lovely oilcloth,' Brenna remarked. 'Nice and thick and shiny. It's hard to believe it's not real wood. Cara! Stop sliding on it, darlin', or you'll make marks. Play with your bricks instead. See, I've brought them with me.' She emptied the bricks on to the parquet-patterned linoleum that did indeed look very real.

'It's not new,' Eleanor said. 'It was laid by the previous tenant.' All the downstairs rooms were covered with the same pattern: upstairs had pale, mottled pink.

They were in the parlour of Eleanor's new house in Tigh Street waiting for the van to arrive with the furniture she'd bought in Frederick & Hughes on Saturday, just enough for her basic needs: two armchairs, a sideboard, a small dining room suite, a bed and a wardrobe, bedding, towels and a few dishes. Once settled, she'd get the rest.

'If that van doesn't come soon, I'll end up sitting on the floor.' Brenna was uncomfortably perched on the sill in the broad bay window. 'Ask the men to bring the chairs in first, won't you, El?'

'I will, don't worry.' Eleanor was similarly perched on the sill. Both were four months pregnant and longed to sit down. She quite liked being called 'El'. It was how Brenna had addressed her throughout the weekend she'd just spent in the Caffreys' house, a highly emotional weekend during which she'd had to come to terms with the fact that she'd burnt all her bridges behind her.

On Saturday afternoon, Nancy had turned up. She hadn't known Eleanor had left until that morning when Nurse Hutton had breathlessly relayed the events of the night before. 'She said she saw you and Brenna leave together, so I came round as soon as I could. Are you all right, pet? I won't say what I think of that husband of yours. I expect you know that already.'

'I feel marvellous,' Eleanor cried. 'I know I shouldn't, but I do. It's as if I've just escaped from jail, but I'm terribly worried about the children. How are they?'

'They're both fine. When I left, Anthony and Fergus were playing snakes and ladders and Marcus was reading Sybil a story.' It would seem that no one had missed her, Eleanor thought. 'Any road, pet,' Nancy continued, 'I've brought your handbag and some clothes and other bits and pieces. I'll put all your other stuff in a trunk and you can send someone to collect it when you're ready. Shall I bring the children round tomorrow to see you?'

'That would be nice.' She wondered if they'd want to come.

Colm offered to collect her trunk and deliver it on the handcart, Nancy said she would make curtains for the house in Tigh Street and Brenna said she'd come and help when everything was delivered. 'I bet you've never made a bed before,' she said slyly, and Eleanor was forced to concede that she hadn't. She was beginning to feel glad that Marcus had thrown her out. *That* life hadn't been nearly as good as this one, children or no children.

Brenna was greatly enamoured with the new house. 'Me and Colm will have big house like this one day,' she'd said earlier when Eleanor had shown her around. 'Colm's going to night school to further his education. One day soon, he'll be giving up the builders' yard for something better.'

'That's good,' Eleanor said absently. She was staring at the ceiling. 'Will you show me how to put the light on before you go? We've had electricity in Parliament Terrace for as long as I can remember. I don't know what you do with gas.'

''Course I will,' Brenna said generously. 'And if there's any little jobs you need doing, Colm'll do them for you.'

'Thank you.' She was about to say how kind he and Brenna were being, when something bounced in her stomach. 'I'm sure the baby kicked just then,' she gasped. 'Has yours kicked yet?' she asked, wanting her baby to be the first.

'No.' A shadow fell over Brenna's face and she turned away. 'If it wasn't that I was getting bigger, I'd swear my baby was dead.'

'What on earth makes you think that?' The hairs rose on Eleanor's neck. It was such a creepy thing to say.

'It *feels* dead,' Brenna said tonelessly. 'It just lies there like a heavy lump in me belly. I've never been able to picture it having a face and arms and legs like the others.'

'Oh, Brenna! You've got too much imagination.'

Before Brenna could reply, the furniture van rumbled to a halt outside and Eleanor went to ask the men to bring in the chairs first.

It was hard to admit, even to herself, that she *wanted* the baby to be dead. She knew she was being desperately foolish, but two of Katie

MacBride's predictions had already come true and any minute now she would lose something very precious. The only things precious to Brenna were Colm and her children and she'd sooner lose the baby than any of them.

They had wondered if, once again, their babies would be born on the same day, within the same hour, possibly at the same minute, but Eleanor's was the first to arrive on the final day of April, after the earth had been cleansed and renewed and was ready for summer.

'It's a boy,' Nancy announced when she came round to Shaw Street with the news. Brenna was likely to drop her own baby any minute and had neither the strength nor the energy to go all the way to the nursing home in Woolton to see her new friend. 'Seven pounds, ten ounces, very handsome and full of beans. She's calling him Jonathan.'

'That's a nice name,' Brenna said dully. 'How is Eleanor?' She remembered the state Eleanor had been in when she'd had Sybil.

'Absolutely fine,' Nancy enthused. 'Since she left Marcus, she's been like a new woman. She didn't need a single stitch and said it hardly hurt at all. She was sitting up, as right as rain, when I went in to see her.'

Brenna sighed. 'I can't wait for me own wee one to come. I feel like a sack o' sawdust, so I do.'

She clutched the bars at the top of the bed and tried not to scream. The effort must have shown on her face as Edie O'Rourke, who acted as unofficial midwife in the area, said gently, 'It won't hurt to make a bit of noise, Brenna. Don't hold it in. It's not doing you any good at all.' Edie had seventeen children of her own and had lost count of her numerous grandchildren. She was a little roly-poly woman with cheeks like apples and a mop of lovely silver hair.

'I don't want to frighten the children.' Cara had been put in with the lads, while a frantic Colm had been despatched at around midnight to fetch the doctor when Edie confessed there was no more she could do: the baby positively refused to budge, despite Brenna pushing and pushing until she could push no more, and the pains that swept regularly over her body: pains the like of which she'd never known before. She still hadn't screamed.

'Has Colm been gone long?' It felt as if he'd been gone for days.

'About half an hour. He'll have roused Doctor Hammond by now and they should be here any minute.' Edie wiped her perspiring face with a flannel, just as a car drew up outside and, seconds later, Colm came pounding up the stairs, followed, more sedately, by the doctor carrying a worn leather bag.

'Is she all right?' Colm gasped.

'She's fine, Colm, luv, if more than a bit weary. Your Brenna's a very healthy girl, it's just the baby . . .' Edie stood aside for the doctor and briefly explained what had happened.

Dr Hammond quickly took in the situation. 'She should be in hospital,' he said brusquely, 'but it's too late for that now.' He opened the bag. 'I'm afraid, Mrs Caffrey, that this is going to hurt rather badly.'

At the first nick of the knife, Brenna fainted. When she came to, the doctor was bending over her, a needle in his hand. He was stitching her up and it hurt like blazes, but not as much as the knife had.

'We've got another boy, Bren.' Brenna managed to turn her head and saw Colm was holding their baby in his arms, his face wet with tears. The tiny boy was wrapped in same the shawl that had been used for their other children. 'Our Rory,' Colm breathed.

'He's awful still and quiet,' she said. 'He's not dead, is he?'

Dr Hammond shook his head. 'No, Mrs Caffrey. Like you, your baby is very tired. He had a hard job coming into the world. He'll perk up in a few days.'

'Are you sure about that, Doctor?' Edie O'Rourke looked doubtful. 'He seems a bit *too* still and quiet to me. I've never known a baby make no sound at all when it came out the womb. There's usually at least a whimper.'

'And what qualifications do you have for saying that, Mrs O'Rourke?' The doctor barked, throwing Edie a scornful look. 'This isn't the first time I've been called to an emergency because you were unable to cope, sometimes too late, I might add. It's about time women like you were banned.'

Edie went very red, but must have decided this was neither the time nor place for an argument. She reached for her coat, saying, 'I'll drop in tomorrer, Brenna, luv, see how you're doing, like.'

The doctor finished his work, gave the baby a cursory glance and said his bill would arrive in the post in a few days. He left and Colm put Rory in his mother's arms.

'How are you feeling, luv?' He couldn't have looked more worn and haggard if he'd given birth to the baby himself.

'As weak as water.' Every ounce of energy had drained from her body. She looked down at the tiny, fragile body that felt as light as a feather. 'He's like a little angel,' she whispered.

'He is indeed.' Colm stroked her hair. 'I was worried I was going to lose you.' He looked close to tears again.

She moved her face so her cheek rested in his hand. 'You won't get rid of me that easy. What are those red marks on the sides of his head?'

Colm grimaced. 'The doctor had to pull him out with something that looked like fire tongues, 'cept they were silver.'

Brenna shuddered at the thought, glad she'd been unconscious at the time. 'He *is* awful still and quiet.' She touched Rory's cheek: it felt unnaturally cold. 'He looks as if he's been carved out of wax,' she said.

'Would you like a cup of tea, luv?'

'I'd love one, Colm, ta.'

Colm gone, she examined the baby all over and was pleased to find him perfect in every way, but wished he didn't feel so cold. She tried to make him suck at her breast, but his little mouth refused to open and he still hadn't opened his eyes. His fluff of hair was a light, powdery gold.

'Look at me, Rory, darlin',' she pleaded, but the pale-blue lids, which looked as if they were made of the finest silk, remained closed.

'Would you like me to put him down in his cot, Bren?' Colm asked when he returned with the tea. 'It's all ready to take him.'

'No, I want to hold him, try to make him warm.' She remembered she'd wanted the baby to be dead, but he'd been born alive and now she desperately wanted him to stay alive, watch him grow until one day he was as big as Colm. It had taken just one look to make him as precious to her as her other children. 'I'm worried about him, Colm,' she said fretfully. 'He's breathing like a little bird, you can hardly feel it.'

'Don't forget the doctor said he'd perk up in a few days. He's just tired, luv, like you.' Colm gave a reassuring smile. 'Hand him over while you drink your tea. By the way, I just looked in on Cara and the lads and they're fast asleep.'

'That's good. In a minute, will you fetch me rosary beads from downstairs? They're in the right-hand sideboard drawer. Oh, and bring the statue of the Blessed Virgin while you're at it, and put it on the mantelpiece so I can see her.' She needed talismans to bring her and Rory luck.

The night was as quiet as the grave, not even the faintest of sounds came from the sleeping city as Brenna nursed the new baby against her breast and willed him to move, get warm, open his eyes. There was something terribly patient, almost noble, about his dear little face, which brought tears to her eyes and made her heart ache so hard it hurt far more than the cuts and stitches she'd had earlier. Somewhere in the far distance, a clock struck four.

Colm lay on the bed beside her, fully dressed. Every half-hour or so, he went down and made more tea.

'You've got two brothers and a sister, Rory, and a big, tall daddy who already loves you to bits. And I'm your mammy, darlin', and I love you more than words can say. Oh, Rory!' she wept. 'I wish you weren't so cold.' She said yet another prayer to the Blessed Virgin to make her baby warm.

Another hour passed and the distant clock struck five. Rory felt no warmer and still hadn't moved. Outside, a door slammed: the street was beginning to stir. Colm made more tea and suggested he fetch the doctor back.

Brenna laid her hand against the baby's chest and could feel nothing. 'I think it's too late for that, Colm,' she whispered.

Colm's face turned ashen. 'Christ Almighty, Bren, he's not gone, has he?'

Brenna nodded. 'It happened only a moment ago. I could almost sense the life flow out of him, whatever life there was.' It was as if a tiny bit of herself had died. 'His little soul's flown straight to heaven.'

The tears flowed freely down Colm's cheeks. He pressed his lips against the baby's forehead. 'Goodbye, Rory,' he murmured, then raised his head and looked Brenna squarely in the eyes. 'After tonight, we're closer to each other than we've ever been before. I can't say how sorry about what happened with Lizzie Phelan, luv, but I swear nothing like that will ever happen again. It's you I love, I always will, and I want to come back to your bed and hold you in my arms and dry your tears when you cry for Rory.'

'All right, Colm.' She stroked his chin, but they didn't kiss. This wasn't the time for kissing with their cold, dead baby lying against her breast. She didn't tell him that things would never be the same as they'd been before, not for her. Although she loved him with all her heart, he'd let her down and, if he'd done it once, he could do it a second time. He'd turned out to be weak, when she'd always thought him strong, and she would never completely trust him again.

Chapter 6

1927

Sybil was being her obnoxious little self. 'It's *my* cake,' she said pettishly. '*I* should be the one who blows the candles out.'

'It's a shared cake,' Nancy told her. 'Half is yours, half is Cara's, and it's got seven candles on each side for you to blow out together.'

'Why can't I have had a cake of my own?'

'Because,' Nancy sighed patiently, 'this is a shared birthday party. Half the guests are yours and the other half are Cara's.'

Sybil sniffed disdainfully. '*I've* got more guests than Cara.'

'No, you haven't, pet. Cara has three and you have three. I'm a shared guest, like the cake.'

'But I want you to be *my* guest, Nancy.'

Nancy rolled her eyes and didn't answer. She noticed that Eleanor had been frowning as she listened to this exchange. As Marcus was raising their daughter, she didn't like to interfere, but thought Sybil was being outrageously spoilt. She was showered with expensive toys and clothes, and got her own way in practically everything, able to wrap her father around her dainty little finger. Should Marcus object to one of her demands, she only had to pout her pretty lips and he would give way. Her smooth blonde hair was topped with a mammoth pink bow and her frock − pink organdie, the skirt and sleeves a froth of frills and lace − had come from Frederick & Hughes and must have cost a mint. Father and daughter had gone together to buy it and afterwards they'd had lunch in the restaurant, something that nowadays Eleanor regarded as a luxury.

Marcus was upstairs, not exactly sulking, but not exactly pleased either that Eleanor was at the party with Jonathan. Sybil was rather taken with Jonathan, had demanded his presence and Eleanor had refused to let him come alone. Anyway, she was Sybil's mother. She had every right to be there.

It was all terribly complicated, Nancy thought sadly. Eleanor came often to see Sybil and Anthony, but only when Marcus was at work. He had made no objection, so Nancy assumed he didn't mind, although he minded today because it was Sybil's seventh birthday and he'd wanted to be present.

'What are you two laughing at?' she demanded when she noticed that Anthony and a frantically signing Fergus were in fits of giggles. Tyrone looked bored out of his mind. He'd always been old beyond his years and girls' birthday parties weren't exactly his cup of tea, at least not when the girls were only seven. Jonathan seemed to be the only one eating and was steadily demolishing the salmon sandwiches. Eleanor was still frowning and Nancy could tell Brenna was cross from her pursed lips. If only Louella Fisk, Anthony's tutor, was here, smoking one of her black cigarettes and giving Nancy the occasional wink at the ridiculousness of it all, lifting her spirits no end.

'Anthony thinks Sybil's dead funny,' Fergus said.

'Why?' asked Eleanor.

Fergus signed the 'why' and it was Anthony himself who replied, but no one could understand him. He had a vacuum tube hearing aid in his room, much too heavy to cart around with its earpiece, amplifier and box for the batteries, so had heard people speak, but not his own voice, so the intonation was completely wrong. He almost disappeared under the table, giggling uncontrollably at the sight of the mystified faces as they tried to make out the words that only Fergus could understand. Nancy hoped he would always find such lack of comprehension amusing.

'He thinks Sybil's a blithering idiot and wants her bottom smacking,' Fergus supplied.

At this, Sybil looked outraged and started to cry. Nancy raised her eyebrows. 'And he finds that funny?'

Anthony must have been able to understand her expression and he nodded. Nancy wondered what it must be like, sitting in this noisy room without being able to hear a single sound. He was twelve and once his deafness had been recognized, he had adjusted wonderfully to his largely silent world, although she was confident he wouldn't have managed so well without Fergus, who'd been his connection to the hearing world for so long.

'Which of the candles do I blow out, the white ones or the pink ones?' Sybil sniffed.

'I thought you and Cara could blow the lot out together, pet, but if you have to have your own, then the pink ones. Pink's your favourite colour, isn't it?'

'I like white better.'

'You can blow the white ones out. I don't mind,' Cara said.

Brenna said exasperatedly, '*I* brought the white ones specially for you.'

'But I don't mind, Mam, honest,' Cara assured her.

'I'm beginning to wish,' Nancy said in a loud voice, 'that I was anywhere else in the world rather than at this party.'

Her comment was conveyed to Anthony who made a sound that might have been 'Hear, hear', but no one was sure apart from Fergus who didn't bother to translate.

'That *child*!' Eleanor gasped as soon as they left the house in Parliament Terrace. Tyrone had gone racing back to Shaw Street with the speed of a wild animal set free from its cage, and Cara and Jonathan trotted alongside their respective mothers. Fergus had stayed with Anthony. 'What Marcus doesn't realize is that he's making a rod for his own back. I daren't think what she'll be like when she's older.'

'She'll be impossible,' Brenna said grimly.

'She's already is,' Eleanor said even more grimly.

'Poor Sybil,' Cara sighed.

'What's poor about her?' Brenna demanded.

'She's dead unhappy, Mam. I can tell.'

Eleanor pulled a face, slightly ashamed. 'I shouldn't complain about my own daughter, should I? It's not her fault she's being spoilt. Anthony is no company, Louella Fisk doesn't like her and she drives Nancy wild. Nancy and I were the best of friends when I was Sybil's age. All the poor child's left with is Marcus. Oh, Cara! Now you've made me feel awful.'

Brenna glanced fondly at her daughter. Cara could be a little imp at times, but she had a lovely, generous nature and compared to Sybil Allardyce she was a saint. 'Would you like to come back to ours for a cuppa?' she asked Eleanor.

'I'd love to, but I'd better not. Mr Fulton will be home soon wanting his tea. He grumbles as much as Marcus did if it's late – mind you, it's lovely not to care. I can get another lodger easier than another husband.' Eleanor grinned. A year ago, when she had discovered her late mother's legacy had sunk dangerously low and fees for Jonathan's schooling would soon be required, she'd taken in a lodger, the irascible Ernest Fulton who complained about everything under the sun. The complaints were mainly ignored: she would fix his blind if it rattled in the wind, but not stop Jonathan from making a noise when he played in the garden, or turn down the wireless to the extent she could hardly hear it herself when Mr Fulton had gone to bed early and protested it was keeping him awake. 'If he doesn't like it, he knows what to do,' she laughed. Eleanor had laughed a lot since she'd left Marcus and hadn't had a single headache since. She even enjoyed accompanying Brenna to Paddy's Market to buy the odd second-hand outfit. Occasionally, she would buy some minor item from Frederick & Hughes, but their clothes were unaffordable nowadays. She didn't seem to mind in the least her change of fortune and gave the impression of enjoying the challenge of trying to make ends meet.

While Eleanor's condition had worsened in monetary terms, Brenna's had improved. Three years ago, Colm had left Phelan's builders' yard to work as an organizer for the Labour Party. He'd learned to drive and travelled the length and breadth of Lancashire and Cheshire in an old battered van, ensuring meetings at the various branches were being properly conducted and internal elections fairly held. His wages were little more than he'd earned before but, as soon as Cara had started school, Brenna had gone to work as a morning waitress in the Park Road Cocoa Rooms; for a woman whose husband held down such an important job it was far more befitting than cleaning.

'Are you going to the Townswomen's Guild tomorrow after-noon, Brenna?' Eleanor asked now. They'd both joined when a new branch had opened not far away in Allerton.

'No, I've got something else on,' Brenna replied abruptly.

'It sounds awfully interesting. Some woman called Lizzie Phelan is coming to talk to talk to us about the time she spent in France with the Red Cross during the war. Nancy's going.'

'I know, Nancy already told me, but I'll be busy.'

'Doing what?'

'Someone's off sick in the Cocoa Rooms and I've offered to do their shift,' Brenna lied. She wasn't prepared to sit in the same room as Lizzie Phelan, worried she might throw a punch at the woman.

'That's a pity. You know,' Eleanor said regretfully, 'I never did a single thing during the war. I could at least have manned a refreshment stall at the station for the troops. Lots of women I knew did things like that.'

'If there's another war you can make up for it then,' Brenna said.

Eleanor shuddered. 'Don't say things like that! There'll never be another war, not in our lifetime. Anyway, they called the last one "the war to end all wars" so we can't possibly have another.'

They parted, Eleanor promising to come to the Cocoa Rooms in the morning if it was a nice day and she took Jonathan for a walk.

Ernest Fulton was in the kitchen when Eleanor arrived home, staring bleakly at the unlit stove. 'There's no tea on the go, Mrs Allardyce,' he complained the second she entered. He completely ignored Jonathan.

'That's because you're early, Mr Fulton,' she pointed out.

'I'm often early on Saturday.'

'Not all that often, Mr Fulton.' He was a door-to-door salesman for Browns Miracle Elixir, supposedly a cure for every ailment under the sun. 'I can't be expected to hang around all day Saturday just in case you come home early once in a while. It's hardly six o'clock and I partly boiled the potatoes this morning and partly fried the sausages. All I have to do is make some gravy and everything will be ready by half six, which is the time you usually come in.' She wasn't a very good cook, but Mr Fulton seemed more interested in quantity rather than quality.

'What about pudding?' he asked rudely.

'For pudding, you shall have a piece of the fruitcake I made yesterday.'

'You know I prefer a hot pudding, Mrs Allardyce.'

'Then I shall put the piece of fruitcake in the oven and make it hot, Mr Fulton. If you like, I'll make custard and you can pretend it's spotted dick.'

He left, unsure if she was making fun of him or not. She knew she was using the poor man as a way of getting back at Marcus, saying things to him that she wished she'd said to Marcus during the years she'd been unfortunate to live with him under the same roof.

'He's a grumpy old man, isn't he, darling?' Jonathan nodded

vigorously. 'Would you like to play in the garden for a little minute before it goes dark? Or shall Mummy make you a nice cup of tea?'

'Tea, please, Mummy, and can I have some digestive biscuits?'

'Of course, darling.' She hugged him, told him he was the most adorable boy in the world and wondered if she was feeding him too much. He was becoming rather chubby. 'I think it best if you have only a single biscuit.'

'All right, Mummy,' he said equably, smiling like the cherub he was although, at five, he was a trifle old to be a cherub. She must go easy on the cakes and sweets in future, but he truly was adorable and she loved pleasing him. By some strange trick of the brain, she always thought of him as the child of Geoffrey, her late fiancé, which was crazy because she and Geoffrey had never made love and he'd died in 1914. Yet somehow, Daniel Vaizey had altogether faded from her mind and been replaced by Geoffrey. It was *him* with whom she'd lain in the rooms in Spellow Lane and he couldn't be with her now because he was dead. The dates, times and names were all wrong, but Eleanor never questioned them. She even considered that her little boy, with his light-brown curls and bright blue eyes, resembled Geoffrey far more than his real father, whose face she could no longer recall.

These days, she hardly ever thought about Anthony and Sybil. She did her motherly duty by going to see them several times a week, but Jonathan occupied such a large part of her heart that there was very little room left for her other children.

'What shall we do tonight?' she asked. 'After the monster has eaten his tea and disappeared into his lair, shall I read you a story? Or would you prefer to do a jigsaw? What about a game: snakes and ladders?'

'A jigsaw, Mummy, the one with the train.' His face broke into a smile of pure happiness that perfectly expressed how Eleanor herself felt. After he'd been put to bed, she'd put on the wireless and listen to a play or some music or read her new library book. Tomorrow was Sunday and they could all sleep in, including Mr Fulton, who wouldn't mind his breakfast being late.

Oh, life was so *good*. Ernest Fulton aside, it really was quite perfect and she never wanted it to change.

'Tyrone!' Brenna screamed the minute she opened the front door.

'He mustn't have come home,' Cara said when Tyrone didn't reply. 'Are you mad at him for something, Mam?'

'No. I was just wondering where he was.' Brenna threw herself into a chair. 'He didn't enjoy that party: it was obvious from the look on his face. Mind you, neither did I. It was dead horrible, in fact.'

'It was all right, Mam.'

'No, it wasn't, girl,' Brenna said sharply. 'All that Sybil did was belittle you: it was *her* party, *her* cake, Nancy was *her* guest. She seemed to have forgotten it was *your* birthday, too.'

'Oh, Mam! It doesn't matter.' Cara looked at her so reproachfully that Brenna felt as if she were the seven-year-old and Cara thirty-one.

'You're right, it doesn't,' she said quickly. She'd been hurt for her child but, as Cara appeared entirely unaffected, no harm had been done. 'Come here a minute, darlin'.' When Cara came, Brenna kissed her cheek and ruffled her lovely red-gold hair. She looked much prettier in her second-hand, cut-down frock than Sybil had in that ridiculous pink creation that reminded her of a blancmange. She looked into her daughter's wide blue eyes and hoped nothing would ever happen to change their look of shining innocence. 'You're too nice, d'you know that, luv? You're a bit like your dad. Me, I fly off the handle at the least little thing. Sit on me knee a minute while I give you a cuddle.'

Cara settled contentedly on her knee. 'I love you, Mam.'

'And I love you, darlin'. That's the difference between the Caffreys and the Allardyces: we all love each other, but it's not something you could say about that family.'

'Anthony loves *me*, Mam. He told our Fergus to tell me. He said he's going to marry me when we grow up.'

'Did he now!' Brenna would have plenty to say about *that* should the occasion ever arise.

'Well, d'you think I should tell her or not, Colm?'

Colm looked up from the exercise book he'd been staring at intently for at least an hour. 'Tell who what, luv?'

'Oh, you!' Brenna said exasperatedly. 'You haven't listened to a word I said.'

'I'm trying to decipher the notes I made at that meeting I went to last night. I took them down so quickly and now I can't make head nor tail of what I wrote.' He laid the book on the table. 'Tell me again.'

'It's Eleanor. She's cross with Marcus for spoiling Sybil, yet she's doing exactly the same with Jonathan. He's five, but she treats him like a wee baby and refuses to let him grow up. *And* she stuffs the poor little lad with food. Fergus said that Anthony thinks he looks like Humpty Dumpty.' She paused and, much to her irritation, Colm grinned. 'It's not funny, Colm. Any road, should I say something to Eleanor or not?'

'Not.' He bent over the book again.

'Is that all you've got to say?'

'You asked for me opinion and I just gave it. Brenna, luv,' he groaned, 'I really should be getting on with these notes. They'll be even more difficult to read by tomorrow. Out of interest, would you be pleased if Eleanor passed an opinion about the way we bring up our children?'

'No, I wouldn't,' Brenna said indignantly. 'Friend or no friend, I'd give her a piece of me mind.'

'Well, there's your answer, Bren. If you value the friendship, I suggest you keep your gob shut, otherwise you'll be in receipt of a piece of Eleanor's mind.'

He returned to his notes and Brenna didn't like to disturb him again. She loved having Eleanor as a friend, improbable though it had once seemed, but would have liked to ask how she could possibly criticize the way her children were being brought up. They weren't perfect, but none had been spoilt. Fergus was still on the quiet side, but being with Anthony had made a big difference, and Tyrone was far too cheeky and full of himself – she'd had to give him a smack earlier for staying out so late, although was sorry afterwards because he looked as if he was coming down with something. All he did was run up and down entries with other lads making a bit too much noise: tonight he'd obviously run himself sick. As for Cara, she'd never given an ounce of trouble.

'Shall I make us a cup of cocoa?' she asked.

'Hmm.' Colm was bent over the exercise book, concentrating hard. There were threads of grey in his coal-black hair and his forehead was becoming lined. He'd done well for a man who'd only been a farm worker back in Ireland, and she supposed it was Lizzie

Phelan she had to thank for that. Brenna's face was sombre when she fetched a kettle of water and put it on the hob. Fortunately, they'd got over that terrible year, culminating in the death of Rory. She caught her breath: the memory of the night her baby had died in her arms was as fresh as if it had happened only yesterday.

She made the cocoa, then sat and watched Colm as he worked. Unlike Eleanor, Brenna didn't consider life to be perfect – it would be foolish not to hope that things might get even better one day – but she was relatively happy with her lot. Despite that one little lapse, Colm was the best of husbands and her children were a blessing. She felt rightfully proud of all three, knowing that they would never let her down.

Earlier that night, Tyrone Caffrey and his mates had been waiting outside the Chesterfield Arms on the corner of Upper Stanhope Street. 'Can you spare a copper, mister?' they enquired nicely of the clientele, predominantly male, as they came out.

About one man in ten, usually the most inebriated, would comply with their polite request and reach in his pocket for a coin, to which the lads would say, 'Ta, mister,' and wait for the next man to accost.

It sometimes happened that a man would take out a handful of coins to search for a penny, whereupon one of the lads – there were four altogether and they took turns – would jerk his elbow and the coins would fall to the ground and roll into the gutter. They'd be picked up, silver first if there was any, and by the time their victim realized what had happened, the lads were nowhere in sight.

It happened again that night. 'You little varmints,' the unlucky man yelled, waving his fists at the empty air.

As soon as they'd reached a safe distance, they stopped running and gathered in the nearest entry, panting for breath. The coins were counted: they had managed to steal two and ninepence halfpenny, a highly satisfactory result.

'What'll we buy?' Tommy Morgan asked.

'Booze,' replied Kevin Plunkett.

'Ciggies,' suggested Squinty Murphy.

Tyrone would have preferred sweets, but it sounded girlish. 'I don't care,' he said recklessly.

'Let's get both. We've got enough. We'll get the booze from Mickey's.' Mickey Gregory sold liquor from the back door of his pub to anyone who asked. He didn't give a damn if the customers were only eleven years old.

Until now, they'd stuck to ale, but that night, Tyrone drank whiskey for the first time. There was a little period, in between the first mouthful and the second, when he felt on top of the world, convinced there was nothing on earth he couldn't do – climb the highest mountain, score magnificent goals for Liverpool, sail around the world all on his own – but once this sensation had passed, all he wanted to do was puke.

Dad would kill him if he knew what he was up to and his mam would scream blue murder, but Tyrone wasn't deterred by the fear of being found out, not even by the bobbies. It all added to the excitement. Nothing he'd done so far in his life could compare with the thrill of picking up the coins and running like blazes, heart in his throat, praying the man wouldn't chase after them. He wouldn't catch *him*, he was the fastest of the four, but might well grab Squinty Murphy who was apt to run into walls and couldn't be trusted not to clat on his mates, resulting in all hell breaking out at home and possibly at school.

Tyrone didn't care about the money, the booze, or the ciggies: the only thing that mattered was the excitement.

While Tyrone tossed and turned in bed, wishing he hadn't drunk so much whiskey, half a mile away in Parliament Terrace, his brother, Fergus, was also unable to sleep. Something had happened that night, something that he'd always known at the back of his mind was bound to happen one day, but now it had and Fergus had been left reeling from the realization that his time with Anthony had come to an end.

Years ago, when Daniel Vaizey had so suddenly and mysteriously left, Mr Allardyce had advertised in the *Echo* for a replacement. By some other mysterious means, a copy of the paper had ended up in New York and the advertisement was read by Mrs Louella Fisk, who wrote stating that she'd learned to sign when she'd married her late husband who had been deaf from birth, that she was a trained teacher and very interested in the vacancy, providing accommodation was supplied.

Within a matter of weeks, Mrs Fisk had settled in Nurse Hutton's old room. Fergus and Anthony liked her straight away, far more than they'd ever liked Daniel Vaizey. She claimed to be forty-five, but winked when she said it so they weren't sure if it was true or not, although why anyone would want to lie about their age was quite beyond them. Tall and as thin as a broomstick, her lips were painted dark red and she smoked black cigarettes in a silver holder. She taught them how to play all sorts of card games and, on Saturdays, under the guise of going to the pictures, she sometimes took them to the dog track and gave them sixpence each to bet with, impressing on them to keep the visits secret.

Fergus had always enjoyed the weekends he spent with Anthony and the arrival of Mrs Fisk made them even better but, in a few months, both she and Anthony would depart for a foreign country millions of miles away. Although he would miss Mrs Fisk, he didn't know how he'd live without Anthony who was as close to him as a brother – in fact, he got on with him much better than he did Tyrone.

He had guessed something was going on. Lately, Mrs Fisk had been making long, transatlantic phone calls. The words 'university' 'genius' and 'remarkable young man' had been mentioned. Tonight, Mrs Fisk had been ensconced with Mr Allardyce in his study for ages and Fergus and Anthony had sat on the floor outside the door listening – at least Fergus had listened and conveyed the gist of the conversation to his friend.

Apparently, Mrs Fisk thought Anthony would benefit from a proper education in a school established especially for the deaf, and such a school – 'The best in the world, Mr Allardyce, I can assure you' – was situated in a place called Florida in the United States. 'It's called the Gaudulet College for the Deaf. I would live close by and provide him with a home.' When Anthony was eighteen, he would transfer to Gaudulet University and Mrs Fisk would then consider her role in his life was over. 'I thought it wise to contact the college before approaching you, and they are willing to take him. The next term starts in January. This is a marvellous opportunity. Your son's talent as an artist is amazing, but it's not just his art that will benefit from expert tuition. He has a brilliant brain that will respond to the expert tuition that I, or any other tutor you might hire, could not possibly provide. What do you say, Mr Allardyce?'

Fergus had told Anthony everything Mrs Fisk had said with his fingers. As he did so, Anthony got more and more excited and

Fergus felt sicker and sicker. Mrs Fisk hadn't mentioned his name once. He'd outlived his usefulness, *his* role in Anthony's life was over.

Mr Allardyce hadn't said much so far, just responded with the occasional grunt. Now he said, 'I think we'd better get Anthony in here, see what he thinks.'

Fergus dragged Anthony to his feet and they raced upstairs. Mrs Fisk shouted, 'Fergus, will you ask Anthony to come down to his father's study, please?'

When Fergus heard the study door shut, he went down and listened again. For a long time, there was silence: Mrs Fisk was telling Anthony in sign language about the wonders of the college in Florida, then Anthony said in his strange voice, 'I want to go.'

'What was that?' Mr Allardyce asked.

'He wants to go,' Mrs Fisk translated.

'Then he shall.'

Later Fergus had asked his friend, 'Won't I ever see you again?'

'Of course you will,' Anthony had replied. 'When I finish university, I shall come back and marry your Cara.'

That would be years and years off, and what made things worse was that in January Fergus would turn fourteen and have to start work. As yet, he had no idea what he would do, but expected he would become an errand boy and deliver things like bread and stuff on a bike. After a few years, he would be promoted to behind the counter of whatever shop it was, and probably stay there for the rest of his life. He wasn't looking forward to it, not a bit, but at least it was better than working in a factory or for a chimney sweep as one lad he knew had done.

Fergus turned over in bed for the umpteenth time and seriously wondered if he'd be better off dead.

Eleanor was furious when she discovered plans had been made for her son's future and she hadn't been consulted, although had to concede that Anthony would be better off in an educational establishment that catered solely for the needs of deaf children.

On New Year's Day, she, Brenna and Nancy went to Princes landing stage to wave Anthony and Mrs Fisk off. The icy wind felt as sharp as knives, making their eyes water and their noses run. It had been deemed too cold to bring the children. Jonathan and Cara had been left with Colm, who had stayed at home to catch up on some paperwork, and Sybil was with Phyllis, the maid, whom she loathed. The feeling was mutual.

They stood in the very spot where the Caffreys had first waited for Paddy when they'd arrived from Ireland seven and a half years before. Marcus stood alone, a dark, brooding figure, hands in pockets, the brim of his black trilby hiding his eyes.

'Where's Fergus?' Eleanor asked. 'I'd've thought he, of all people, would want to see Anthony off. They were such tremendous friends.'

'He couldn't come, he started work today,' Brenna said a trifle shortly. She was only there to keep Eleanor company. So far as she was concerned, Anthony Allardyce could go and jump in a lake. He'd proved anything but a friend over the last few months. Fergus had been useful enough while he'd lasted, but cast aside like an old rag when his usefulness had come to an end. Now Anthony had other fish to fry and, while a flurry of arrangements were being made for his future, Fergus had been sidelined or ignored, even told not to bother coming some weekends. He'd been deeply hurt, she could tell. 'I hope we're not going to wait until the boat sails,' she said. 'Any minute now and I'll freeze to the spot.'

'Let's just wait until they appear on deck and we'll give them a wave and leave,' Nancy suggested. 'They won't want to hang around either.'

'I'll go along with that,' agreed a shivering Eleanor. 'Oh, there they are now.' She waved energetically. 'Bye, Anthony. Bye, darling.'

Before the women left, Brenna approached Marcus Allardyce. 'Thank you for giving Fergus a job in your office,' she said shyly. 'It's much appreciated.'

Marcus smiled bleakly. 'He's a bright boy, Fergus. He seemed to think he was destined to be an errand boy, but he's capable of much better than that. Let's say the job is in return for all he did for Anthony. That was much appreciated too, Mrs Caffrey.'

He was ever such a strange man, Brenna thought when they were on their way home on the tram: kind one minute, horrible the next. Years ago, Eleanor had told her the reason she'd been thrown out into the rain and, while there was no excuse for such monstrous behaviour, a man couldn't be blamed for losing his temper when he discovered his wife was expecting another man's child.

'If you'd like to come back to Parliament Terrace,' Nancy said, 'there's some freshly made pea and ham soup that'll warm the cockles of your heart.'

'That's just what I need,' Eleanor cried. 'How about you, Brenna?'

'I can't wait.' Brenna forgot about Marcus Allardyce, but he didn't forget her. For weeks afterwards, he savoured their short conversation and the recollection of her wondrous smile. Then she shifted back to the corner of his mind where she had always been and where she always would be.

Part Two

Chapter 7

1939

'Sybil!' someone shouted. 'Sybil Allardyce!'

Sybil winced. She didn't recognize the voice, but it couldn't be one of her friends as none would shout so loudly in a public place, even though the noise was deafening. She and, it seemed, several hundred other women were in Renshaw Hall registering for military service in the war that was about to start at almost any minute. There were at least a dozen desks where particulars were being taken and a long queue at every one.

All of a sudden, a pair of thin arms grasped her shoulders. 'Sybil! It's me, Cara Caffrey. Are you joining up too? Oh, isn't it exciting!'

'Yes,' Sybil muttered, shaking off the arms. The last time she'd seen Cara was nearly three years ago when they'd both been sixteen. She'd been tall enough then, but had grown even more and her head, with its thick mass of red-gold hair, could be seen above that of every other woman in the hall.

'I'd like to be a Wren,' Cara said, 'but I don't think we'll be given a choice. We could end up in the Air Force or the Army.'

Sybil also fancied becoming a Wren. 'That's right,' she said in a clipped voice, wishing Cara would go away. Her friend, Betsy Billington-Clarke, had gone to look for the Ladies and she didn't want her to come back and find her in the company of someone as common as Cara Caffrey whose accent was a mixture of Liverpudlian and Irish and who was hatless, gloveless and wearing a startling red frock that clashed violently with her hair. She was conscious of her own neat blue rayon frock spotted with daisies and little pillbox hat to match, both from Harrods. To her dismay, at that very moment, Betsy appeared at her side, mopping her brow with a lace-trimmed handkerchief.

'Phew! It's hot in here. Sorry I was so long, Sybil, there was a queue for the Ladies a mile long.' She smiled at Cara. 'Hello. I'm Betsy Clarke.'

'And I'm Cara Caffrey. Nice to meet you, Betsy.' Cara's answering smile stretched from ear to ear as she shook hands. 'Look, I'd better run. Me friend, Sheila, is keeping me place in the queue over there and she's nearly reached the front. Tara, Sybil. Tara, Betsy.'

'Isn't she lovely?' Betsy enthused when Cara had gone. 'I noticed her before, she's outstanding. Such gorgeous hair and, unlike so many tall women, she looks quite comfortable with her height. Is she a friend of yours?'

'No!' Sybil shuddered at the thought, rather resenting Betsy being so taken with Cara. 'Her mother knows mine, that's all.' She turned on her friend. 'What happened to the "Billington"? Since when have you been just Betsy Clarke?'

Betsy laughed. 'Since I entered this hall. Billington is my mother's maiden name and Daddy added it to Clarke when they got married. I've always hated having a double-barrelled name, it's frightfully snobbish, and today's my chance of getting rid of it.'

'I always wanted one,' Sybil confessed, 'but Wallace-Allardyce is a terrible mouthful.'

'Terrible,' Betsy agreed. She fanned her face with her hand. 'Didn't anyone think to open a window in the middle of June? You know, I don't think this queue has grown any shorter since I went to the Ladies. I never dreamt there'd be such a crowd wanting to join up. The women of Liverpool must be extremely patriotic.'

'If she comes home and ses she's joined up, I'll kill her,' Brenna promised the empty parlour. 'War's men's work, women should take no part in it, least not in the fighting. I already told her that but young people today, they just won't listen.'

She noticed an overflowing ashtray on the floor beside an armchair and tut-tutted loudly. The local branch of the Labour Party had held a meeting in the room the night before and always left the place a mess, although she couldn't very well expect them to take home their spent fags and bring their own cups and saucers so she wouldn't have to use her own when she made them a drink. They were quite a nice crowd, but next time she'd provide more ashtrays.

She flicked a duster over the room, plumped up the cushions on the grey moquette three-piece of which she was so proud, breathed on the mirror and polished it, then, giving the room a final glance, went upstairs to make the beds, singing along to the wireless as she went. 'Smoke gets in your eyes . . .' she warbled tunefully.

They hadn't moved to a bigger house as she'd always wanted. When it came right down to it, Colm couldn't bring himself to leave. The house was his brother's legacy and he didn't want to part with it. 'Our Paddy *died* for this house,' he said emotionally.

When Brenna suggested they let it and use the money towards the rent on somewhere nicer, he'd looked at her if she'd proposed he rob a bank or join the Conservative Party. 'I'm not going to become a *landlord*, Bren,' he gasped, horrified.

Brenna hadn't minded too much. She was also fond of the house and would have found leaving a wrench, remembering how thrilled they'd been to get it. She was quite happy to settle for improving the place, decorating it from top to bottom – the entire family had mucked in and helped – and there'd been money enough to buy decent, if not new, furniture once Fergus, then Tyrone, had gone out to work, followed four years later by Cara who worked in Boots' Cash Chemists with a very nice crowd of girls. By then, Brenna had given up her job in the Cocoa Rooms, feeling the family were flush enough. They'd had electricity installed, a bath put in the washhouse and a gas cooker in the kitchen, and had been contemplating having the range removed and replaced with a nice cream-and-brown tiled fireplace, when Tyrone left home and married Maria Murphy. Not only did it mean there was one less wage coming in, but they found themselves having to buy things for the baby that arrived about six months later, making Brenna a grandmother at the age of thirty-nine.

She stroked the pillow on Tyrone's bed, hardly used for almost five years. She was still convinced it had all been a set-up. Tyrone was too soft-hearted by a mile.

These days, the house in Shaw Street was as busy as a station with meetings of one sort or another held in the parlour two or three nights a week. Hardly a day would pass without people coming to see Colm on Labour Party business, and Cara often had her friends around. Brenna and Eleanor had been elected to the committee of the Townswomen's Guild and they took turns meeting in each other's houses. She'd had to buy a little notebook and enter the dates of all the various gatherings so they wouldn't clash.

She heard the latch go on the back-yard door and a few seconds later Eleanor shouted, 'Yoohoo! It's only me, Bren.'

'I'm making the beds, I'll be down in a minute,' she shouted back. 'Put the kettle on while you're waiting.'

'I've just been to see Nancy,' Eleanor said when Brenna appeared and turned the wireless off. 'She said Sybil's also gone to Renshaw Hall to join up or sign on or whatever it is you do. She must have made up her mind very suddenly, as she didn't mention it when she came on Sunday. Apparently, Marcus is terribly upset – he hasn't said anything, but Nancy can just tell. Sybil's been at school in London for three whole years and he was expecting her to stay home for a while. I suppose he's lonely, what with Anthony settled in America and showing no sign of coming back.'

'I wonder if Sybil and our Cara will be in the same regiment,' Brenna mused. 'Do women go in regiments?'

'I've no idea. Oh, Bren!' Eleanor said tearfully. 'This war when it starts is going to be perfectly horrible. Last night, Mr Chandler warned we might go short of food and would I mind if he started growing vegetables instead of flowers in the greenhouse. I agreed, of course.'

'I could do with going short of food for a while.' Brenna patted her expanding midriff. Lately, all her clothes had started to feel uncomfortably tight and her mirror reflected a distinctly matronly figure. She looked enviously at Eleanor whose shape at forty-two was still that of a young girl.

'It's not funny, Bren.'

'Do you see me laughing?' Brenna asked indignantly. 'Any minute now, our Cara will come home and announce she's an admiral in the Navy or something and our Tyrone will be called up, although they'll never take Fergus, not with his poor eyesight – I never thought I'd be pleased the poor lad has to wear glasses. There's gasmasks under the stairs along with rolls of tape to stick on me winders to stop them shattering 'case a bomb drops outside, ration books and identity cards in the sideboard, and the other day I bought Lord knows how many yards of blackout material for Nancy to make into curtains.' She paused for breath. 'Colm's already become an air raid protection warden – as if he didn't have enough to do already – and the Townswomen's Guild is helping to organize the evacuation of children when the war actually starts.'

'I know, Bren, aren't I helping with that, too?'

'Of course you are, darlin', I hadn't forgot,' Brenna assured her with a gracious wave of her hand, adding grimly, 'That eejit Hitler has turned the whole of Europe upside down, so he has. He needs putting over someone's knee and given a good spanking – I'd do it meself if I could get me hands on him.'

'I'm sure you would, Bren,' Eleanor said dryly. 'Have you noticed we no longer say, "if war starts," but "when"? Oh, I wish women ran things instead of men. If we were in charge, no one would know the meaning of the word "war".'

It was all quite dreadful, Eleanor thought, shuddering, as she passed the newly built air raid shelters and sandbagged buildings on her way back to Tigh Street.

War! The last one had been bad enough, but this new one would involve civilians on the ground. She looked up at the blue sky and tried to picture it filled with enemy planes and bombs raining down on the innocent people below, but it was quite beyond the bounds of her imagination. Twenty-five years ago she'd lost Geoffrey and now she was faced with the fear of losing her darling Jonathan. He was only seventeen and still at school, but in a matter of months the schoolboy would be considered old enough to fight for his country. And he was such a delicate, sensitive young man she wasn't convinced if he could stand up to life in the forces.

She arrived home to find Oliver Chandler in the greenhouse looking thoughtful. 'I shall have to buy a gardening book,' he announced. 'All I can think to plant is tomatoes.'

'Tomatoes would be very useful,' Eleanor said, glad to have something mundane to talk about. 'They can be eaten fresh, bottled, or made into soup or chutney.'

'What an enterprising lady you are, Mrs Allardyce!' Mr Chandler gave her his charming, whimsical grin. He had only been living there for six months, her fifth lodger since Ernest Fulton had retired and gone to live with his sister in Morecambe. Fortyish, slightly built, with smoky brown hair and eyes to match, as well as an irresistible grin and a posh accent, Eleanor was a tiny bit in love with him. She wasn't on the lookout for a lover or another husband – she was still married to Marcus – but wouldn't have minded having a mild flirtation with Mr Chandler, and accompanying him to the pictures or the theatre once in a while, but he'd never asked and she had no intention of dropping hints. He was the perfect lodger, never complaining, cleaning his own room and even cooking the occasional meal. He and Jonathan got on well and he frequently helped the boy with his homework. His own work was highly secret – he worked for the Admiralty in an office down by the Pier Head.

She was about to leave him to his musings in the greenhouse, when he said, 'I've been meaning to ask, Mrs Allardyce, if you would be willing to let out your spare bedroom? One of my colleagues will shortly be transferred to Liverpool from London and will be looking for somewhere to live.'

It had never crossed her mind before to let the fourth bedroom. Until Oliver Chandler had come along, she'd never been keen on lodgers, considering them an intrusion into her life, but she'd needed the money and her various lodgers had provided more than enough.

'I'll need to think about that, Mr Chandler,' she told him. She wondered if the colleague was a woman and there'd be all sorts of hanky panky going on under her roof, but remembered she had indulged in quite a bit of hanky panky herself, even if it was quite a while ago. 'I'll let you know when I've made up my mind.'

'If it helps, make up your mind, that is,' he said, flashing his appealing grin, 'the chap concerned is a brilliant mathematician with a PhD from Cambridge University. His name is Lewis Brown and, like me, he is a perfect gentleman.' He grinned again and Eleanor was lost.

'Oh, all right,' she smiled. 'When will he move in?'

'In a month or so.'

'There's hardly any furniture in that room.'

'That's all right, Lewis will bring his own.'

The manager of Boots hadn't minded Cara and Sheila taking time off for such a patriotic reason. On the way back, they nipped into the Kardomah in Bold Street and treated themselves to a cream tea to celebrate their imminent departure from Liverpool for a life of excitement, adventure and possibly a dash of danger on top.

When she arrived home, there was a mouth-watering smell coming from the kitchen and she realized she was starving, the cream cake having not dulled her appetite a jot – Mam claimed she had the appetite of a horse.

Mam was hovering in the living room and threw her a glowering look. 'Did you do it?' she asked sharply.

'Yes, Mam, I did.' Cara threw herself into a chair, her long slim legs stretched out, creating a hazard for everyone to trip over. 'Sybil Allardyce was there and hundreds of other women. I'm not the only girl in Liverpool who wants to do their bit.' For some reason, Mam was dead set against her joining up.

'You can do "your bit", as you call it, here at home,' Mam said in the same sharp voice. 'There's no need to go scurrying off to some foreign country.'

'She mightn't be sent to a foreign country, Bren,' Dad said reasonably. He was sitting at the table reading the paper as he waited for the meal to arrive. Fergus was also there, looking very fed up: lately, he looked fed up all the time.

'Oh, but Colm, she could be sent to Timbuctoo or somewhere,' Mam wailed. 'It's not fair. I'll be desperately worried about her every minute of every day. You expect your sons to go off and fight, but not your one and only daughter.' At this, Fergus winced.

'She won't do any fighting either, Bren. They won't be sending women to the front line.'

'Any road, Mam, we've all got to have medicals and I might not pass.' She only said it to calm her mother down a bit, but it had the opposite effect.

'*You*,' Mam snorted loudly, '*you* not pass a medical! You're as fit as a fiddle. I'd have something to say to any doctor who dared turn you down.'

Dad glanced over the paper and winked at his daughter. 'She's a bundle of contradictions, your mam.'

'And what about that nice boyfriend of yours? What's he got to say about you joining up?'

'Mam!' Cara burst out laughing. 'Last week, you claimed Richie Larkin wasn't nearly good enough for me. This week he's "nice". He doesn't care if I join up or not. We weren't intending to get married or anything.' So far, Cara hadn't met a single man she wanted to marry.

'Are we having anything to eat tonight or not, luv?' Dad gave

Mam a pained look. 'Something in the kitchen smells awful good and it'd be interesting to see if it tastes as good as it smells.'

'It's beef stew with dumplings,' Mam said, looking flustered. 'I'll fetch it.'

She returned with the stew in a big serving dish, plonking it on the table with a too-loud thud. Taking off her pinny, she sat down with another thud. 'There's two dumplings each, so no one's to take more than their fair share,' she barked, and Dad said there was no need for anyone in the house to join the forces as they had their very own sergeant major on the premises. Mam said if he wasn't careful she'd give him a thick ear and Dad hit her with the rolled-up paper. With that, everyone started laughing, but they didn't laugh for long, because at that very minute the back door opened and Tyrone came bursting in.

'I've left Maria,' he announced in a flat voice, 'and this time it's for good.'

Cara sighed, Fergus groaned and Dad said, 'Not again!'

'I only wish it were for good,' Mam said angrily, 'but knowing you, you'll go back the very second Maria snaps her fingers.'

'Don't interfere, Bren,' Dad muttered, which was just about the worse thing he could have said.

'Don't interfere! *Don't interfere!*' Mam shrieked. 'Maria Murphy tricked our son into getting married and you tell me not to interfere?'

'She was expecting his baby, Bren. I wouldn't exactly call that a trick.'

'He was only eighteen,' Mam countered.

'So was she,' Dad countered back.

Tyrone ignored the argument, sat down, reached for the ladle and helped himself to stew.

Cara wondered how they were to share eight dumplings between five. Feeling rather saintly, she took just one, leaving the others to sort out the remaining seven.

Five years ago, all hell had broken loose when Annie Murphy had come to the house in flaming temper and announced her daughter, Maria, was expecting a baby and it was all the fault of their Tyrone.

'It can't possibly be our Tyrone,' Mam had spat. 'He's only a lad and he'd never do such a thing.'

'Lad or not, our Maria's up the stick and it was your Tyrone who put her there.' Mrs Murphy had folded her arms stubbornly. 'They'll just have to get married – she's already three months gone, so the sooner the better.'

'He's much too young to get married! It's all a trick. Your Maria's no better than she ought to be. Our Tyrone would never go with her – he'd never go with anyone, he's been too well brought up for that.'

'He wasn't well brought up enough to stop him from going thieving with our Squinty,' Mrs Murphy sneered, 'or breaking into cars if there was something worth nicking on the back seat. If you like, Mrs Caffrey, I'll give you a whole list of the things that lad of yours has been up to, despite him being so well brought up.'

Mam's answer had been to slam the door in the woman's face, then collapse in Dad's arms, sobbing uncontrollably. 'She's lying, isn't she, darlin'? Our Tyrone would never do any of those things.'

'I dunno, luv,' Dad said miserably. 'We'd better ask him when he comes home.'

'Where is he?'

'He's taken some girl to the pictures,' Fergus supplied.

It turned out that Tyrone was indeed the father of Maria's baby and guilty of a whole host of crimes. 'I only did it for fun,' he explained, as if Mam and Dad would understand. 'I've been going straight since I was sixteen.'

Mam was too upset to rant and rave, but somehow managed to blame Mrs Murphy for everything, even the thieving. 'That Squinty lad led Tyrone astray – his mam never even tried to control him – and Maria's got a terrible reputation. Our Tyrone's such an easygoing lad, wanting to please everyone.'

Tyrone and Maria had got wed straight away, but the two mothers had been sworn enemies ever since. It took Mam a long while, but she eventually grew to like Maria, who in fact was very pleasant, extremely pretty and nothing like the good-time girl she'd been made out to be. The marriage wasn't a happy one, even though the young couple loved each other very much. Tyrone's head had held all sorts of plans for the future that didn't include having a wife and child at eighteen and had ended with him becoming very rich, and Maria had confessed to Cara that she'd had every intention of going to Hollywood to be a film star. 'But now I'm stuck living in me gran's parlour with a baby and another on the way, and no hope of a place of our own, not on Tyrone's wages.' Tyrone had had to give up his electrician's apprenticeship, where he earned only shillings a week, and take up labouring, which paid a little bit more. Mam and Dad had felt obliged to dip into the money they were saving for a new fireplace to buy a pram and a cot and the hundred and one other things that a baby needed.

Now Tyrone was twenty-three, father to two little boys, Joey and Mike, whom he loved as desperately as he did Maria, although would never admit it, and still living with Maria's gran and an unmarried uncle who was a penny short of a shilling. About once a month, he left his little family and came home to be petted and fussed over by Mam, or Maria would take the boys and go to stay with her mother. Dad said it was nothing to be alarmed about: they were living in too close quarters and just needed a rest from each other now'n again. They usually returned to each other within a day.

'Any minute now,' Tyrone said tiredly as he helped himself to a second dumpling, 'me call-up papers will arrive. I can't wait to get in the forces.'

'I know, lad.' Mam patted his hand comfortingly. 'I'll keep an eye on Maria and the lads, so there'll be no need to worry about them.'

Tyrone sniffed pathetically and said in a namby-pamby voice, 'I know you will, Mam.'

Mam went to fetch the rice pudding and let Tyrone have the skin off the top. Cara and Fergus gave each other a secret grin. Afterwards, Mam went to wash the dishes – Cara would dry them later – and Dad offered to take the lads to the pub. Tyrone accepted, but Fergus said he'd sooner read a book and went upstairs.

'If anyone calls for me,' Dad said, 'tell them to come round to the Bakers' Arms, I'll be there till half past seven, or put them in the parlour to wait.'

'All right, darlin',' Mam promised.

All of a sudden, the house was quiet. Cara stayed at the table with a second cup of tea, the reflection of the sun in the windows of the houses behind almost blinding in its intensity, making her blink. It only happened at this time of the year when the days were at their longest. It came to her how much she would miss her family if – when – she left. She hadn't thought about it before and the feeling was so raw that it almost took her breath away. It would be unbearable, not seeing Mam and Dad every single day, not eating meals in this room that was as familiar to her as the back of her hand, sleeping in the box room in Uncle Paddy's bed. Mam had let her pick the wallpaper – blue with pink roses – and Nancy Gates had sewn the blue curtains and another curtain to fit over the wooden frame that Dad had made for a wardrobe.

She stared at the mantelpiece, at the little statue of a lady in a crinoline with a lacy parasol over her shoulder. Mam continually moved it around the house: it was her favourite ornament, Cara's too. She'd wanted to play with it when she was a little girl, but had never been allowed to touch it. 'That's real china, that,' Mam used to laugh. It was years before Cara realized it was a cheap thing that had been bought for coppers in a second-hand shop. She took the statue off the mantelpiece and nursed it in her hand, unable to imagine life without this almost worthless object somewhere close at hand.

'Mam!' she cried. 'Oh, Mam! I've made a terrible mistake.'

Her mother appeared in the doorway, her pinny back on and suds up to her elbows, looking concerned. 'What's the matter, darlin'?'

'I wish I hadn't joined up! Will I be able to back out of it, d'you think?'

'I expect so, but why would you want to do that, Cara?' Mam sat beside her and put her wet arm around her neck.

Cara buried her face in her mother's ample bosom. 'I'm frightened, Mam. I don't want to leave home.' She expected her mother would be relieved, but she was wrong.

'You'll get over it, darlin'. Just give yourself a couple of days and you'll be looking forward to it again.'

'I thought you wanted me to stay!'

'Oh, my dear, lovely girl,' Mam breathed, ''course I want you to stay. I want you to stay with all me heart, but that's just me, being selfish as usual. You're nearly nineteen and have your own life to lead. I've no right to stop you, have I?'

'You're never selfish, Mam.'

'Indeed I am, darlin'. I'd've liked you and Fergus and Tyrone to stay in this house for ever with me and your dad, for us never to grow old, but just be one big happy family till the end of time.' She stroked Cara's cheek and Cara felt her lips brush the top of her head. 'I can't think of anything that would have made me happier. But it wouldn't have made *you* three happy, would it? You've got lots of years ahead of you, darlin', and you're going to have a wonderful time. What's this?' She'd noticed the little statue in Cara's hand.

'I used to love her when I was little,' Cara sniffed, 'but you'd never let me play with her.'

'She's one of the first ornaments I ever bought for the house: I was so proud of her.' She folded Cara's fingers around the statue. 'Take her with you, darlin'. You never know, she might enjoy going travelling with you. Now, do us a favour: go upstairs and persuade that brother of yours to take you to the pictures. I'm fed up with him lying upstairs night after night pretending to read, when all he's really doing is wishing he could go in the forces. Edward G. Robinson's on at the Gaumont in *The Last Gangster*: he's an ugly little bugger, but I always quite fancied him. In fact,' she said impulsively, untying her apron, 'I wouldn't mind going meself. I'll leave a note for your dad. C'mon, darling, rouse your brother and we'll be off.'

It was almost half past seven and Sybil was still out. Marcus drummed his fingers on the desk and a coldness settled over him: she'd turned against him. It had happened while she was at school in London where she'd changed from a young girl into a young lady. Each time she'd come home on holiday, she'd been more withdrawn: not from Nancy, or from Eleanor, the mother who'd deserted her, or from her friends, just her father. He got the distinct impression she actively disliked him. Last Christmas, she hadn't come home at all, but had stayed with friends in Sussex.

Perhaps he'd loved her too much – was it possible to love someone too much? He hadn't thought so. Sybil was the light of his life. He adored her. There was nothing on earth he wouldn't do for her: lay down his life, if necessary. Clothes, jewellery, money, had been heaped upon her. Anything she asked for, he made sure she got. If Sybil requested a new dress, he would buy two. When she'd asked for pearl earrings, he'd got a necklace and bracelet to match. He'd planned to buy her a mink coat for her twenty-first and this year, now that she was old enough, a sports car – she'd had lessons in London and could already drive.

He hadn't minded the long months she'd been away at school, knowing that the holidays would soon come and she'd be home. Originally, he'd wanted her to go to a proper finishing school in

Switzerland, but the situation in Europe had been too dangerous, what with that chap Hitler strutting all over the place.

The drumming of his fingers was the only sound in the house. He stopped, leaving a silence so oppressive that the hairs stiffened on his neck. If Sybil joined the forces, she could be away for years and the house would always be quiet like this. So far as he knew, Nancy was still in the basement. If she were, any minute now she'd be off to one of her meetings. He supposed he could go to his club, but wasn't in the mood. The talk would inevitably be about the war – some of the chaps were looking forward to it, easily done if you were too old to fight. They expected the conflict to last about six months, at which point Hitler would surrender, having been given a bloody nose. Marcus was considered a Jeremiah when he argued they were wrong. The powerful German war machine had been years in the making, whereas Britain, after years of appeasement and a crazy belief in 'peace in our time', was only now scrambling madly to catch up.

Recently, H.B. Wallace had turned over exclusively to war work and now produced asbestos sheets for the Navy. For the moment it meant they were over-staffed but, as at least half the workforce was young enough for active service, this would be remedied as soon as the war began – a couple had already been called up. Indeed, they could actually end up with a staff shortage.

There was a knock on the study door. 'Enter,' he called, and Nancy Gates came in. Nancy was getting more ugly as she grew older, he thought. Now in her mid-sixties, her hair had turned completely grey and her big chin had collapsed into the folds of her neck, reminding him strongly of a giant tortoise. He hadn't grown fond of Nancy with the years, but he was used to her and would be upset should she ever leave his employ. He'd expected she might depart when Eleanor did, but she'd stayed on, perhaps for Anthony and then, when he'd gone, for Sybil, although she'd never forged the same warm relationship with his daughter as she'd had with his wife, something he suspected was nothing to do with Nancy, but Sybil keeping her distance.

'Is there no sign of Sybil yet?' she asked.

'No. She must still be with her friend, the one she went with to Renshaw Hall.' He couldn't remember the girl's name.

'I thought she might have phoned, but you know what youngsters are like: it never crosses their minds people might be worried about them.' Nancy shrugged. 'Cara Caffrey only went and did the same this morning: joined up, like. Brenna's as mad as hell.'

'It seems like only yesterday the girls were born,' Marcus said, remembering the tiny baby in Brenna's arms only minutes after her birth. He wished he could bring himself to ask Nancy to sit down – he could probably find more to talk about with her than any of the members of his club – but she might think he was need of company and the last thing he wanted was pity.

'I was thinking that very thing earlier today: as you get older, the time seems to fly by. Well, I'll be off now. I'm taking a First Aid course and this is me first night. It might be useful if we have air raids.'

'Good for you,' he said cordially, rather surprising himself – and Nancy: her thick eyebrows shot up in surprise.

Perhaps he should get involved in some sort of war work: the Home Guard, for instance, or Civil Defence. There was bound to be something useful he could do rather than sit at home moping for the daughter who didn't have time for him any more.

At nine o'clock, he turned on the wireless to be met by the familiar chimes of Big Ben followed by the latest news. Nothing much had happened, just another few miles covered in the grim, remorseless march to war. He turned off the set and went to bed, but didn't fall a sleep, not until he heard Sybil come home, by which time it was approaching midnight. He thought about getting up and remonstrating with her, gently, of course, but changed his mind. It would only get on her nerves and turn her against him even more.

Sybil was relieved to find that only the hall light had been left on and the rest of the house was in darkness. Daddy had obviously gone to bed and it meant she wouldn't have to face his reproachful eyes, making her feel as if she'd badly let him down by coming home so late. Mummy, now, was completely different. There were no demands from either side and they saw each other when they felt like it. Lately, Sybil had begun to wish her mother had taken her with her when she'd walked out all those years ago.

After leaving Renshaw Hall, she and Betsy had done some shopping, had tea, then gone to the cinema to see *Gone With the Wind*, a picture that was sheer magic the whole way through and had lasted for almost four hours. They'd left the cinema in a daze and had caught a taxi back to Betsy's house in Calderstones to have supper. Betsy's elder brother had been there with an old pal from school and the four of them had sat talking for hours. At one point, Betsy had suggested she ring her father and explain where she was, but Sybil had said there was no need, although she knew Daddy would be sick with worry until she returned.

She wondered if, deep down, she still loved her father, but wasn't sure. Over the last few years he'd driven her wild. He was much too possessive, too interested in her every single movement, too involved in her life, not realizing she wanted some privacy now that she was older. At times, she couldn't help herself, but was deliberately cruel, wanting to hurt him for some horrid reason, actually enjoying the wounded look on his face when she told him to mind his own business, or for Christ's sake to leave her alone.

She'd been rehearsing a stiff little speech for when she came in – 'You don't own me, I can stay out as long as I like' – and, on the way up to her bedroom, felt rather piqued to find Daddy in bed and she wasn't able to make it.

Within a fortnight, Cara was called back to Renshaw Hall for a medical that she easily passed, and was informed she'd been assigned to the ATS – the Auxiliary Territorial Reserve – in other words, the Army. She would have preferred to be a Wren, but reckoned it was no use complaining. Sheila, her friend, had changed her mind and decided to stay in Liverpool.

On the following day, Fergus Caffrey marched into Renshaw Hall and volunteered to fight for King and Country. His spectacles were in their case in his pocket, along with a copy of the sight chart that Cara had learnt by heart the day before and frantically scribbled down in the Ladies, minus the last line, which she'd forgotten. Fergus had spent the previous night memorizing it and passed the medical as easily as his sister, reeling off the letters on the chart that was merely a white blur. He could hardly believe it when told he would join the Royal Infantry and his orders would arrive within a fortnight.

When he got home, Cara looked at him questioningly. He made the thumbs-up sign. She grinned and mouthed, 'Good!'

Fergus decided to leave it a few days before he told Mam, who was still a bit upset over Cara. After he'd eaten, he changed his shirt and went out, his spectacles on his nose. He walked until he came to a pub where he was unlikely to be recognized, as he didn't want the news getting back to Mam before he was ready to tell her himself. Once inside, he ordered a whiskey.

'I'm celebrating,' he told the elderly barman. Fergus wasn't the sort of person who normally conversed with strangers, being much too shy, but tonight, given half the chance, he would have been happy to make a public announcement. 'Joined up today. I'm going in the Royal Infantry.'

'In that case, laddie,' said the barman, 'this is on the house.'

'And the next one's on me,' declared the customer who was holding up the bar next to Fergus. 'Better still, give the lad a double and I'll pay half.' He pumped Fergus's hand. 'Good luck, lad. Give them Jerries hell.'

'I will indeed,' Fergus said modestly.

In no time, he was surrounded by men who wanted to shake his hand, slap his back, wish him luck and urge him to do unspeakable things to the Jerries. He left the pub hours later as pissed as a lord and as happy as a lark, having never enjoyed himself so much since Anthony had gone to America.

Anthony had broken Fergus's young heart. That the boy with whom he'd been so close could drop him like a hot brick the minute he'd outlived his usefulness had cut him to the quick. The confidence gained from being Anthony's friend had been completely sapped and he was reduced to being the timid child he'd used to be, terrified of his own shadow. He still hadn't got over it and couldn't imagine trusting another person again.

He was grateful when Mr Allardyce offered him a job as a clerk with H.B. Wallace. It was a better job than he'd ever expected, but he found clerical work as dull as ditchwater, yet was still there after eleven years because there was nothing else he wanted to do – not until there was talk of war and Fergus realized what he wanted more than anything was to join the Army and fight for his country.

But there was a problem. At about the age of eighteen, he'd noticed the figures he was reading were getting smaller and when he tied his shoelaces they looked very far away. A visit to an optician – Mam had insisted on coming with him and it made him feel dead embarrassed – had revealed the fact that he was short-sighted and needed to wear spectacles permanently.

Most young men would have been shattered at the idea of wearing glasses, but Fergus loved his. They provided a shield for him to hide behind, although they had then become a barrier to him joining the Army. Today, though, with the help of his sister and a great deal of guile, he'd climbed the barrier and was now a member of His Majesty's Armed Forces. All he had to do was keep his head down and always follow the chap in front, after making damn sure it would never be him.

Lewis Brown, Eleanor's new lodger, arrived in Tigh Street in a white, two-seater sports car, a silk scarf tied casually around his neck and wearing a red-and-grey striped blazer and baggy flannels, followed a few hours later by his furniture in a van: a gorgeous antique desk, a worn, but comfortable-looking leather armchair, a four-poster bed and a set of damson-coloured curtains that were almost too heavy to lift. He'd only brought the minimum, he explained, just a few favourite pieces, his friend, Oliver, having explained there wouldn't be all that much room.

Lewis was about thirty-five, a well-built Scot, with dark tousled hair and smouldering black eyes, his romantic good looks reminding Eleanor of the poet Byron.

'*Smouldering* eyes!' Brenna hooted when Eleanor attempted to describe him. 'You've been reading too many books, El, and seeing too many pictures.'

Perhaps Eleanor had for, within a week, she was a tiny bit in love with both her lodgers: Lewis Brown for his thoughtful silences that usually ended with him saying something terribly significant and clever in his deep, gruff voice, and Oliver Chandler for his tempting smile and extrovert manner. Both were utterly charming and the best of friends, and she felt incredibly lucky to have them in her house.

On Lewis's first Sunday there, he and Oliver set to work and prepared a meal for the three of them – Jonathan had gone to play cricket – braised lamb followed by chocolate mousse accompanied by two bottles of wine. Eleanor recognized the label on one. 'That used to be my favourite,' she remarked. 'It was one of the last wines to come out of France before the last war.'

'I see you are a wine expert, Mrs Allardyce,' said Oliver Chandler.

'Hardly. I only remember this particular one. My father had an extensive wine cellar, which my husband inherited.'

'What did your late husband do?' Lewis Brown enquired.

'He's not late, we're still married, but separated some years ago. He also inherited my father's company and lives less than a mile from here.'

Was it just her imagination that both men looked slightly disappointed? Eleanor wasn't sure, but later that day she resolved to ask Marcus for a divorce. He would almost certainly refuse, if only out of sheer spite, but it wouldn't hurt to ask.

On Tuesday, she telephoned Nancy to see if Marcus would be in that night. 'Well, pet, he's not likely to tell me if he'll be in or out, is he?' Nancy said. 'But I reckon he'll be in. These days, he's in most nights. I think he's given up on that club of his.'

'What about Sybil?' She'd sooner her daughter wasn't around.

'Sybil's just the opposite, she's hardly ever in.' Like Cara, Sybil's hopes of becoming a Wren had also been dashed and both girls were leaving for a camp in Lincolnshire on Monday.

Eleanor felt the years fall away when she knocked on the door of Marcus's study and he called, 'Enter.'

She threw back her shoulders and went in, reminding herself that he no longer had any power over her and could do her no harm. Should he lose his temper or slam his fist on the desk then she was free to do the same. His head was bent over the papers on his desk and he didn't look up, no doubt thinking she was Nancy and he would look up when he felt like it.

'Good evening, Marcus,' she said quietly. He looked up then and she was shocked by the thinness of his face and the haunted, terribly sad look in his grey eyes. She sat down quickly in the chair in front of the desk before he had the opportunity to nod in its direction, giving her permission, as it were, to sit: in the past, he'd often left her standing during one of his tirades about something or other. She'd intended coming straight out with her request for a divorce, but felt deterred by the look in his eyes. 'How are you, Marcus?' she asked instead. She'd bring up the subject in a minute.

'Well,' he said heartily, although he didn't look it. 'Very well.'

'Good. I suppose the house is in an uproar with Sybil leaving for Lincolnshire in only a few days.'

'You could say that. Are you likely to see her before she leaves, or have you forgotten you have a daughter?' he asked coldly.

'I haven't forgotten, no. She came to tea the other night to meet my new lodger and on Sunday I'm taking her and Jonathan to a farewell lunch at the Adelphi. We've met quite a few times since she came home from London, Marcus.'

'I hadn't realized.' He looked crestfallen. Sybil obviously hadn't bothered to tell him.

'I love her,' Eleanor said simply. 'I concede we don't share a bond, like some mothers to do with their daughters, like Brenna does with Cara, for instance, but I still love her. I suppose we're more like friends than mother and daughter.'

'I'm pleased to hear it.'

She looked at him quickly, thinking there'd been a trace of sarcasm in his voice, but his face showed no hint of it. He looked sad and defeated. She deduced it was Sybil who had reduced him to the same state as he'd reduced *her* when she'd lived with him in Parliament Terrace.

'Why are you here, Eleanor?'

'I came . . .' She paused, not wanting to make him even more miserable than he already was, then remembered he'd never shown her an ounce of pity in the past. 'I came to ask if you will give me a divorce,' she said. 'You could give desertion as the reason, it would create less scandal than adultery.'

'For you or for me?' His mouth twisted in a dry smile.

'For you. Make it adultery if you wish. I'm not in the least bothered if people shun me. Nancy, Jonathan and the Caffreys already know the truth and they're the only people I care about. I doubt if my lodgers give two hoots about my background.'

He looked slightly surprised. 'You've told Jonathan?'

'He knows you're not his father, I had to tell him that. I said his real father was dead. I've never spoken about it to Sybil, but she must surely have guessed the truth – she realizes Jonathan is only her half-brother.'

'I see.' He shrugged. 'I'll phone my solicitor tomorrow.'

'Thank you, Marcus.' She was astounded that it had been so easy.

'Out of interest, are you asking for a divorce after all this time so you can get married again?'

It was none of his business, but he'd been so civilized about everything she didn't mind answering. 'No, I just want to be free, although I might get married again. I'll just have to see.' She smiled, feeling extraordinarily happy. 'You never know, Marcus, one of these days you might want to marry again.'

He laughed bitterly. 'There is absolutely no chance of that.'

Eleanor believed him. It would have stunned them both had they known that within eighteen months Marcus would have a new and very beautiful wife the same age as his daughter.

Brenna was about to lose all three of her children. Cara was off to Lincolnshire on Monday and on Wednesday Fergus would leave for Kent – she was amazed he'd managed to pass the eye test. Tyrone, resentful at being left behind, had gone that very day to the Army Recruiting Office to volunteer, not prepared to wait for his call-up papers to arrive.

'Maria and the lads will be better off without me,' he'd said the night before.

'I doubt it,' Brenna replied. 'Joey and Mike love you to bits and so does Maria – and you love them back. Don't deny it,' she added when Tyrone opened his mouth to do that very thing.

He groaned. 'Maybe I do, but it's hell on earth living in that place, Mam. We've got no room to breathe and I'm bound to be called up one day, so I'd only be going sooner rather than later.'

Brenna would rather he went later, after she'd got used to Cara and Fergus being away – if she ever did. 'What about Maria?' she asked. 'What's she got to say about it?'

'I haven't talked it over with her. It's always too noisy. Her gran's deaf and she and that mad uncle yell at each other all the time and the lads can't get to sleep. Oh, Mam!' he looked on the verge of tears. 'It's dead horrible in that house.'

'There, there.' Brenna tenderly patted his shoulder. There was a catch in her voice. He looked so young, far too young to have the responsibility of a wife and family. 'Maria won't thank you for leaving her and the lads behind in her gran's, will she, darlin'?'

Tyrone sniffed pathetically. 'Once I'm out the road, they can go and live with her mam. They get along just fine, it's only me Mrs Murphy won't speak to.'

'They can come and live here,' Brenna said instantly. 'There'll be two spare rooms once Cara and Fergus go.' She should really discuss it first with Colm, but felt sure he would agree that they didn't want their grandchildren living under Annie Murphy's roof, Tyrone coming home when the war was over to find them hardened criminals. That Squinty still lived with his mam, the lad who'd nudged Tyrone off the straight and narrow and would no doubt do the same with his old mate's little sons.

Colm, the most easygoing of husbands, had said later it was fine with him and that he hadn't been looking forward to living in an empty house. 'Any road, I'll be out most of the time. It's you who'll have the extra work, luv.'

Brenna said that she didn't mind a bit. In fact, she'd love to have Joey and Mike there all the time and it'd be one in the eye for Annie Murphy. And if Maria decided to send the lads to Southport as evacuees, they could all go to see them on Sundays in the van and have a nice day out at the same time.

Now she was waiting for Tyrone to come home and announce he'd joined the forces. She made a cup of tea and walked around the house drinking it, feeling restless, knowing she would never be able to sit still. Everyone said tea was the first thing that would be rationed because every leaf had to be imported from places like India and Ceylon and the Merchant Navy couldn't be expected to risk their lives so the population could enjoy never-ending cuppas. Unknown to Colm, because he wouldn't approve and would regard it as unpatriotic, Brenna had a secret hoard in the cupboard under the stairs. Every day she bought a quarter from a different shop – she could do without most things, but not tea.

She was pouring a second cup when Tyrone came in. There was something about his pale, set face that made her go cold. 'What's the matter, son?' she asked.

'I've been rejected, Mam,' he said in an appalled voice. 'There's something wrong with me heart.'

'There never is!' she gasped, going even colder.

'Yes, there is, Mam. It's got a murmur or something. The doctor said it's nothing to worry about, it's not dangerous, and lots of people have them and they never even know, but it means I can't go in the forces.' He sat down at the table and burst into tears. 'Oh, Mam! I feel like a bloody invalid.'

'Tyrone, me darlin' boy.' She took him in her arms and at the same time the coldness left and a feeling of relief spread over her. The doctor had said it wasn't dangerous and it meant that she'd have at least one of her children left. Tyrone could sleep in his old room with Maria – the beds could be shoved together – and Joey and Mike in Cara's, one at each end of Paddy's old bed.

There was no doubt about it, she thought, feeling deeply ashamed, she truly was the most selfish woman alive.

It was a breathtaking August day. The sun shone brilliantly out of a luminous blue sky and the air positively sparkled. It was far too nice a day to see your daughter off to war.

'It doesn't seem right,' Brenna said to Colm on the way to the station. Cara had gone early to make sure she got a seat.

'What doesn't seem right, luv?' Colm asked.

'That the Good Lord should give us such glorious weather at the same time as there's a war about to start. It's too much of a contrast: the sun reminds you of how good life can be. I'd sooner it was raining and the sky was as black as soot: it'd be more fitting.'

'The Good Lord might be responsible for the weather, I wouldn't know, but he's not responsible for the war, Bren,' Colm said soberly. 'Wars are caused by human beings for all sorts of different reasons. This time it's to stop a madman from taking over Europe and turning it into a fascist state with all the evil that goes with it. It'll be a just war, Bren, a war that had to happen because good men couldn't sit back and let Hitler have his way.'

'I know.' Brenna sighed. Until recently, Colm had been a pacifist and it had taken a just war to make him change. 'I only wish our Cara wasn't taking part in it.'

The platform was crowded with excited young women and their less than excited relatives – most looked extremely tearful. A train was chugging out, discharging clouds of grey smoke. The smell reminded Brenna of the cellar where they'd once lived and the fumes from the fire, which had so badly affected her baby daughter's chest. And now that same daughter was tall and lovely and about to leave home for a new and quite different life. It wasn't often these days that she prayed to the Blessed Virgin, but she did so now, imploring her to keep her precious Cara safe and well.

Cara, with her mane of red-golden hair and bright red frock, was easily spied halfway along the platform. Fergus and Tyrone had already arrived, having taken time off work to bid their sister goodbye. The train hissed and snorted, steam rising from underneath, like an impatient dragon anxious to escape the confines of the station and fly off to some strange, foreign land.

'Mam!' Cara threw her arms around Brenna's neck and then embraced her father. 'I'll write and let you know how things are as soon as I can.'

'You'd better had!' Brenna threateningly. 'If we don't hear from you by the end of the week, your dad'll drive to Lincolnshire looking for you. Have you saved yourself a seat, girl?'

'I've put me bags on one, Mam.'

'Don't do anything I wouldn't do, sis,' Fergus joked. The last few weeks, he'd been on top of the world and it was Tyrone who was down in the doldrums. Brenna thought how unpredictable life was. The son she'd thought she'd have at home was going away, and the one she'd expected to go was staying.

Cara said, 'Mam, Sybil Allardyce is over there with her mam and dad. Nancy and Jonathan are there, too.'

'I'd forgotten Eleanor would be here.' Brenna went over to say tara to Sybil. She'd never particularly liked her, but this wasn't the time to let it show. The girl was dressed up to the nines in a navy-blue linen costume and white hat, gloves and bag. She kissed her and urged her to look after herself. 'You and our Cara are like family. The September girls must try and stick together if they can,' she advised.

'Yes, Mrs Caffrey,' Sybil said curtly. Like the train, she looked impatient to be off.

Eleanor and Nancy came back with Brenna to say goodbye to Cara. 'All these goodbyes,' Nancy sighed. 'They make me feel restless. If I was young enough, I'd join the Army meself.'

'Is Mr Allardyce coming down with something?' Brenna asked. 'He doesn't look very well.'

'He's upset that Sybil's leaving,' Eleanor explained, 'and it doesn't help that she's being so horrid to him.' She shook her head disapprovingly. 'Sometimes my daughter can be a real bitch.'

Minutes later, the guard blew his whistle and there was a brief commotion as the girls piled on to the train. Cara's head appeared at a window and she waved madly at her family. 'Tara Mama, tara Dad.' She blew kisses at Fergus and Tyrone. 'Tara, everyone.'

'Tara, Cara,' Brenna cried. 'Take care of yourself, me darlin' girl.'

The train gave a massive snort and the wheels began to move. Brenna ran along the platform, dodging in and out of the waving crowds, determined to stay as close to her daughter for as long as possible, but Colm caught up and put his arms around her waist, holding her back.

'Let her go, luv,' he whispered.

'I don't want to let her go, Colm. I want her here with us.' She began to cry – huge, painful sobs that threatened to tear her guts apart. She remembered then that in another forty-eight hours, she would have to go through the same desperately horrible experience when Fergus left.

'Every mam and dad on the platform probably feels the same.' By now, the train had disappeared and only the smoke remained, melting into wisps and puffs that floated away in front of their eyes. Colm led her towards the exit. 'Come on, Bren, let's go home.'

Marcus stood and waited until the train could no longer be seen or heard. Only then did he turn and join the crush to leave. Everybody seemed subdued and dejected. Ahead, Brenna and Colm walked, their bodies pressed close together. Fergus and Tyrone waited at the entrance to the platform for them to catch up. Eleanor linked Jonathan's arm – he was an overweight, unhealthy-looking boy – and Nancy was on her other side, all three involved in an animated conversation that appeared to demand lots of waving of hands.

He seemed to be the only person alone. Would he feel better, he wondered, if he had someone to share his all-consuming misery, someone he could tell how much he missed Sybil, who would know exactly how he felt because they would miss her too? Eleanor hadn't been too concerned to see her daughter leave – she was happy enough with Jonathan and her lodgers – but Nancy had lost most of the people close to her, who'd either died or gone away: her parents, her brothers, Herbert Wallace and his wife, Anthony, now Sybil and Cara Caffrey, whom she'd helped to deliver nearly nineteen years ago in the basement of the house in Parliament Terrace. She would surely understand how he felt.

Marcus quickened his pace until he caught up with the trio. 'I thought I'd go home for a while rather than back to the factory,' he said to Nancy. 'I wondered if you'd like a lift?'

'Oh, but I wasn't . . .' She looked into his face. 'That's very nice of you. I'd like a lift home, thank you.'

He was aware of the sympathy in her eyes. She had clearly intended going somewhere else, but had changed her mind because she felt sorry for him. His face stiffened. He hated the thought of looking so wretched that he invited compassion. 'I've just remembered,' he said harshly, 'I have an important appointment this afternoon. I won't be going home, after all.'

'That's all right,' Nancy said kindly, and he could tell she'd seen right through him and it made him feel even worse.

It seemed to Brenna that the entire country took a collective breath and held it in while they waited for something to happen. Eleanor had an Anderson air raid shelter built at the bottom of her garden, as did everyone who had a house with a garden. But the Caffreys only had a yard and were required to go to the nearest public shelter if there was a raid. Brenna had no intention of doing any such thing. She cleared out the cupboard under the stairs, which would probably be just as safe, although a bit squashed once she, Tyrone, Maria and the lads were inside.

They'd moved into the Caffreys' house a few days ago. The lads loved having a room to themselves and Maria said it was the first time she'd slept the whole night through in ages. Brenna had never realized what an admirable person her daughter-in-law was: a loving mother to her two little sons and patience itself with Tyrone, who'd been in a desperately dark mood ever since the Army had rejected him. She insisted on doing her own washing and her share of the housework at which she was inclined to be a bit slapdash, but Brenna put the blame for that on Mrs Murphy for not showing the girl a good example — she'd like to bet the Murphys' house was a tip.

'Are you going to let the lads be evacuated to Southport, darlin'?' Brenna enquired one day. 'Me and Eleanor are helping to organize it.'

'I'd sooner not, least not straight away. I'd sooner wait until the raids start, that's if they ever start at all.' Maria's pretty face was grim. 'And if they do have to go, I'm going with them. I'm not having strangers looking after me kids.' Which was exactly what Brenna would have done had she been in Maria's position.

Government leaflets poured through the letterbox: how to tape your windows, use a stirrup pump, take your gas mask with you everywhere . . .

Brenna duly taped her windows and put up the blackout curtains. From outside, every house looked like a funeral parlour. Some people she knew just disappeared, having gone to stay with relatives in the country or to another country altogether: Australia, Canada, the United States . . . Shops and a few small firms closed down, the owners having been called up for military service: the young milkman was replaced by his father and the postman gave way to a postwoman.

Cara wrote to say that once she had finished her basic training she was going to Bedford on a driving course, and Fergus telephoned the Allardyces to say he'd just been informed he was being sent to France early the following day and didn't have time to write. Nancy came hurrying round to Shaw Street with the news and told them Mr Allardyce said they could use his telephone any time they wanted.

'That's kind of him,' Brenna said, touched, although she'd always had free use of Eleanor's phone.

The air raid siren was tested several times during the day, scaring the living daylights out of the population who tried not to imagine what the inhuman wail would sound like in the middle of the night bringing the ugly message that a raid was about to start and bombs would drop from the sky at any minute.

The weather in August was the finest that Brenna could remember: each golden day followed by another just as lovely, yet bringing the threat of war even closer.

On the final day of August, the threat seemed more like a promise when it was announced that mass evacuation would take place the following day.

Half a dozen coaches waited at Our Lady of Mount Carmel, gleaming in the morning sunshine, when Brenna arrived the next morning. Eleanor was already there as well as a straggling line of children, most accompanied by mothers who were loudly cursing

Hitler for having to send their children away because Liverpool was about to become a place where it was no longer safe to be.

'How long will it be for?' one demanded angrily of Brenna.

'I don't know, darlin',' she confessed. 'No one does, not even the good Lord himself.'

She helped the alternately brave, weeping or giggling children on to the buses. Some were dressed in their best clothes, but she pitied the families who'd be landed with the poor little ragamuffins whose mothers hadn't bothered to come and who smelled as if they hadn't had a wash in weeks. They'd brought nothing with them: no clothes, not even a toothbrush.

The last coach was about to leave when Maria arrived with Joey and Mike and a giant suitcase. 'I've decided to go after all,' she said breathlessly. 'It doesn't seem fair on the kids to stay.'

'Tara, darlin'.' Brenna took the girl in her arms. 'I'll miss you and the lads something awful. You've hardly been there five minutes, but the house won't seem the same with the three of you gone.'

There was a lump in throat as she watched the coach drive away, Joey and Mike on the back seat waving furiously. This was the third time she'd had to say goodbye to people she loved and she prayed it would be the last.

That was the day the blackout began and that night a nightmarish darkness fell over the city. For the first time, Colm left to take up his official role as an air raid warden, and Tyrone went to the pub, driven half-mad with despair at the way things had turned out – people had already started to ask when he would be called up.

'What am I supposed to tell them, Mam?' he'd asked.

'The truth, darlin'.'

'I don't want to tell them the truth and if I did, they'd probably never believe me. They'll think I'm just a shirker, too scared to fight.'

Brenna sat alone in the house, pulling the curtains tightly closed when it grew dark, unable to hear the faintest sound outside. On such a warm night, there'd normally have been plenty of people about. The street lights would be lit by now, women would be jangling on their doorsteps, children still playing out. But most of the children had gone away and the women were, like her, shut inside wondering what on earth the world had come to. She was unwilling to turn on the wireless, worried what awful news she might hear.

The next day, Friday, Hitler invaded Poland, a signal that all hell was about to break out, and at ten o'clock on Sunday morning it was announced on the wireless that the prime minister, Neville Chamberlain, would speak to the nation at quarter past eleven.

'This is it, Bren,' Colm said ominously.

'I'll invite in some of the neighbours.' They were one of the few houses in the street that had a wireless. Brenna wondered if her old neighbour, Katie MacBride, would have predicted the war in the leaves had she still been alive, but Katie had passed away years ago.

By quarter past eleven, the house was full to bursting with people standing in the hall and sitting on the stairs. They heard the prime minister tell them that their country was now at war with Germany, finishing with, 'May God bless you all. May He defend the right, for it is evil things that we shall be fighting against – brute force, bad faith, injustice, oppression and persecution – and against them I am certain that the right will prevail.'

Chapter 8

Sybil buried her head beneath the bedclothes, but the voices were only slightly muffled by the stiff-as-a-board sheet and blankets so coarse you could have struck matches on them. The pillow felt as if had been stuffed with cobbles.

'Bleedin' hell,' someone groaned. 'I wanna pee already. I only went just before lights out. I'll never find me bleedin' way to the bog in the dark.'

'Pee out the winder,' someone else suggested. 'Some lucky soldier will get a great, big hard-on if he spies your arse hanging out.'

'Yeah! But what'll *she* get,' asked a third someone.

'The clap?'

There was a burst of laughter. 'The clap' was another term for venereal disease and Sybil could see nothing funny about it. Since she'd joined the Army, she had lost all sense of humour and was convinced it wouldn't return until she left. She would never understand how Betsy Billington-Clarke had managed to become a WAAF. It was rumoured that the RAF and the Navy took all the superior girls, leaving the dregs to the ATS. Sybil preferred to think it was all the luck of the draw, otherwise where did that leave her? Or, come to that, Cara Caffrey, who was a bit rough, but could hardly be described as 'dregs', like most of the common-as-muck girls in the billet to whom it had come as a shock to find they were expected to shower every morning. 'At home, I only had a bath once a month,' one had said. They didn't go to the lavatory, but to the bog, 'for a pee', or even 'a piss', and they never washed their hands afterwards. They came out with swear words that Sybil had never heard before.

The worse part though, the very worst and most nauseating part of all, was that after breakfast they were expected to carry out all sorts of menial tasks like cleaning the kitchen and the lavatories, which

169

required kneeling down to scrub floors. Had they never heard of a mop? Sybil had never actually used a mop, but thought it must be easier. The officers' mess also had to be dusted and tidied – the officers had their own little bar where alcohol and light refreshments were provided and there were comfortable armchairs, pictures on the walls and a vase of flowers. The lower ranks had to spend all their leisure time in the billet or go for walks in the uninspiring country lanes that surrounded the camp.

The most nauseating job was collecting the used sanitary towels from the women's lavatories and burning them in the furnace. The smell was enough to put you off food for the rest of your life. Was this why she'd joined the Army?

Cara was asleep at the other end of the twenty-four-bed billet. She seemed to have settled in well and made a few friends. Everybody liked her – apart from the drill sergeant who picked on her most unfairly, Sybil had to concede – whereas *she* was openly referred to as a 'toffee-nosed bitch'. *She* hadn't made a single friend, didn't know a single name apart from Cara's and only spoke to people when she had to. So far as she was concerned, it could stay that way until the war was over.

'I'll never like it here,' she muttered into the rock-hard pillow. 'Never, never, never.'

Cara wasn't asleep, but crying quietly into her own uncomfortable pillow. She badly wanted to go home. What sort of madness had prompted her to join the forces? It had all seemed like a jolly game and she'd expected to have loads of fun, but had been as miserable as sin since the day she'd arrived three weeks ago.

For one thing, the camp was situated in a flat, desolate area as different from Liverpool as it was possible to imagine, miles away from the shops and picture houses and ordinary human beings. Used to the hustle and bustle of a big, busy city, she found the isolation unnerving and faintly threatening. The September weather was lovely, but they weren't far from the Lincolnshire coast and it could be chilly some mornings. It affected her more than the others because her skirt was too short and she had to roll up the legs of her long, khaki knickers in case they showed. Longer skirts had been ordered especially for her, but there'd been no indication as to when they would arrive. It was also cold at night: all the camp buildings were made of wood and had been thrown up in a hurry so none were lined. She dreaded to think what it would be like in winter, but fortunately basic training would be over by then and she would be transferred somewhere else, hopefully warmer.

Sergeant Major Fawcett who took them for drill was a bully and the most bad-tempered, ill-humoured person she'd ever met in her life. Perhaps, because she was the tallest, he noticed her more than the other girls and picked on her all the time.

'Caffrey, you're out of step,' he would bawl.

'Caffrey, don't you know your left from your right?' This when virtually every other girl had also turned the wrong way.

'Caffrey, you great big dollop, don't slouch. Remember, you're now a member of His Majesty's armed forces. Walk tall, girl, be proud.'

Cara had reached the point where drill had become torture and she was finding it hard to stop herself from crying the whole way through. The other girls had noticed she was being picked on – it would have been impossible not to – and were very sympathetic. There was nothing they could do to protect her from the sergeant major's invective other than call him names, not loud enough for him to hear, but sometimes managing to bring a smile to Cara's agonized face.

'If I ever come across that bastard in the dark,' one of the London girls had muttered the other day, 'I'll knee him in the balls so hard that he'll choke on the bleedin' things.'

'Oh, shut up, you revolting, pig-headed creature,' Peggy Cross had whispered only that morning when Cara had been accused of having two left feet. 'Don't let him upset you, love, he's not worth it.'

Peggy was a schoolteacher, already regretting she'd abandoned a promising career and a very annoyed fiancé for the Army. 'I thought I was being patriotic, but now it seems more like downright foolishness.' She was four years older than Cara and they'd become good friends.

At the far end of the dormitory, the London girls were joking among themselves. They were a good laugh, as well as being as tough as old boots, and their hearts were made of pure gold. Sergeant Major Fawcett's ears would have caught fire had he been able to hear the names they called him – names Cara wasn't prepared to repeat, not even in her head.

She sniffed dejectedly into the pillow and slipped her hand underneath to where she kept the china lady that Mam had insisted she take with her. Perhaps it'll bring you luck, darlin'. Well, so far it hadn't, although Mam would never know. When she wrote home, she claimed everything was the gear and she was having a marvellous time, often having to write the letter again, or even a third time, when she noticed tears had fallen on to the paper, smudging the ink and making a lie of all the cheerful things she had written.

One good thing had happened. A few days ago they'd been set a series of tests to establish the sort of work that would most suit them and she'd done really well, boosting her badly dented confidence no end. The result of this was, when basic training finished, she was being sent to Bedford on a driving course with four other women: Peggy Cross, Fielding, Childs and Sybil Allardyce. Becoming a driver was far preferable to catering, domestic work or working in an office. Peggy was really pleased, but Cara had no idea what Sybil felt about it – it was hard to tell how Sybil felt about anything. She kept herself to herself and no one would have guessed that she and Cara had known each other before. Perhaps, having been at boarding school for so long, she didn't mind being away from home.

'Wake up, girls,' Corporal Smithson bellowed in the foghorn voice that sounded bizarre coming from such a dimunitive figure. 'Wakey, wakey, wakey.' The light was switched on and she walked the length of the dormitory, kicking the foot of each bed as she passed. The kick would carry through the metal frame like an electric charge and the sleeper would be shocked awake.

'You'll be pleased to know, girls,' the corporal continued gleefully, 'that according to the weather forecast, the sun has decided to give our little part of the world a miss today, the wind has risen and it's started to rain. You'll enjoy drill more than usual this morning.' She kicked a few more beds. 'Up you get, Fielding. You too, Atkinson. Why, Caffrey, if you haven't grown a few more inches during the night! Allardyce! That is *not* an Army issue nightdress. Where d'you think you're staying – the Savoy? That reminds me, Allardyce, Captain Muir would like to see you in her office at half past eleven. Now, girls, I'm going to stand outside these 'ere showers and if anyone comes out and they're not sopping wet, they'll be sent back in and their lovely porridge will go cold.'

'It's pitch-dark outside. It's still the middle of the night.'

'It's only pitch-dark, Fielding, because you've yet to open your eyes. It's five to six and the beginning of another scintillating day. Get up and face it with a smile.'

'Ugh!' Fielding pretended to be sick. She was a sparky little girl, smaller even than the corporal. She only looked about fourteen and had something to say about everything.

'You're a sadist, Corporal,' Peggy Cross grumbled. 'You're really enjoying this, aren't you?'

Corporal Smithson grinned. She was really quite nice and everyone liked her. 'I'm enjoying it enormously, Cross. Buggering you lot around gives me enormous pleasure.'

The girls stumbled out of their beds, shivering even in their thick pyjamas, grabbed their towels and shuffled into the showers. The water wasn't exactly cold, but nor was it exactly warm. They emerged, still shivering, and hurriedly began to get dressed. The trouble with a uniform was you couldn't just throw it on: shirts, collars, ties, jackets and caps all had to be coped with and shoes had to be laced, not to mention the khaki woollen stockings that made the slimmest of legs look like tree trunks.

They left the building, still struggling with buttons, caps askew, hoping they wouldn't encounter an officer who'd tell them they were a disgrace to the service and order them to go back and not come out until they were properly attired.

In the half-light – in any sort of light – the camp presented a dismal sight, but particularly so this morning in the drizzling rain under a bleak grey sky: a vast concrete parade ground where puddles had already formed, surrounded by single-storey huts; six billets for the girls and more than a hundred men, the officers' mess, administration buildings, a gymnasium and the canteen towards which the women were eagerly heading, aching for a hot drink and something to eat. It might have been because they were hungry all the time that the food didn't taste so bad, not even the porridge you could stand your spoon up in, the over-done bacon, the greasy eggs and the sausages that always smelled a bit off.

Breakfast over, the girls were told what tasks awaited them that morning. Cara was detailed to help in the laundry, one of the few jobs she didn't mind. They returned to their hut and changed into overalls, tying a cotton square turban-style over their hair. Poor Sybil had to burn the sanitary towels for the second or third time and her face was like thunder as they straggled across the parade ground to the various sites.

While the laundry was one of the least unpleasant jobs, especially if all you had to do was iron dozens of shirts, it was also perilous in that men operated the giant gas boilers. They were new recruits like themselves, and some were very nice. Others, though, seemed to regard every female soldier as a slag who would make no objection if her bottom was pinched or her breasts stroked. Cara had been forced to threaten one with an iron when his arms sneaked around her waist and he cupped her breasts in his hands.

'All right, miss, all right,' the man had said, laughing as he backed away, making Cara even madder. 'I didn't realize you were a lesbian.'

The word meant nothing to Cara, she'd never heard it before.

One had slid his hand between Peggy's legs and she'd hit him with a wet towel, nearly taking an eye out with the corner. He had screeched in pain and had to visit the First Aid post, returning with a bandage over the damaged eye.

'I bet you won't try that again,' Peggy said coldly, not the least bit sorry.

That morning, laundry detail passed without incident. Cara felt relieved, although it meant that ten o'clock, time for drill, was drawing ever closer. But perhaps the gods were smiling on her today, because when they were back in uniform and had assembled on the parade ground, Sergeant Major Fawcett announced they were going on an exercise. Anything was preferable to drill, she thought.

'Today, me lovelies, you are going to march to Henslow. A lorry will pick you up at four o'clock and bring you back.'

'Henslow's a good twenty miles away, Sarge. We mightn't have reached there by four,' Fielding shouted. She seemed to have appointed herself the group's spokesman.

'If you miss the lorry, you'll just have to march back, won't you? Oh, and don't forget to wear your greatcoats.'

'Do we have to, Sarge?'

'Yes, Fielding,' the sergeant major said patiently. 'It's all part of the exercise. Besides which, it's raining. We don't want you catching a chill, do we?'

'I'd sooner catch a chill than wear my greatcoat. It weighs a ton. Are you coming with us, Sarge?'

'No, I'm not. You're going on your ownsomes. There's a list of things to take with you in the billet.'

'A list—' Fielding began, but got no further because Sergeant Major Fawcett's patience snapped and he bawled, 'Dismissed!'

Back in the billet, they read the list of things to take with a mixture of dismay and anger.

'A change of uniform!'

'Billy cans and cutlery!'

'Spare boots!'

'A groundsheet, for God's sake. Why on earth will we need a groundsheet?'

'*Candles!*'

'It's all part of the exercise. It's a test to see if we come back alive. If we don't, we're out of the Army.'

They began to stuff the things into their haversacks, groaning mightily, and groaning even more when they shrugged into the greatcoats that felt as if they were made of lead. With the haversacks on their backs, they could hardly move.

Sergeant Major Fawcett stood by the camp gate and ticked off their names as they left. 'Where's Allardyce?' he barked when there was no sign of Sybil.

'She has to see Captain Muir at half past eleven,' Fielding informed him. 'Lucky old her.'

'There's no need for that attitude. You're about to have a nice day out and I bet Allardyce is kicking herself for missing it.'

'Oh, yeah!'

They marched for about half a mile along a dreary country lane, by which time shoes had begun to pinch and shoulders to ache. Rain dripped off their caps and trickled down their necks, the temperature had warmed up considerably and they were melting in the heavy coats. They were seriously considering staging a mutiny and risking being expelled or cashiered or whatever it was called when you were chucked out of the Army, when they heard something approaching from behind and turned to see a single-decker bus trundling towards them, its destination Henslow. They stood in the middle of the lane, leaving the driver with no choice but to mow them down or stop his bus.

He stopped and they piled inside and sat among the bemused passengers, mainly women with shopping bags.

'We're just showing initiative, that's all,' said Peggy Cross. 'That's what you're supposed to do in the face of the enemy: show initiative. Has everyone got enough money for the fare?'

'It doesn't matter about paying.' The young bus conductor grinned at them broadly and explained he was about to join the Army himself. Fielding, whose mouth was never still, began to sing 'Roll Out the Barrel' – she had a wonderful singing voice – and everyone joined in, including the passengers. The bus stopped frequently to let on more astounded passengers who were only too willing to take part in the entertainment on what, until then, had been an exceeding dull grey morning. Cara did an Irish jig in the aisle, Fielding tap-danced to 'Twelfth Street Rag', only slightly hindered by her heavy shoes, and the London girls did 'Knees Up Mother Brown' showing yards of khaki knickers. Everyone was in the very best of spirits: they hadn't had to walk twenty miles in the rain and felt they had got their own back on the Army, Sergeant Major Fawcett in particular.

When they got to Henslow, despite Corporal Smithson's prediction, the sun was shining and the driver said it was quite the nicest journey he'd ever made in his bus and, if they wanted, they could leave their haversacks and overcoats in the bus station to collect later. The girls showed their gratitude by showering him and the conductor with kisses.

Any other time, they would have regarded Henslow as nothing out of the ordinary, but today it seemed an enchanted place as they dispersed into its shops and cafés. Cara, Peggy and Fielding made for the nearest Woolworth's to buy make-up, sweets and scented soap – Army-issue soap smelled like week-old kippers – then to a fish and chip restaurant because, as usual, they were starving. Later, they bought biscuits, tea and condensed milk to help relieve the boredom of the long evenings spent in the billet.

Later still, they all met up at the pictures where they sat on wooden benches to watch an ancient film, *The Blue Angel*, in which Marlene Dietrich sang 'Falling in Love Again'. They came out, singing at the top of their voices, trying to ape Marlene's husky distinctive style, raising smiles from everyone around.

They collected their coats and haversacks, waited for the lorry and sang all the way back. It had been a glorious, truly enjoyable day and they'd felt like themselves again, no longer just a tiny cog in the big, impersonal Army machine.

'You know,' said Fielding as they climbed out of the lorry, 'I think I might come to like Army life, after all,' and everyone agreed, including Cara.

That morning, at about the time the bus was arriving in Henslow, Sybil was sitting in Captain Muir's outer office waiting to be called in. The captain's beautifully modulated voice could be heard on the telephone. She was the daughter of a lord and married to a Member of Parliament and why she wanted to see her, Sybil had no idea. She wasn't aware she'd done anything wrong other than hate the Army with all her heart and soul, although the captain wasn't likely to know that unless it showed on her face.

Perhaps she was to be told off for her attitude. If asked, she'd admit the truth and say how much she loathed the Army and rather hoped she'd be thrown out and could go home to Daddy. He could fuss over her all he liked and she wouldn't mind a bit.

The door to the office opened and Captain Muir said, 'Ah, Allardyce! Come in, won't you, and sit down.'

'Thank you, ma'am.' Sybil entered the sparsely furnished room, its only adornment a framed photograph of the King at his coronation, and seated herself in front of the desk. She savoured the discreet hint of expensive perfume.

'You should have waited for me to sit first,' Captain Muir said with a slight smile.

Sybil was taken aback. 'I'm sorry.'

'That's all right. It takes time to learn the rules – not that that's a rule. It's just common courtesy to let a senior officer sit first. I would have to do the same if I was with someone of a higher rank.'

'I'll remember in future, ma'am,' Sybil promised.

'Good.' The woman didn't speak for a while. Her brow puckered, as if she were thinking deeply, her long, white hands joined together by the fingertips. 'How are you liking the Army, Allardyce?' she asked eventually.

Sybil had been prepared to confess her loathing for the Army, but now that she was face to face with the elegant, self-assured Captain Muir her nerve failed her. The woman was good-looking in an aristocratic way, with a thin, straight nose, large eyes that were almost violet, and skin the texture of finest porcelain. Her dark-brown hair was cut manishly short, but on her it looked quite feminine, and her uniform fitted her slim body so perfectly it must have been specially tailored. Sybil didn't want to admit to such a distinguished figure that joining the forces had been a big mistake and she'd like to go home. She wanted Captain Muir to like her and this wouldn't be achieved by confessing her true opinion.

'I'm slowly getting to like it, ma'am,' she lied. She doubted if the captain would believe her if she claimed to be loving every minute. 'Some of the girls in the billet take a bit of getting used to.'

'You're a very mixed bunch: a few factory girls, shop girls, clerks, a schoolteacher, an artist, a couple of girls like you who've come straight from school and another couple who were halfway through their university courses but gave them up to join the forces. Oh, and I forgot, you have an actress.'

'An actress!' Sybil hadn't dreamt her fellow recruits came from such diverse backgrounds. She had thought herself the only properly educated one there.

'Yes, an actress: Juliette Fielding. She's twenty-one, but is such a tiny little thing that she usually plays juvenile parts.'

'The name rings a bell. I think I may have seen her in a West End show.' Sybil could hardly believe she was sharing her billet with a professional actress. She wondered why she was being told all this. Perhaps the thought communicated itself to the captain because she said, 'The reason I wanted to speak to you, Allardyce, is I wondered if you would be interested in being sent for officer training?'

'Me? Be an officer?' Sybil had rarely been so surprised in her life.

'You have the right attitude. You haven't plunged in and made half a dozen best friends in the first few weeks. You appear to be extremely self-contained. You're well educated, obey orders without complaint – I've been told you didn't object to burning the sanitary towels when you were asked to do it a third time this morning.'

'I didn't like it, ma'am,' Sybil confessed.

'No, but you didn't complain. Most girls would have considered they were being picked on.'

178

'I was beginning to think that I was.' A thought struck her. 'Was I being asked to do that horrible job as a test?'

The captain smiled. 'Perhaps, and I promise it won't happen again. About the officer training, what do you think?'

'I'd love it, ma'am, I really would.' It would make all the difference in the world. She would have a room to herself, spend her evenings in a comfortable armchair in the officers' mess, mix with people like Captain Muir. It would put an entirely different slant on Army life.

She sprang to her feet when the captain stood and came round and shook hands. 'Keep the news under your hat for now, Allardyce, until after you've finished your basic training, then I seem to remember you were being transferred to Bedford to take a driving course.'

'I can already drive, ma'am. My father arranged for me to have lessons while I was at school in London.'

'I don't suppose you know what goes on under a car's bonnet?'

'I'm afraid I haven't a clue.'

'Then it wouldn't hurt to find out. Officer training finishes a few weeks before the driving course does. You can join it then and learn the mechanics of a car.'

'Yes, ma'am.'

That night in the billet, Sybil sat on her bed and carefully studied her fellow recruits, trying to work out who had been the schoolteacher, the artist, the university students, the girls who, like her, had come straight from school. She'd been inclined to bunch them altogether and consider them a common lot, but taken individually most seemed perfectly respectable. She felt slightly ashamed of her rush to judgement, influenced by a handful of coarse types.

Fielding, the actress, was treating everyone to a perfect imitation of Marlene Dietrich singing 'Falling in Love Again', while sat astride a chair wearing only her vest and knickers for some reason. She was an incredibly pretty girl with long blonde curly hair that she kept tied in a knot beneath her cap, although now it flowed like a cape around her childish shoulders.

When the song had finished to loud applause, Sybil said, 'I once saw you on the West End. It was a wonderful show, all about the

Great War. At the end, you sang "Keep the Home Fires Burning" and everybody cried.'

There was a stunned silence, then half a dozen voices cried, 'Were you on the *stage*, Fielding?'

'I was indeed,' Fielding said modestly. She began to twirl like a top down the space between the beds, until she tripped over a shoe and collapsed, laughing, on the foot of Sybil's bed.

'You know,' a slightly older woman said thoughtfully, 'we've been living together for three whole weeks, yet we know nothing about each other. What did you all do before you came here? Where do you come from? And I don't even know anyone's first name apart from Cara's.'

'Who's Cara?'

'I am.' Cara raised her hand. 'Cara Caffrey. I used to work in Boots Cash Chemist's in Liverpool. And that's Peggy Cross who just spoke.'

'I was a schoolteacher in Guildford,' Peggy said.

'I'm Juliette Fielding,' said Fielding, bowing graciously, 'and I'm an actress and I've lived all over the place.'

'My name's Annie Black and I was a clerk with an estate agent in Portsmouth.'

'I'm Joan Drummond. I left art college a year ago and worked for an advertising agency in Piccadilly, but it's my ambition to become a portrait painter. I'm going to be a draughtswomen when we finish training and I'm very pleased about it.'

'I used to help me old dad sell fish in Billingsgate Market. Me name's Lily Salmon, and if anyone finds that funny, I'll give them a punch in their bleedin' gob. Oh, and when I finish me training, I'm gonna be a cook and I'm not pleased about it a bit.'

'I'm Elizabeth Childs, but everyone calls me Liz. I got married in April on my eighteenth birthday, but my husband was called up, so I thought I might as well join up too. I worked as a receptionist for the Gas Board in Leeds and I'm really thrilled I'm going to learn to drive.'

One by one, the girls spoke, giving their names and occupation and where they came from. As they did, they became real people with their own quite different backgrounds, no longer just anonymous recruits in a khaki uniform. Sybil couldn't help herself, she felt quite moved.

'What about you?' Lily Salmon said when Sybil was the only one who hadn't spoken. 'You're the one who started this, so you can't cop out.'

'I'm Sybil Allardyce from Liverpool. I joined up straight from school.'

'Now that we all know each other, let's have a party,' Fielding shouted. 'I bought some groceries this afternoon. Let's pool everything. Put the kettle on, someone.'

Water was fetched and a giant kettle put on the stove to boil, biscuits were produced, saccharine tablets, half a dozen packets of Smith's crisps, a wedge of bunloaf, sweets, a jar of jam, although there was nothing to spread it on, coffee, condensed milk, a bottle of brown sauce, bottles of lemonade and dandelion and burdock. Sybil brought out the box of expensive chocolates her father had sent: there were just enough to have one each.

The kettle took an age to boil on top of the black cylindrical fire that gave off hardly any heat. When it did, they made the tea and coffee and, clutching their tin mugs, gathered around the fire, adding the chocolate wrappings and anything else burnable that they could find which would provide a moment's warmth. Crisps were dipped in the brown sauce, biscuits in the jam and Sybil's chocolates were kept to the last, a final treat after a feast that had been more unusual than enjoyable, although it was something they would remember for a long time. Afterwards, they chatted to each other quietly, singing occasionally, until Corporal Smithson arrived to turn out the lights.

'What's this?' she yelled. 'A soirée? If everyone's not in bed in five minutes, the lights are going out and you can get undressed in the dark. I don't suppose,' she added in a wheedling tone, 'you've got a cup of tea left?'

Another night like that and she'd wish she hadn't agreed to become an officer, Sybil thought as she lay between the stiffly starched sheets. It had been enormous fun and the girls were much nicer than the ones at school. There'd been a great feeling of camaraderie, which she'd never experienced before. Still, she'd only be another three weeks with this particular crowd before being transferred to another camp where she'd have to get to know a completely new set of girls. Cara was taking the driving course and that Liz woman, but she had no idea who else. When it came right down to it, she'd be miles better off as an officer with her uniform specially tailored, a room of her own, and in a position to give orders rather than take them, even if it meant she'd never experience a feeling of camaraderie again for the rest of her life.

Basic training was over. The not-so-new recruits could march in strict formation without putting a step wrong and Sergeant Major Fawcett had ceased to be an ogre. Now they were about to be split up and transferred to camps all over the country. Many tears were shed as they bid each other an emotional farewell. They'd lived together a mere six weeks, but it felt like a lifetime. They swore they'd meet up again one day: 'We're bound to, aren't we? After all the Army's not all *that* big.' It made parting so much easier if they could believe it.

Before being sent on their various courses, they'd were given five days' leave to see their families.

Travelling in wartime was a nightmarish experience. Cara had to catch three trains to Liverpool, all so packed that she had to sit on her kit bag in the corridor with hardly room to bend her legs, surrounded by troops who fought their way out when the train stopped to fetch her cups of tea and sandwiches or, on one occasion, an Eccles cake that looked as if it had been sat on. They told each other their life stories, sang for miles on end, making the exhausting journey far more bearable than it might have been. She had no idea what had happened to Sybil whom she'd expected to travel with her, but hadn't been around when they'd made their goodbyes.

It was almost midnight when she reached Liverpool, having given the Bedford address to half a dozen soldiers who'd promised to write to her. Only then did she discover what the blackout was really like. It was as if someone had laid a dark blanket over the city and she felt totally disorientated when she stepped outside Lime Street station. There was hardly any traffic about and the few vehicles to be seen had had their headlights reduced to a tiny slit. She was wondering if it would be best to go back into the station and stay in the waiting room until daylight, when someone bumped into her, nearly knocking her over.

'Bloody hell, I'm sorry,' said a male voice, and she vaguely glimpsed a hand reaching out to steady her. By then, she was able to make out the slight difference between the feathery blackness of the sky and the solid blackness of the buildings across the road. She could see stars and the hint of a moon playing hide and seek between the clouds.

'Where are you off to?' asked the owner of the voice.

'Back inside the station, I think, although I was intending to go to Toxteth. Do you know if the trams are still running?'

'No idea. I'm headed for Childwall. I'll give you a lift on me motorbike, if you like. I came to meet me brother, but he must have missed the train.'

'I've got a kit bag with me.'

'That's all right. I'll tie it on the back. I left the bike parked over there.' He took her arm and led her across the road. 'I've got used to driving without hardly any lights, although I'll have to crawl along.'

About quarter of an hour later, the bike drew up outside the house in Shaw Street and Cara climbed off, untied the bag and thanked her Good Samaritan. 'I'm dead grateful, I really am. Thanks . . . I don't know your name!'

'Charlie Green. What's yours?'

'Cara Caffrey.'

'Tara, Cara.' The bike zoomed away and became lost in the night.

'Tara, Charlie,' Cara whispered. They would never recognize each other if they met again, yet she'd just spent a good fifteen minutes with her arms around his waist and her head pressed against his shoulder.

She pulled the door key through the letterbox and let herself in. The house was in darkness, everyone must be in bed. 'Mam,' she cried. 'Dad, it's me, Cara, and I'm home.'

Mam screamed when she saw her and said she'd lost too much weight, but Dad claimed he'd never known her look so well.

'Have you heard from our Fergus lately?' she asked. 'He only wrote me a single letter the whole time I've been away.'

'He's in France with the British Expeditionary Forces having a fine old time,' Dad replied. 'He'll probably write and tell you soon.'

Tyrone appeared and his face seemed to shrivel a little when he saw his little sister in uniform. 'What's it like, sis?'

She shrugged. 'OK.' It wouldn't do to tell him Army life was the gear, although Mam was bound to have shown him her letters. 'How's Maria getting on in Southport?'

'She hates it. If there's no raids soon, she's bringing the lads home.'

'Least it means you've got your own bed to sleep in, darlin',' Mam said, 'otherwise your dad would have had to doss down on the settee in the parlour and you could have slept with me.'

At this, Dad made a face behind Mam's back and Carla smiled. She was home!

It was hard to fit everything into just three days – she'd lost a whole day coming and would lose another travelling to Bedford. On the first day, she went to Boots so the girls behind the counter, most of whom she'd known since she left school, could see her in her uniform, then for a stroll around the familiar shops where she had the strangest feeling that she belonged somewhere else, not Liverpool, and not just in a single place, but with the Army and the various unknown towns and villages where she would live over the next months or years, depending on how long the war lasted.

On the way home, she called on Nancy Gates, whom she loved almost as much as she did Mam and Dad.

'Well, this is a sight I never thought I'd see,' Nancy gasped. 'Cara Caffrey in a uniform! By my reckoning, you can't be more than five or six years old – it only seems that long since you were born in the next room while your poor dad roamed the streets looking for a bobby.'

'I'll be nineteen next week, Nancy.'

'I know you will, pet. It's just me. Time passes so quickly I can't keep up with it. Sit down and I'll make you a cuppa. Tomorrow, you must come to tea – I'll make a cake, it can be a birthday party in advance, as it were.' She took a while getting to her feet and her bones creaked audibly. 'I'm going rusty,' she snorted. 'I need a damn good oiling.'

'Is Sybil back? I thought we'd be on the same train, but she just disappeared.'

Nancy looked surprised. 'Didn't she tell you? She's been sent on an officer training course. She only rang last night to tell her dad. He's pleased, naturally, but dead disappointed she's not coming home.'

'An officer!' Cara wasn't even faintly impressed. 'Poor thing. Me, I'd hate to be an officer. They never have any fun.'

'They might, pet, on the quiet, like. It's just that they can't be *seen* having fun.'

'An officer!' Mam shrieked. 'Sybil Allardyce, an officer! Why didn't they pick *you* to be an officer, I'd like to know?'

'I don't speak like her, do I, Mam? She went to a dead posh school. Any road, like I just told Nancy, if they asked me to be an officer, I'd turn it down.'

'Good for you, Cara,' Dad said approvingly from his armchair. 'You're a working-class girl and I'd sooner you stuck with your class.'

'Don't worry, Dad, I will,' Cara assured him.

When Marcus came home from work, he was greeted by the sound of laughter from the kitchen. He was about to go to his study, when he heard Brenna Caffrey's distinctive voice, the Irish accent as strong as ever. 'Tell Nancy about the day you flagged down that bus,' she urged. 'Go on, darlin'.'

Marcus retraced his steps and stood, listening, at the top of the kitchen stairs.

'Well,' began another voice, 'we were ordered to march to Henslow, a town twenty miles away, but we could hardly walk, let alone march . . .'

It was Cara Caffrey, he realized, home on leave. He'd been expecting Sybil, had bought tickets for the Empire Theatre where he'd met Eleanor, asked Nancy to get in some extra nice food, but the night before last Sybil had rung to say she wasn't coming home because she being transferred straight away to another camp for officer training. He wished she hadn't sounded so exultant and had thought to say she was sorry they wouldn't see each other. Instead, she had just rung off with a careless, 'Bye, Daddy. I've no idea when I'll be home again.'

Cara had almost finished her tale. 'That night,' she said, 'we had a feast in the billet. It was the night we all got to know each other properly. Until then, everyone had been dead miserable.'

'You never told us you were miserable,' Brenna said accusingly. 'You said you were having a marvellous time.'

'I was lying, Mam.' Cara laughed. She had the same attractive, husky laugh as her mother.

Marcus stood chewing his lip for a few seconds before venturing downstairs. It was, after all, *his* kitchen.

'I thought I heard voices,' he said. Four women were seated around the table: he hadn't realized Eleanor was there. She wouldn't be his wife for much longer, the divorce proceedings had begun and soon they would both be single again. He attempted a smile. 'Good evening, ladies.'

'Hello, Marcus.' Eleanor smiled back. 'What do you think of our daughter? According to Oliver Chandler, she'll be made a second lieutenant, the lowest rank.'

'It's very good news,' he said stiffly. 'How are you liking Army life, Cara?'

'I'm loving it, Mr Allardyce,' Cara replied, and Marcus noticed a spasm of hurt pass across Brenna's face.

'Your dinner's in the oven, but would you like to sit down and have a cup of tea with us?' Nancy asked. 'We were just about to cut Cara's birthday cake, although I know it's a week early.'

'That would be very pleasant, thank you.' It was only the second time in the almost thirty years he'd lived in the house that Marcus had sat at the kitchen table. The other time, he recalled, had been Sybil's first birthday party when Eleanor and Daniel Vaizey had appeared so much in love. He'd always thought Eleanor such a feeble, pathetic person, yet she'd turned out to be strong, taking in lodgers to support herself and Jonathan. And now it was *him* who was feeble and pathetic, made so by the daughter who was slowly breaking his heart. He suggested to Nancy that she fetch a bottle of wine from the cellar, 'So we can toast Cara's health – and Sybil's too.'

Nancy went to get the wine, but not before giving him a curious look. He had got used to Nancy's curious looks of late, as if she were wondering what the hell had happened to the man who had ruled the household with a rod of iron, had even thrown his pregnant wife out into the rain. That man was dead, he wanted to tell her, or perhaps the man had never been real in the first place, but acting a part. Now the play had come to an end, and the man no longer had a role in anyone's life but his own.

The glasses were filled and Marcus raised his. 'Happy birthday, Cara.'

Cara blushed slightly. 'Thank you, Mr Allardyce.'

He'd seen the girl on countless occasions, but had never really *looked* at her before. She was as beautiful as her mother had once been – no, more so. Brenna had never had such a slender neck or such gentle blue eyes. Her voice was softer and there was a freshness about her, an air of innocence, that her mother, raised in the school of hard knocks, had never had. And now, just as he had once wished the mother was his wife, he wished Cara was his daughter because he knew, as surely as he would ever know anything, that she would never treat him the way Sybil did.

On Cara's third and final day in Liverpool, she was invited to dinner at Eleanor's along with Mam and Dad.

'She only wants to show off her lodgers,' Mam laughed. 'She claims it's like living with Clark Gable and Robert Taylor and she's not sure which one she loves the most: Clark or Robert.'

Oliver Chandler and Lewis Brown were undoubtedly dead gorgeous and Cara could quite understand Eleanor's predicament. They had prepared the meal and waited on table, reminding her of Laurel and Hardy the way they worked together.

'Is the gravy ready, Oliver?'

'It is indeed, Lewis. Are the potatoes nice and floury?'

'They're perfect, Oliver.'

'Shall I slice the beef or will you?'

'You do it. You're much better at it than I.'

'Who do you think is the handsomest, Cara?' Eleanor whispered.

'I'm not sure, but I think Clark Gable looks more like Leslie Howard.'

Jonathan was there. Cara remembered what a lovely, chubby baby he'd been, but he'd grown up awfully stout. Eleanor was doing her best to stop him from going in the forces by persuading him to go to university, but Jonathan was against the idea.

'I'd never get in, Mummy,' he said patiently, as if he'd had the same argument before. 'I'm not terribly clever.'

'Don't be so modest, darling,' Eleanor cried. 'You're top in everything at school.'

'No, I'm not, Mummy. I'm top in English, that's all, and hopeless in anything to do with science.'

'Then you can take English at university, darling.'

'Except I don't want to, I want to go in the forces, preferably the Royal Air Force.' He beamed at Cara. 'I want to learn to fly a plane.'

'It'll do him good, El,' Mam said encouragingly. 'You can't stop your children going their own way, I should know, I've tried hard enough in the past, but it never got me anywhere.'

When the meal was over, Lewis took Cara for a ride in his white sports car, showed her how to use the gear lever and explained what the pedals were for. 'I have just two words of advice,' he said. 'Stay calm. Whatever you do, don't get flustered, even if it means you're slower off the mark than the next chap. Just take it easy and you'll be all right.' He smiled wistfully. 'You know I'm envious of you, Cara – or dead envious, as they say in Liverpool. I wish I were off to war tomorrow. I almost feel tempted to volunteer, I'm not too old at thirty-seven.'

'Eleanor would miss you,' Cara remarked.

'Not nearly as much as she'll miss Jonathan: he seems quite determined to join up the minute he turns eighteen, if not before.'

She felt sad leaving Mam and Dad behind, but it was almost with a feeling of relief that she boarded the train for Crewe where she would change and take another train to Birmingham, then change again for one to Bedford. At least that was the plan. She might have to change another half-dozen times with the railways in such a state of chaos.

This time she was armed with a flask of tea, enough sandwiches to feed the five hundred, a large piece of her own birthday cake and a box of sugared fruit from Oliver and Lewis.

'Aren't they the most charming men you could ever meet?' Eleanor had breathed that morning when she'd brought the fruit, along with a pretty quilted bag full of toiletries, her own parting gift.

As the thought of Lewis Brown had been the first to pop into Cara's head when she'd woken up that morning, she heartily agreed.

She arrived in Bedford after a surprisingly comfortable journey: the trains had been on time and only moderately crowded, she'd only had to change twice and had actually found a seat on the final stage. All the food had gone, most given away to civilian passengers who weren't allowed to buy refreshments from the kiosks that only served military personnel. She gave her address to an elderly woman who'd been so grateful for a cup of tea and a sandwich that she wanted to send Cara something in return.

'The Army is lucky to have you, dear, and I'm lucky to have met you. I'll never forget your kindness today.'

Cara found Peggy Cross and Fielding in the billet where they'd saved her a bed and were in the middle of unpacking. They whooped and flung their arms around her – it was lovely to start off in a new camp with ready-made friends.

'Have you saved a bed for Liz Childs?' she asked.

'She's not coming back,' Peggy explained. 'I saw her name wasn't down on the list of names for the billet, and when I asked they said she'd discovered she was pregnant. That other girl's name isn't there either, Sybil something-or-other, the snooty one.'

'Sybil Allardyce. She isn't coming, she's gone for officer training,' Cara told them.

'So, it's just us,' Fielding cried. 'The Three Musketeers. Let's stay together if we possibly can till this bloody war ends. United we stand . . .'

'. . . divided we fall,' the others chorused.

'We'll have a great time here,' Peggy said gleefully. 'We'll be learning something useful, not like last time, and this camp has a mess for the lower ranks and they hold dances at weekends. Bedford's only a bus ride away and there's loads of cinemas – I noticed *Gone with the Wind* is on: I'm dying to see it.'

'Me, too,' Cara enthused.

'I've already seen it, but I'd love to again.' Fielding raised her voice and spoke in the accent of the American Deep South. 'I'll think about it tomorrow, at Tara. Tomorrow, I'll think of some way to get him back. After all,' she declared, throwing back her head dramatically, 'after all, tomorrow is another day.'

Two other girls in the billet who looked very lonely as they unpacked their kit bags raised their heads in surprise.

Peggy folded her arms and frowned accusingly. 'Have you just told us the end of *Gone with the Wind*, Fielding?'

Fielding grinned. 'An awful lot happens before then, Peg.'

'I'd sooner not sit through a picture for nearly four hours knowing how the bloody thing ends.' She flung her pillow at the unrepentant Fielding, who merely stuck out her tongue.

'If you're going to see *Gone with the Wind*, can I come with you?' one of the girls asked timidly. 'I don't know a soul here.'

'Neither do I, and I'd love to see it, too,' said the other.

'Let's put a notice on the board and we can all go together,' Cara suggested. 'If there's time, we can have a cup of tea afterwards.'

'Or something stronger,' said Peggy.

'Or something stronger,' Cara echoed.

The next few months were very intense. She took to driving like a dream and always remembered to stay calm, as Lewis Brown had advised. The instructor, Sergeant Drummond, expressed his pleasure every time she had a lesson, unlike Sergeant Major Fawcett who'd made her feel a failure.

'You've got a gift for this, Caffrey. You're a natural driver and there's not many of them around.'

There were lectures every day with diagrams showing how the engine worked that she managed to understand. She knew, before taking a vehicle out, that the ignition system had to be checked, as well as the battery, the leads to the distributor and the alternator, that she had to make sure the tyre on the spare wheel was fully inflated and there was enough fuel in the tank, enough water in the cooling system and enough oil in the engine.

'Imagine if you were in the middle of the desert on your own and the vehicle broke down, what would you look for?' asked Sergeant Kelly, a bluff, red-faced man with four daughters of his own, who considered himself a father figure to the girls on the course.

'An ice cream cornet,' shouted Fielding.

'And after you've eaten the cornet, Fielding, what then?'

'I'd check the things you've told us to check, Sarge, and if they were all right, I'd stand on top of the vehicle and scream for help.'

Evenings were spent in the mess, at the cinema, or in public houses where eyebrows would be raised when they went in. Until the war, the only women seen in pubs without male escorts were of doubtful reputation, and the influx of quite respectable girls in uniform was taking a bit of getting used to. Occasionally, a barman would refuse to serve them, but plenty of male customers would leap forward and buy them drinks. Mostly, they only drank lemonade, but Peggy Cross was partial to a gin and It and Fielding drank Guinness. 'It gives me muscles,' she claimed, flexing her tiny, bird-like arms.

The tests had marked Fielding out as a promising driver, but no account had been taken of her stature. She had to take a pillow when she had a lesson otherwise she was hardly big enough to see through the windscreen and people would dodge out of the way, thinking the oncoming vehicle was driverless.

Saturday night dances in the mess were the best of all. There were two men for every girl and, by the end of the evening, they'd been danced off their feet and would limp back to the billet, exhausted.

'I know I shouldn't say this,' Cara confided to her friends one night when they got back after a particularly hectic evening in the mess, 'but I'm almost glad there's a war on. I was perfectly happy living at home, but I didn't realize how awful dull me life was until I left. Since I've been in the Army, I've felt quite different. Me brain's moved into a higher gear or something.' Her emotions lay beneath a very thin surface and she cried easily and laughed a lot. She was very conscious of the pathos of the young men, some even younger than her, who were being sent overseas after Christmas and had asked if she would be their girlfriend.

'I'd like to have a girl to write to,' one had said to her only that night. His name was Brian and he hadn't yet started shaving. His eyes were still a baby blue. 'Have you got a photo I can stick on my locker?'

'I'll have one taken,' Cara promised.

Christmas was fast approaching and the course would come to an end in January. Yet again they would part from women to whom they felt closer than they ever had to their friends back home.

'How can we make sure us three stay together?' Fielding asked one morning when they were having breakfast.

'I suppose we could ask,' Peggy mused.

'Who?'

'I've no idea.'

'That's a lot of use. Most of the men are staying together.'

'Only because they belong to a particular regiment: us girls are just anonymous drivers and we don't belong anywhere,' Cara explained.

'But that's not fair!' Fielding said plaintively, pretending to wipe away a tear.

'There's nothing fair about the Army, Fielding. I'd have thought you'd know that by now.'

'There's a notice in the billet asking who wants to be sent

overseas. If we put down our names, bracketed them together and wrote NOT TO BE SEPARATED, do you think that'd work?'

'Do we want to be sent overseas?' Peggy looked doubtful.

'I'd love it,' Cara said instantly. Fergus was having a great time in France where he seemed to do nothing much except lounge in cafés and drink wine.

'It'd be more exciting than staying in England,' Fielding said. 'Ah, come on, Peggy, me girl. Imagine us strolling down the Champs-Elysées or climbing the Sphinx.'

'It's not a sightseeing tour we'd be going on,' Peggy pointed out. 'Oh, all right. Tom is already so fed up with me, it can't make things any worse.' Tom was Peggy's fiancé and sent complaining letters every week accusing her of deserting him, which she had, Peggy conceded, but had felt the urge to do her bit and thought he'd understand.

They returned to the billet, put their names on the list and were making their way to the lecture hall when they saw a smart young woman coming towards them. She wore an expensive fur coat and carried an equally expensive leather suitcase. It took a good minute for Cara to recognize Sybil Allardyce.

'Sybil!' she cried, hurrying towards her. 'Have you been posted here?'

'Only for a few weeks,' Sybil said stiffly. 'I'm an officer now, Caffrey. You should salute me and address me as ma'am.'

'Oh!' Cara fell back with the strong feeling she'd been put in her place.

Peggy butted in. 'You're wearing civilian clothes . . . *ma'am*, and we're only expected to salute the uniform, not the person.'

Sybil's face went very red. 'I'll see about that – what's your name?'

'Cross . . . *ma'am*.' Peggy invested as much sarcasm as she could muster into the word. Fielding was doing her very best not to giggle.

'You might find yourself on a charge, Cross.' Sybil was blustering now, clearly aware she was on the losing side. 'And you, Private, what's your name?'

'Fielding . . . *ma'am*. You said you saw me on the West End. Apparently, I made you cry.' Fielding had suddenly acquired a cut-glass accent, and now Cara had the urge to giggle.

Sybil didn't answer. She marched away, leaving the three women to laugh until they cried, holding each other up as the tears poured down their cheeks.

'What a bitch!' Peggy said eventually when she'd got her breath back. 'It's a wonder she didn't order us to carry her suitcase.'

'I don't think much of your friends, Caffrey.'

'Our mothers are friends, that's all. Sybil Allardyce is no friend of mine.' She'd always thought of Sybil as a sort of friend, but no longer.

Sybil signed in and was shown to her room, feeling very put out when she saw there were two beds when she'd expected to be on her own. The sound of hysterical laughter was still ringing in her ears. She'd got off to a really bad start. There'd been no need to jump down Cara's throat like that, but she'd been so keen to advertise the fact that she was an officer and hadn't been prepared for Cara's unexpected approach. It wouldn't have hurt to explain their changed positions in a more courteous way.

She groaned and began to unpack, hanging the uniforms she'd had made in the wardrobe. The tailor had been instructed to send the bill to daddy. At least she actually had a proper wardrobe, not like the first camp where there was only a locker and a hook to hang things on. And her room-mate would be from her own class, not some awful woman who'd worked in a factory or a fish market and whose every other word was a curse. What's more, she'd only be in this camp for a fortnight before being transferred elsewhere. She'd volunteered to be sent overseas and was unlikely to meet Cara and her friends again while she was in the Army.

The door swung open and a hearty voice cried, 'I was told you were here. Allardyce, isn't it? We're going to be room-mates, but not for long. I'm Cordelia Butcher, known as Butch to my friends and enemies alike. How do you do?'

Sybil's slender hand was shaken forcefully by a stout, red-faced woman of about thirty with skin like an elephant's hide. 'How do you do, Butch?' she said faintly.

'I'm very well, Allardyce, very well indeed,' Butch boomed. 'Don't think much of this shitty place, though. D'you know they don't stock beer in the officers' mess, only shorts. I like a slug of whiskey as much as the next chap, but only if it's washed down with a pint of brown ale. Bloody bad show, I must say. Well, Allardyce,

I'll love you and leave you, I only came to say hello.' She half closed the door, then opened it again. 'I say, I hope you're a sound sleeper. People tell me I snore like a fucking rhinoceros, so I apologize in advance if I keep you awake.'

The door closed. Sybil put her hands over her face and groaned again.

They were going home for Christmas for a whole week. On the morning of their departure, a parcel arrived for Cara. She opened it curiously and found a little black velvet box that held a ring with three sparkling blue stones, accompanied by a letter – the notepaper smelled of lavender and the writing was very shaky.

> Dear Cara
> I do hope this arrives in time for Christmas. I had meant to send it before, but have been ill. It belonged to my grandmother and has always been very precious to me. I shall never forget your kindness on the train.
> Sincerely yours,
> Louise Appleton (Miss)

There was no return address.

'Oh!' Cara felt quite overcome. She showed the ring to Peggy and Fielding. 'Isn't it beautiful? It looks almost real. All I did was give her a cup of tea and a sarnie.'

Peggy took the ring and examined it. 'It *is* real, at least it's real gold: twenty-two carat. I'm no expert, but they look like genuine sapphires too. If so, it's worth a mint. I'd leave it at home if I were you, Cara. We're not allowed to wear jewellery apart from wedding rings and you don't want to leave something that valuable in your locker.'

The weather was appalling. The entire country was covered in a thick carpet of snow and great lumps of it threw themselves at the train windows all the way to Liverpool. At Birmingham, where Cara changed trains and the platforms were packed with troops, all the non-military passengers were ordered off and told to wait for the next one, including mothers with small children, the elderly and the infirm.

That night, she showed the ring to her mother.

'It's lovely, darlin',' Mam gasped. 'Here, let's try it on a minute.'

The ring fitted the third finger of Mam's right hand perfectly – it was too big for Cara's. 'Keep it for now, Mam,' she said impulsively. 'You can give it me back once I'm home for good. I was going to leave it behind, any road.'

'Oh, I couldn't possibly, girl, I might lose it.' She waved her hand, admiring the way the stones flashed and sparkled. 'Eleanor hasn't got a ring like this.'

'You can just wear it for best, luv,' Dad said. 'Seems silly to let it lie in a drawer when you fancy it so much.'

'Oh, all right,' Mam replied in a tone that implied she'd been forced into wearing the ring, while continuing to admire it on her hand.

Maria and the lads had returned from Southport. 'It's nothing but a phoney war,' Maria snorted. 'If there wasn't a shortage of food, you'd hardly believe there was a war on. Nothing's hardly changed.'

Cara didn't point out that thousands of seamen had already lost their lives, their ships sunk by the German Navy – the U-boats were the worst, slithering silently under the water, the ships oblivious to the danger lying beneath. Maria wasn't the only person who claimed the war was phoney, even the newspapers complained that nothing was happening.

It was a strange Christmas. The awful weather didn't help and, although Mam and Dad did their best to be cheerful, Cara could tell it was an effort. Tyrone was in a foul mood, despite being taken on by the Mersey Docks & Harbour Board as an improver, which meant he would finish his apprenticeship as an electrician on full pay. He was still bitter he wasn't in uniform. Even Nancy Gates seemed down in the dumps.

'I wish this damn war would start properly,' she said to Cara. 'It's the waiting that's getting to me, knowing that the sky's about to fall in any minute.'

'I've done something awful,' Cara confessed. 'Don't tell Mam, I'll tell her meself when the time comes, but I've put me name down to serve overseas. She'll have a fit, she's already worried to death about our Fergus. I almost wish I hadn't done it.'

'It's your life, Cara, not your mam's, and you've only got the one. You must do with it whatever you wish.'

The only place where everyone appeared to be having a good

time was in Eleanor's house in Tigh Street. Oliver and Lewis had somehow managed to get a turkey, a Christmas cake and two bottles of sherry. Eleanor was in a state of high excitement when the Caffreys turned up for tea on Christmas Day.

'It's been the best Christmas I've ever known,' she gushed. 'I must be the luckiest woman alive: my divorce has come through, Jonathan's promised to go to university and I've spent the day with the two of most adorable men alive.'

'They'll never take me at university,' Jonathan whispered to Cara. 'I only told Mummy I'd go to keep her off my back.'

Cara had been back in Bedford a week when she and Fielding were informed they were being sent to Malta as soon as the driving course finished, but Peggy was destined for North Africa. Although she put in a written request to the commander of the camp asking if she could go to Malta with her friends, the next day she was called into the staff sergeant's office where the request was bluntly refused.

'You're in the Army now, Cross, not the Circle of Friends. You'll go where you're told and it's just too bad if you're unhappy about it.'

'Our Cara's being sent to Malta,' Brenna told Colm a few days later when he returned from work. She waved Cara's letter. 'There'll be no fighting there, will there, darlin'? It'll just be like one long holiday, same as with Fergus.'

'We'll just have to see, Bren,' Colm said easily, although he felt fearful. France was like a time bomb, likely to go off at any minute, and whoever held Malta held the key to the Mediterranean. It had a fine natural harbour that Germany would, quite literally, kill for. If there was one place in the world where he didn't want his little girl to go, it was Malta.

Chapter 9

Malta 1940

'Caffrey,' Corporal Culpepper yelled. 'Captain Bradford wants taking to Grand Harbour and he's asked for you. *Caffrey!*' he bellowed when Cara didn't instantly appear.

'Coming, Corpy, coming. Give us time to get up off me behind.' She put down her half-drunk tea, seized her cap and jacket, and hurried into his office.

'No cheek, now, Caffrey,' the burly corporal said, grinning. 'And a very nice behind it is too, I must say,' he remarked, smacking his lips and about to give it a pat as Cara passed. She dodged out of the way just in time: Corporal Culpepper was too free with his hands.

She walked through the workshop where two mechanics were down the pit working on the underside of a lorry and a car was having its windscreen replaced. Outside, on an expanse of oil-stained concrete where the vehicles were parked, Fielding was washing a car, almost invisible inside her overalls. 'Did Culpepper get you?' she shouted.

'Not this time,' Cara said grimly. She slid into the first staff car in the line, a giant Humber Hawk painted khaki, drove it a short distance along the dusty road to Marzipan Hall, where she stopped, jumped out, opened the rear door and waited for Captain Bradford to emerge. Marzipan Hall wasn't the real name of the huge building where the senior and clerical staff of the British Royal Artillery had their offices and billets, but the glazed yellow bricks must have reminded the first arrivals of a cake and the name had stuck. It had been built two centuries ago for an Italian duke and there were more than forty rooms within its impressive interior. Cara and nine other women drivers were billeted in an abandoned farmhouse a stone's throw away, their services available, not only to the officers of the Royal Artillery, but the Royal Ordnance, the Royal Service and the Royal Infantry Corps who were scattered around the island.

Captain Bradford emerged through the magnificent, carved doors. 'Morning, Caffrey,' he said shyly. He was a small, kindly man of about fifty, completely bald, who seemed nervous with women. Unmarried, he'd joined the Army in the Great War and had made it his career. Cara always tried her best to put him at his ease. It must have worked, as he always asked for her when he required a driver.

'Morning, sir.' She stood stiffly to attention and saluted, then gave him a glowing smile.

'Nice day for the cricket,' he remarked as he climbed in the back.

'Is it, sir?'

'Don't they play cricket in Liverpool, Caffrey?'

'I imagine they do, sir, but my family were only interested in football.'

'Liverpool or Everton?'

'Liverpool, sir. It's the Catholic team, you see.'

'Ah, yes, you're a papist, aren't you, Caffrey? You must feel at home in Malta: it's overrun with churches and every day is a saint's day.'

'I'm enjoying it very much, Captain.' As if to prove the accuracy of his words, she had to slow down while passing a tiny procession of women and children carrying embroidered banners and garlands of flowers, led by a priest bearing a wooden cross. They were singing a hymn she didn't recognize and were probably on their way to the little roadside shrine she came to a few minutes later.

'Which saint is it today?' the captain asked.

'I don't know, sir. We're not all *that* religious in Liverpool. We only go mad at Easter and Christmas and have processions in May. I took part in a few myself when I was young.'

The captain chuckled. 'You're not exactly old now, Caffrey.'

He lapsed into silence while she drove through the barren countryside. There was nothing pretty about Malta: the scenery was rugged and the soil more red than brown, although she understood it would improve in spring when fields would be full of blossom. The temperature for March was remarkably warm and the mid-morning sun blazed through the windows, making the car feel like an oven.

'Do you mind if I open a window, Captain?'

'Not at all, my dear. That's better,' he said when the window had been wound down. 'Feeling the heat, are you?'

'Just a bit.'

'You're not used to it yet, that's why. It'll be cooler when we reach the coast.'

Cara ran her finger around the inside of her collar. It felt damp and she couldn't wait to reach the coast. As Malta was a mere seventeen miles long and nine miles wide and Marzipan Hall was situated between Mdina and Rabat near the centre of the island, it never took long to reach anywhere. Cara went to Mass in St Paul's Cathedral in tiny Mdina every Sunday. Rabat, a much bigger place, with plenty of restaurants and two cinemas, was where she spent most of her leisure hours, as it saved hitching a lift to Valletta, the capital.

Ten minutes later, she was driving down Mediterranean Street on the outskirts of Valletta, a cool breeze ruffling her hair. The air smelled salty and fresh.

The Grand Harbour was lined with an odd mixture of ships, ranging from the grim, grey shapes of naval vessels, rusty cargo boats and brightly painted fishing smacks, to a few elegant yachts bobbing lazily in the clear, blue-green water.

The road curved and she was passing St Elmo's Palace when Captain Bradford asked her to stop outside a little café that was just opening on the far side of the road: tables and chairs were being put outside by a young waiter with film star looks. 'I have a meeting here, Caffrey, and it won't be over until midday.'

'Shall I come back and fetch you then, sir?' She checked her watch: it was twenty-five to eleven.

'Hang around, my dear, it's only an hour and a half. Do a bit of sightseeing – and take that jacket off. An hour or so, and you'll be melting in that thing.'

'Thank you, sir.'

The captain disappeared inside the café. Cara parked outside, gleefully removed her jacket, and rolled up her shirtsleeves – they'd been forbidden to do so until summer arrived. She strolled back to the harbour, bought a coffee from a stall frequented by fishermen and sat on the wall watching the morning's catch being unloaded, although she hated the sight of the poor fish being thrown into slithering, silver heaps, their heads rising in desperation as they gasped their last breath.

The fishermen eyed her curiously. She was so different from their own women: tall with red-gold hair and, what's more, wearing a uniform, whereas their women were small and dark and dressed like peasants. Malta was another world and she was still getting used to the place as well as the temperature.

With the sun warm on her back and the sky like blue velvet, not a cloud in sight, the sea shimmering like silk with barely a ripple in it, she wondered what it was like in Liverpool on this particular March morning. In Mam's last letter, posted two weeks before, she'd said the weather was just as bad as at Christmas. 'Every morning there's snow up the window sill,' and Cara shuddered at the thought, although it came with a wish to be in front of a roaring fire in Shaw Street, all snug and cosy, with a cup of hot tea in her hand. The wish swiftly fled and she stretched out her legs to the sun and had another wish, that she wasn't wearing thick, khaki stockings and could get a tan.

It came to her how much more she knew of the world than her mother. Mam had only travelled from Ireland to Liverpool where she'd stayed put, never leaving its environs except for the occasional day out in New Brighton or Southport, yet she loved anything new. She would like Malta with its strong, Catholic traditions and numerous shrines and churches, its never-ending saints' days and religious festivals, usually accompanied by a thrilling display of fireworks.

'Miss! Hey, miss.' The shouts were coming from behind. Cara turned and saw three sailors jumping up and down on the deck of their ship, waving frantically. She waved back and they cheered. 'What's your name?' one yelled.

'Cara Caffrey,' she yelled back.

'Where are you from, Cara?'

'Liverpool.'

The smallest sailor leapt about in a frenzy of delight. 'I'm a scouser too, from Edge Hill. Me name's Ernie Thomas.'

'I'm from Toxteth: Shaw Street.'

'What'cha doing tonight, Cara?'

She shrugged extravagantly and spread her hands. 'I don't know. I might be on duty.'

'If you're not on duty, we'll be in St Patrick's Bar in Merchant Street from eight o'clock on. Bring a friend.'

'Bring two friends.'

'I'll try. I can't promise anything.' She backed away, laughing. She had no intention of meeting the sailors whether she was on duty or not, but hadn't liked to turn them down. They continued to shout as she crossed the road, having remembered that Merchant Street was no distance away and it had a market every day except Sunday. There was still more than an hour to go before the captain finished his meeting.

She wandered up and down the vibrantly covered stalls that mainly sold food, although a few displayed local craftwork: gold and silver filigree jewellery, decorated glass, ornaments fashioned out of limestone. She was particularly enamoured with the lace-work – she'd already noticed women sitting outside their houses working away with their lace-makers' cushions – Mam would love a tablecloth or a bedspread. As Cara had only a few Maltese lira with her, she contented herself with two lace-trimmed hankies for now.

At quarter to twelve, having exhausted the market, she walked slowly back to the café where she was to collect Captain Bradford, sat at a table outside and ordered coffee from the waiter with the film star looks.

'You are a very good-looking lady,' he announced when he came with the drink.

'And you are a very handsome man,' she said in return and couldn't resist a smile when he blushed to the roots of his hair and almost ran back into the café.

'This is the life!' she whispered. It was like being paid to have a holiday of a lifetime. Lulled by the sun, she must have fallen asleep, because when she opened her eyes, she was startled to find a young airman sitting opposite, grinning widely.

'You looked like Sleeping Beauty,' he said. 'I was thinking about kissing you awake, but was worried you might turn into a frog.'

It was Cara's turn to blush. 'How long have you been there?'

'An hour, two, I'm not sure.'

'Liar.' She looked at her watch. 'I've only been here five minutes.'

'Are you waiting for the Army top brass?'

'Yes, Captain Bradford.' She saw a grey saloon car had been parked behind the khaki Humber.

'I'm here for Captain Chapman. My mum wanted me to be a pilot and she's a bit disappointed I'm only a driver. But I've got a stripe. See! I'm a lance corporal. I never expected to get a stripe and I'm terribly proud.' He pointed to the stripe on his sleeve and Cara started to laugh. He was a most appealing young man, if not exactly handsome. About twenty-one, his hair was light-brown, cut very short, and she suspected it would have been curly if allowed to grow longer. His eyes were as blue as hers, his mouth much too wide and his nose looked as if it had been broken and badly repaired. He must have been in Malta quite a while as he was very tanned.

'I hope you're not laughing at my stripe,' he said, pretending to be hurt.

'No, you, I'm laughing at you.'

'Is it my nose you find so funny? It must have broken in my mother's womb. I can't think of any other reason for its odd shape.' He twisted his nose, as if trying to straighten it, making Cara laugh even more. 'You clearly consider me quite hilarious, Miss . . . ? He raised his eyebrows questioningly.

'Caffrey, Cara Caffrey.'

'I'm Christopher Farthing, known as Kit, and if you dare call me Penny Farthing, I shall cry – I cried all the time at school. How do you do, Cara Caffrey?' He held out his hand and she shook it. His fingers were long and brown and his grip so strong it almost hurt. Cara felt a sensation in her breast, a feeling of something she couldn't describe, perhaps because she'd never had it before.

He was holding her hand for far too long – maybe he would have held on to it for ever had the door to the café not opened and Captain Bradford came out accompanied by two other men: one a naval officer, the other in the blue-grey uniform of the Royal Air Force. Cara's hand was released, Kit Farthing sprang to his feet and saluted, and Cara did the same: there were times when she felt like a jack-in-the-box.

'We'll meet again, won't we?' Kit whispered as they walked towards the cars.

'I hope so,' said Cara.

After delivering Captain Bradford to Marzipan Hall, Cara parked the car and was heading in the direction of the workshop when she came face to face with Sybil Allardyce who was just coming out. Sybil's eyes narrowed and she said coldly, 'I should put you on a charge for that, Caffrey.'

Cara groaned inwardly as she gave a rather limp salute. 'For what, ma'am?'

'For removing your jacket and rolling up your sleeves.'

Ever since the day in Bedford when she'd demanded they salute her and they'd refused because she wasn't in uniform, Sybil had borne Cara and Fielding a grudge. She picked on them constantly and hadn't appeared to notice that she usually came off worse, particularly where Fielding was concerned. It was real bad luck that they'd all been transferred to Malta.

'Captain Bradford told me to take my jacket off, ma'am.' Cara cursed herself for not putting it on before, but she'd had something far more important on her mind while she'd driven back – in the shape of a young airman with the wonderful name of Kit Farthing.

'He had no right to,' Sybil barked. 'And why have you been gone for so long? It must be two and a half hours.'

'The captain asked me to wait, ma'am.'

'He had no right to do that either.' She marched away, having come off second best, as usual. Stationed in Marzipan Hall, she was the officer in charge of transport, her job to ensure that all vehicles were regularly serviced, that there was always enough petrol in the pump and spare parts available in the workshop for minor repairs. Requests for a driver were directed through her office and passed on to Corporal Culpepper, whose own office was in a sectioned-off corner of the workshop next to the women's rest room. Unfortunately, the girls had to pass through his office to get in and out, and were at the mercy of his roving hands.

'Your friend's been looking for you. She looked on the verge of apoplexy,' Fielding said when Cara went into the poky little room. There was another girl there, Adele Morgan, who was deeply engrossed in a book. She looked up and gave Cara a brief smile.

'How many times do I have to tell you, Fielding,' Cara said mildly, 'that Sybil Allardyce is no friend of mine.' She threw herself into a chair. 'I've brought you a prezzie.'

'What's a prezzie?'

'A present.' She took the lace hankies out of her pocket. 'I got one for meself at the same time. Now listen here, Fielding, on no account are you to blow your dinky little nose on this. It's to be kept for best.'

Fielding curtsied as she took the handkerchief and made a great show of weeping into it. 'Aw shucks, ma'am,' she cried – she'd

recently got into the habit of speaking in the American vernacular –
'I'm touched, I truly am. Fancy you thinking of little ol' me.'

Cara groaned. 'Why I ever made a best friend of an actress, I'll
never know.'

'Am I, Caffrey? Am I really your best friend?' Fielding looked at
her curiously.

'Of course you are.'

'I love you, Caffrey.' The pretty, impish little face was serious for
once.

Cara looked at her uncertainly, never quite sure whether Fielding
was pretending or not. Because she genuinely loved this maddening,
irrepressible, garrulous person as much as she would have done a
sister, she was about to say, 'I love you too,' when Fielding said
gruffly, 'When this war's over, I'd like us to get married and have
children.'

'Oh, *you!*' Cara looked for a cushion to throw, but there weren't
any – Fielding must have had more cushions thrown at her than
anyone else on earth. 'I'm hungry,' she announced instead.

'Shall I fetch you a sarnie – or is it a butty? I'm not sure,' her
tormenter asked.

'Neither am I, but I'd like one, and a nice cold drink.' One big
advantage of Marzipan Hall was that the canteen was open from
early morning until late at night.

'How about you, Morgan?'

'I wouldn't mind a cold drink, thanks.'

'Your wish is my command.' Fielding bowed and was gone.

'Is she all there?' Morgan enquired. She was a dreamy Welsh girl
whose head was always buried in a book.

'I don't think she is, no.'

'Was she really an actress back in Blighty?'

'Yes. Apparently she was on the West End.'

'Oh, well, I suppose that accounts for it.' Morgan returned to her
book.

It was easy to get irritated with Fielding, but she was the least
boring person Cara had ever met and she was glad to have her as a
friend.

Sybil ground her teeth as she walked back to her office. She thought
of asking Captain Bradford if he'd really given Cara permission to

remove her jacket and asked her to wait in Valletta, but on reflection it seemed a rather petty thing to do and it might look as if she were questioning his decisions. He seemed to have taken a shine to Cara and always asked for her when he wanted a driver.

She would never forget that day in Bedford. She'd felt so proud of herself, her first day as an officer completely ruined by Cara, Fielding and that other woman whom she'd never seen again. If she closed her eyes, she could still hear the sound of their helpless laughter. They laughed at her still, although it might have been just her imagination that she could hear them chuckling when she walked away.

She was sitting behind her desk, still fuming, when Lieutenant Alec Townend popped his head around the door and she forgot all about Cara and Fielding. 'Is it still on for tonight?' he asked.

'Why yes, of course,' she twinkled.

'Drink first, film second, meal third,' he said briskly. 'OK with you?'

'You sound as if you've got it all organized and it's fine with me,' Sybil said admiringly. 'Are we going to Rabat or Valletta?'

'Rabat. We can walk that far, save organizing transport.'

'Do you know what film is on?'

'An old musical with George Raft and Alice Faye: *Every Night at Eight*. I hope you haven't seen it.'

'No, and I adore George Raft.'

'I think Alice Faye's rather the bee's knees, so it looks as if we'll both enjoy ourselves.'

'I'm sure we will.'

Alec winked and closed the door. He wasn't a very attractive man, being short and rather tubby with a nondescript face and an over-weening sense of his own importance. He was twenty-four and had been a solicitor in his father's firm before being called up. Tonight would be their first time out together. Sybil didn't particularly like him, but she'd sooner go out with a man any day, even one she didn't like, than a crowd of tedious women. Flirting was a much more satisfactory way of passing the time compared with gossiping, and she scorned all-women gatherings: there was nothing productive or enjoyable about them and she refused all invitations from the female officers to join them for dinner or a drink or the pictures, preferring to stay in her room and read a book if there was no man available. She'd had a few women friends: Betsy Billington-Clarke, for instance, who'd been useful in her way and had a very good-looking brother, but Betsy was a rare exception.

She sometimes wondered what Mummy and Daddy would say if they knew what she'd been up to when she was at school in London. Weekends, they were allowed to do as they pleased and Sybil used to go to a bar in one of the best West End hotels and allow herself to be picked up – men seemed to find her enormously attractive in her prim, schoolgirlish clothes. It was one of these men who'd taken her to see the review that Fielding had been in. Afterwards, they'd gone back to the hotel and she'd slept with him. Any minute now, she'd sleep with Alec Townend. It was the way she liked the evening to end, and it couldn't end that way with a woman!

Cara was staring into the black, oily engine of a lorry, and trying to deduce why it wouldn't start, when a voice said, 'One of the leads to the distributor is loose.'

'I'd just noticed that for meself,' she said tartly. Turning, she found Kit Farthing staring into the engine with her and the strange, unidentifiable sensation that she'd had when they'd shaken hands returned with a vengeance. 'Oh, it's you!' she said shakily, self-consciously patting her turbaned head and wishing she was wearing something more attractive than a pair of greasy overalls that were too short in the leg. Kit looked very smart and spruce in his well-pressed uniform. His hair had grown a fraction since the other day and looked curlier. He was very slim, almost gawky, and about four inches taller than she was – it made a change to be looked down on. 'What are you doing here?'

'My chap had the minutes of that meeting typed up and asked me to deliver them to your chap. Now that my mission has been accomplished, I thought I'd seek out Sleeping Beauty and say hello.'

'Hello.' Her tongue seemed to have frozen in her mouth.

'Hello, Cara.' Kit sounded completely normal, so she clearly wasn't having the same effect on him as he was on her, although there was an expression on his agreeable, verging-on-ugly face that was as unidentifiable as the feeling in her chest. 'Are you likely to have a break soon?' he asked lightly.

'What time is it?' She'd forgotten she had a watch.

He consulted his own. 'Nearly eleven.'

'Half eleven I stop for a drink.'

'Can we go for a walk then?'

Cara dropped her eyes. 'All right.'

'Don't forget to put the distributor lead back,' he reminded her when she was about to close the bonnet of the lorry.

She'd forgotten all about it. Lorries, engines and their various parts no longer seemed all that important.

He was twenty-one and from Lancaster, he told her on the short stroll through the arid countryside as far as Marzipan Hall. 'It's the capital of Lancashire and hardly any distance from Liverpool.'

'What did you do there?' she asked. She'd already told him she'd worked in Boots and had described her family and the house in Shaw Street.

'I was a librarian. I love books,' he said simply. 'All I ever wanted to do was work with them. When you think of all the information they hold, the stories they tell, the time and commitment that's gone into writing them, the pleasure they give, the good they do – teaching people everything from how to repair a car to understanding Einstein's theory of relativity, and – oh, all sorts of things.' He stopped and looked at her uncomfortably. 'I sound a bit like a book myself. I'm going on about it too much.'

'No, you're not.' He'd made her think of books in an entirely new way. 'I must say, you don't look like a librarian.'

'Oh, please don't say you thought I was a boxer!' he said, scandalized. 'Or a rugby player. It's this damn nose! At school, I always avoided rugby like the plague. I can't stand games where people are likely to hurt me.' He gave a pathetic sniff. 'I'm not nearly as tough as I look.'

Cara burst out laughing. 'I'm glad. I far prefer librarians to boxers.' She would never tell him he looked far more like the latter than the former.

They arrived at Marzipan Hall. 'Would you like a drink?' he asked. 'Captain Bradford told me to have a beer in the mess and put it on his bill – he's a decent old stick, isn't he?'

'Really nice,' Cara agreed. 'I'm afraid I wouldn't be allowed in the mess in overalls.' She'd removed the turban, combed her hair, but there hadn't been time to change her clothes. 'Any road, I'd better be getting back.'

'Can I see you again? I'm off duty tonight.' She could tell from the way he said it – slightly anxious, a little bit nervous – that the invitation, casual though it was, meant as much to him as it did to her.

'I'm off duty too,' she said.

'Then I'll pick you up at about seven,' he said eagerly. 'I think I can get my hands on a car. We'll go to Rabat. Would you like to see a film or have a meal?'

'I'd love a meal.'

'We can talk while we eat.' He took her hand in his and, by the time they'd got back to the section where she worked, Cara had the strongest feeling that she was in love with Kit Farthing and, as he told her a month later, he'd fallen in love with her before they'd even spoken: 'When you were sitting outside that café, fast asleep, my Sleeping Beauty, my one and only Cara, snoring her adorable head off in the heat of the midday sun.'

'I never was snoring!' she protested.

'Yes, you were,' he insisted. 'I could hear you from miles away. When we get married, we'll have to have separate rooms or I shall never sleep a wink.'

Cara took the mention of marriage calmly in her stride. It was the way things happened in wartime when you weren't certain where you'd be this time next week, or even if you'd be alive. The uncertainty, the feeling of danger, induced in people a sense of urgency and they made decisions within an hour that would normally have taken weeks, and courtships that, in less hectic times, would have continued a whole year, lasted a mere month because people needed to know where they stood.

Just now, Malta was a place of peace and tranquillity, although there were frequent practice air raids when the siren would go and everyone had to rush to shelters underground. But it wouldn't always stay that way. The small island provided a crucial supply base between Europe and North Africa where troops from both sides were massing in preparation for battle. Hitler wouldn't just sit back and let the Allies hold on to such a vitally important position, not without a fight.

Any road, it seemed the natural thing to do, to promise herself to Kit, stay faithful to him until the war was over – the general opinion seemed to be this would happen within a year – then get married and settle down somewhere between Liverpool and Lancaster so they could easily visit their families – Kit had a brother and two sisters as well as a mum and dad – and have children. She'd like four: two girls and two boys. She drew in a deep, sharp breath, so blissfully happy that she could hardly think clearly any more. Now she knew what the strange feeling was that she'd had in her breast: it was happiness mixed with love for Kit and she took it for granted the feeling would never go away.

Sybil saw them together one night in a café in Rabat. They were with Fielding and another Air Force chap: slim and boyish, exceptionally handsome. The pair seemed to be getting on well, laughing heartily over something. But the other two, Cara and her companion, had eyes only for each other, talking quietly, smiling occasionally and holding hands across the table. Every now and then, the man would lift Cara's hand to his lips and kiss it, and the look he would give her – and she him! It was obvious they were madly in love. The man wasn't even faintly handsome, but there was something about him, about his face – at first, Sybil couldn't figure out what it was – something decent and good, she decided, and terribly romantic. She reckoned he would make a marvellous lover. Had he and Cara made love yet? she wondered.

'I say, this crab is delicious,' Alec Townend remarked. 'What do you think, darling?'

'Delicious,' Sybil murmured. Lately, he'd begun to get on her nerves. He was so *dull*. She couldn't recall him once saying anything remotely interesting. She'd give him up and start going out with someone else – that other lieutenant, John Glover, who'd invited her to dinner the other day. Sybil pushed the crab away and twisted restlessly in her chair, wishing she'd been sent somewhere more exciting. Like Alec, Malta was very dull. Nothing happened. She glanced across the crowded restaurant, full of servicemen and women. There was a space in the middle for people to dance and a few had got up and were dancing to the little local band playing 'I'm in the Mood for Love'. It had been in that film she'd seen with Alec the first time they'd gone out together. Tonight, it sounded very amateurish, as if the band weren't used to playing that sort of music. Cara and her chap were up, she noticed, and they moved slowly around the floor, wrapped so tightly in each other's arms they could have been one person.

For some reason, Sybil felt tears come to her eyes. *That* was what she wanted, for someone to love her, not in the possessive, suffocating way that Daddy did, or in the indifferent way of the mother who'd deserted her and only really cared for Jonathan, but the way the young airman loved Cara.

Once a month, Cara was allowed a weekend off duty. She and Fielding usually managed to swap weekends with other girls so they would have the time off together. So far, all they'd done with their free days was treat themselves to a few extra hours in bed, laze around the farmhouse – last time, they'd cut each other's hair, as it was a nuisance having to put it in buns and plaits so it didn't touch their collars – go to the pictures in Rabat and explore the many street markets, or hitch a ride to Valletta and do the same things there.

In May, when she told Kit about the forthcoming weekend, he said, 'If I try and wangle the same time off, shall we go to Gozo for a few days? It only takes half an hour on the ferry.' Gozo was a small island off the northern tip of Malta.

'I'd love to, but will Mac be able to come for Fielding? I can't leave her behind all on her own.' Peter McShane was Kit's best mate and known as Mac: small and strikingly handsome, he came from Newcastle and was happily married with two children. A shop assistant in his old life, he'd become friendly with Kit through their shared love of books. They often went out in a foursome and his relationship with Fielding was entirely platonic, but they had the same wicked sense of humour, laughing at things that normal people wouldn't have considered remotely funny.

Kit kissed her nose. 'If it means you won't come without Fielding, then I shall fetch Mac, even if he has to be bound and gagged first.'

There'd been no need for Mac to be bound and gagged. When the men arrived early on Saturday morning on the old rattling bikes they'd managed to acquire from somewhere, Mac looked as keyed up as Kit about the weekend ahead. All four wore civvies for the first time: the men in grey flannels, Aertex shirts and sports jackets, and Cara in her red frock and a white cardigan. Fielding wore a drawstring blouse and dirndl skirt in which she managed to look even smaller.

They waited at the side of the road for the bus to Gozo. On such a perfect May morning, the warm air sparkling like champagne and filled with the scent of the blossom that carpeted the surrounding fields, it was hard to believe there was a war on, that only the other day Winston Churchill had replaced Neville Chamberlain as prime minister of Great Britain, that yesterday Germany had invaded the Netherlands, Belgium and Luxembourg, that vicious battles were raging throughout Europe.

The bus came, a miniature single-decker packed with elderly women clad in long, black garments. They must have got up at the crack of dawn as they were laden with baskets of fruit and vegetables from the markets of Rabat. Cara and Fielding took the last empty seats and Kit and Mac had to stand.

A small shrine was attached to the screen behind the driver, a painting of Jesus encased in a heart-shaped frame with a little scooped ledge underneath containing holy water. As the bus stopped frequently to let people on and off, usually more elderly women, passengers would dip the fingers in the water and make the sign of the Cross. It looked very ostentatious, Cara thought. She'd sooner keep her religion to herself, not flaunt it.

A priest boarded the bus, hardly out of his teens, and a woman at the front, who looked about ninety, struggled to her feet and gave him her seat. He took it with a curt nod. Snorting loudly, Fielding stood and indicated to the woman to have her seat. She looked nervously at the priest before taking it.

It was much too hot on the crowded, noisy bus. Mac was smoking – he smoked a lot – and the atmosphere was fuggy: it was hard to breathe. Cara began to feel sleepy as they trundled along the narrow, otherwise deserted roads, passing tiny villages, each with its own enormous church. Kit was holding on to the back of her seat and she could feel his knuckles against her neck. She hadn't told Mam or Dad about him, yet they were virtually engaged: Mam would only demand to know if he was a Catholic and Dad would ask about his politics. As Kit was an atheist and had no time for politicians of any party, they would both be unhappy with her choice of husband and she had no intention of getting involved in heated arguments by letter as to why she should or shouldn't marry him.

He bent and said, 'We're nearly there,' and she felt his lips against her hair. His fingers caressed her neck and she looked up at him and smiled. 'I love you,' he mouthed.

'And I love you.' She said it so quietly, she wasn't sure if he'd heard. But they both knew how much they loved each other, yet kept on saying it. She wondered if she would sleep with Kit on Gozo. They hadn't discussed it, but she had a feeling it would happen and her veins tingled with a mixture of anticipation and trepidation. They could only spend one night away as they had to be on duty early on Monday morning, but it could be a turning point in her life, the time when she ceased to be a girl and became a woman.

The bus stopped at Cirkewwa from where the ferries ran to Gozo, the remainder of the passengers got off, their places immediately taken by those disembarking from the ferry that had just docked. Mac bought four beers to soothe their dry throats – it didn't matter that the beer was warm – and they proceeded on to the ship, gratefully breathing in the crisp fresh air, enjoying the gentle motion of the boat as it took them on the thirty-minute journey to Gozo. The blue water was as clear as a diamond, reminding Cara of the ring that Louise Appleton had sent, and fish of every size and colour could be seen swimming aimlessly in its depths. One came shooting up towards her and she stepped back in alarm, but it was only a mirror image of a gull diving towards the water, hitting it with a muffled splash and a spurt of creamy foam.

Fielding said she felt as if she'd escaped from prison and didn't care that she would be recaptured the day after tomorrow. 'Until that happens, I'm going to have the time of my life. There's a war on, and who knows when we'll be able to do this again?'

Mac said, 'Hear, hear,' but Cara and Kit just looked at each other and didn't say anything.

Victoria, Gozo's capital, was a hilltop citadel, its 400-year-old walls standing like a giant candle in the centre of the island. In one of the confusing maze of narrow streets was a cheap hotel that Mac had been recommended. It took a while to find, even with the aid of a map. A flat-fronted house within a row of similar buildings, it was situated in a curved alleyway of shallow steps. The owner, a smiling, bejewelled woman in a long, flowered dress, spoke English well and could even understand Mac with his slight Geordie accent. Most Maltese had at least a smattering of the language, the island having been a British colony for more than a hundred years.

Mac reserved two double rooms for the night. Cara wasn't sure whether to be pleased or disappointed that it seemed Kit had no intention of sleeping with her. She came to the conclusion she was a little bit of both.

'I'd like to have a wash and change my shirt,' Mac announced when the terms had been negotiated.

A few minutes later, the men having disappeared, Cara and Fielding entered their ground-floor room. The roughly plastered walls were painted white and the floor paved with caramel-coloured stones. There was a gaudy rug on each site of the double bed that was covered with an extravagantly lacy white spread. The curtains on the tiny windows were also white, and a black crucifix with a brass figure of Christ hung on the wall.

'It's nice and cool in here.' Fielding threw herself on the bed. 'It's a bit like a nun's cell. Is that what nuns sleep in, Caffrey, a cell?'

'I can't remember, but I'm pretty sure they don't go in for lace bedspreads.'

They spent the afternoon lazily exploring the rambling streets of Gozo with its crumbling medieval buildings, museums and craft shops, stopping frequently to escape the blazing sun for an invigorating cup of coffee or a glass of highly alcoholic Maltese wine. There were a surprising number of people about, many from the military like themselves. Now that Cara knew that she would end the weekend as she'd started it, a virgin, the tension she'd felt before, thrilling though it had been, ebbed away and she felt more at ease.

At six, the girls returned to the hotel for a rest and to get changed. Kit and Mac remained in a bar and promised to collect them in an hour's time.

'Don't you dare get squiffy,' Fielding said threateningly.

'As if we would,' Mac said in a hurt voice.

As soon as they reached their room, Cara took off her dress and lay down on the bed, exhausted. She noticed a silvery gauze dress hanging outside the wardrobe. Sleeveless, with a self-coloured petticoat underneath, it had been exquisitely embroidered with silver thread around the neck and hem. She'd never seen Fielding in it before.

'That's pretty,' she remarked, 'the dress, I mean.' Her own imitation silk two-piece from C & A would look very drab beside it.

'I wore it in a play and they let me have it afterwards.' Fielding was washing herself from head to toe with a flannel. Her tiny body was perfectly formed, her breasts like small pink roses and her recently shorn blonde hair a mass of miniature ringlets. Cara was about to say, 'You remind me of a doll I used to have,' but thought she might take offence. Instead, she asked, 'What made you join the Army, Fielding?' She'd asked before, but had never received a satisfactory answer as to why a relatively successful actress who could also sing and dance had given up her career for the forces.

'Just felt like it, that's all.' She pulled on white knickers and a bra, fastening the bra at the front, then twisting it round, the way Cara did.

'I don't believe you. You're losing valuable time building up your career.'

'Why did you join the Army, Caffrey?'

'You know quite well why. I had this dead-end job and wanted some excitement, but being on the stage must be exciting enough for anyone. Why are you keeping secrets from me when I tell you everything?' she asked accusingly.

'Oh, all right,' Fielding shrugged nonchalantly, 'if you must have an answer: I was jilted at the altar by the love of my life. Will that do?'

Cara shook her head. 'Not if it's not the truth, no.'

'My entire family were killed in a road accident and I just had to get away from everything I knew. Does that suit you, Inspector Caffrey?'

'You mentioned your father only the other week.'

'I've got a deadly disease and am likely to die any minute?'

'It'd been discovered when you had a medical.'

Fielding stared at her exasperatedly, then her face changed and she began to cry, hard, wracking sobs that made her whole body shudder. She didn't cover her face, just stood, arms hanging at her sides, her face twisted with grief. 'My baby died,' she sobbed. 'He died in my womb and they had to take the womb away so I can never have more children. The man, the father, did a bunk. I joined the Army because I wanted to die. My baby's *dead*, Cara, and I don't want to live any more.'

Cara leapt out of bed and took the weeping girl in her arms. 'Oh, Fielding, I'm so sorry. I shouldn't have persisted. I never realized it was such a terrible thing. What was wrong with your baby?'

'He was too big for my womb, almost twenty-five pounds, and it was beginning to split.'

'Twenty-five . . . Fielding, you bloody liar!' Cara pushed her away and she fell on to the bed, helpless with laughter.

'Well, you refused to believe the real truth,' she said, almost choking on the words.

'You've told so many lies I don't know what the real truth is.'

'My first answer was the true one. I was jilted, not exactly at the altar and not exactly by the love of my life, although I thought he was at the time.' She looked briefly sad and Cara suspected it was genuine, although you could never tell with Fielding. 'It can sometimes be a bit boring on the stage, especially if you're in a long run, so I joined up for the excitement, just like you. And I thought it would look good on my resumé. Don't forget the war was only supposed to last six months.'

'You really had me fooled,' Cara said indignantly. 'You can be a bitch sometimes, Fielding.'

'And you can be a nosy bugger, Caffrey.'

They had dinner outside in a tree-lined square situated in the very heart of Victoria. Cara could never remember what she ate, only that they all drank far too much wine and, by the time the food had gone, the world had taken on a different hue and everything appeared bigger than normal, sounds were sharper, and she felt as light as air and so much in love with Kit that it made her want to cry.

'Are you all right, darling?' he asked tenderly.

'I've never felt more all right in me life,' she replied.

The setting sun was melting into a sky that had suddenly turned purple with gashes of gold and looked as if it was on fire. Mac had brought a camera and took a picture with Cara and Fielding in the foreground. 'I'll let you have copies if it comes out OK,' he promised. 'I think I might have had the camera pointing the wrong way and it's taken a photo of my nose. Either way, it won't look up to much in black and white.'

The interior of the restaurant was darkly lit, a candle fluttering on each table, smoke rising from the inevitable cigarettes, and a pianist, hidden from view, accompanied by a violinist dressed as a gypsy, a red bandana tied around his long, black hair, a gold hoop in his ear, played familiar tunes from Hollywood films: 'Let's Face the Music and Dance', 'Change Partners', 'The Way You Look Tonight'. He wandered in and out, pausing at each table, his black, passionate eyes resting on the women, making them feel wanted and adorable, at least for tonight.

The pianist began to play 'A Foggy Day in London Town' just as the gypsy reached their table for the second time. Fielding said, 'I sang this in a show once.' Never backward in coming forward, and spurred on by the wine, she began to sing at full throttle and the gypsy flashed encouragement with his eyes. Fielding stood and followed him into the restaurant, a tiny, moth-like figure in her silvery dress. Cara noticed Mac's eyes following her every move and was shocked because the look in them was anything but platonic.

Fielding's voice wasn't strong, but it throbbed with feeling. Everyone had stopped eating and people came from across the square, drawn by the haunting voice, although it was impossible to imagine a foggy day anywhere on such a glorious night.

'If I was at home right now,' Kit said in a low voice, 'I'd be getting ready for bed. It's Saturday and I might have been to the pictures or a concert. I might even have stayed in and read a book, never knowing that in another part of the world people were sitting under the stars listening to an angel sing.' He looked at Cara. 'Am I dreaming this, or is it real? Are *you* real?'

'It's all real,' she assured him. 'Really real.'

'Me, I'd've been to a footy match this afternoon,' said Mac. 'By now, the kids'd be in bed and me and the wife would be falling asleep in our chairs and half listening to the wireless.' He frowned and shook his head. 'I can't imagine going back to that life, not after this one.'

'You've got no choice, mate,' Kit said.

'I don't suppose I have.' Mac stood and held the chair for Fielding, who'd finished her song to loud applause, not just from the diners, but the small and appreciative crowd that had gathered outside. From inside the restaurant, a voice shouted, 'Jolly good show, Fielding.'

Mac's arm rested along the back of Fielding's chair. She took one of his cigarettes, although she didn't normally smoke. They seemed very close tonight, not just physically.

For another hour, they sat around, until dusk had turned to darkness and half a moon had appeared in the starry, navy-blue sky. Mac began to yawn. Cara actually nodded off for a second and was glad that no one noticed.

Kit stretched. 'It's time we were getting back.' For some reason he looked rather strained.

'But the night is only young,' Fielding cried. 'Can't we go to a club?'

'It's quarter past eleven,' Kit said. 'If there are clubs on Gozo, they'll close promptly at midnight because tomorrow's Sunday. No work and no play on the Sabbath day, that's what I was taught at school.'

They danced back to the hotel, arms crossed, hands linked, the girls in the middle, singing 'The Lambeth Walk'.

'Shush!' Mac chided when arrived.

'Shush yourself.' Fielding gave an extra-loud 'Oi!'

The door had been left unlocked and they went inside, shushing each other, unable to see in the dark, windowless foyer. Cara couldn't remember if the place had electricity. 'Does anyone know where our room is?' she whispered plaintively.

'It's here.' She felt herself being guided through a door: it closed behind her. Here it was lighter as the curtains hadn't been drawn and the light from the half-moon was just enough to see by. She became aware that it was Kit, not Fielding, standing by the door, leaning against it. She couldn't make out the expression on his face, but felt extremely angry.

'I'll go away if you want,' he said in a tight voice. Perhaps he could see the expression on *her* face.

'Where are Fielding and Mac?'

'Where do you think? The other bedroom.'

'But . . .' It wasn't supposed to happen that way. Mac was married. Surely Fielding didn't intend to sleep with a married man? 'Did you arrange this beforehand with Mac, that you come into the room with me?'

'I had to, didn't I?' Kit said tersely.

Cara backed away. 'It seems really sordid, planning it in advance so Mac knew you wanted to sleep with me before *I* did.'

'I've wanted to make love to you since the day we met. I thought you would have guessed that by now. I rather hoped you might feel the same.'

'I do, I did. I'm not sure how I feel now.' This wasn't how she'd imagined it would happen. She'd wanted it to be perfect, but it had started off all wrong.

'Cara! I've never done anything like this before. I had no idea how to go about it. I didn't know whether to ask you first or . . . or what to do.' He sounded on the verge of tears. 'It seems I've made a perfect mess of everything. It doesn't matter, I'll spend the night somewhere else.' He was about to open the door when she ran towards him, putting her hand on his arm.

'Don't go. I'm sorry, but I'm all in a muddle. I've spoilt things, haven't I?'

'No, it was me.'

'It was *me*.' There was silence for a moment, then they fell into each other's arms: half laughing, half crying as they stumbled towards the bed.

'Tell me if I do anything wrong,' Kit murmured as he began to kiss her.

It hurt, badly, and wasn't nearly as wonderful as she'd expected, although she swore to Kit that it was: she was too tense and he was nervous. Afterwards, they fell asleep in each other's arms and that was enough for now, to feel the weight of his arm on her waist and the beat of his heart close to hers and knowing she was no longer a virgin.

It was still dark when Cara woke with the terrifying feeling that she was about to die. Shakily, she got out of bed and just managed to make it to the sink where she vomited so much that her ribs ached and her insides felt as if they were being scraped with a spoon.

'It's all that wine.' She'd woken Kit and he was holding her over the sink. Despite her utter wretchedness, Cara was aware he had nothing on and neither did she. Waves of embarrassment swept over her already shuddering body and she was sick again. 'Oh, you poor darling,' Kit was saying.

He helped her back to bed, fetched a glass of water and mopped her brow with a wet flannel until she fell asleep again.

The next time she woke up it was broad daylight: the sun poured into the white room and all over Gozo, church bells were ringing and she remembered she'd have to go to Mass. To her surprise, Kit, looking very grave and thoughtful, was sitting up in bed. 'Do you still love me?' he asked the second she opened her eyes.

'I'll always love you,' she said sleepily. 'Why did you ask such a silly question when you already know the answer?'

'I was worried you might have second thoughts after last night – as first nights go, it was pretty disastrous.'

'It wasn't your fault I was sick.'

'The disaster occurred before you were sick: it might even be *why* you were sick,' he said forlornly. 'It happened far too quickly and I noticed you grimace more than once.'

'Only because it hurt, but it might not hurt if we do it again.'

He slid down the bed and took her in his arms. 'Are you sure? Do you feel up to it?'

'I'm not sure, no,' she said regretfully. 'On second thoughts, I feel as weak as a kitten.'

'Then we'll leave it until another time.'

'All right.' Cara sighed contentedly.

'You know what I think?' he said softly in her ear.

'What?'

'I think we should get married: now, next week, as soon as possible. If we can survive a night like that one, we must be made for each other.'

Her heart stopped for a second. 'Will the Army and Air Force give us permission?'

'All we have to do is ask. What do *you* think, darling?'

'I think we should ask.'

By Monday morning, the night on Gozo was already merely a memory that would linger for ever in her mind. Cara tried to think who to ask if she could marry Kit Farthing – he was setting things in motion his end that very day.

'There's only Allardyce,' Fielding said glumly. They were lying underneath a lorry looking for a leak in the petrol tank. It provided a quiet place to talk. Cara still didn't know what had gone on between her and Mac when they'd spent the night together. Perhaps they had, platonically, shared a bed, or Mac had slept on the floor, or they'd made passionate love the whole night long – it was no use asking Fielding, who wouldn't hesitate to lie if it suited her. Any road, it was none of Cara's business.

'Sybil's the last person in the world I'd want to ask for anything, let alone permission to get married.'

'I don't blame you, although you could always claim you were preggers, then she'd have no alternative but to say yes.'

'I wouldn't bank on it. I might get sent home in disgrace.' Cara sighed. 'I've got no alternative but to ask her, have I?'

'Not really, and Caffrey, if you're going to ask, do it quickly. I've never been a bridesmaid before and I'm looking forward to it.'

'Have you two gone asleep under there?' a voice thundered, and Corporal Culpepper's face appeared upside down at the side of the lorry. 'How long does it take to find a leak in a petrol tank and why does it need the two of you to do it?'

'Ask *him* if you can get married,' Fielding whispered. 'He's bound to give you permission if you promise him the first night.'

'Come in,' Sybil shouted when Cara knocked on the door of her office in Marzipan Hall.

Cara entered, stood stiffly to attention in front of the desk and saluted. Sybil looked up. She had been reading a letter and seemed rather distracted. She threw the letter down and Cara saw it was handwritten. The little office was rather soulless and hardly bigger than the box room in Shaw Street where she'd used to sleep. There were numerous charts on the wall, a large map of Malta with red pins indicating various positions and the inevitable picture of King George VI, this time in military uniform. Cara thanked the Lord she was a driver, as she would have hated being stuck in such a place without a soul to talk to for hours on end.

'I've heard from Mummy,' Sybil said in a perfectly normal voice, not the strident tone she usually used. 'Jonathan joined up secretly, behind her back, and she's distraught.'

'Didn't he turn eighteen the other week? He was likely to get his call-up papers any minute.' Cara stood at ease, as it didn't appear that Sybil was likely to tell her to.

'Yes, but he's still at school and Mummy's been desperately trying to get him into university.'

'Jonathan said they'd never take him at university, he's not clever enough.'

'When did he tell you that? Why don't you sit down a minute, Cara?'

'At Christmas.' Cara pulled forward a chair. There was no need to wonder why she was suddenly Cara and not Caffrey, why she'd been asked to sit. Sybil must need someone to talk to and Cara was her only link with home.

'I didn't manage to get home for Christmas.' She looked as if she wished she had. 'I haven't seen Jonathan since the war began. Oh, and Mummy says your mother isn't being much help. She keeps saying it'll be the making of him for some reason and it makes Mummy feel even more upset.'

'It's just Mam's way,' she said apologetically. It seemed odd to be making excuses for a mother who was hundreds of miles away. 'She was dead upset when me and our Fergus joined up.' Mam considered herself the perfect mother and had always claimed that Eleanor had never stopped treating Jonathan as a baby. 'He'll grow up a sissy,' she would say warningly, as if Dad or one of her own children could do anything about it. But Jonathan had proved her wrong and gone his own way, despite all the pressure from his own mother. 'What's he joined?' she asked Sybil. 'The Army, the Navy, or the Air Force?'

'The Fleet Air Arm,' Sybil sighed.

'I'm sure he'll like it. He seemed anxious to get away.'

'So long as he doesn't end up dead.' Her eyes blazed briefly, then she sighed. 'I always loved Jonathan more than anyone. He was the only person who didn't want anything from me.' She picked up the letter, stared it unseeingly and let it fall back on the desk. 'I couldn't stand Anthony, always making fun of me. I was glad when *he* went away.'

Cara didn't know what to say. She was glad when the telephone rang. Sybil picked up the receiver, listened for a moment then said, 'I'll see to it straight away.' She dialled a number, drumming her fingers impatiently on the desk until the person answered at the other end. 'Corporal Culpepper? Major Hull wants a driver to take him to Republic Square, Valletta.' She replaced the receiver without saying goodbye or thank you, looked at Cara, as if surprised to see her there, and asked, 'Were you here for a reason, Caffrey?'

'Yes,' Cara said bluntly. 'I came to ask permission to get married.'

'Who to?' Once again she glanced at the letter, as if she couldn't get it off her mind.

'Lance Corporal Christopher Farthing, he's in the RAF.' Cara bit her lip, wishing now that the telephone hadn't rung, as it seemed to have nudged Sybil into being Allardyce again and her usual obnoxious self. It wasn't solely self-interest, but also a feeling of pity for the girl who seemed so terribly lonely, that made her say, 'I was going to invite you to the wedding, ma'am. I thought it would be nice to have someone there from home – Mam always called us The September Girls.'

To her relief, Sybil looked pleased. 'Why, thank you, Caffrey, I'd love to come.'

Cara was leaving Marzipan Hall, feeling exultant, when a staff car drew up and Fielding leapt out. 'I've come for Major Hull. What did Allardyce have to say?'

'She didn't say yes or no, but she's accepted an invitation to the wedding.'

Fielding groaned. 'You shouldn't have asked *her*. She'll put a bad spell on it.'

'She's terribly unhappy, I felt sorry for her.'

'Idiot! You're too soft-hearted by a heart by a mile, Caffrey.'

'Not all that soft-hearted, I also thought it might help swing things my way.'

Fielding grinned. 'All you have to do now is set the date.'

It wasn't until the beginning of July that everyone concerned would have a whole day free at the same time – and Cara and Kit an extra day for a brief honeymoon in Gozo.

'We'll stay at the same hotel in the same room,' Kit said, kissing her tenderly, 'and we'll do much better this time. It's a pity we haven't had a chance to practise.' Since they'd met, they'd only seen each other about once a week, twice at the most, when he would come haring along on his bike, usually with Mac. They never had the opportunity to be alone in a place where they could do any more than kiss. It wouldn't be any different when they were married, but at least Cara would have his ring on her finger and that would be, almost, enough for now. They were only young and there'd be plenty of time to make love in the future: there'd be time for all sorts of things in the future that they couldn't do now.

Cara invited all the girls who shared the farmhouse, although knew that some would be on duty and unable to come. Corporal Culpepper insisted on giving her away and didn't demand any other privileges.

The army chaplain had agreed to marry them in the little makeshift chapel behind Marzipan Hall that had once been a stable. It would be a civil ceremony as it was no use asking a priest to officiate at what would be a mixed marriage. Even in Liverpool, such a thing would never have been tolerated.

'You'd have to agree to become a Catholic and it'd take months and months,' Cara said, knowing Mam would do her nut at the idea of her only daughter not getting married in a Catholic church. She'd asked Sybil not to tell Eleanor about the wedding: she was bound to tell Mam, and if Mam found out, she'd swim all the way to Malta if she thought she could put a stop to it.

Cara and Fielding were in the mess listening to the BBC World Service when it was announced that Germany had invaded France. There was a united groan and Cara's thoughts immediately went to her brother, Fergus, who'd been in France for months, waiting and no doubt dreading that this very thing would happen. The Netherlands had already surrendered. Would France be able to hold the German Army at bay? If it didn't, Great Britain would stand alone, with only the English Channel separating it from an enemy that seemed set on conquering the world.

May drifted into June, by which time Belgium had fallen and France seemed on the brink. Thousands of British and French troops had been evacuated to Britain from the French port of Dunkirk, but Cara had absolutely no idea if Fergus was among them. She couldn't stop worrying about her gentle brother, imagining his mangled body lying in a muddy ditch in a strange country. It made the war feel very close and personal. A few days later, it came even closer.

It was morning, almost seven o'clock, and the girls in the farmhouse were squabbling over the single bathroom, when the air raid warning sounded, as it had done many times before to signal a mock raid. They didn't go down the cellar as they'd been instructed but, after a slight pause, continued with their squabbling, until someone said, 'Hush!'

They hushed and, in the ensuing silence, a distant rumbling noise could be heard.

'Aeroplanes!' Fielding ran over to a window. 'I can't see a thing,' she cried. 'What's that?'

'What's what?'

'I just heard an explosion. There's another – and another. Oh, my God!' She turned to face the girls. 'It's an air raid, a proper air raid. They're dropping bombs on Malta.'

The raids continued during the afternoon and early evening, eight altogether, all directed at the area of the dockyards. More than thirty people were killed and many more were injured. Malta had had its baptism of fire and blood – and this was only the beginning.

Chapter 10

June 1940

Fergus Caffrey was just an average soldier. He'd never disgraced himself, nor had he shone. Anxious to please, he was nevertheless a mite too clumsy, forever tripping over things. The other men liked him because there was nothing to dislike about someone so inoffensive who could have easily become a target for bullies, except that Fergus was tall, well built, more than averagely good-looking and popular with women.

This had rather surprised Fergus and he'd eventually put it down to the fact the women were French and couldn't speak English and he was English and couldn't speak French and it was difficult to be tongue-tied with someone you couldn't converse with except by signs. And if there was one thing he was good at, it was conversing by signs – he'd had enough practice with Anthony.

Until a few weeks ago, he'd enjoyed his time in France with the British Expeditionary Force. There'd been no sign of the enemy and little to do except make his bed, keep himself and his part of the billet clean, stand to attention when required and carry out the various tasks that were apportioned to him as best as he could without his glasses. As his job as an accounts clerk had been unutterably boring, he didn't find the various tasks as tedious as the other men. He rather enjoyed repainting doors and window frames white, although they didn't need it – the only reason was to 'keep idle hands busy', according to the corporals and sergeants who nowadays ruled his life.

His wish to fight for his country had paled rather once he'd been taught how it was done – he doubted if he could ever bring himself to thrust his bayonet into the belly of a young soldier no different from himself apart from the fact he happened to be German, but he didn't regret joining up: *someone* had to do the dirty work necessary to keep his country democratic and free.

Now though, weeks later, Fergus had no idea how he felt about anything. His brain was in a state of total confusion as he trudged along a road somewhere in France, nipping out of the way of cars and horse-drawn carts laden with furniture and bundles of bedding and sometimes small children that occasionally passed him. Those less lucky pushed handcarts stacked with the possessions of a lifetime and the even less lucky carried the stuff in giant suitcases or in awkward bundles on their backs with things like kettles and teddy bears poking out and, in one case, a violin.

These people were refugees fleeing from the advancing German Army and that's what Fergus had become, a refugee. But, unlike the others, he had no idea where he was going or what part of France he was in. He was just following these wretched people because he didn't know what else to do. There were a few other troops in the fleeing crowds, in their twos or threes or all alone. Perhaps, like him, the single ones preferred their own company at a time like this.

Every now and then, a German plane would swoop out of the summery blue sky and strafe them. There'd be a concerted dash for the ditches on each side of the road, but not everyone was quick enough to escape and the plane would fly away, its work done, leaving the women to weep, the men to groan and the children to scream when they found their dead, dying or injured loved ones left lying on the bloody road. It reminded Fergus of the game they'd played at school: musical chairs. Everyone had to grab a seat when the music stopped, but there was always someone who wasn't quick enough and they'd be out. In the end, only the winner would be left and, in the game now being played, there was no doubt who the winner would be and it wasn't *his* side.

This must be what hell was like – perhaps he'd died along with many of his mates and he was in hell for all eternity, although he didn't know what he'd done to deserve it. He'd missed Mass a few times in France, but that wasn't a mortal sin, not deserving of such horrendous punishment.

His feet were killing him. There were holes as big as spuds in his socks and his heels were raw and bleeding. There was nothing to stuff in his boots except bits of newspaper that quickly turned to shreds. He had no spare socks. In fact, he had nothing: no rations, no money, no kit of any description. Everything had been lost or left behind, even his rifle – he didn't know where. His glasses must have fallen from his pocket: he'd used to wear them occasionally to write letters home and no one had ever commented. It was strange, but his sight had actually improved since they'd been lost, as if every part of his body, including his eyes, was alert to the danger he was in.

Fergus felt as if he had just taken part in another game rather more skilled than musical chairs: chess. The four armies – the British, French, Belgium and German – had been the pawns that had been moved aimlessly around by blindfolded men who couldn't see the board. One minute, Fergus and his comrades had been advancing, then discovered they were retreating. They'd think they were on the winning side when, in reality, they were losing. The tanks promised in support hadn't put in an appearance: expected and longed-for rations hadn't turned up. Rumours abounded: that Churchill was in Paris, that the Belgians had surrendered, that the much-vaunted Maginot Line hadn't stopped the enemy dead in its tracks as anticipated; instead, they'd thoughtlessly marched right round it. Calais and Boulogne had been taken and British troops were to be evacuated from Dunkirk. And it was to Dunkirk that Fergus hoped and prayed he was heading as he limped along a pretty country lane in France in the company of a pitiful collection of ordinary human beings whose worlds had been torn apart.

He passed the body of a very old man sprawled in the ditch, a deep hole in his chest. A small dog lay beside him, very much alive and barking tiredly. The sight left Fergus cold. He'd already seen worse, including good friends blown to pieces in front of his eyes.

'Gets to you, doesn't it?'

Fergus didn't bother to turn and see who had spoken. He was past caring about such niceties as good manners and had lost count of the people who'd tried to speak to him that he'd dismissed with a rude shrug. He shrugged again.

'Hang on a minute. I just want to take a shot of the old man and his dog.'

He turned then, to see a thin, white-faced lad, no more than sixteen, wearing what looked very much like a school uniform: flannels, navy-blue blazer, white shirt and striped tie, holding a camera aimed at the ditch. There was a click, the lad nodded as if satisfied, wound the reel of film to the next exposure and put the camera in the leather satchel slung over his shoulder.

'Isn't that a bit ghoulish?' Fergus asked, stirred out of his torpor by this strange sight.

'It isn't if you're a professional photographer,' the lad said airily.

'You don't look old enough to be a professional anything. What the hell are you doing here? Are you English, French or what?'

'I'm English and I'm taking photos for my dad's newspaper. I came over yesterday with my granddad on his fishing boat.'

'Came over from where?' Fergus's already confused brain couldn't cope with this perky young individual who looked as if he'd been on his way home from school when transported by magical means to the nightmare that was now France.

'Folkestone. You've no idea what's happening, have you?' This was said so patronizingly that Fergus felt like giving the little bugger a clock around the ear.

'Has anyone?' he grunted.

'*I* have,' the lad said boastfully. 'My dad's editor of the local paper, the *Folkestone Courier*, so what with my granddad having a boat, I've been more or less in the thick of things. Since last Monday, thousands of British and French troops have been evacuated from Dunkirk. Boats like my granddad's have come from all over the country to help. I stowed away and nipped off when we got here to take photos and make notes. It'll be the scoop of a lifetime and Dad'll be really proud of me.' For a moment, he looked slightly worried. 'I expect him and Mum are wondering where I am.'

'I expect they are,' Fergus said dryly. 'How old are you?'

'Fifteen. What's your name, by the way? I'm Julian Mellor.'

'Fergus Caffrey.'

Julian Mellor took a notebook and the stub of a pencil out of his blazer pocket and made a note of the name. 'Are you Irish, Fergus?'

'Liverpool Irish,' Fergus grunted. He looked hungrily at the satchel. 'Have you got anything to eat in there?'

'I've only got chocolate left. It's from the lunch Mum made me for school yesterday, I've been making it last out. Would you like some?'

'Please.'

'It's a Mars bar. Here, have it all,' he said impulsively. 'We're only a few miles from Dunkirk, then it'll be home and proper meals again.'

'Ta.' Fergus licked his lips as he tore the paper away from the

Mars bar and was about to bite into it when he became aware that a small boy had stopped in front of him and was staring longingly at the chocolate. The child's face bore the expression of someone very much older, for he too had passed the old man and the dog, walked in the blood spilled on the road, witnessed the same terrifying sights as Fergus, except Fergus was twenty-five and this child looked no more than six or seven.

'Marcel!' A woman a few yards ahead who was wearily pushing a pram piled high with suitcases must have noticed the boy was no longer at her side. 'Marcel!' she called again. She wore high-heeled shoes, a pink flowered frock, a straw picture hat and lace gloves. Fergus wondered if there was a baby in the pram.

'Here you are, kiddo.' He thrust the chocolate at the boy.

'*Merci, monsieur,*' he said politely and ran to catch up with the woman.

'Are we really only a few miles off Dunkirk?' Fergus asked, thinking wistfully about the Mars bar.

'About two or three. Whoa! Looks like we're going to be strafed again. You'd better duck, Fergus.'

Fergus stared, transfixed, at the plane zooming towards them, so low that he could actually see the face of the pilot, see the goggles over his eyes. He never quite knew what came over him. It wasn't courage, he was quite sure of that, but more a feeling of sheer foolhardiness when he saw the woman in front swerve the pram towards the ditch, so sharply that she knocked the Mars bar out of the little boy's hand and he stooped to pick it up. Bullets were hitting the road in a dead straight line, raising little clouds of dust, and the line was heading straight towards the child.

With a roar that was a mixture of rage and despair, Fergus leapt forward, scooped up the lad in his arms and threw him into the ditch, landing on top of him with a thud that winded them both. Something bit his leg and he screamed at the same time as the little lad began to cry, not because he was hurt, but because he'd lost his Mars bar.

It had become a crazy world when you actually felt glad that you'd been shot in the leg and could no longer walk. It meant that other people had to take over this important function for you, like the troops that appeared from nowhere, made a seat with their hands and in turns, carried Fergus as far as Dunkirk where the harbour was chock-a-block with sunken ships. There was something almost biblical about the sight of thousands and thousands of men sitting and lying on the beach in the blazing sunshine and others standing in water up to their necks as they waited to be rescued.

But, fortunately for Fergus, he'd been shot in the leg and it meant a stretcher was called for. He was placed with the wounded, given a drink of water, his boots removed and told he'd be put on the next hospital ship as soon as it arrived. It didn't matter that his leg was giving him gyp, his destiny was no longer under his control and he was quite happy about it.

Ever since the fighting in France had begun, Brenna and Colm had talked well into the night, unable to sleep because all they could think of was Fergus: Fergus being shot, blown up, bayoneted to death, taken prisoner.

'He was always terrified of his own shadow, poor little lad,' Brenna sobbed, entirely forgetting that Fergus was now a grown man six inches taller than his mam. 'I could hardly believe it when he volunteered to fight.'

'He hasn't got it in him to fight,' Colm said soberly. 'I bet he made a hopeless soldier.'

During the day, Brenna lived by the wireless, waiting for reports of the battle taking place across the Channel, while people kept bringing Colm little snippets of news they'd just come by. 'Our lads have been cut off at the mouth of the Somme,' he was told. 'There's no escape for them now.'

'Churchill has ordered the Admiralty to send ships to Dunkirk to rescue the British Expeditionary Force,' he was told another time.

Over the next few days, Brenna and Colm hardly ate or slept as they waited for news of Fergus, praying that he was still alive, that he had managed to reach Dunkirk where the troops were gathering, that he'd been taken on one of the armada of ships that had been sent to bring them safely home: the naval vessels, the pleasure craft, the fishing boats, the ferries, and the little yachts and motor launches that had volunteered for this mission of mercy.

'Colm!' Brenna screeched. She flew into the yard to meet him the very second he opened the back door. 'Oh, Colm!'

'What's the matter, luv?' he asked, going pale.

'Nancy came round earlier to say our Fergus had phoned. He's in hospital in Folkestone and he's hurt his leg, but he's safe.' She flung herself into his arms and began to cry. 'I was convinced he was dead, Colm.'

'So was I.' They clung to each other and said a silent prayer that their son was safe. Colm's face glowed. 'He's come through Dunkirk. I never dreamt one day I'd be proud of our Fergus.'

'He gave Nancy the address of the hospital, so you can write to him, darlin', tell him how proud we are.'

A few days later, Colm and Brenna had more reason to be proud. A picture appeared in the *Liverpool Echo* of an unrecognizable man face down in a ditch on top of a small boy whose terrified face could just be seen above the man's shoulder.

'*Brave Liverpool soldier, Fergus Caffrey, risks his life to save French child from German bullets on way to Dunkirk,*' proclaimed the caption, and underneath, 'Just one of the acts of heroism witnessed by photographer, Julian Mellor, who spent two days with the troops as they made their spectacular escape from France.'

Two weeks later, in the middle of June, Fergus arrived home in an ambulance, his leg heavily bandaged, and walking with the aid of crutches. He already felt uncomfortable about the photo in the *Echo* that Mam had sent, but cringed with a mixture of embarrassment and shame when he saw the banner strung across the street with 'WELCOME HOME, FERGUS' painted on it. As if on cue, people came pouring out of their houses, surrounding him and shaking his hand, a photographer from the paper took his photo and requested an interview, Mam cried her eyes out and even Dad looked close to tears. His two little nephews, Joey and Mike, went round, busting with self-importance, and telling people, 'He's our uncle.' However, the thing that touched him most was when his brother, Tyrone, squeezed his shoulder and said gruffly, 'Well done, Ferg,' because he knew how much Tyrone wanted to be in his shoes and what a much better job he would have made of being a soldier.

Colm had given up his job as organizer of the Labour Party – or the job had given up on him, he wasn't sure. The country was being run by a Government of National Unity: Labour's Clement Attlee had been appointed Churchill's deputy and Colm's all-time hero, Ernest

Bevin, was Minister of Labour, so there was no longer any need for members to meet and plot the downfall of the Tories. They were perfectly satisfied with what they had and, consequently, meetings were poorly attended. Added to that, there was no petrol to be had for the van and it had been laid up for the duration.

There being no shortage of work for an able-bodied fellow of forty-six, Colm soon found another job, this time in a munitions factory in Kirkby as a quality control inspector. He retained close links with the local Labour Party and acted as unpaid agent, arranging social events, dealing with the correspondence that had been reduced to a trickle since the war began, and still hosting the monthly meetings in the parlour of the house in Shaw Street that were attended by a handful of party stalwarts.

Six weeks ago, when Ignatius Herlihy, the elderly and ailing Labour Member of Parliament for the seat of Toxteth and Dingle, had passed away quietly in his sleep, it had fallen to Colm to arrange the by-election. His first task had been to circulate members with the news and, after a decent interval for Ignatius Herlihy's funeral, ask for prospective candidates willing to stand for the vacancy in what was a safe Labour seat. He'd already received an application, sent with indecent haste, from a chap by the name of Bertram Gilbert who worked for Bevin in the Ministry of Labour.

In all, ten applications were received, giving the individual's personal details, their record in politics and a photograph. Colm had called a special meeting in his parlour so the applications could be discussed and the hopefuls invited to a selection meeting at some future date.

'There's four local applicants, four from London, one from the Isle of Wight and one lives in Scotland: Glasgow to be precise,' he told the assembled crowd of three: Bill Randal, eighty if a day and pedantic to his bones; Jessie Connors, almost as old as Bill and his sworn enemy, automatically disagreeing with everything he said; and Chris Pitt who was about Colm's age, a sensible chap who only spoke when he had something worth saying.

'I think we should forget about the ones from the Isle of Wight and Glasgow,' Bill said. 'The Government has asked us not to travel if our journey's not really necessary. It seems unpatriotic to ask people to come so far – it's unpatriotic of them to apply, come to that,' he growled. 'We should scrub that pair out.'

'Don't be daft, Bill,' Jessie said scornfully. 'If they want to come, we should let 'em. Pass the details around, Colm, there's a luv. Let's see what the buggers have to say for thereselves.'

'One's from a woman,' Colm said casually.

'A woman!' Chris sounded surprised. 'I'd like us to send a woman to Parliament. What's her name, Colm? Is she one of the locals?'

'She's called Elizabeth Phelan, she's forty-two and lives in Wallasey. She's been a member of the party since she was eighteen, apart from a little break when she joined the Communists.' Colm was surprised at how steady he managed to keep his voice.

'The Communists!' Bill spat. 'I don't want to be represented by an ex-Commie.'

'I remember Lizzie Phelan! She used to be in this branch,' Jessie cried. 'Me, I never thought all that much of her, she was much too pleased with herself. Mind you,' she added hastily, 'it doesn't bother me in the least that she was a Communist for a while.'

The arguments raged furiously back and forth between Bill and Jessie, with Chris getting in only the occasional word. Colm hardly spoke at all. In the end, it was decided to invite all four local applicants and two of the London ones to the selection meeting, a decision that took two noisy hours.

Everyone went home, but Colm stayed in the parlour and stared at the photograph of Lizzie Phelan. Unless it was an old one, she'd hardly changed a bit. Her hair was different, curly when it used to be straight – perhaps she'd had it permed. It was an unsuitable photo for the purpose intended, as she was posing like a film star, one shoulder forward and smiling pertly at the camera. He read her neatly typed resumé for the umpteenth time. She hadn't worked as a secretary for years and had come up in the world since then. For a while, she'd worked for an international agency in Paris, then for the same agency in New York. A matter of weeks before the war began she'd come home and was now living over the water with her sister and working for an engineering company in Chester that produced parts for tanks. Colm smiled. It was just like Lizzie to give up a comfortable, well-paid job abroad and return home to take a job in a factory.

She'd made him feel good about himself, Colm remembered with a touch of nostalgia. She was the one who'd convinced him he had a brain. It was all due to Lizzie that he'd started to read books: George

Bernard Shaw, Bertrand Russell, Thomas Paine's *The Rights of Man*, introducing him to a world he hadn't known existed. If it weren't for her, he'd still think himself lucky to have a job like the one in her father's builders' yard. Yet their affair, if you could call it such, had been brief and unpleasant and had nearly wrecked his marriage.

The photo was still in his hand when Brenna burst in. 'Have they gone? I didn't hear them. D'you want a cup of tea, darlin'?'

'Please, luv.' With a feeling of guilt, he shuffled the papers and photos together. 'I've got to write to this lot, tell them whether to come or not, then sort out the selection meeting.' He hoped there'd be more members there than the three who'd come tonight.

He arranged for the meeting to be held in a room over a pub and turned it into a social event by asking people to bring a few refreshments. Brenna was a member of the party, although she found the meetings boring and never came. Under different circumstances, he would have suggested she attend to swell the numbers, but suspected that, even after all this time, Lizzie Phelan's name would be like a red rag to a bull, so didn't mention it and hoped she wouldn't find out until the matter was over and done with. The odds against Lizzie being selected were virtually nil and she'd disappear out of his life for another twenty years – or perhaps this time it would be for ever.

She was by far the best candidate, speaking clearly and concisely, no histrionics or thumping of fists on the table like the male applicants who'd already had their turn – Colm had arranged the speakers alphabetically so Lizzie was next to last. She talked of justice and fairness and her hope for a better world, a world in which women played a bigger part. 'Especially in Parliament,' she said. 'I'm sure you men wouldn't like it if the governance of the country was almost entirely in the hands of the opposite sex.'

She was then subjected to ten minutes of questions, far tougher than those asked of the men, and some quite rude.

'Why aren't you married?' Bill Randal wanted to know.

'Because I've never met a man I wanted to marry,' she replied coolly.

'Didn't you want children?' one of the women demanded.

'As I'm not married, that question is irrelevant.'

'Do you think it's right that women should be in Parliament when there's a war on?'

'I can't think of a single reason why not. It's women who supply the young men who fight the wars for us and they should have a say in the matter.'

Of the thirty-one members who had come to the meeting – five of them women – only two gave Lizzie their vote. Colm was one and Charlie Pitt the other. She was too clever by half for the men and too pretty for the women. What's more, she was unmarried and both sides reckoned there was something dangerous about a woman who had such a narrow waist and pointed breasts, who wore nail polish to match her lipstick, a smart lilac hat to match her smart lilac frock, silk stockings and the highest heels they'd ever seen.

Colm Caffrey recognized the danger most of all. It had been his intention merely to shake Lizzie Phelan's hand, thank her for coming and wish her good luck in the future but, when the meeting was over and Bertram Gilbert had been chosen as the prospective parliamentary candidate for the seat of Toxteth and Dingle, Colm couldn't resist inviting her downstairs to the bar for a drink. He admired her unwillingness to compromise: her speech had expressed her own beliefs and hadn't just told the audience what they wanted to hear. He admired the way she'd dressed as herself, with her nail polish and silk stockings, not in some drab outfit that wouldn't have raised a single hackle.

'You've hardly changed,' he said. 'I'd have recognized you anywhere.' There was scarcely a line on her face and her brown eyes were as bright and vivacious as those of a young girl. She had lost none of her enthusiasm for life or her dedication to making it better, not just for herself, but for everyone.

'And you look far too old for your years, Colm,' she replied with her usual bluntness. 'Why didn't you stand for the seat? You'd have easily won.'

'It didn't cross me mind,' he confessed.

'You underestimate yourself, you always did,' she said crossly. 'You're honest and truthful and would make a marvellous Member of Parliament. I'm surprised your wife didn't try and talk you into it.'

'Brenna doesn't think like that.' Brenna loved him, but she wouldn't consider him capable of becoming a politician.

'She doesn't realize the sort of husband she has. It's about time you started aiming a bit higher, Colm. You know what they say: the sky's the limit.'

He'd only been in Lizzie's presence five minutes and he was already thinking there was nothing he couldn't do. She did wonders for his ego. She produced a packet of cigarettes and offered him one.

'No, ta.' He took the silver lighter from her hand and lit the cigarette for her, conscious of the curve of her cheeks, her long, dark lashes, the way her pink lips puckered with the first puff. 'What's it like living in Wallasey?' he asked.

'Wallasey's fine, but my sister's house is terribly cramped. I'm moving to Liverpool shortly. I've got a job as personnel officer in a munitions factory in Kirkby.'

Colm caught his breath. 'That's where I work.'

'No doubt we'll come across each other from time to time.'

'No doubt we will,' said Colm.

Back in Shaw Street, after a cup of tea and having described the events of the evening to Brenna, omitting all mention of Lizzie Phelan, Colm went upstairs and examined his full-length reflection in the mirror, something he hadn't done in a long while. He saw a tired, round-shouldered man with blurred features, greying hair and the beginnings of a pot belly. His entire body seemed to have sagged and he looked smaller than he'd used to – no wonder Lizzie had said he looked old for his age. He threw back his shoulders, pulled in his belly and straight away looked younger and taller.

After practising a few times, he went down and said to Brenna, 'I think I'll buy meself a new suit, luv, before they go on coupons, like.'

'But there's years of wear in that one, darlin',' Brenna cried.

'Yes, but it's dead old-fashioned. The lapels are too wide and I quite fancy a single-breasted jacket. And I've never liked the colour. I fancy a nice, dark grey.' He couldn't think what had possessed him to buy brown. 'You should have seen the one this Bertram Gilbert chap wore. It probably came from Savile Row and cost a small fortune.'

Brenna laughed. 'You just stick to Burtons, the fifty-shilling tailors. I don't know where this Savile Row place is, darlin', but it's not for the likes of you and me.'

Which, Colm thought, most unfairly, was just like Brenna. She didn't aim high enough.

Eleanor's eyes popped when she opened the door and saw him outside, as well they might, Marcus thought, as he'd never visited the house in Tigh Street before. She looked very pretty in a blue blouse and white skirt, her sunburnt legs bare. He found it hard to believe that this smiling, carefree woman was the little mouse he'd married.

'Good morning.' He tipped his hat. 'I'd like us to have a little talk, if you don't mind.'

'Of course, Marcus.' She graciously stood aside to let him in and he removed his hat and entered an attractive hallway with white woodwork and flowered paper on the walls. 'It's the door at the end,' she said. 'I'm sorry it's in a mess, but I'm in the middle of making a patchwork quilt.'

A treadle sewing machine stood in the corner of the sun-filled room, a colourful quilt flowing from it on to the floor, and squares of brightly patterned material were spread on the table. The French windows were open and he glimpsed a small garden with neat rows of vegetables and a greenhouse packed with climbing plants, reminding him of a jungle. He sat in a small armchair covered in flowered cretonne.

'Would you like a drink?' Eleanor asked. 'There's tea, some rather bitter coffee or lemonade.'

'Nothing, thank you. I was sorry to hear about Jonathan,' he said when she sat opposite in a matching chair.

She waved a dismissive hand. 'I was terribly upset at first, but I'm used to the idea by now. Jonathan can't wait, he's leaving on Saturday. I'm dreading it, but it would be pointless to make a fuss. I shall just have to grin and bear it the way Brenna did when her children left – and now Fergus has come back a hero.' She folded her hands on her knee and looked at him expectantly. 'What did you want us to have a little talk about?'

He coughed awkwardly. 'I was thinking of making a will . . .'

'You're not ill, are you?' she asked quickly, interrupting.

'No, but they say the air raids could start any minute and the odds against being killed have shortened rather for us all. The other day, I remembered that half the house in Parliament Terrace is yours—'

She interrupted again. 'It's taken a long time for you to remember that, Marcus, almost twenty years.'

'I know, and I'm sorry,' he said humbly. 'It didn't cross my mind until I began to think about a will, and I realized I couldn't leave the house to Sybil because I only owned half of it.'

'You can have my half with pleasure,' Eleanor cried. 'I shall never, never live in that house again. *This* is my home now, and I shall stay here until I die. Sybil can have it with my compliments, although I can't see her living in it. She'll probably sell it and buy something a bit more modern.'

As he would be dead if that happened, he didn't care what Sybil did with the house. 'If I give you the address of my solicitor, would you mind writing him a letter to that effect?'

'Of course not, I'll do it today,' she said cheerfully. 'But what about Anthony? Shouldn't he and Sybil share the house? In fact, surely there's no need to make a will if I write the letter? As we are no longer man and wife, everything will automatically go to the children.'

'It's for precisely that reason I wanted to make it. We haven't heard from Anthony in years – at least *I* haven't. Have you?'

'Not since he was eighteen, no. Since then, I've written to him loads of times, but he didn't reply.' She didn't look even faintly upset about it. Jonathan had filled her life to the exclusion of her other children. Although she claimed to love Sybil, he suspected it was more from a sense of duty on her part that she kept the relationship going.

'That's six years ago,' he said sternly. 'The last letter I sent him was returned unopened and marked "No longer at this address". He doesn't deserve anything. If I should die, I don't want him coming back to claim his share of the house, wanting to sell it or wanting to keep it, when Sybil would sooner do the opposite. They never got on and things could get very unpleasant.' There were two things that could set a family at each other's throats: money and property.

Eleanor sighed. 'I suppose you're right. I'm sure Anthony must be doing well in America, else we'd have heard.' Her eyes narrowed. 'Although I wonder how he *is* getting on.'

'Unless he writes and tells us, we shall never know.'

A black cat came wandering through the window and jumped on her knee. She stroked it and it began to purr loudly. 'This is Tosca,' she said. 'She's a stray. Oliver christened her Tosca because she miaows like an opera singer he once heard.'

Marcus smiled thinly. He hated cats.

'There's just one thing, Marcus,' she went on. 'My father had an emerald tiepin and a ring to match. Mummy bought them for him when they got married. I'd like to have them, please. I don't understand legal things, but perhaps you could leave them to me in this famous will of yours?'

'I shall bring them round tomorrow,' he said promptly, 'and anything else you might like to have.'

'Just the ring and the tiepin, they're all I want.' She smiled at him sweetly. 'Oh, Marcus! If only you'd always been so kind. There'd never have been any need for me to leave. We could have been happily married all this time.'

They shook hands politely and he left for the factory, although he would quite liked to have stayed in the sunny room with the half-made quilt and the black cat – and Eleanor. He had never loved her and never would, although they could perhaps be friends. But it was probably too late, as it was too late for so many other things.

The house wasn't the only thing that belonged to them both, Eleanor remembered when Marcus had gone and she sat down again at the sewing machine: her father had also left them half the company each, something he had conveniently forgotten. When she'd first left home – been *thrown out* of her home – she'd been too scared to approach him and demand her share of the profits. But in no time at all she was taking in lodgers and managing perfectly well on her own. She'd felt so proud and had wanted Marcus to know that she didn't need him or the money that legitimately belonged to her. Tomorrow when he came, she'd remind him about the company. It would be something for Jonathan to inherit. Marcus was right: if the raids started, she was as likely to die as anyone and perhaps it would be wise if she also made a will.

She abandoned the quilt, wrote the promised letter to Marcus's solicitor and decided to take a trip into town and deliver it by hand. While there, she would arrange an appointment to make a will of her own. She also wanted to buy some remnants of material for the quilt as she didn't have enough and had used up all the odds and ends of stuff she could find in the house.

With Jonathan's imminent departure put firmly to the back of her mind, she quite enjoyed the day. Perhaps it was Marcus's visit, reminding her of the old days, that made her savour the freedom she now had to do as she pleased. She had coffee in Frederick & Hughes, bought two Revlon lipsticks, both the same shade – it was rumoured that cosmetics, like so many other things, would soon be in short supply – a detective magazine for Fergus who, Brenna reported, was bored out of his skull stuck in the house, some colourful remnants and four yards of crêpe de chine to make a frock: it had been a surprise to discover she was handy with a sewing machine.

On the way home, she called on Nancy and found her in the middle of making an eggless sponge cake, eggs having virtually disappeared from the shops.

'How do they turn out?' Eleanor enquired curiously. As more and more food was being rationed, she was finding it difficult to feed her lodgers.

'A bit like two pancakes stuck together with jam, but his lordship seems to like them. Do you realize tea will be on ration as from the first of July? It's only a few days away.'

Eleanor shuddered. 'How on earth will we manage with only two ounces a week?'

'All we can do is try.'

'You're right.' Very soon, she'd have to manage without Jonathan. Compared to that, tea was a very minor sacrifice.

'He's out,' Brenna announced when Eleanor called in Shaw Street with the magazine for Fergus. 'An ambulance came for him this avvy to take him to a military hospital over the water for an assessment or something. Would you like a cup of tea? Oh, and as from next week, you can bring your own. I'm not prepared to give away a leaf of me precious two ounces, not even to me best friend in the world.' No one knew about the secret store that she was keeping for emergencies.

Jonathan had changed out of his school uniform and was in the kitchen wearing old flannel trousers and a short-sleeved shirt when Eleanor arrived home.

'Hello, Mummy.' He lifted his face for a kiss and she complied with pleasure.

240

'Hello, darling. We're having corned beef salad for tea. Everything's ready and we'll eat as soon as Oliver and Lewis come.'

'They're already here. They're upstairs having a fight.'

'A fight!'

'Well, a very heated argument.'

'What about?' She felt startled. Oliver and Lewis rarely had a difference of opinion let alone an argument, and certainly not a heated one.

'I don't know what about, Mummy. I wouldn't dream of eavesdropping.'

Eleanor had no such inhibitions. She went to the bottom of the stairs and listened. Raised voices were coming from Lewis's room.

'But how could you do this to me, Lewis?' Oliver wailed.

'You've already asked me that a dozen times, Ollie,' Lewis replied in his lovely deep voice with its Scots burr, 'and my answer never varies: I'm not doing anything *to* you. I'm joining up. I want to see some action, not sit pushing pieces of paper around while other men fight this dratted war on my behalf.'

'That's frightfully selfish of you, Lew.' Eleanor could detect a sob in Oliver's response.

'Actually, old chap, it's the very opposite of selfish. Perhaps you'll understand once you've calmed down a bit.'

'I shall never calm down, Lew.'

'Yes, you will. Another year or two and I'd've been called up anyway, and it won't be long before it's your turn.'

Oliver had begun to cry. 'I don't know how I'll live without you.'

'You'll manage, my dear old chap. Now, come over here and let me dry those tears for you . . .'

Eleanor felt tears come to her own eyes. What a beautiful friendship they had! If only all men loved each other the way Oliver and Lewis did, there'd never be a war again.

'Well, young man, I think we can confidently say you'll walk again,' the doctor chortled. He was fiftyish, short and tubby with flaming red hair and millions of freckles. Fergus didn't chortle back. An ambulance had brought him to the military hospital in Bebington, but he'd walked into the doctor's office and it was obvious to anyone with eyes in their head that he was already walking again, although he still needed crutches, as it hurt to put his weight on the injured leg.

'And,' Dr Worthington continued jovially, 'you'll be discharged from the Army as unfit for service.'

Was this another joke? 'Do you mean that?' Fergus gasped.

'Every word,' he was assured with a grin. 'The bullet entered the back of your knee, shattering the bones. You'll have to have an operation to have a metal sleeve inserted and it means you won't be able to bend your knee like you could before, not with so many nuts and bolts inside you. You'll end up with a bit of a limp and we can't have a limping soldier on parade, can we?' He spoke as if he actually owned the bloody Army.

'I suppose not,' Fergus said weakly.

'I suspect that's the best news you've heard in years.'

'What, that I'll walk with a limp for the rest of me days?'

'No, that you're being discharged from the Army.' He was like one of those Cheshire cats, grinning all the time. 'If I were you, I'd be dancing for joy despite a shattered knee. You've done your stint, emerged a hero and now you can sit the war out from a safe distance. You'll even get a few shillings pension.'

'But I wasn't a hero.' Fergus felt tears come to his eyes. He sat up on the bed feeling uncomfortable with the grinning doctor looking down on him. 'I was terrified most of the time and when I threw meself on top of the little French lad, I wasn't even thinking.'

'People aren't brave if they feel no fear, and when you threw yourself and the boy into the ditch, you were behaving quite spontaneously, with no thought for yourself.' The man had stopped grinning and looked sober for a change. He slapped Fergus's good knee. 'You're a hero, young man, and don't you forget it. Now, I'll send a card with the date and time of your operation: it'll probably be mid-July. Would you like a wheelchair to take you out to the ambulance?'

'No, ta. I'd sooner walk. Tara, Doctor, and thanks.'

I'll not be wearing this uniform for much longer, Fergus thought, as he transported himself skilfully along the corridor towards the exit – he was becoming a dab hand with the crutches. He tried to work out how he felt about losing the uniform, but wasn't sure. His brain was still as muddled as it had been in Dunkirk.

'Are you Fergus Caffrey?' A young nurse with jet-black hair cut in a fringe appeared at his side. Fergus nodded.

'We saw your photey in the *Echo* and heard you were coming in. We're both from Liverpool, you see.' A second nurse had appeared at his other side. She was tall and blonde and reminded him of his sister, Cara.

'We've been waiting outside Doctor Worthington's office to have a look at you 'cos the photey only showed you from the back.' The black-haired nurse giggled. 'We didn't expect you to be so good-looking. And you really suit them glasses.' Fergus had acquired a new pair of spectacles. He wasn't quite sure if he needed them or not, but felt more comfortable with them on.

'*Really* good-looking,' echoed the blonde one. 'I'm Pamela by the way, and she's Betty.'

Fergus felt slightly dizzy. 'Pleased to meet you, Pamela and Betty.'

'Do you mind if we come with you as far as the ambulance?' Betty enquired.

'As long as it won't get you in trouble.' He felt even dizzier.

Pamela laughed. 'Oh, we're always in trouble for something or other, so it doesn't matter, does it, Bet?'

'No. How long will it be before you can go dancing again, Fergus?'

'I'm not sure.' Fergus had never been to a dance in his life. He was beginning to enjoy the attention of the two pretty nurses. 'I might not be able to dance any more. I've got to have an operation and the doctor ses I'm likely to end up with a limp.'

'Would you like me and Betty to teach you to dance again?'

'I would like that very much, thank you.'

'Would it be all right if we came to see you? You'd have to give us your address, of course.'

'I'd like that very much, too.' The limp apart, there seemed no end to the advantages of having a German shoot you in the leg.

Chapter 11

Cara slammed her foot on the brake, the car screeched to a halt, and she leapt out and was sick at the side of the road.

'Are you all right, Caffrey?' A concerned Captain Bradley poked his head out of the rear window.

'I'm sorry, sir. It's just my tummy, it seems to be a bit upset.' She felt dead embarrassed as she made her unsteady way back to the Humber and slid behind the wheel. 'I think it must be all the excitement.'

'Of course, you're getting married soon — when is it?'

'The day after tomorrow, sir.' She reached for the ignition, but the captain leaned forward and put his hand on her shoulder.

'Have a little rest before we set off again. I'm in no hurry. Would a little drop of whiskey help? I have a flask in my pocket.'

'That's kind of you, Captain, but I think it might make it worse.' Just the thought of whiskey made her feel nauseous and the blazing sun didn't help. Lately, the heat had been getting her down. She felt as if she was being slowly roasted in an oven, despite not wearing a jacket and having rolled up the sleeves of her shirt.

'Are you getting married in our little chapel in Marzipan Hall?'

'Yes, sir, at midday.' It was just over forty-eight hours away.

'I might pop in if that's all right, wish you good luck.'

'You'd be more than welcome, sir,' she said warmly.

'Have you had any more news about your brother?'

'Not since we last spoke, sir, no. He was going to hospital for an assessment the other day, but I've no idea how he got on.' It had been an enormous relief to get a letter from Mam saying Fergus was safe, if not exactly well.

'Strange thing, Dunkirk,' the captain mused. 'They managed to turn an ignominious defeat into a glorious victory. Clever chappie, Churchill.'

'Indeed he is, Captain.' She was beginning to feel better. At least her heart had stopped racing and her tummy was settling down. Nothing could be done about the sun except to escape from its blistering rays – the sooner, the better. 'I feel OK now,' she said and started up the car again. She was taking the captain to Valletta for a meeting in the same café where she'd met Kit three months before.

Like last time, the meeting was being held in a private room upstairs. When Captain Bradley had disappeared, after asking her to wait and saying he wouldn't be long, Cara removed her cap, settled in a dark corner where it was as cool as it was likely to get in Malta in July, and ordered a cold drink from the waiter with the film star looks. A few minutes later, the same Air Force official as before arrived, but when Cara looked in the hope his driver was Kit, it was a much older man. She didn't mind too much; she wanted to be alone with her thoughts.

It wasn't excitement that was upsetting her tummy, but the consequence of the night she'd spent with Kit in Gozo: a baby. She recalled how much it had hurt, that Kit had called it a disaster, yet it had been the beginning of the new life that was now growing inside her.

She hadn't told Kit, not yet. It had only been the other day that she'd realized the sickly feeling she had every morning, the urge to vomit at the most inconvenient times, going off her food, particularly anything fried, were because she was pregnant and that her life, which had already changed out of all proportion over the last year, was about to change again. She'd thought that she and Kit would continue to see each other regularly, a few times a week, but it would seem this was not to be.

She loved the Army, but as soon as they were married, she would have to leave, go home and have his child, then sit and wait for the war to end and for him to return to a ready-made family.

Her mind was already made up that she would go to Liverpool. She wanted to be near her mother at such a crucial time, although there wouldn't be room in Shaw Street with Tyrone, Maria and the lads already living there. If Lewis Brown had been tempted to volunteer as he'd mentioned that time they'd met, perhaps she could take over his room and become one of Eleanor's lodgers. The rent could be paid out of the allowance she would get from the Army for being Kit's wife.

It would mean telling Mam that she and Kit had got married

months ago and there'd be hell to play for not telling her before, particularly when she learnt it wasn't in a Catholic church. But it would be better than her knowing Cara had been two months pregnant when the wedding took place: she'd take it for granted that she'd *had* to get married. Cara remembered how long it had been before she would so much as speak to Maria for having to marry Tyrone; she wasn't prepared to live under the shadow of her mother's anger until the time came for her to be forgiven, however long that might take.

On the night before her wedding, Cara invited the girls from the billet to Marzipan Hall for a drink in the mess – the two girls on duty reluctantly had to stay behind. They went early at half six, because Kit and Mac were coming at about eight. They raced each other on their bikes all the way from Valletta. Kit usually won, as his legs were the longest.

Within an hour, the girls were in a state of acute inebriation, apart from Cara who stuck to lemonade. Their merriment was infectious and everyone in the crowded mess willingly attached themselves to the end of the chain when they danced the conga, joined in the hokey-kokey and 'Knees Up, Mother Brown', sang 'We'll Meet Again', 'Roll out the Barrel', 'Here Comes the Bride', and every other song they could think of. Cara was kissed and wished good luck so many times she lost count.

Fielding was doing a perfect imitation of Charlie Chaplin when Corporal Culpepper appeared looking extremely cross. 'Is there a single one of you that's sober?' he demanded. The girls fell silent, shuffled their feet and tried not to giggle.

'Only me,' Cara said.

'In that case, Caffrey, get yourself to Valletta in a hurry and collect Lieutenant Banks from headquarters – they haven't got a car to spare, someone else would have brought him. Major Winkworth-Blythe wants him urgently for some reason, probably fancies a game of cards. I've brought a car with me: it's outside, the key's in the ignition and there's a tin hat in case there's a raid. Don't forget to put it on the minute the siren goes.' There'd been two or three raids every week since the first one in May.

'But what about Parker and Hughes?' Fielding cried. Parker and Hughes were the drivers who'd stayed behind.

'Parker's gone to Hal Far to collect someone off a plane: Hughes cut her hand this afternoon and it looks like it's going septic. I had to send her to First Aid.' Culpepper's eyes flashed thunder. 'Are you questioning my orders, Fielding, you little twerp?'

'No, Corpy, but Cara's getting married tomorrow and it hardly seems fair.'

'I know damn well she's getting married tomorrow. Aren't I the one who's giving her away? And I doubt if Major Winkworth-Blythe would see anything unfair about it. *Caffrey!*' the corporal barked. 'Are you still here? Didn't you hear me say something about hurrying?'

'I'm on my way, Corpy.'

It seemed more unfortunate than unfair, Cara thought as she climbed into the car. She'd been enjoying letting her hair down. She was on the verge of moving away when the passenger door opened and Fielding tumbled inside, her hat on back to front and carrying her tie.

'You'd think you'd just robbed a bank,' Cara remarked.

'Thought I'd come with you,' Fielding gasped. 'Drop me off at that shrine by Barracca Gardens and I'll meet up with the blokes. They always come that way and Mac can bring me back on the handlebars of the bike.'

'I'm sure he'll love that.'

'He probably will. I say, Caffrey, this seat's awfully uncomfortable.'

'That's because you're sitting on a tin hat.'

'D'you think it's Culpepper's?' Fielding put the hat on the floor and rested her feet on it. 'If you wear it, you'll probably get nits or something.'

'I don't know who it belongs to.'

'Are you looking forward to tomorrow?'

''Course I am. It'd be pretty peculiar if I weren't. That's a daft question to ask, Fielding,' Cara said as an afterthought.

'I wish you were having a white wedding.' Fielding sighed. 'If I were a proper bridesmaid, I'd wear a purple crinoline and a big lacy hat with a bunch of pink roses on the brim and carry a matching bouquet.'

Cara laughed. 'I don't fancy having a purple bridesmaid and you'd look gruesome dressed like that. It's the sort of thing you'd wear in a pantomime.'

'I think I might have done once, perhaps it's where I got the idea from.'

'If you weren't so pissed, you might want to dress a bit less colourfully.'

'You're probably right.' She lapsed into silence, but not for long. 'What sort of dress would you wear, Caffrey, if you were a proper bride?'

'I'm going to be a proper bride and you're going to be a proper bridesmaid. It's just that we'll be in uniform, that's all.' Oh, but she would have loved to be married in white: a plain, classical style, no frills, no ribbons, no bows, and a waist-length veil secured by a circle of lilies of the valley. She visualized her mother in the front row of the church, full of airs and graces and all done up in powder blue or salmon pink and a gigantic hat with layers of net. Dad would give his only daughter away – it was a coincidence, but Mam had written to say he'd bought a new suit, dark grey, from Burtons the tailors. It sounded perfect for a wedding.

Suddenly, thinking of her father, Cara wanted to cry. Unlike Mam, he never lost his temper, had hysterics, criticized, or so much as raised his voice. He was just *there*, for Mam, for her, for everybody. 'I've got the most wonderful dad in the whole world, Fielding,' she said, choking on the words.

'I'm sure you have, Caffrey.'

'I wish he could be there tomorrow to give me away.'

'Anyone'd be better than Culpepper: King Kong, for instance, or Doctor Crippen.'

'Fielding! Can't you ever be serious?' Cara hid a grin. 'I'm terribly upset because my father can't be there and all you can do is joke.'

'I think I might be incapable of being serious.' Fielding rolled herself into a ball on the seat, just like a kitten. 'I'm going to have a little nap.'

'Fine company you are,' Cara snorted, but Fielding had the enviable ability to fall asleep the very second she closed her eyes and had already started to snore.

Cara hummed 'Here Comes the Bride' as she drove along the deserted road. The night was warm, but bearable, the setting sun a giant orange ball in the faintly darkening sky. There were no smells, all the flowers had withered in the heat. The fields she drove through lay fallow and nothing would grow again until autumn when she would no longer be in Malta, but Liverpool, by which time her baby would have started to show. She caught her breath. It was all so new, so unexpected. To think that in a few weeks, Malta would have just become a memory, like everything that had happened in her life. People often brought back souvenirs from places they had been, and she would have a husband and a child to remind her.

She was just coming up to Barracca Gardens when two men on bikes came into view, pedalling like maniacs. She nudged Fielding, sounded the horn and braked. 'I can spy those blokes you were on about.'

Kit arrived first. He stuck his head through the window and kissed her. 'Hello, darling. This time tomorrow . . .' He left the rest unsaid, just looked at her, and the love in his eyes made her want to weep.

'I know.' This time tomorrow they would be in Gozo putting everything right that had gone wrong before. 'I can't wait,' she breathed.

'Neither can I.'

She could have sat there for ever just looking into his eyes, but remembered Lieutenant Banks, waiting to be collected from headquarters. 'I have to go,' she said, 'but I've got something very important to tell you later.'

'Tell me now,' he demanded.

'No, later.' She laughed. 'Shall we meet in the mess? We can have a drink with the girls.' She would almost certainly pass him on the way back and get there first.

He kissed her again. 'OK.'

She started up the car. Mac was already on his way, wobbling all over the road, with Fielding, in fits of giggles, seated on the handlebars. She waved. 'Bye, Caffrey.'

The siren sounded to indicate an imminent air raid when she stopped outside headquarters and she felt a trickle of fear. She'd never been in Valletta during a raid. Plenty of bombs had fallen in other parts of the island, but their main target was the docks.

Lieutenant Banks was waiting, tapping his thigh impatiently with his stick. He looked pointedly at his watch when she stopped. 'You're late, Caffrey,' he snapped when he climbed in the back.

'I drove as fast as I could,' Cara replied stiffly, adding a reluctant, 'sir'. The lieutenant was young, arrogant and always made her feel as if she'd just crawled from under a stone. Fielding could do a perfect imitation of his posh accent with its strangulated vowels and clipped consonants.

The Italian planes were already visible approaching Malta, the silver fuselages reflecting the setting sun, turning them into dazzlingly exotic insects, deadly insects, Cara thought with a shudder, bearers of death and destruction.

'Haven't they ever heard of camouflage?' the lieutenant sneered.

Cara drove out of Valletta as quickly as she could, accompanied by the dull thud of exploding bombs. Through the rear-view mirror, she could see the sky gradually filling with black smoke. Please God, don't let me be killed before tomorrow, she prayed. It seemed terribly important that she stay alive until she had married Kit. To her horror, a bomb fell somewhere over to her right and she could feel the ground shake. Lieutenant Banks didn't speak and she wondered if he were frightened, too. Smoke and flames blotted out the sun. She pressed her foot on the accelerator and the speedometer shot up to seventy. She'd never driven so fast before, but had to slow down when she saw the two bikes about fifty yards in front. Mac must have worn himself out because Fielding was now sitting on the pannier of Kit's bike. Cara sounded the horn when she overtook them and the men rang their rather rusty bells in reply.

Lieutenant Banks tut-tutted irritably. 'Irresponsible idiots!'

Cara accelerated again. She had driven about half a mile when the ground shook again. She looked left, right and straight ahead, but could see no sign of where the bomb had fallen. It must have been behind. She looked in the mirror, but all it reflected was black smoke.

'Caffrey!' snapped Lieutenant Banks.

'What?'

'Why have you stopped?'

She hadn't realized that she'd stopped, only that she was staring into the mirror, waiting for the bikes to appear.

'*Caffrey!*'

Now she was out of the car, walking back the way she'd come, *running* back, looking for the bikes.

Where were they? They hadn't been all *that* far behind. Why didn't they come, riding through the smoke, Kit, Mac and Fielding, laughing over their narrow escape?

She was nearing the crater where the bomb had fallen when she came to a contorted heap of metal. It was Mac's bike, one of the wheels spinning, making a slight whirring sound. There was no sign of Kit's, but she could see Kit himself, his tall body spread-eagled on the ground, perfectly still. He looked unhurt, but when she got closer, all prepared to smile and kiss him better, she saw he no longer had a face to kiss.

Mac's body was as tangled and twisted as his bike and Fielding lay on her side, as if she'd just closed her eyes and gone peacefully asleep. One of her arms was about six feet away.

Something snapped inside and Cara fell to her knees and began to scream, and continued to scream and scream until someone dragged her roughly to her feet.

'Come on, Caffrey,' Lieutenant Banks said curtly. 'You're not doing any good here. Let's get back to Marzipan Hall and call an ambulance.'

The car had been reversed until it almost reached the crater. Cara was pushed into the passenger seat, her feet nudging the tin hat she'd forgotten to wear, and the lieutenant drove like the wind, while bombs continued to fall and the sky was slowly disappearing behind a veil of smoke.

'Did you know any of those people?' he asked at one point.

'I knew them all,' Cara replied in a deadpan voice.

The Army was being very understanding. She was being sent back to Liverpool for a week's compassionate leave and it was up to her whether she came back to Malta or preferred to be transferred elsewhere.

'But you don't *have* to go,' Sybil told her. 'If you want, you can stay in Malta.'

'I can't,' Cara said. 'I'm expecting a baby.' It was almost two days since the bomb had dropped on the road and, so far as she knew, Sybil was the first person she had spoken to. She reckoned no one knew what to do with her, that's why she was being sent home. A doctor had been and told her to buck up, she'd soon get over it. He'd given her tablets to help her sleep, but she wasn't ill, didn't need to go in hospital, yet wasn't fit to go back on duty. People kept coming into the room, sitting on Fielding's empty bed and saying how sorry they were. But Cara just lay staring at the ceiling and not saying a word. Now it seemed that someone high up must have decided they wanted shot of her and the best thing was to send her home to recover, although Cara knew that she would never recover from the sight that had met her on the road to Valletta; it would stay with her until her dying day. She wished now she'd told Kit about the baby, so he would have known he was about to become a father before he died.

'That changes everything,' Sybil said practically. She didn't look particularly surprised. 'You'll be discharged from the Army, although it'll take a couple of weeks for the discharge papers to come through.'

'But I don't know where to go,' Cara said piteously, 'Mam will kill me – discharged for getting pregnant! You know what she's like. She thinks the Caffreys are superior to everyone else and she'll be dead ashamed on top of everything else. She wouldn't want me at home for all the neighbours to see, even if there was the room.'

'My father would be the same.' Sybil chewed her lip. 'Is there no one else you can stay with?'

'I can't think of a soul.' Cara wept.

'You know what I'd do if I were in your position? I'd go and see Nancy Gates. She seems to have answers for everything.'

'But she's bound to tell Mam; they're friends.'

'No, she won't.' Sybil shook her head emphatically. 'Not if you tell her in confidence.'

Cara was inclined to believe this was true, but it didn't solve all her problems. 'Mam will wonder why I'm not writing to her any more.'

'Still write, but send the letters to me and I'll post them on to your mother and send hers to you. I won't mention a word about this to my mother either.'

'You're being awfully kind, Sybil.'

'I'm your superior officer and it's my job to look after you,' Sybil said a touch prissily. 'Under the circumstances, I couldn't very well be *un*kind.' She got to her feet and smoothed her hands over the creases in her skirt. 'Unless you want to hang on for the funerals, I'll arrange transport home as soon as possible; it'd probably be best if you went by plane in your condition, rather than ship. Wear uniform, but leave everything else behind apart from your personal possessions. Have you got a bag of your own?' Cara nodded; she still had her old suitcase. Sybil opened the door. 'It's no use wishing you a pleasant journey, not with the way you must be feeling, but I hope it goes without a hitch. By the way, if you see my father, give him my regards.'

'I'd like to go as soon as possible, please.' She had no wish to hang on for the funerals. Kit was dead and nothing else mattered. Later, when she packed, she threw away the little china lady Mam had given her. It hadn't brought her a shred of luck and she never wanted to see it again.

As Sybil had hoped, the journey went smoothly but Cara felt sick the entire way, not just because she was pregnant, but because of the way things had turned out. She'd been expecting change, had been looking forward to finding somewhere to live, having the baby, waiting for Kit to come home. She had imagined sending him the baby's photograph, describing its day-to-day progress. 'He can sit up, walk, say "Mummy" but I'm teaching him to say "Daddy" too.' She had a feeling that the baby was a boy. But now she didn't even have a photo of Kit and she was worried she would forget what he looked like, because all she could remember was Kit without a face.

She flew on a naval cargo plane, the only woman in a handful of passengers. The few seats were hard and uncomfortable, the engines grated noisily and there was a lot of turbulence. With each mile, her spirits, already low, sank even lower, until she felt as if she were at the bottom of a deep, black pit from where there was no escape and where she was destined to spend the rest of her days. There wasn't a single thing to look forward to, not even the baby. She'd wanted it before, but then Kit, the father, had been alive. Now she would give birth to a child who would be stigmatized all its life because it was a bastard. How would she support it? What sort of job could she get with a baby to look after?

It was late afternoon when the plane landed at an airfield in Suffolk where it was only fractionally less hot than it had been in Malta. Was she expected? Cara wondered, as she followed the few passengers to a single-storey building where she was glad to see refreshments were being served. She couldn't be completely dead inside as she was dying for a cup of tea.

She was seated in a comfortable easy chair, drinking the tea, having refused the sandwiches and cakes pressed on her by a middle-aged woman in a flowered overall who was in charge of the food stall, when a young airman approached.

'Private Caffrey?'

'That's me.'

'I'm Connors and I'm to drive you to London, Euston Station to be precise. I understand you're heading for Liverpool?'

Cara nodded. Connors was small and dark and remind her very much of Mac. She felt the urge to cry, but tightened her lips, determined not to. 'That's right.'

'We'll go when you've finished your tea, there's no need to hurry.'

Connors never stopped talking the whole way to Euston Station. Fortunately, he didn't seem to mind if he received a reply and seemed quite satisfied with Cara's occasional accommodating grunts.

The station was crowded to the point of suffocation, as if the entire population of an overheated London had decided to leave the capital, all at the same time and in the same direction. The air smelled of soot and smoke. Cara identified the Liverpool train and her heart sank when she saw it was packed to capacity, with passengers stuffed like sardines in the corridors.

'You'd better get on quick, luv,' a porter warned. 'It's leaving in a minute.'

A door opened and eager hands reached to pull her on; soldiers, a whole regiment of them. Cara gulped; she wasn't in the mood to spend an uncomfortable few hours with a pile of raucous soldiers who'd flirt with her and expect her to flirt back. But she had no choice. She was about to allow herself to be yanked on board, when a man in railway uniform caught her arm.

'Come and sit in the guard's van with me, luv.' He led her towards the dimly lit van. 'I noticed you before. You look like death warmed up, if you don't mind me saying. Feeling a bit under the weather, are you?'

His name was Cecil and he came from Liverpool. 'Anfield, right next to Liverpool Football Club. Trouble is, I support Everton.'

Cara travelled home in the company of two dogs in a cage, a rabbit in a hutch, several bikes, two large prams and Cecil, who shared with her the flask of cocoa made by his wife, then left her alone to wallow in her misery. 'You don't look as if you feel much like talking, luv.'

It was the last thing she felt like doing, along with virtually everything else she could think of.

★

Nancy Gates was fast asleep after an exceptionally hectic day. Since the war started, Nancy had twice as much to do. At the outset, she had given up her political activities and joined the Red Cross, the Townswomen's Guild and had, recently, the Women's Voluntary Service. Apart from looking after Marcus, she gave First Aid lessons once a week, having gained a certificate, attended sewing days with Brenna and Eleanor, knitted socks for servicemen and could now turn a heel without looking at the pattern. This particular day had been spent pushing a handcart round Toxteth, knocking on doors asking for salvage.

'Anything will do: paper, metal, old tyres, jam jars, old light bulbs, batteries and books – the books are for the forces, not for scrap.'

The main response had been: 'I'll have a look, luv. Call back again tomorrer and I'll let you have what I've got.'

Not normally one to go to bed early, no matter how exhausted she might be, Nancy had nevertheless thought it wise to turn in before her usual time of midnight, as it seemed tomorrow was likely to be as hectic as today.

She had no idea how long she'd been asleep when she became aware that someone was hammering on the basement door. She considered ignoring it, telling herself it was probably a drunk come to the wrong house, when a woman's voice called, 'Nancy.' The woman sounded desperate.

Groaning, she staggered out of bed, put on the thick woollen dressing gown that she wore winter and summer, pushed her large feet into a pair of men's slippers and went to answer the door.

At first, she thought there was no one there until her eyes got used to the dark and she could see a woman sitting on the bottom of the basement steps. Her heart turned over.

'Brenna!'

'It's me, Cara. I was beginning to think you'd gone away.'

'Lord Almighty! You gave me quite a turn, pet. I couldn't see you were wearing a uniform and it's almost twenty years since I opened the door and found your mam sitting in exactly the same position.'

'I'm sorry, Nancy. Can I come in?'

'Of course, pet. What on earth are you doing here?' she asked when the door was closed and a thick curtain pulled over it so not a chink of light would show. Automatically, she filled the kettle and switched it on. There was plenty of tea as she'd managed to convert Marcus from tea to coffee so he hardly used any of his ration.

'I don't know where to start,' Cara whispered. The poor child looked done in. Her eyes were red-rimmed, her face pale and her long neck drooped like the stem of a dying flower.

'Try the beginning, pet,' Nancy suggested gently. She couldn't begin to guess what had brought Cara back from Malta to the house in Parliament Terrace or why hadn't she gone straight to her mam's.

'The other day,' Cara said tiredly, 'I was going to get married, but the . . . the man got killed the night before and now I'm expecting his baby and I don't want Mam to find out. Sybil said you'd know what to do.'

Nancy could hardly believe her ears. Her heart turned over a second time. 'You poor girl! What a terrible thing to happen.' She put her arm around Cara's thin shoulders and led her to a chair. 'You really need your mam at a time like this, pet.'

'No!' Cara shook her head emphatically. 'Mam will shout and scream and I couldn't stand it, not right now. I want to be somewhere quiet. I'll face Mam when the baby's born, I'll feel stronger then.' She began to cry, hard racking sobs. 'Kit's dead and I'll never love another man again.'

'How did he die, Cara?'

'It was a bomb, it tore his face off. Oh, Nancy, I can't get it out of me mind.' She closed her eyes. 'I can see him now, lying in the road, Mac too, and Fielding. One of her arms had been torn off.'

'Cara, my poor, dear girl.' Nancy felt like crying herself. That Cara, so sweet and blameless, should suffer such a tragedy only confirmed her long-held belief that there was no such person as God. A halfway decent God would never allow such an horrific war to start in which young men had their faces blown off and innocent people were slaughtered in their thousands. Any God worth his salt wouldn't let someone like Hitler be born into His world, let alone permit him to flourish.

There followed a long silence during which Nancy could think of nothing to say and Cara seemed to fall asleep, yet remained sitting up in the chair. Nancy wondered how long she'd been travelling. Outside, there wasn't a sound to be heard. It used to be possible to hear the trams hurtling along Upper Parliament Street, but these days they just crawled along like ghosts in the blackout, their lights hardly visible until they were right on top of you. On any normal midsummer night, there'd still be plenty of people about, singing at the top of their voices as they made their way home from the pubs and picture houses, but things were no longer normal. Nancy wondered how long it would be before they were, and hoped she'd be alive to see the day.

Cara whimpered in her sleep and she wondered what on earth she could do for the girl. She was right about her mother. Brenna had a kind heart, but couldn't control her temper and would be no good for Cara the state she was in. The poor girl would be inundated with questions and more questions, castigated for being pregnant, given no peace. She needed a quiet place to grieve for the man called Kit and think about her future with Kit's child.

Well, there's nothing I can do right now, Nancy thought. Perhaps I'll think of something tomorrow. In the meantime, she'd ask Marcus if it was all right if Cara stayed the night. The old Marcus would have thundered a derisive, 'No,' but she felt the new one would be quite amenable to the idea. Like her, he kept late hours and would almost certainly be listening to the wireless in his study.

Marcus listened to every single news bulletin in the hope Malta would be mentioned, although it rarely was. He recognized the strategic importance of the island, knew that the Italians had been bombing the place since May, but that was all. He was worried about Sybil, wishing she would write more often. Cara Caffrey wrote to her parents regularly and Nancy supplied him with any news there was.

He sighed, turned the wireless off and stared at the virgin-white blotter on his desk. He couldn't remember when he'd last done work in his study and was even losing interest in the factory, as it ran quite smoothly without him. The workers that were left were fully occupied with producing asbestos sheeting for the Navy; new business was no longer required and neither was he. He kept meaning to get involved in the war effort, but it meant mixing with other people when he'd far rather be alone, yet at the same time he felt utterly sick of his own company. 'There's no pleasing you, Marcus,' his mother used to say, he couldn't remember for what reason.

There was a tap on the study door and he called, 'Come in, Nancy.' He quite welcomed a visit from his housekeeper. Lately, they'd been having quite interesting discussions about the war, although not usually at such a late hour, just past midnight, he noticed, glancing at his watch.

'I've got someone downstairs, Mr Allardyce,' Nancy announced. 'It's Cara Caffrey and she's in terrible trouble, poor child. I wondered if she could stay the night? I always keep the bed in Eleanor's old room aired, in case we have an unexpected visitor, like.'

'What sort of trouble?' he asked. He was astonished that Cara should be under his roof when he'd assumed she was in Malta with Sybil.

Nancy explained Cara's situation with a great deal of dramatic waving of her big hands, finishing with, 'She's asleep now and I don't know what to do with her. If necessary, she can have my bed and I'll sleep on the couch, but seeing as there's beds to spare upstairs . . .'

'Put her in Eleanor's old room, but what about tomorrow? Where will she go then?'

Nancy shrugged. 'I dunno. It seems it was Sybil who sent her to me, so I'll just have to think of something, won't I? Oh, and don't mention this to anyone, will you? Cara doesn't want Brenna to know she's home.'

It took quite a while for Cara to deduce where she was when she woke up in an opulent bedroom with black lacquered furniture and a turkey-red carpet. She sat up, head thudding, and took in the cream, satin-striped wallpaper, the red velvet curtains around which daylight glimmered. A fancy white-and-gold clock on the wall showed it was quarter past nine.

Was this a dream? Had the whole thing been a dream, including Kit? She pressed her hands against her swollen eyes and remembered that she'd left Malta early the previous day. The plane had landed in Suffolk and a young airman called Connors, who'd been very like Mac, had driven her to Euston Station where she'd caught the train to Liverpool, then had walked through the blackout to Parliament Terrace to see Nancy.

That's where she was, in the Allardyces' house and it wasn't a dream, but real. She faintly remembered Nancy helping her upstairs, helping to take off her uniform.

'You can sleep in your petticoat. It won't hurt for once. Now, come on, pet, into bed you get. You'll feel better in the morning.'

And Cara *did* feel better, although only in her body, not her head. She would never feel better in her head, but she felt fitter after a good night's sleep in a quiet room where she felt completely safe and cut off from the world and everyone in it except for Nancy Gates – Mr Allardyce would have gone to work by now. Where she would sleep tonight was a different matter altogether.

She wondered if it were possible to have a bath. She got out of bed, pulled back the curtains and gaped at the sight of the tall building, very close, that blocked out any chance of sunlight reaching the room. It was the Protestant cathedral, she remembered, still not finished after almost thirty years. The room must be at the back of the house.

Her suitcase was on a chair beside the bed. She opened it and pulled out her red dress. It was badly creased, but she put it on all the same and went to look for Nancy.

Marcus was wandering around the house wondering what to do with himself, whether or not to go into the factory, or shut himself in the study, when he met Cara coming down the stairs. They both jumped; he'd forgotten she was there and no doubt she'd thought he'd be out by now.

'How are you feeling today?' he asked.

'Better,' she said bravely. 'Much better.'

'I'm sorry about what happened, Nancy told me about it.'

'So am I. Thank you very much for letting me stay in your house last night. Oh, in case I forget, Sybil said to give you her love.' He doubted that very much; she was just being kind. 'I was just about to ask Nancy if I could have a bath.'

'Of course, there's plenty of hot water and there's a bathroom next to the room where you slept.'

'Cara? Is that you, pet?' Nancy must have heard them talking. 'There's a pot of tea made down here.'

'I'll be down in a minute.' She looked at him with her big blue eyes bright with unshed tears. 'Will you excuse me?'

Marcus nodded and stood aside to let her pass. She disappeared down the stairs to the kitchen. He followed and stood at the top, listening.

'I looked in on you earlier, and you were dead to the world,' he heard Nancy say. 'I thought it best to let you sleep, wake up in your own time, as it were. How d'you feel this morning?'

'Much better,' Cara said again, although Marcus suspected it was a lie. 'I've just been speaking to Mr Allardyce. He's awfully kind, isn't he?'

Nancy chuckled. 'You're probably the first person in the world to say that.'

'Oh, but he is!' Cara protested. 'He was kind to our Fergus too when he gave him a job in his factory. I remember Eleanor used to call him all sorts of names, I can't think why.'

'I expect Eleanor had her reasons. Look, pet,' Nancy said seriously, 'I was awake half the night wondering what to do with you and I haven't come up with a single idea. There's homes for unmarried mothers, usually run by some church or other, but they're terribly strict places, not very pleasant.'

'I don't mind,' Cara cried. 'Anywhere will do. It'll only be for seven months, then I shall have to sort meself out.'

She was so naive, Marcus thought. Somehow, she'd managed to reach the age of nineteen without having learnt that people could be very cruel, that not everyone thought the same as she did. He moved swiftly to his study when he heard Nancy say, 'I'll just take Mr Allardyce up a cup of coffee.'

'What's happening with Cara?' he enquired innocently when Nancy came in.

'All I can think of is a home for unmarried mothers,' she replied. 'I feel awful, if the truth be known. I feel as if I'm letting her down – Sybil, too.'

'You can't do the impossible,' he said. 'Look, why not let Cara stay here for however long it takes for her to have the baby? Then you won't be letting either her or Sybil down.'

'Do you really mean that?' Nancy looked at him with disbelief.

'I wouldn't say it if I didn't mean it,' he snapped. Did she think him such an ogre that he was incapable of a single kind gesture? It would make a change to have someone living in the house who liked him: no one else did.

Cara never left the house, not even for Mass. She wasn't remotely happy, but she was in the perfect place to be *un*happy. Nancy was out most of the day, Mr Allardyce spent most of time in his study or at the factory, and she had had the run of the house except for Tuesday and Friday mornings when the cleaner came and Cara locked herself in her room.

'Mrs Clegg is the only paid help left,' Nancy said. 'Time was we had a maid, someone to do the washing and a woman who came in Sundays to make the meals. These days, I send the washing to the laundry and look after the place meself. But your mam and Mrs Clegg know each other, so you'd best keep out of her way.'

It was a gloomy house, full of dark shadows and cool even on the warmest of days. Nancy would come in, mopping her brow, saying, 'By jingo, it's hot out there,' but Cara preferred the house the way it was after the scorching heat of Malta.

She never got bored, even if she spent half the day lying on the bed wishing things had gone differently and she was Mrs Christopher Farthing. Sometimes, she wrote letters to Kit, telling him how she felt, then tore them up in floods of tears. She wrote to Mam and Dad, pretending she was in Malta, and sent the letters to Sybil who sent them all the way back to Liverpool with a Maltese postmark, then did the same with the letters that arrived for Cara.

Sybil declared herself tickled pink with the idea of Cara living in Parliament Terrace. 'Daddy must have had a brainstorm,' she wrote. 'I've only ever known him to be pleasant with me. He must be mellowing in his old age.'

Sometimes, Mam or Eleanor came to visit Nancy, or they both came together, and Cara would sit on the stairs, listening to her mother's loud voice, heart thumping, worried she might creep up and find her there – what her reaction would be was beyond the bounds of even Cara's vivid imagination.

According to Mam, Fergus was having a whale of a time, girls coming to see him every night, even taking him to the pictures and teaching him to dance. He'd been discharged from the Army. Cara winced when she heard this. Her own discharge had arrived, but it wasn't for an honourable reason like Fergus.

According to Mam, since Fergus had come home, Tyrone was even more steeped in despair than he'd been before. 'I don't know what to do with him, I really don't,' Mam declared. 'And neither does Maria. All he does with them poor kids is bite their heads off.'

There were lots of novels in the parlour with 'This book belongs to Eleanor Wallace' written on the flyleaf. They were by authors such as Jane Austen, George Eliot and Charles Dickens. Never one for reading much, nevertheless, Cara found that once she'd started a novel, she became so absorbed she couldn't put it down.

Only one thing spoiled Cara's quiet, limited existence in the house in Parliament Terrace and that was the air raids that had started in July, at first the bombs dropping harmlessly in fields damaging only the crops. Next month, the raids became more frequent and the bombs crept closer. The docks were hit, the Customs House, Mossley Hill church, and ordinary streets with ordinary houses where a lot of people died, people who'd done no harm to anyone in their lives.

Nancy and Mr Allardyce stayed in their beds and ignored the raids, but Cara woke the very second the siren sounded – that's if she'd gone asleep in the first place. She couldn't understand how anyone could sleep through the hideous wail of the siren, the drone of the approaching planes, followed by the dull thud of bombs exploding all over the city.

With every raid, Cara relived the night in Malta when she'd lost Kit. Everything would come back, as if it had only happened yesterday, and she would go downstairs in the pyjamas that were now too small for Nancy, yet were too big for her, sit in the kitchen and try to read her book, but found it impossible to concentrate. There were public shelters not far away, but even if there had been no chance of seeing someone she knew, the stoutly built house probably offered more protection than a shelter in the case of a direct hit.

During these quiet times in the kitchen, Cara reviewed her own situation. She wasn't the only woman in the world who had lost a loved one. She would never cease to mourn Kit, but the fact she was single and pregnant was probably common to a lot of young women in wartime and she was one of the luckiest, living where she was in a comfortable house with Nancy to look after her. As Mam would have said, she'd landed on her feet – she'd said the same thing when Fergus had got the job with H.B. Wallace. Then, as now, it was the much-maligned Mr Allardyce who'd turned up trumps.

September came and the raids were even heavier. Nancy remarked they'd woken her; Mr Allardyce said he'd found them rather worrying. The next time Cara went down to the kitchen in the middle of the night, Nancy was already there in her dressing gown in the process of making tea. Five minutes later, Mr Allardyce, wearing a grey silk robe, joined them, just as an explosion rocked the house.

'Bloody hell!' Nancy gasped. 'That was close.'

That was the night the cathedral was hit, destroying many of the stained-glass windows. Next day, Nancy reported the building was surrounded by craters. 'There's one right outside our back door.'

From then on, every time the siren went, all three would meet in the kitchen, Mr Allardyce with a couple of bottles of wine from the cellar, which he shared with Nancy; Cara preferred tea. By the time the raid was over, she would be the only clear-headed person there.

'If I'm going to die,' Nancy said once. 'I'd sooner do it when I'm as drunk as a lord, rather than as sober as a judge.'

'Hear, hear!' echoed Mr Allardyce.

An unlikely camaraderie developed between them and they began to play cards during the raids, aces high and poker, using cutlery for money, each knife, fork or spoon worth a thousand pounds. Cara had learned to play poker in the Army and was good at reading people's faces and guessing if the cards they had were good or bad. She would throw in thousands of pounds' worth of spoons and end up winning a fortune, even if the cards in her hand were hopeless.

'I'll be a millionaire in no time,' she laughed one night when the all-clear sounded and she collected her winnings. Her expression changed. 'I can't remember the last time I laughed,' she said in a shocked voice.

'Let's hope it won't be such a long time before you laugh again.' Nancy patted her hand. 'Now, put that cutlery back in the box. It'll be needed tomorrer.'

Nancy had found loads of baby clothes in the drawers in Nurse Hutton's old room. 'They just need a wash,' she declared, 'get rid of the smell of mothballs.'

'They're lovely,' Cara breathed as she sorted through the pretty embroidered gowns, hand-knitted cardigans, booties and bonnets, a satin christening robe, a crocheted shawl, dozens of warm vests, pretty socks and loads of napkins. Everything was white and some things looked as if they'd never been worn. Nancy said there was a pram in the cellar and a cradle in the loft. 'Will Mr Allardyce mind if I have them?' Cara asked.

'He won't mind a bit.' Nancy winked. 'He likes you. It's not often Marcus likes someone, but he does you. Any road, pet, that's the baby clothes sorted, but what about you? You're already bursting out of that frock and you've still got another four months to go. There's probably some of Eleanor's old frocks still in her wardrobe. I'll see if I can turn two into one and make you a maternity frock.'

'Thank you, Nancy, I don't know what I'd have done without you – or Mr Allardyce.' Cara looked at her shyly. 'I like him too, by the way.'

She was reading when he went into the living room, her feet on a stool, but put the book down immediately she saw him. He got on better with her than he'd ever done with Sybil.

'Hello.' Her smile lit up the room. 'What's it like outside? It looks awfully cold and windy. I watched people go past snuggled inside their coats and holding on to their hats.'

'It's exactly that,' Marcus said, 'cold and windy, a typical November day. What's that you're reading?'

'*Pickwick Papers*, it's dead funny. Have you read it?'

'I did when I was a child.'

She snorted. 'You must have been a very clever child. Me, I only read comics.'

'I liked comics too,' he conceded. He noticed there were a handful of coals burning in the grate giving off hardly any heat. 'That's not much of a fire,' he remarked.

'We're virtually out of fuel. All of a sudden there's a shortage and we've only a little bit of coke left. No more will be delivered until Friday, and then it won't be much. I hope you don't mind, but Nancy lit that just for me. She's got visitors, else I'd be in the kitchen helping to make tea. It's lovely and warm down there. I made some fairy cakes earlier,' she said proudly. 'I don't know what they'll taste like, they're little more than flour and water and a bit of margarine.'

'I'm sure they'll taste very nice.' He liked the way she'd said '*we're* virtually out of fuel', as if she belonged there and they were all mucking in together. By now, she genuinely was better and the fighting spirit she'd inherited from her mother had come back, although her face sometimes bore an expression of utter desolation if she thought no one was looking. 'I've bought you something,' he said bashfully. He fetched the Frederick & Hughes carrier bag he'd left in the hall and gave it to her. 'Call it a late birthday present.' She'd turned twenty about six weeks ago.

'What is it?' She delved into the bag and brought out the turquoise velvet dressing gown he'd got that afternoon. 'Oh! Oh, it's *beautiful!*' Her face turned pink and she clutched the gown to her chest. 'Oh, Mr Allardyce, you shouldn't have. It's not right. You've already been incredibly generous, letting me live here, like. This is too much.'

'To tell the truth,' he said, making a joke of it so she wouldn't feel so embarrassed, 'I'm sick of seeing you in those giant pyjamas. And this house gets very cold in the winter and we won't be able to have fires in every room as we used to. Try the thing on, see if it fits,' he suggested.

She put it on and twirled round a few times. 'What d'you think?'

'Very smart.' He nodded. 'Very smart indeed.'

'It's lovely and warm,' she breathed, smoothing her hands over her stomach as if she was caressing the baby inside. She sighed. 'Poor thing, he doesn't what lies ahead of him, does he?'

'What do you mean?' He was at a loss to know why she thought it was a boy.

'He won't have a name, only mine, and that's not worth anything.'

Marcus thought of something he could do about that, but he'd wait until he knew her better.

The next time Mam came to see Nancy she was in a terrible mood, understandably given the circumstances. The night before, a bomb had dropped in the next street and the front windows in the house in Shaw Street had been shattered in the blast.

'Colm's taken the day off to fix them, but all he can fit is plywood for now. It'll be desperately miserable inside. Joey and Mike had fits of hysterics when it happened and Maria screamed her head off. And didn't I have to cope with everything on me own? Colm was out, him being an ARP warden, like, and our Tyrone wasn't there. He never is; he just sits in the pub until it closes and, if there's a raid, the pub stays open until the all-clear goes, although they're not supposed to.' She paused for breath. 'And our Fergus! Well, all I can say is I'm dead disappointed in our Fergus. You know that woman he's been knocking around with?'

'You mean Jessie Clifford?' Nancy queried.

'Indeed I do,' Mam huffed. 'The one with the dyed blonde hair and eyes like cockroaches. Well, didn't he only go and spend the whole night in her house! Not only is she ten years older than him, but she's got a husband in the Merchant Navy. I called him every name under the sun when he came back this morning, but he told me to mind me own business.'

'Well, it isn't really any of your business, is it, pet?' Nancy said mildly.

'It is while he's living under *my* roof, Nancy. If only our Cara were home,' she continued fretfully. 'She's got a sensible head on her shoulders and at least she'd be someone to talk to. But nowadays even she only writes once a fortnight when she used to write every week.' She sniffed wretchedly. 'All me kids are letting me down, Nancy.'

'Don't be daft, Brenna,' Nancy said a touch impatiently. 'Fergus isn't letting *you* down by seeing a married woman and Tyrone can't help being depressed. As for Cara, I expect she has loads to do in Malta. You're lucky she writes once a fortnight. I can't remember when Marcus last had a letter from Sybil.'

Then Mam began to cry and Cara went upstairs, ashamed of herself for eavesdropping, feeling dead sorry for her mother, but at the same time a bit irritated that she expected her children to be perfect. She didn't know, not yet, that Cara was the most imperfect of them all.

The raids continued, becoming even more destructive, as hundreds and hundreds of German bombers flew over Liverpool, dropping their lethal cargo on the city, as if intent on wiping it off the face of the earth. The atmosphere in the kitchen became more animated, even rowdy, when they played cards. The longer the raid continued the more wine Nancy and Marcus drank – he'd insisted Cara stop calling him Mr Allardyce. Nancy, whose language could be earthy at the best of times, cursed loudly at every explosion, and Marcus, normally so unsmiling and serious, discovered a dry wit when in his cups. They both made Cara laugh, even though she knew they could all die at any minute and she was worried sick for her family in Shaw Street. Yet she thought she couldn't have endured the raids in a better place or with such enjoyable company.

★

Christmas came and by now she was huge, the baby due to arrive in about six weeks. December had been relatively free from attacks, but a few days before Christmas the siren went at half past six, signalling the start of a heavy bombardment that lasted until the early hours of the morning. The next night, the city suffered an assault that continued for almost twelve hours and Christmas Eve saw no let up.

They couldn't play cards, laugh or joke, not while the carnage continued outside. It was half past one on Christmas morning when the all-clear went, and the sound had never been so welcome. Cara climbed the stairs to her bedroom with a heavy tread and a heavy heart. What sort of crazy world was she bringing her baby into? At the top, she paused by the window on the landing and drew the curtain back. It was as if every part of Liverpool was on fire, the flames turning the sky livid red. This was surely what hell must look like, she thought angrily. She could hear the urgent clang of fire engines and the scream of ambulances as they raced along the streets. How many people had died tonight? Her father had been out in all this mayhem and she prayed he was all right and that Shaw Street was still standing and everyone there was safe. Nancy had promised to check first thing in the morning, *Christmas* morning, normally such a joyous occasion, a time for giving and receiving, for prayers and carols and going to Mass, not for grieving and checking if people were dead or alive.

The baby gave her a fierce kick. She hugged her stomach and promised him that he would be all right, that she would keep him safe, although she knew the promise was an empty one. If ever there was another war, mothers would have no say in whether their sons would be sacrificed in order to restrain one man's vanity and his insane desire to force his will on the world.

It was an icy cold day at the end of January when Cara's baby arrived. She was in the kitchen, still in her dressing gown, having breakfast when she had the first contraction, but didn't mention it to Nancy until the second one came.

'I'll ask Marcus to alert the midwife,' Nancy said calmly.

Cara had refused to see a doctor during her pregnancy, claiming she felt exceptionally well and that there was no need. And, she added, she preferred to have a midwife in attendance when her time came.

'But what if there are complications?' Marcus had asked, looking worried.

'We can call a doctor then,' Cara said simply.

He came rushing into the kitchen now, looking flustered. 'I've called the midwife. I told her to come round straight away.'

Cara laughed. 'But there's no need, she'll be sitting around with nothing to do for hours. I've only had a few mild contractions. Whoops! There's another.' She winced. 'That one hurt.'

'I think you'd be best in bed, pet,' Nancy said. 'I'll start boiling some water.'

'But I don't want to go to bed!'

'And I don't want you having the baby on me kitchen floor. Get to bed this very minute and I'll bring you up a cup of tea.'

'You're trying to make me out an invalid,' Cara said sulkily. She went upstairs reluctantly, Marcus hovering anxiously behind. She was just about to open the door of her room, when a wave of pain made her double up in agony. Marcus helped her into bed just as the front door bell rang.

'That'll be the midwife.' He virtually ran out of the room. A few minutes later, the midwife, rosy-faced and briskly efficient, entered, followed by Nancy with pans of hot water and old sheets.

'You're far too early,' Cara told them sternly. 'The baby won't be born for ages yet.'

'Let me be the judge of that, young lady. Now, lie down flat and lift up your nightie.'

Cara giggled and did as she was told and, as the midwife told her colleagues a few hours later, 'It was almost as if the mother lifting her nightie acted as a signal to the baby, because it came shooting out, taking us all by surprise, the mother most of all. Oh, and it was a girl, a beautiful little girl, absolutely perfect – magnificent pair of lungs on her, too. She weighed a fraction under nine pounds and she's to be called Kitty.'

Kitty quickly established herself as ruler of the household. When she was asleep, Nancy and Marcus tiptoed around, worried they would wake her. Awake, and her golden curls, so much like Cara's, would be admired, her blue eyes with their long lashes, her little pink mouth and long white limbs.

'She's going to be tall, like you,' Nancy said to Cara.

'Isn't she!' Cara said gleefully. Once she'd got over the shock of her son turning out to be a daughter, she'd fallen head over heels in love with Kitty, who only cried when she was hungry or her nappy needed changing and otherwise was no trouble at all. 'I can't believe I'm a mother,' she said in an awed voice.

'What about your own mother, pet?' Nancy asked gravely. 'Isn't it about time she knew about Kitty? You said you were going to tell her after the baby had been born.' By now, Kitty was a fortnight old.

Cara hung her head. 'I know, but I've only made things worse, living here all this time and Mam not knowing a thing about it, haven't I? She'll be even madder now than she would have been before. If I'd gone straight to Shaw Street when I got back from Malta, she'd have got over it by now.'

'But you couldn't have lived there,' Nancy reminded her. 'There wasn't the room – your Fergus has to sleep on a camp bed in the parlour – and, even if there had been, Brenna wouldn't have been exactly keen on the whole world knowing her daughter was having a baby on the wrong side of the blanket. I love your mam, Cara, but she has her faults like everyone else, including meself. The thing is, though, you can't keep Kitty a secret for ever. You can't stay inside the house for ever, either. It's cold now, but as soon as the weather improves the baby will need fresh air – you could do with some yourself an' all. What happens if you're out and you come face to face with your mam?'

Cara groaned. She'd got herself into a terrible predicament and didn't know how to get out of it.

March blew itself in, and with it came clear skies, a weak sun and an increase in the temperature. Cara started to take Kitty for walks very early in the morning when there was hardly anyone about. She pushed the pram around the centre of the city, seeing for the first time the huge crater in Hanover Street, not far from Frederick & Hughes, Eleanor's favourite shop, the spot where a mine had fallen, only just missing the Adelphi Hotel, and other familiar buildings reduced to heaps of rubble. The Town Hall had been damaged and incendiary bombs had set St George's Hall alight, although the building still stood and had been roped off. She saw many other ugly sights on her early morning walks – and this was only the tip of the iceberg. The dock area had been the chief target of enemy bombs and, according to Nancy, the destruction there was horrific – all over the city there were similar sights, evidence of man's inhumanity to man, something she would never understand for as long as she lived. Yet Nancy said people were standing up to the bombing with incredible courage. There'd be no sign of panic. 'Stalwarts,' she called them.

'I'm glad you can't see this, sweetheart,' Cara said to Kitty, snugly tucked up inside the big pram in which Anthony, then Sybil, had once been pushed. The raids had been fewer since the year began, with none so heavy as those just prior to Christmas, and Kitty had slept through every one. Her little world consisted of warmth and food and being loved, and Cara wanted to keep it that way for as long as she possibly could.

At the beginning of April, Cara announced she was going away for a few days. 'To London. There's someone there I want to see.'

Nancy expressed her astonishment. 'Are you taking Kitty?'

Cara wouldn't have dreamt of moving outside the door without Kitty, let alone going all the way to London. 'Of course. She's still being breastfed, isn't she?'

'It'll be an awful journey, pet, taking a baby on the train all the way to London.' She still looked doubtful. 'How long did you say you'd be gone?'

'Three days and two nights, that's all.'

Marcus proved even harder to convince that she and Kitty would be all right. Cara managed to assure him that she wouldn't come to any harm, but he then began to worry she wouldn't come back.

'I'm leaving tomorrow, Wednesday, and I'll be back on Friday,' she promised, 'and I hope by then you'll have been to see the doctor.' Lately, he'd been complaining of a sharp pain in his stomach.

'I hate doctors.' He shuddered.

'I'm not so keen on them either, but you need something for that pain. Promise me you'll see one,' she said in a wheedling voice.

'All right, I promise,' he said grudgingly.

On the day of her departure Marcus insisted on ordering a taxi to take her to Lime Street Station and came with her so he could carry her suitcase on to the train and make sure she found a seat.

'Are you sure you're coming back?' he asked anxiously when they said goodbye through the window.

'I'll see you on Friday,' Cara told him firmly.

After an uneventful journey – Kitty behaved admirably the whole way, gaining loads of admirers – they arrived at Euston mid-afternoon where Cara hailed a taxi and asked the driver to take her to 57 Greek Street. The driver gave her an odd look and, when they reached their destination and he got out to get her suitcase from the boot, he said, 'Are you sure you've got the right place, love?'

'It's the address I was given,' Cara explained. She thought the street looked rather sordid. It appeared to consist mainly of small shops with neon lights blinking in the windows, some with letters missing. Number fifty-seven was called Raz ma tazz and she assumed it should be Razzmatazz.

The taxi driver was still hovering. 'There's a door here for flats one, two and three. D'you know which one you want, love?'

'Number three.'

'That must be the top floor. Shall I ring the bell?'

'Please.' She appreciated his obvious concern, even though she couldn't understand the reason for it.

He pressed the bell for what seemed like ages and it was still ringing when the door was opened by a small, dishevelled figure who said irritably, 'I was asleep. What's up? Have the Germans invaded or something?'

Cara stepped forward. 'Hello, Fielding.'

'Caffrey!' the small figure gasped. 'What the hell are you doing here? How did you know where I lived?'

'Sybil Allardyce gave me your address and I've come to see how you are.'

'I'm absolutely fine.' Fielding burst into tears. 'No, I'm not, Caffrey. If the truth be known, I wish I'd been killed when that bomb exploded, I really do.'

'If there's anything I can do to help . . .' Having made sure Cara and Kitty were going to be all right, the taxi driver appeared ready to sort out Fielding, but Cara thanked him for being so kind and said that, now that she was there, her friend was going to be OK.

Chapter 12

Much to Eleanor's relief and Jonathan's annoyance, he had so far remained on British soil in a place called Thurso on the northernmost tip of Scotland. Mother and son prayed every night at cross purposes; Eleanor that he'd stay where he was, and Jonathan that he'd be posted to a place where there was some action to be had. He came home on leave every few months, leaner and fitter, and spoiling for a fight with the Jerries.

'Everyone in the forces is doing their bit towards the war, including you, darling,' Eleanor would try to convince him, but Jonathan refused to be convinced.

'I'd sooner be in Liverpool any day, Mummy,' he would say sulkily. 'There's far more going on. You even had an incendiary bomb in the garden.'

Eleanor was very proud of her incendiary bomb that had done little damage except to the Brussels sprouts Oliver had planted in readiness for Christmas. They'd both been in the Anderson shelter and Oliver had put the flames out with the stirrup pump that he had never imagined using. A bomb in your very own garden was really something to boast about, unlike Brenna having her windows smashed; that happened to loads of people.

She'd managed to coax Oliver out of the decline into which he'd fallen when Lewis Brown had joined the Navy – Lewis was now a first officer on a destroyer somewhere in the Atlantic – and they were now romantically entwined in the way she'd always dreamt about. All those nights they'd spent together in the shelter while bombs fell all around them had created a rapport that she hoped would never be broken.

Just as Oliver was the perfect lodger, he was also the perfect lover, giving her merely an affectionate kiss on the cheek at the end of a highly enjoyable evening spent at the cinema or the theatre. As this was the limit of Eleanor's desires, she was completely satisfied. She was terribly fond of him and he of her, and although they flirted madly, the flirting ended outside the doors of their respective bedrooms. She was, she thought frequently and rather selfishly, having an extremely good war: provided Jonathan stayed in Scotland, that was.

At the time when Cara was halfway to London on the train, Eleanor put on her hat and coat, collected her gas mask and made her way to Brenna's.

Brenna had been very down lately. Tyrone was being his usual beastly self and Fergus was still seeing that ghastly Jessie Clifford woman. Brenna had threatened to throw him out, but Fergus had, in turn, threatened to move in with Jessie, and poor Brenna was left floundering, not knowing what to do. Colm, so easy-going, wasn't being much help, telling her not to get so agitated.

Eleanor was inclined to think that Colm was right. Fergus was twenty-six and a war hero. He had a very responsible job as head of a section in Littlewoods, the pools company, now turning out barrage balloons. Even his mother had no right to tell someone like Fergus how to lead his life. If ever Jonathan did such a thing, Eleanor thought a trifle sanctimoniously, she would reason with him, not upbraid him.

'Yoohoo!' She entered the back door of Shaw Street. 'Brenna, it's only me.'

'I know it's only you,' Brenna said grumpily from the chair in the living room where she appeared to be staring into space. 'You're the only one who shouts "yoohoo".'

'Where are Maria and the boys?'

'Round at her mam's. Some days I hardly see them.'

Eleanor wasn't surprised. Right now, she wouldn't want to be stuck in the house all day with Brenna. 'How are you today?' she asked brightly. Her friend was letting herself go and had recently put on more weight. Her lovely hair was turning grey and was badly in need of a trim, and she wore an unflattering brown frock and not a scrap of make-up. Without being aware of what she was doing, Eleanor patted her own flat stomach and adjusted her hat over her smooth, brown hair, as if to convince herself that *she* looked fine, particularly in the camel coat that had once been long, but she'd converted to three-quarter length and made a hat to match out of the piece she'd cut off.

'Same as usual.' There followed the usual tirade with which Eleanor was becoming rather bored. Tyrone was being a pain, Fergus was being a pain, Colm wasn't being the least bit sympathetic.

'Perhaps he doesn't think there's anything to be sympathetic about,' Eleanor suggested helpfully. 'After all, Tyrone and Fergus are his sons as much as yours. If they don't bother him, he's probably wondering why you let them bother you.'

'You're a big help, I must say.'

'Sometimes, Brenna, you get a bee in your bonnet and you won't let it go.'

'What's that supposed to mean?' Brenna asked in a surly voice.

'Things bother you, but you won't give up, no matter what. You won't be happy until Fergus has split up with Jessie Clifford, yet the more you get on to him, the more stubborn he will be. It only stands to sense, Bren.'

'Since when have you been the expert on how to deal with kids?' Her face turned red with anger.

Eleanor could tell she was about to lose her temper, something she'd sooner avoid. She said gently, 'I don't claim to be an expert, I just don't like seeing you unhappy, that's all.'

'I'm not unhappy, I'm as mad as hell.'

'Is there a difference?'

At this, Brenna did lose her temper. 'Oh, go away, Eleanor. I thought you'd come for a chat, not to give me a lecture. I'm not prepared to take advice from you or anyone on how to be a mother.'

'Oh, all right.' Eleanor sprang to her feet. 'I'll love you and leave you. Bye, Brenna.'

She left, not in the least disturbed by their little spat. They often had them and Brenna would soon come round. She decided to go and see Nancy and was surprised to find a big, black car parked outside the house in Parliament Terrace.

'It's the doctor,' Nancy explained. 'He's come to see Marcus.'

'Is he ill?' She'd never known Marcus have more than a touch of flu.

'He keeps getting a bad pain in his stomach. This morning, Car . . . I mean, I insisted he call the doctor.'

'Poor old thing!' Eleanor had never expected she'd feel sympathy for the man who'd been her husband, but he'd become far more likeable of late. 'I've just been to see Brenna. She was in a foul mood and virtually threw me out.'

'The other day, she left in a huff when I tried to offer some advice.'

They both agreed that Brenna wasn't interested in advice and that she was inclined to let herself go if life wasn't running as smoothly as she felt it should.

You've got a bee in your bonnet and you won't let it go.

Brenna vaguely remembered Colm saying something similar years ago when she was on at him about Lizzie Phelan. Mind you, she'd had a right to worry, for hadn't Colm gone and slept with the damn woman? About a year ago, she'd heard that Lizzie had turned up out of the blue wanting to be the Labour candidate when old Ignatius Herlihy and gone and died. Lizzie hadn't won the nomination – hell would have to freeze over before Brenna would have voted for her – and had disappeared again by the time Brenna found out what had happened. She wasn't surprised Colm hadn't said anything about it.

Now she had a bee in her bonnet about Fergus and Jessie Clifford, finding it hard to accept that her darling son, who'd been such an amenable, well-behaved little lad, would actually defy his mam and continue seeing that slut Jessie when she'd specifically ordered him not to.

'I'm not a child any more, Mam,' he'd said haughtily the other day.

'You are in my eyes, lad.'

'Maybe you need glasses, too.'

The other night, Colm had told her not to worry. 'He's only after one thing, the sex. He's being a man, luv, and that's the way men are.'

'Oh, so you'd do the same thing if you were in his position?' Brenna had screamed.

'I'm not going to answer such a daft question, Bren.' With that, he'd gone to the pub. Tyrone was already in another pub, Fergus was with Jessie Clifford, and Maria and the lads were still at her mam's.

I'm driving everyone away with me moods, Brenna thought now, including Eleanor, whom she'd actually told to go away, when she would far rather she'd stayed. Perhaps it was the change – her periods were getting thinner and becoming irregular. Since Rory had died in her arms, she'd never wanted another baby, but it gave her a horrible, empty feeling to think that now she couldn't have one if she tried. At the same time, she felt slightly better knowing that her behaviour wasn't entirely her own fault, but due to her body going haywire.

She went upstairs for a more flattering frock, combed her hair, put on a bit of lippy and went to see Eleanor, only to find she wasn't in, so went to see Nancy instead and found Eleanor there. The two women were so pleased to see her in a good mood that Brenna felt quite gratified. They all sat round the table and had a long, detailed and very enjoyable discussion about the change. It turned out a far better day than she'd expected, but she couldn't resist having a go at Fergus that night when he was getting done up to see his fancy woman.

'Who does the flat belong to?' Cara asked. It was obviously an actor, as the walls of the bright, cheerful, very untidy and not very clean living room were full of theatre posters. The furniture was very old, but there were lots of colourful cushions thrown about and the walls were painted pink. Pink frilly curtains hid the blackout on the window and a striped blanket was thrown over the rackety settee on which Cara sat and breastfed a hungry Kitty, who curled and uncurled her tiny hands in blissful satisfaction.

'What makes you think it isn't mine?' Fielding asked churlishly. She was seated in a massive armchair that dwarfed her tiny figure, watching Cara and the baby with fascination. The left sleeve of her blouse was empty and flopped about untidily whenever she moved. Their conversation was very disjointed, hopping from one subject to another, not always waiting for answers. After her initial bout of tears, Fielding had adopted an attitude of tough cynicism mixed with extremely bad temper.

'If it *is* yours, all you have to do is say "me".'

'Well, it's not me, but this chap called Aubrey who's sitting out the war in California: Los Angeles to be precise. He got a part in a film and decided to stay when the war started.'

'I don't blame him.'

'No one in their right mind would. The lease is up at the end of

July and I'll have to find somewhere else. I couldn't possibly afford to renew it.'

'But I thought you got a pension!'

'I do.' She laughed bitterly. 'It's *nearly* enough to buy the groceries.'

'But that's not fair!' Cara said angrily. 'Our Fergus gets a pension, but all he has is a bit of a limp. Someone in your condition should get far more.'

'I'll have you know, Caffrey, that I'm in perfect condition apart from being minus an arm.'

'You look a wreck if the truth be known.' Her small face was pasty and wizened, her eyes bloodshot. Her lovely blonde hair had lost most of its curl and hung in lank clumps on her shoulders. Kit had taken most of the force of the bomb; Fielding, sitting behind him on the panier of the bike, had been left alive, if badly injured. She'd been flown to England and spent four months in a coma in a hospital in Birmingham where she could have died at any minute. Six weeks later, having recovered consciousness, she'd been transferred to a convalescent home in Bournemouth, but had walked out after another month. No one had known where she was until she applied for her pension. Sybil had sent her address to Cara with one of Mam's letters.

'Where does the money come from to buy all the gin and stuff I saw in the kitchen?' she asked. There'd been at least a dozen empty bottles on the floor.

'I busk,' Fielding said simply.

'What's that?'

'I sing outside Piccadilly Underground Station. I could make a mint if I did it all day.' Her face twisted in a sour smile. 'Everyone feels sorry for me, you see; poor wretched girl with only one arm. Trouble is, I get tired very quickly.'

'Oh, Fielding!'

'Oh, Caffrey!' She made a face. 'Would you like to see my arm? I've got about three inches left and the end has turned into a shrimp. Perhaps I could join the circus. "The Girl with a Shrimp for an Arm." I'd make a great attraction. I could learn to juggle and play the piano, although not both together.'

'Stop it!' Cara said, so sharply that Kitty paused briefly, hands still, then started to suck noisily again. 'Sorry, sweetheart,' she whispered.

'She's awfully like Kit,' Fielding commented.

'Is she? I think so too, but thought I might be biased. Fortunately, she hasn't got his nose. You know,' she said softly, 'for a whole twenty-four hours after the accident, I thought you were dead. Kit and Mac obviously were and I assumed you were too.'

'You *saw* us?' Her jaw dropped in astonishment.

'When the bomb went off, I stopped the car and waited for the three of you to come riding through the smoke. When you didn't, I ran back and found . . . well, you know what I found.' Cara closed her eyes and visualized the horror of the scene for the umpteenth time. 'What's that?' she asked, alarmed, when she heard piercing screams from directly below the window. By now, it was pitch dark and the blackout was upon them.

'Just the girls having a fight,' Fielding said serenely. 'It's nothing to worry about.'

'What girls?'

'The working girls, the pros – *prostitutes*,' she said impatiently when Cara continued to look bemused. 'The street's full of them. If it's not them fighting with each other, then it's their pimps beating them up. Don't tell me you don't know what a pimp is, Caffrey?' she groaned when Cara looked at her vacantly. 'What sort of world have you been living in?'

'A different sort of world from you, obviously.'

Fielding explained what a pimp was and Cara said, 'No wonder that nice taxi driver gave me a funny look when I told him your address.'

'You didn't *have* to come,' Fielding said huffily. 'Perhaps you wouldn't have if you'd known what the area was like.'

'I *did* have to come,' Cara said simply. 'I'd have come if you'd been living on the moon. I wanted to see you. I had to know how you were.' She hoisted Kitty on to her shoulder and began to rub her back.

'Why are you doing that?'

'To bring up her wind. Is there anywhere I can put her down to sleep after I've changed her nappy?'

'Only my bed. You two can sleep together and I'll doss down on the settee.'

'Are you sure?'

'Unless you and Kitty would prefer to doss down on the settee, yes, I'm sure.' She got to her feet, the sleeve hanging limply by her side. 'Would you like another cup of tea?'

'Yes, please. Is there anything to eat in this place? I'm starving.'

'There's a fish and chip shop around the corner. I'll go and buy some in a minute.'

'Is that all you eat, fish and chips?'

'Yes, except for the days I don't eat anything at all.'

'I suppose you drink instead. Oh!' Cara said exasperatedly. 'Fielding, my friend, you're not doing yourself any good living like this. Couldn't you have gone to live with your father?' Fielding had never been exactly forthcoming about her family.

'He lives in Devon and only came to see me once in hospital. I haven't heard from him since, although that's hardly surprising as he doesn't know where I am and probably doesn't want to. My mother died when I was fourteen and, within a year, he'd married this bitchy woman called Barbara who couldn't wait to see the back of my brother and I. Roger joined the Army and we lost touch. I moved to London, took acting classes and went on the stage. I haven't been home since.' She dried her nose on her sleeve. 'I keep going to do things with my left arm, but it isn't there. You're very lucky, Caffrey, having a proper family.'

'I haven't seen a single member of my family since I came home from Malta,' Cara said. 'I'll tell you about it another time.'

Kitty gave an unladylike burp, Cara changed her nappy and took her into the bedroom for a sleep. The bedroom was as untidy and as unclean as the rest of the flat. Fielding said she'd go for the fish and chips, having forgotten all about the tea, and Cara asked if she could use the phone she'd noticed under the mess on the sideboard. 'I want to ring someone in Liverpool and tell him I've arrived safely.'

'Help yourself. I won't be long.'

Marcus answered the phone at the other end, as she knew he would. 'It's me,' Cara said. 'Everything's fine. Did you go to see the doctor?'

'He came to see me. He wants me to go into hospital to be X-rayed,' Marcus grumbled.

'When are you going?' she asked sternly.

'I'm not sure if I want to. They might find something wrong with me.'

'But that's the whole point of being X-rayed, to discover the reason for the pain. Have you got it now?'

'Only slightly.'

She was about to accuse him of lying through his teeth, when Kitty set up a desperate wail and she said, 'I'll have to go, Kitty's crying. She's probably wondering where on earth she is.' Cara credited Kitty with a great deal more intelligence than any normal two-month-old child.

'I can hear her from here. Goodbye, Cara. Let me know what train you're catching on Friday and I'll meet you at the station.'

The line clicked, she'd gone to attend to Kitty, but Marcus kept the receiver against his ear, her voice and the sound of the baby crying lingering in the silence. After a while, he replaced the receiver in its cradle and got painfully to his feet. The ache in his side was anything but mild. Since the doctor had poked every inch of his stomach that morning, he was convinced it had got worse. There was something terribly demeaning about lying on the bed with your trousers down to your knees and having your stomach prodded by a man half your age. Dr Langdon, who'd delivered Anthony and Sybil, had retired many years ago and could be dead by now for all Marcus knew.

If only Cara were there! Last night, when he'd been groaning in his sleep and she'd come to see what was wrong, something wonderful and entirely unexpected had happened . . . He wanted to think about that, not this ferocious, nagging, never-ending pain. He shouted down the stairs for Nancy, wanting to ask if she'd make a hot water bottle to rest on his stomach but, when she didn't come, he remembered she was out, but had promised to be back by seven.

'In case there's a raid,' she'd said. Wherever she might be, Nancy always rushed home if an air raid started, preferring to be in her kitchen than anywhere else on earth.

Marcus had no idea where the hot water bottles were kept. He shivered, the house felt unusually cold for March – almost April – or perhaps it was just him. These days, no matter how wealthy a person might be, there was a limit to how much coal they could buy. He could understand the poor burning their furniture when it was cold and, had he been in a fit condition to drag one of the heavy sideboards or bookcases into the yard and saw it to pieces, he might have felt tempted to do it himself.

His stomach felt as if it was being pierced by a knife. I'll go to bed, he decided. It was the best place to be when he felt like this. Lately, he'd been keeping a supply of Aspro tablets in the desk drawer. He took four, although the packet advised two, and staggered upstairs.

Within half an hour, the tablets had done their work and he was asleep. When Nancy came home, knocked at the study door, found it empty and saw the box of Aspros on the desk, she took for granted he was in bed. She returned to the kitchen, made herself some supper, and retired to her sitting room to listen to the wireless, hoping there wouldn't be a raid. The house seemed unnaturally quiet without Cara and the baby. They hadn't been gone a day and she was already missing them badly.

Marcus had no idea what time it was when he was woken by the pain, so severe that he screamed out loud, 'Help! Somebody help me!' Then, 'Cara! Cara, come quickly,' followed by a whimpered, 'Please!'

But Cara didn't come as she'd done the night before and he remembered she was in London. 'Nancy,' he yelled, but Nancy was now fast asleep two floors below in the basement.

He needed the doctor, an ambulance. The pain wasn't natural, something was badly wrong. Marcus practically fell out of bed. If he could reach his study, he could phone for help. But he could hardly stand, the pain wouldn't let him. He managed to crawl as far as the door, managed to open it and crawl on to the landing, where he was faced with the daunting prospect of getting down the stairs. He grasped the banisters, hauled himself to his feet and shuffled down the stairs like an old, old man, very slowly, one at a time, pausing for breath. Halfway down, a wave of dizziness swept over him and he tried to sit down, but toppled forward instead and landed head first at the bottom, stopping just short of the grandfather clock with its loud tick and creaking pendulum.

At some time during the night, he regained consciousness, although was unable to make out where he was or why there were such strange ticking and creaking noises close to his head. His face was covered with something cold and sticky.

'Cara,' he whispered. 'Cara, my darling girl, where are you?'

When a horrified Nancy found him next morning lying in a pool of blood, there was hardly any life left in him and his body felt as cold as ice. She telephoned for an ambulance and watched him being taken away on a stretcher, knowing for certain that she would never see Marcus Allardyce alive again.

'This is a nice street,' Cara said. 'What's it called?'

'Piccadilly,' Fielding told her. 'I thought we could stroll as far as Green Park, then cut through to Oxford Street.'

'Sounds fine to me.' Some of the buildings looked as if they'd been there for centuries and the shops were terribly posh. Women, beautifully dressed and liberally perfumed, drifted in and out, looking as though war was the very last thing on their minds. There was no sign of bomb damage. The siren had gone the night before, but all the activity had sounded very far away. 'In London,' Nancy had said once, 'it's the poor that are getting the worst hammering, the East Enders, who live close to the docks. Least in Liverpool, rich and poor alike get an equal share of Hitler's bombs.'

They arrived at Green Park, which looked very pretty, the trees covered with a spattering of pale-green buds as they prepared for summer. 'I'd love to have had a wander round,' Cara said, 'but me arms are already aching from carrying Kitty.' She wished it had been possible to bring the pram – it would have gone in the guard's van, but not the taxi.

'I'd offer to carry her for a while, but as you can see I've only got one arm to ache.'

'When we get to Oxford Street, can we stop for a cup of tea?'

'We'll go in Selfridges, and this afternoon I'll take you to see Buckingham Palace and the Houses of Parliament.'

'I came to see you, Fielding, not the sights of London.' She seemed much better this morning and Cara was glad that she'd come. Her visit had stirred her out of her torpor. Last night, they'd talked until the early hours, right through the raid, reliving their time in Malta with Kit and Mac, especially the weekend in Gozo.

'That's when I fell in love with Mac and he with me,' Fielding confessed. 'We slept together, although it was the last thing we'd ever intended doing. Until then, our relationship had been entirely platonic. We both knew nothing would come of it because he would never have left his wife and children.'

'You know,' Cara mused, 'this is the first time I've ever given a thought to Mac's wife. She must have been devastated when he was killed.'

'And what about Kit's family, His mum and dad? Are you going to take Kitty to see them some day? After all, they're her grandparents.'

'I've written to them twice, told them about Kitty, but never got an answer. It would seem his family don't want to know.' There was still the matter of Kitty's other grandparents to sort out, something she wasn't looking forward to a bit.

'Are you going to get a false arm?' she asked when they were in Selfridges restaurant waiting for their tea and crumpets. Kitty was wide awake and getting fidgety. In a minute, she'd take her to the Ladies and change her nappy.

'Actually, I thought about getting a hook,' Fielding replied. 'It would be handy in a fight.'

'Can't you possibly be serious for a minute? Cara rolled her eyes impatiently, thinking it was quite like old times, trying to get some sense out of Fielding. 'Wasn't there some famous actress who had a wooden leg?'

'Yes, Sarah Bernhardt.' She laughed derisively. 'The thing is, she was brilliant and I'm not.'

'I bet she couldn't sing like you,' Cara said stoutly. 'You can't spend the rest of your life busking, Fielding.'

'I can if I want.'

'Don't talk such utter rubbish, of course you can't.'

'It was when I was singing "A Foggy Day in London Town" in that café in Gozo that Mac fell in love with me,' she said in a soft voice, eyes misty as she recalled that glorious night, the night when Kitty had been conceived.

'When did you fall in love with him?' Cara asked, interested.

'When I saw him watching me sing "A Foggy Day in London Town". I could tell from the expression on his face what was happening and realized I felt the same.' She cocked her small head on one side, like a bird. 'Are we lucky to have such wonderful memories, Caffrey, or would we be better off without them?'

'Lucky,' Cara said firmly. Kitty was squirming on her knee. She jumped up and took her to the Ladies where she changed her nappy and kissed her rosy cheek. 'Really lucky,' she told her little daughter.

After an exhausting day, they returned to the flat in Greek Street at teatime. Fielding went to buy fish and chips and Cara slowly climbed the stairs, Kitty in her arms, by now weighing a ton. Two women were coming down, heavily made up, one with long, dark hair, the other dyed a brassy blonde. Their skirts looked awfully tight and were far too short.

'What a sweet little baby,' cried the blonde. 'How old is she, dearie?'

'Two months. Her name is Kitty.' These must be two of the 'girls' Fielding had spoken about the night before. They might even have been involved in the fight outside.

The dark-haired one, she looked no more than Cara's age, chucked Kitty under the chin. 'She's a real little bobby dazzler,' she said in a strong scouse accent.

'Are you from Liverpool?' Cara asked.

'Yes, Pickwick Street in Toxteth.'

'I'm from Shaw Street, it's only just round the corner.' It was only now that Cara noticed the girl had yellow, sickly eyes and her face was covered with spots. Worried Kitty might catch something, she muttered, 'I'd better go, excuse me,' and hurried up the final flight of stairs. She was unlocking the door, when a voice from below shouted, 'Hey, you up there! Have you never heard the saying, "There but for the grace of God go I?" If things had gone different, it could've been *me* carrying the baby and *you* with the scabby face. Just remember that next time you turn up your nose at an innocent working girl.'

Cara slammed the door behind her and leaned against it, panting. 'Really, *really*, lucky,' she gasped.

Early next morning, she rang Marcus to tell him she was catching the half past ten train. It was supposed to get into Liverpool at half past two, but who could tell in wartime? She was surprised when Nancy answered and was about to tell her the time of the train, but didn't have the chance, because Nancy said, 'Cara! Oh, I wish I'd known your number.'

'Why?'

'Because Marcus is dead, pet, that's why. He died yesterday morning. I couldn't let you know.'

Cara could hardly believe her ears. Marcus *dead*! She sat heavily on the settee and the springs creaked in protest. 'But how did he die?'

'It might have been peritonitis as a result of a burst appendix or it could have been the fall downstairs. No one knows for sure, not yet. There's going to be a post-mortem today and he's being buried on Monday.'

'I'll still catch the same train home,' Cara said hurriedly, 'the half past ten.'

'Don't do that, pet. There'll be ructions if you and Kitty turn up now. Let's get the funeral over first, we can deal with the fireworks later. Come on Tuesday, but give me a ring first. I might have something to tell you.'

'All right,' she said obediently. Nancy always knew best. An unpleasant thought struck her. 'But if poor Marcus is dead, there's no point in me coming back, is there, least not to Parliament Terrace? The house will belong to someone else.' Eleanor, Sybil or Anthony, or all three together. 'The last thing they'll want is me and Kitty living there.'

'Come on Tuesday, Cara,' Nancy said firmly. 'By the way, I forgot to say, Sybil's on her way home from Malta and Jonathan will be here.'

'All right,' Cara said again.

Despite all the things Eleanor had said about him, that Brenna didn't doubt were true, she'd always liked Marcus Allardyce. Even the night he'd chucked Eleanor out in the rain was understandable given the reason for it. With her, he'd never been anything but polite and she would always be grateful to him for giving Fergus a job when Anthony had left him in the lurch and he'd felt so down.

It had been upsetting to learn he'd died in such a desperately horrible way, from loss of blood after falling down his very own stairs. 'I didn't hear a thing,' Nancy wailed. 'If I'd known he'd fallen, I'd've called the ambulance. He was good company during the raids,' she said. 'We'd drink a bottle or two of wine between us and end up pissed rotten.' Apparently, an inebriated Marcus had even been known to crack a joke or two, something Eleanor found difficult to believe, but had to concede Nancy wasn't the sort of person who'd lie.

Brenna wasn't going to the funeral. She had agreed to stay in the house and get on with the food so Nancy could go. Eleanor, who had taken care of all the arrangements with the help of Oliver Chandler, had sent notice of Marcus's death to the *Liverpool Echo*, which had published a long, quite flattering obituary – 'A good employer, respected by his workers,' and so on. Eleanor had no idea how many people would come back from the cemetery for something to eat. Less than a dozen, and they could have a cup of tea, more than that and it would have to be wine or sherry; there was plenty of both in the cellar, but not much tea left in the caddy.

On the day – a nothing sort of day, neither cold nor warm, sunny or dull – after the funeral cortege had driven away, Brenna remained in the kitchen to get on with making the salmon sandwiches – she'd contributed a large tin of pink that she'd been keeping for a special occasion, although hadn't dreamt the special occasion would turn out to be a funeral. She boiled a kettle of water just in case tea was needed and had just decided to treat herself to a cup, when the front doorbell rang and she went upstairs to answer it.

A tall, handsome woman dressed all in black, diamonds flashing on her ears and neck, stood outside, leaning heavily on a stick.

'I'm sorry,' Brenna said, 'but they all left for the cemetery ages ago, although they should be back soon. Would you like to come inside and wait in the parlour?'

'Thank you,' the woman said coldly, giving Brenna a haughty look. 'I saw the cortege leave, but I'm a semi-invalid these days and have difficulty getting in and out of cars. I merely came to pay my respects to the family when they arrive home. I know what it's like to lose someone, my husband died many years ago.' She made her stiff way into the parlour and sat down with great difficulty.

'You obviously live close by if you saw the cars leave,' Brenna commented, thinking she looked awfully young to be an invalid, not much more than her own age.

'Next door. Aren't you going to take my stick?'

'If you want.' The woman clearly thought she was a servant. Brenna put the stick in the umbrella stand in the hall. There was still a stain on the carpet where Marcus's head had lain that Nancy had been unable to remove. She was careful not to step on it. 'Would you like a cup of tea or a glass of wine or sherry while you're waiting?' she enquired.

'Sherry, please, very dry.'

Brenna looked carefully at the woman. 'Have we met before? Not recently, a long time ago. There's something dead familiar about your face.'

'I doubt that very much.' The words, said so cuttingly, were a deliberate snub, as if to say she didn't mix with people of Brenna's type who answered doors and brought drinks. At any other time, Brenna would have taken offence, but today was Marcus's funeral and it didn't seem to matter. She took a last glance at the woman as she closed the door, noticing the way the jewels glinted in her ears and on her neck. She had reached the kitchen and was pouring the sherry when she remembered where she'd seen her before – the memory had stuck with her ever since.

It was the day they'd arrived in Liverpool twenty years ago and there'd been a party in the next door house. Brenna had been clinging to the railings, looking in, while the rain poured down and her body was being assailed by contractions heralding the imminent arrival of Cara. She'd been thinking how unjust it was that she, her husband and children were outside in the cold and wet having had hardly a bite to eat all day, while the well-dressed, well-fed people on the other side of the window were having a wonderful time. She'd wondered why fate had treated them so differently. In particular, she'd noticed a woman with glittering earrings and a plume in her hair who had, in turn, seen Brenda peering through the window and closed the curtains with an angry flourish. The same woman was now sitting in the Allardyces' parlour, a semi-invalid and a widow. Fate was still treating them differently, but now it was Brenna who possessed the real riches, a good husband, good health, three children who caused their mam an awful lot of worry, but were basically the best in the world.

'I'll never complain about anything ever again,' Brenna promised herself for about the hundredth time in her life. This time, the promise didn't even last the day.

She was home again, feeling sad – well, you couldn't expect to come home from a funeral feeling happy – peeling 'taters for the tea, glad to be under her own roof again, when Eleanor came into the kitchen, still in her black costume, but minus her over-feathered hat.

'I wasn't expecting to see you again today,' Brenna remarked. 'I thought you'd be too busy with Sybil and Jonathan. And what happened to the yoohoo?'

Not only did Eleanor ignore this, she didn't even smile. In fact, she looked so serious that Brenna began to wonder if someone else had died. 'You know Marcus's solicitor was there today, don't you?' she said in a neutral tone.

'Yes, you said he was going to read the will after everyone had gone.'

'And that's exactly what he did. I just thought that you might like to know that Marcus has left the house and all his money to his wife.'

'That's only to be expected, isn't it? He probably made the will before you and him were divorced.' Had Eleanor come all this way to tell her the patently obvious?

'No, it was a new will made only last week on the day he saw the doctor and only hours before he died. He asked Nancy to witness his signature.'

'That's odd.' The words took a few seconds to sink in. 'That's *really* odd.'

'I thought so too, until the solicitor explained that Marcus had married again just before Christmas. He showed us the marriage certificate. His new wife's maiden name is Cara Caffrey, who, according to Nancy, has a little girl called Kitty and has been living in Parliament Terrace since last July.'

'*What!*' The kitchen began to swim in front of Brenna's eyes. She stumbled into the living room and collapsed in a chair. '*My* Cara?'

'How many other Cara Caffreys do you know?' Eleanor asked coolly. She had followed Brenna and stood, leaning against the sideboard with her arms folded. Eleanor only folded her arms when she was terribly cross about something.

'But I don't understand,' Brenna said faintly. 'Are you saying our Cara has been living less than a mile away since last July?'

'So it would seem.'

'But I get letters from Malta every other week!'

'She sent them to Sybil who sent them back to you and did the same with your letters.' She sniffed disapprovingly, but it came out more like an angry snort. 'It was all very sneaky and underhand and I told Sybil as much.'

'And Cara had a baby by Marcus?' Her voice had gone all quivery and old.

'I didn't say that, no.' Eleanor's voice was the opposite, hard and crisp. 'Apparently, Cara was already pregnant when she came to the house and Marcus let her stay. Kitty was born on the twenty-fifth of January. Maybe he married her so Kitty would be legitimate. From the date on the marriage certificate, they did it when the Towns-women's Guild had their Christmas Bazaar and Nancy – all of us – were out all day. They went to a Registry Office in Chester, clearly wanting to keep it quiet.'

Brenna was beginning to recover some of her composure as her brain began to grasp the enormity of what had happened. 'So, our Cara has been living in Parliament Terrace since July and Nancy didn't say a word about it? She's actually had a baby *and I didn't know!*' She jumped to her feet. 'I'm going round there this very minute to have it out with Nancy Gates. How dare she keep something like that to herself?'

Eleanor stepped forward and spread her arms, creating a human barrier. 'You'll do no such thing, Brenna Caffrey,' she rasped, eyes blazing. 'Nancy was asked to keep a confidence and that's what she did. I've confided in her myself enough times in the past.' Her lips curled in disgust. 'Trust you to put the blame on someone else. Hasn't it crossed your mind to wonder why Cara didn't come home to her mother instead of throwing herself on Nancy's mercy?'

'What d'you mean?'

'What would your reaction have been if Cara had come home and confessed she was pregnant?'

'I would have bloody killed her,' Brenna said belligerently.

'That's precisely why she went to Nancy and not you.' Eleanor refolded her arms and the two friends glared at each other with animosity. 'About a year ago,' Eleanor said, 'Marcus asked me if I'd give up my share in the house so he could leave it to Sybil, our daughter. I agreed willingly, but I would never, *never* have done so if I'd thought for one moment it was going to be left to someone else.'

Brenna licked her lips, unable to think of a single thing to say, but Eleanor hadn't finished with her yet. 'This whole mess can be laid at your door, Brenna. Had Cara felt able to tell you she was pregnant, none of this would have happened. There'd have been no need for her to live in Parliament Terrace. Nancy suspects Marcus fell in love with her and he adored Kitty. Oh, and before you start accusing Cara of something or other, she knows nothing about the will. She didn't seduce him, according to Nancy they didn't have any sort of relationship, they were just friends.'

'Where is Cara now?' Brenna asked limply.

'In London, staying with someone. She's coming back tomorrow.

Marcus was alive when she left and it was her who insisted he see a doctor. I'm not blaming Cara for anything, Brenna; she's a sweet girl, I've always liked her. I'm blaming you.'

'What did Marcus look like?' Fielding whispered.

'He was very handsome for an older man,' Cara whispered back. 'Tall and dark-haired with hardly any grey at all, and a Clark Gable moustache.'

'Did you . . . you know?' Fielding winked.

'Shush!' Cara glanced covertly at the other people in the carriage, but they all seemed to be involved in conversations of their own. 'You've got a really dirty mind.'

Fielding winked again. 'That's not an answer.'

'It's the only answer you're going to get.' She saw that Kitty had gone asleep with her dummy in her mouth and tried to remove it, but perhaps a tiny part of her brain was still awake and she positively refused to give it up. 'Little madam,' she murmured softly.

That morning, Tuesday, as Nancy had requested, Cara had telephoned before leaving for the train, to be given the startling news that Marcus had left her everything except the factory in his will. 'So you'll be coming back to your own house,' Nancy had said gravely.

'But that's not fair,' Cara gasped. 'I couldn't possibly take it.'

'Marcus obviously thought it fair, pet. He and Eleanor were divorced and she's already got a house, even if it's only rented, Jonathan isn't his child, and Anthony seems to have disappeared off the face of the earth. That only leaves Sybil, and Marcus must have decided he'd rather you had the house than her.'

'All right,' Cara said. It still didn't seem right, but if it was what Marcus wanted for her and Kitty . . . 'I'll be back later today. I'm not quite sure what time.'

'Everyone knows about Kitty, but I only gave them the bare facts. It's up to you to fill in the details. I didn't mention Kit.'

'Thank you, Nancy.'

She'd put down the phone and shouted, 'Fielding, how do you fancy living in Liverpool? It seems I've been left a house.'

Now Fielding's large suitcase and Cara's small bag were on the rack above their heads on the inevitably crowded Liverpool-bound train – two young women with a baby had quickly been found seats.

'What's the house like?' Fielding asked.

'It's a big mausoleum of a place, rather cold,' Cara explained. 'The kitchen's the nicest room, really huge, and you'll love Nancy. She's the housekeeper and does all the cooking.'

'Will she housekeep and cook for you?'

'I certainly hope so,' Cara replied with feeling. 'The house wouldn't be the same without Nancy, although I hope I can afford to pay her wages. She said Marcus had left me his money too, but she didn't say how much. If there isn't enough, we'll just have to use your pension.'

'I wouldn't mind,' Fielding said easily. She was excited at the idea of going to Liverpool. Perhaps she would never be her old self again and this was as close as she'd ever get, but she looked miles better than she'd done when they'd met last week. Cara had insisted on giving her hair a good wash and her blonde curls had returned to their former glory. Her face had lost its wizened look, although a few lines remained that she hadn't had before, making her look older. Malta had turned both girls into women. Cara couldn't imagine ever feeling young again.

'Cara!' a voice yelled. '*Cara!*'

Cara searched for the owner of the voice among the crowds on the platform at Lime Street Station, and saw her brother, Fergus, struggling to reach her.

'Cara!' He picked her up and twirled her round, regardless of Kitty squashed between them.

'Mind the baby,' Cara gasped.

'Ah, yes, the baby, let's have a look at her.' Cara removed the shawl from Kitty's face and Fergus examined her carefully. 'She's not much like you,' he said eventually.

'She's more like her father. How did you know we'd be on this train?'

'I didn't. I phoned Nancy before I left work and she said you still hadn't arrived, so I walked up from Exchange Station and they said the London train was expected any minute. I waited, just in case you were on it and you were! Jaysus, it's great to see you, Cara.'

'It's great to see you, Fergus.' She marvelled at the change in her brother. Quiet, desperately shy Fergus had emerged from his shell, a loud and exuberant young man with laughing eyes behind a pair of flattering, horn-rimmed glasses, and a face beaming with confidence.

'Where's your luggage?'

'Someone carried it off the train for me – there it is, right behind you. The big case belongs to Fielding.'

'Who's Fielding?'

'I am,' said Fielding.

'She's my friend from the Army,' Cara said. 'She's going to live with us in the Allardyces' house.'

'How do you do, Fielding?' They shook hands politely. 'Have you got a first name?' Fergus asked. 'I'd sooner call you by that seeing as I'm no longer in the Army.'

'It's Juliette,' Fielding said graciously. 'I'm no longer in the Army either.'

'Why not?'

'It's silly, I know, but they draw the line at one-armed soldiers.'

'Ouch! I'm sorry, I didn't notice,' Fergus groaned. 'How did you lose it?'

'I've no idea,' Fielding explained, wide-eyed, 'I just woke up one morning and it wasn't there. I'm always losing things, but it's the first time an arm has gone missing.'

'Take no notice of her, Fergus,' Cara said. 'She has this desperately weird sense of humour that takes some getting used to. Shall we go? I think the situation calls for a taxi, don't you?'

'You're late,' Mam snapped when Fergus arrived home. 'Your tea's in the oven. Sit down and I'll fetch it.'

'In a minute, Mam.' Fergus sat down nevertheless. 'I've just seen our Cara,' he announced. 'I met her off the train and we went back to Parliament Terrace. That's why I'm late.'

Mam nearly jumped out of her skin. 'Did you, son? What does she look like? Did she have the baby with her?'

'Cara looks fine, except she seems much more grown up than when she went away. The baby, Kitty, isn't a bit like her. Cara said she takes after the father.'

'Did she say who the father is?' Mam asked eagerly.

'He was an airman called Kit Farthing.' Fergus had been told the whole story from beginning to end and had promised to pass it on to

Mam, to save Cara having to do it, and giving Mam time to come to terms with things in her own good time.

'*Was* an airman?' She'd noticed the past tense.

'He and his friend were killed by a bomb the night before he and Cara were to get married.'

'She never mentioned anything in her letters about getting married,' Mam said pugnaciously.

'That's because he wasn't a Catholic and they were getting married in a Protestant church and she knew you and Dad wouldn't approve.' Fergus flinched as he waited for the explosion that duly followed.

'*What?*' Mam shrieked. 'Me own daughter getting married in a . . .' She stopped, unable to finish the sentence, as if words had failed her.

'But she didn't, did she, Mam?' Fergus said patiently. 'Kit got killed before it could happen.'

'She married Marcus Allardyce in a registry office.'

'That's because she had no choice. All Mr Allardyce wanted was to give the baby a name. I'd've thought you'd be pleased about that, Mam. It's better than having a bastard granddaughter.'

Mam slammed her fist on the table and Fergus flinched again. 'Don't you dare use that word in this house, Fergus Caffrey.'

Fergus shrugged. 'Illegitimate, then.'

'I suppose I can expect Cara to come and see me later, full of excuses,' Mam said bitterly.

'No, Mam, you can't.' Fergus knew what he was about to say would only make matters worse, but he plunged ahead. 'She ses you're to go and see her, but not until you've calmed down. She's not prepared to listen to you screaming your head off.'

At this, Mam's face crumpled and she burst into tears. 'No one understands,' she wept. 'No one cares about the way she's treated me. Me own daughter, lying and cheating and sneaking around Parliament Terrace for months on end, pretending to send letters from Malta, marrying Marcus Allardyce and, worst of all, sleeping with some airman and having his child.'

Fergus was tempted to say that, if he'd been Cara, he might well have done the same. Lying, cheating and sneaking around were far preferable to coming home and telling Mam that you were pregnant. But she already looked awful, her face haggard and drained of colour, and he remembered the foggy night his tempestuous mother had come storming into St Hilda's Convent, shouting for her lads, bringing them back to this very house that she'd endeavoured to make as comfortable as possible for them all. She loved her children to the point of obsession. Unfortunately, she also thought she *owned* them and they must live their lives according to her own strict rules. But now there was a war on and her children had changed. He had faced death and killed men before escaping from Dunkirk. Compared to that, sleeping with Jessie Clifford, a cheerful, kind-hearted soul, was a trite thing, and he resented being harangued every time he went to see her. As for Cara, who'd seen the dead body of her husband-to-be only hours before they were to be wed, she no doubt felt the same and wasn't prepared to put up with Mam making a scene.

'Don't cry, Mam,' he urged, putting his arm around her, feeling almost like crying himself because he loved her so much, but not enough to forget he was a grown man who wasn't prepared to do as he was told for the rest of his life.

'I can't help it, son. I suppose you're like Eleanor and blame me for the whole thing. Last night, your dad more or less did the same. It seems it's all my fault.'

'That's not true, Mam.' He sighed. 'I'll have me tea now seeing as it's ready.' He didn't remotely feeling like eating, but didn't want to upset his mother even more by turning down the meal she had so lovingly prepared.

Nancy was in her element. She loved having her kitchen full of people and now Cara and Kitty were back, along with Cara's strange, badly wounded little friend, Fielding, whom she had immediately taken to her heart. Fergus had been and gone, and now Colm had arrived and was hugging his daughter so tightly, as if he never wanted to let her go. He released her and turned to look at Kitty, cooing happily as Nancy nursed her in her brawny arms. She passed the baby to her granddad and saw tears come to his eyes as he touched her sweet little face. He said, 'I wish things could've been done differently, Cara, luv.'

'So do I, Dad,' was all Cara said fervently, and Nancy could tell the matter was over between them. Colm understood. Cara had been forgiven and that was that.

Colm hadn't been gone for long when Eleanor came. She'd been in a right old temper the day before when the will had been read, but it seemed she'd got over it for she smiled at Cara and kissed her on the cheek. 'I don't quite know what to say, dear, only that I'm glad Marcus found happiness during his last few months on earth.'

'I think he did,' Cara said shyly.

'Good,' Eleanor said briskly. 'Now, where's the baby? I'm longing to see her.'

And *that* was all right too, Nancy thought, beaming contentedly at everyone. Now, there was only Brenna to come round and everything would be perfect. She completely forgot about Sybil.

Mummy had had no idea how to get in touch with her when Daddy had passed away so suddenly. It was no use writing a letter that would have taken ages to arrive, she wasn't sure if it was possible to send a telegram to someone in the Army, so Oliver Chandler, her friend, had stepped into the breech and telephoned Army headquarters in London and someone there had promised to contact Sybil in Malta.

Perhaps it was because she was already in such an awful state that the news had upset her so dreadfully. She put down the phone and couldn't stop crying. Too late, she realized that her father was the one person in the world on whom she could totally depend. When Cara had said, months ago, that her mother wouldn't want her living at home while she was expecting a baby, Sybil had replied, 'My father would be the same,' knowing it wasn't true, because Daddy would have forgiven her anything. He might disapprove, might even *say* he disapproved, but he would have taken her into his home and heaped gifts upon her in the way she'd used to think of as suffocating, but now would have welcomed with all her heart.

But now Daddy was dead and she'd made a terrible mess of Malta and her career in the Army. Lately, she'd been wondering if he could buy her out, but wasn't sure if it were possible in wartime.

It was all the fault of John Glover, the other lieutenant she'd gone out with after she'd finished with Alec Townend. After a while, she'd allowed him into her bed, but he was a violent, sadistic lover with unnatural tastes. Within a few days, she'd had enough, but finishing with John wasn't as easy as it had been with Alec. He came into her office at least a dozen times a day, not to plead with her to go out with him again, but to insult her and call her names she'd never heard before. He telephoned as many times, hurling at her the same insults. Other officers began to ask her out and Sybil would accept, only to find they expected to make love on the first date.

'John and Alec said you were a whore,' one said to her nastily. 'Who do you think you are, turning up your nose at me?'

John must have discovered she'd slept with Alec and it seemed as if everyone in Marzipan Hall knew it too. The men looked at her with brazen insolence and the women with hostility. If only she had some friends among the women, but she'd studiously avoided them. She felt sure she wasn't the only woman there who'd slept with two men, but it was her misfortune that one of them had been John Glover who was determined to make her pay for ditching him.

For months now, she'd felt ashamed and very alone, staying in her room at night, the door locked, because occasionally someone would try the handle and say loudly, 'Can I come in for a shag?' followed by titters, as if there was more than one man outside.

It was all too horrible for words and now Daddy was dead and she didn't think it possible to feel more miserable than she did just then. She put her hands on the desk and pushed herself wearily to her feet. She'd ask Major Winkworth-Blythe, who was in overall charge of Marzipan Hall, if she could have a week's compassionate leave. It wasn't always possible to be sent home from Malta – it was too far away – no matter who had died, but it wouldn't hurt to enquire.

'The major is busy right now, ma'am,' she was crisply told by the female clerk when she entered the outer office.

'Can I wait?'

'Suit yourself, ma'am,' the woman said, shrugging.

It was an hour before a senior officer emerged from the major's office. Sybil jumped to her feet and made to enter, but the clerk said sharply, 'Kindly wait until I've asked if Major Winkworth-Blythe is willing to see you.' She picked up the phone and spoke a few words. Another five minutes passed before a buzzer went and she said, 'He'll see you now.'

Sybil marched into the room, stood to attention and saluted. 'Lieutenant Allardyce, sir. I've just heard that my father has died suddenly and I would like to go home for the funeral.'

'Ah, yes, Allardyce.' Major Winkworth-Blythe was a well-bred, distinguished-looking man with charming manners who'd been a high-ranking diplomat before the war. He regarded Sybil with a certain amount of sympathy. 'I think that can be arranged,' he said mildly and her heart leapt with joy. 'In fact, Allardyce,' he went on, 'I've been wondering what to do with you for some time. It would seem you've gained a somewhat risqué reputation and I don't think your presence here is entirely desirable.' He coughed delicately. 'I had already requested that you be transferred elsewhere and have been awaiting a decision on your next posting. That decision arrived this morning. You are being sent to a training camp in Suffolk. Under normal circumstances, you would be allowed a week's leave and that should give you time to attend your father's funeral.' He gave her a gentle smile. 'I realize, Allardyce, that you have been as much sinned against as sinning and Lieutenant Glover is also being moved elsewhere.'

'Thank you, sir,' Sybil gulped, feeling her face turn scarlet with a mixture of shame and embarrassment.

'I wasn't over-specific when I asked for your transfer, just wrote "doesn't fit in", and that could cover many reasons. You will take up your new posting without anyone being aware of the truth of what happened here.' He nodded dismissively. 'Come back in half an hour and my clerk will have your papers ready. Good luck, Allardyce.'

Now she was back in Liverpool with Mummy – Jonathan had only been allowed a few days' leave and had gone straight back to Scotland after Daddy's funeral. The day after tomorrow she would present herself at the camp in Suffolk. She wasn't particularly looking forward to it, but it was preferable to Malta. She resolved that never again would she give any man she met a second glance.

In a way, the awfulness of Malta had been rather overshadowed by the equally awful events back home. She still kept hoping it had all been a mistake, that any minute the solicitor would telephone and say that Cara Caffrey shouldn't have been mentioned in Daddy's will, or that it was a forgery and Daddy had had nothing to do with it.

'But Nancy witnessed it, darling,' Mummy had pointed out last night when they got home and Sybil had expressed, very forcibly, her opinion that there was something very suspicious about the will, that it couldn't possibly have been Daddy's wish not to leave his darling daughter anything at all. 'Mr Maplin, the solicitor, expressly brought his clerk with him so he could witness it, too. Daddy was there the whole time.'

'But don't forget Daddy was in a terrific amount of pain, maybe he wasn't of sound mind.'

'I'm sure Nancy would have noticed if he was – and Mr Maplin.'

'I think we should contest it,' Sybil said heatedly.

'You do whatever you wish, darling, but I'm afraid you won't have my backing.' Mummy stroked her hand. 'And such a thing would be terribly expensive. *I* don't have enough funds to embark on a long legal battle. I intend to sign the factory over to you and Jonathan straight away so you will have the income from that. If you want to waste it on court action, it's up to you.'

Cara had come back from London earlier today and Mummy had actually gone to see her, which Sybil considered a traitorous thing to do. She returned, saying the baby was the sweetest little thing and Cara had brought a friend back with her, Fielding, whom Sybil might know as she'd been in Malta, too.

'She lost her arm in the same air raid that killed Cara's fiancé, yet she's being so brave about it. Me, I'd have gone to pieces, I really would,' Mummy twittered.

Sybil had gone up to her room where she sat on the bed and brooded over the idea of Cara and Fielding living in *her* house, one of them possibly sleeping in *her* bed, using the things on *her* dressing table – the silver-backed mirror and brush set that Daddy had bought her one Christmas, the jewellery kept in a marquisette box, the clothes still hanging in the wardrobe.

Impulsively, she got off the bed and ran downstairs, shouting, 'I'm going for a walk, Mummy.'

'But, darling,' Mummy cried, 'it's pitch-black outside and there might be a raid.'

Sybil's answer was a slam the door. She stood on the step, waiting to get used to the darkness, for the sky to separate itself from the houses opposite and, as the buildings gradually took shape, she set off for Parliament Terrace.

She had remembered to bring her front door key, but took ages finding the keyhole so she could let herself in. Inside, she became entangled in a thick curtain covering the door, but managed to fight her way through and was then faced with a dilemma. Should she make her presence known by shouting? Or creep upstairs and remove everything that belonged to her? It struck her that she'd had no right to let herself in. The house no longer belonged to her, but to Cara Caffrey, who had, somehow, managed to trick poor Daddy into leaving it to her.

She crept along the hall. There were people in the kitchen. She recognized Nancy's voice and another, only faintly familiar. Fielding, she realized after a while. Insolent, brazen-faced Fielding, whom she'd never liked, was actually sitting in what should have been *her* kitchen, talking to Nancy.

It's *not your kitchen, not your house*, a little voice reminded her. *You have no right to be here.*

The best thing would be to ask Mummy to collect her things – she should have thought of that before, but her brain wasn't working properly at that moment. She was about to leave when she noticed a light shining underneath the door of Daddy's study. She crept along the hall and listened outside, but was met with complete silence. All of a sudden, she felt a desire to sit in Daddy's chair, touch the things on his desk, something he'd used to do, as if the feel of them gave him some satisfaction.

She opened the door and came face to face with Cara Caffrey, who was sitting behind the desk, tears streaming down her cheeks.

'Hello, Sybil,' Cara said softly. She didn't look even faintly surprised to see her. 'I was just sitting in your father's chair. This was his favourite room. He spent nearly all his time in here.'

'Do you think I didn't already know that?'

'Of course. What a silly thing for me to say! I was just having a little cry alone – this is the first minute I've had to meself since I got back. I've just put Kitty down to sleep, she's worn out with all the attention she's had tonight.' She made a welcoming gesture with her hand. 'Come in and sit down.'

How gracious of her, Sybil thought, inviting me into my own father's study. She went in and closed the door, but didn't sit, deeply resenting the way Cara looked so very much at home.

'What did you do to Daddy to make him leave everything to you?' she asked, making a great effort to keep her voice steady and reasonable, when she really wanted to scream and yell.

'Do?' Cara wiped the tears off her cheeks with the back of her hands. 'I didn't do anything. I've no idea why he should have been so generous.'

'But he loved me more than anyone else in the world!' she wailed. It was impossible to keep her voice steady and she didn't feel even remotely reasonable. 'You must have done something to make him prefer you over me.'

'I didn't, Sybil, honest. He was nice to me and I was nice to him. I told him often how grateful I was that he'd taken me in – I've no idea what I'd have done if he hadn't.'

'It was all my idea that you approach Nancy for help,' Sybil sullenly pointed out.

'I know, and I'm very grateful for that, too.'

She wished Cara wasn't being quite so calm, as if she were determined not to lose her temper no matter what Sybil said. She would have much preferred a shouting match.

'There is something,' Cara added quietly. 'I think you should have written to him more often. The whole time I was here, you only sent him the one letter and he kept it on his desk for ages. I often came in and found him reading it. In a way, I think I took your place. I told him all about Marzipan Hall and what it was like being in Malta – *you* hadn't. The letter you sent was only a single page and was obviously dashed off in a hurry.' Her voice wobbled slightly. 'He was a terribly lonely man, Sybil and, after a while, I think he began to look upon *me* as his daughter.'

'Men don't usually marry their daughters.'

'He only did it for Kitty's sake and I accepted for the same reason. I wouldn't have dreamt of marrying Marcus otherwise and he wouldn't have dreamt of asking.' Cara stood and came round to the front of the desk. If she comes any closer, Sybil vowed, I'll slap her face, but Cara stopped a few feet away and gave her an imploring look. 'I'd like us to be friends, Sybil. It was dead good of you to pass on my letters to Mam and hers to me. I don't know how I would have managed without your help. Now, we're both related in a way and there'll always be a room for you in this house whenever you want it.'

She held out her hand, but Sybil ignored it. 'I shall never set foot in this house again,' she spat. 'I shall ask Mummy to collect all the things from my room and keep them at hers. I take it you have no objection?' she added sarcastically.

'Of course not.' Cara's narrow shoulders heaved in a sigh. 'Take anything you want.'

'Cara!' There was a knock on the door and Nancy came in. She looked surprised when she noticed Sybil there. 'Oh, hello, pet. I didn't realize you were here.'

'I'm just going – and I'm never coming back!' Sybil rushed out of the room and both women were silent until the front door banged shut.

'Poor old thing.' Nancy shook her head. 'Her father wanted to give her the sun, moon and stars, but she threw them back in his face, so he gave them to you and Kitty instead.'

Chapter 13

It was one of the oldest tricks in the book and he'd fallen for it, hook, line and sinker. For as long as he lived, he would never make a bigger mistake.

The three Irish men were playing rummy for tanners in the Black Horse, a pub on the Dock Road, when he dropped in for a pint after work. When they saw him watching and asked if he'd like to play a hand, he'd done so willingly, although had always considered rummy an old woman's game.

Tyrone Caffrey had inherited his Uncle Paddy's fondness for playing cards for money. No matter how low the stakes, it gave him the same tingling, faintly unsettling, but highly enjoyable feeling he'd had when he and his mates had shaken down drunks for coppers.

The men's names were Barry, Johnno and Titch; the latter was well over six feet tall. At first, he'd considered them a bit gormless and wasn't surprised to find himself winning every game. By eight o'clock, when the men had to go, he'd won over thirty bob and was surprised when they suggested they meet the next night for another game. Just try and stop me, he'd thought exultantly. It was like taking buns from a baby.

The following night, he didn't win quite so much, but a quid was better than a kick up the backside and he returned home feeling mightily pleased with himself, having arranged to meet them again at the same time in the same place tomorrow.

'Have you ever played blackjack, Ty?' Barry asked when they met. 'It's an American game otherwise known as twenty-one.'

'A few times,' Tyrone replied. Blackjack was a man's game, faster and more skilful, far preferable to rummy.

They cut to deal and Tyrone's card was the highest. Being the dealer was a distinct advantage in blackjack and he easily won the first game. This must be my lucky night, he crowed inwardly when he cut the highest card again and again and was up by twelve and a tanner in no time.

Then everything began to change, so suddenly that it left him breathless. The games speeded up, the men stopped joking and became more businesslike, and by the time eight o'clock came and they had to leave, he discovered he'd lost all his winnings and was down by a further ten pounds – they'd stopped using money when he'd spent all he had on him and Barry was writing the figures down in a notebook.

'Hard luck, boyo,' Johnno said sympathetically. 'Don't worry, I'm down almost as much as you, but we'll win it back again tomorrer night, eh?'

'Sure thing,' Tyrone gulped. He *had* to win it back. There was no other way he could get his hands on ten pounds.

'Oh, he'll be back tomorrer night, that's for sure, won't you, boyo?' Barry said with a smile that didn't quite reach his eyes. 'Don't forget, we know where he lives and we know where he works. If he doesn't come, we'll just have to go and fetch him.'

He'd told them where he worked, but did they really know where he lived? By now, he considered them more sinister than gormless. If Johnno hadn't lost so much, Tyrone might have suspected he was being set up. He hoped and prayed his luck would change tomorrow. He didn't care if he came out of the experience with nothing in his pocket. All he was interested in was clearing the ten-pound debt.

The next night was a disaster. It had taken Tyrone, who'd always thought of himself as a canny bugger, quite a while before the penny dropped and he realized the Irishmen were cheating. There was something suspicious about the cards they used, a yellowing pack with smudged backs, and Tyrone suspected they were marked. And although Johnno had lost the night before, it didn't matter because they were working as a team and it had been just a ruse to make him believe he hadn't been singled out. He must be the biggest idiot under the sun to be so easily duped. He threw his cards on to the table and said flatly, 'I've had enough. I don't know how much I owe, but I'll never manage to pay it back.' He'd never been short of nerve, but couldn't pluck up the courage to accuse the men of cheating, and couldn't see what use it would be if he did. They'd only deny it.

Barry silently totted up the figures in his notebook, his expression hard and calculating. 'You owe just over twenty-four quid, boyo, and you're going to have to pay it back, if not in cash, then in kind.'

'What d'you mean by that?'

'We've seen your house in Shaw Street, it's not exactly a hovel. There must be goods in there worth twenty-four good ould English pounds that you can take to the pawnshop.'

'It's not my house. It belongs to me mam and dad.' They really had been to see where he lived. Terror gripped Tyrone's heart like a fist.

'Does your dear ould ma not own a decent bit of jewellery?' Barry asked in a silky voice. 'Has your da got a watch? What about your wife's wedding ring? Does the family have a wireless, a nice chiming clock, some good china, a canteen of cutlery?'

'Me mam doesn't have any jewellery and I can't possibly take me wife's ring or me dad's watch. Or any of those other things,' he added.

Barry thrust his face into his so that their noses almost touched. 'Well, boyo, either you pay us what you owe, or you'll find yourself with both your legs broke in so many places that you'll never walk again, not even with crutches. The choice is yours. You've got twenty-four hours to come up with the cash. If you're not here by eight o'clock tomorrer night, you know what'll happen.'

Tyrone didn't doubt that Barry meant every word.

That night, he didn't sleep a wink as he tried to think of ways of getting together the twenty-four pounds, ranging from holding up a bank, to staging a robbery in his own house when everyone was out and taking the stuff to the pawnshop. The first was no good as he didn't have a gun, and the second because pawnshops usually demanded some sort of identification and they'd be the first places the coppers would look when Mam reported the burglary. It was no good thinking up a reason to get Maria to hand over her ring, as it was hardly thicker than a thread of cotton and had only cost three pound, two and sixpence in the first place.

It wasn't until he was back at work next day that Tyrone remembered Cara's sapphire ring that Mam had been looking after all this time. Only the other day, she'd muttered bitterly, 'I bet she'll turn up any minute wanting it back.'

So far, there'd been no communication between Mam and Cara, so the ring was still somewhere in the house. There'd be no need to pawn it, as it was gold with real stones, obviously worth well over twenty-four pounds. He'd give it straight to the Irish men, tell *them* to pawn the bloody thing, so there'd be no record of Tyrone Caffrey having been near a pawnshop. There'd be ructions when Mam discovered it had gone, but she hardly ever wore it so it would be ages before she found out, and all he'd have to do was claim he knew nothing about it – he was good at pretending innocence when he was as guilty as sin.

He decided to fetch the ring at dinnertime when there was more chance of the house being empty – Maria and the lads at her mam's and his own mam gone to the shops. He easily found the little dark-blue velvet box in which the ring was kept in the top dressing table drawer, underneath a pile of hankies. He opened the box to make sure the ring was inside and it twinkled at him brilliantly. Tyrone heaved a sigh of relief and put it deep into his trouser pocket, then sank on to the bed, feeling dead ashamed.

What a way for a 24-year-old man to conduct his life, stealing jewellery from his mother. He resolved that never again would he play cards for money. Trouble was, he was always on the lookout for a bit of excitement, but now see where it had landed him!

He stood, groaning when he thought of the example he was setting for his lads. He'd never been much of a dad, spending far too much time in the pub. Weekdays, he didn't set eyes on them; they were in bed when he left for work and in bed when he got home. Recently, Joey had been asking to be taken to a football match, but Tyrone had better things to do with his Saturday afternoons and had told him to sod off.

'I'll take him on Sat'day,' he vowed. 'And I'll take them both to the park on Sunday, Maria an' all.' Tyrone genuinely loved his wife and sons, although he'd never given them much reason to love him. Once all this horrible business was over, he'd take Maria away for the weekend, somewhere quiet where they'd have a bit of peace. It wouldn't exactly be a second honeymoon, as they'd never had a first, but the break would do their marriage good. She'd been a good, loyal wife who'd stuck by him through his moods, hardly ever complaining. He almost wished she'd come back so he could tell her how much he loved her, but it was time he returned to work.

Groaning again, Tyrone left the house, feeling the box with the ring in rubbing against his thigh. He would leave the Irish men waiting until the very last minute, until about five to eight, before he turned up with the ring. It wouldn't hurt to let them sweat a bit.

'I may as well be living in this place by meself,' Brenna declared aloud when she went in and found the house empty. Maria and the lads spent more time at Mrs Murphy's than they did at Shaw Street, Tyrone was either at work or the pub, Fergus at least had the decency to come home for a meal before making his way to Jessie Clifford's and she wasn't seeing all that much of Colm who for months now had been working late, leaving no time to eat before taking up his duties as an ARP warden. Some nights, she didn't see him until the early hours and he'd even taken to working some weekends.

She slammed the shopping on the table with unnecessary force. Everything had gone wrong. She hadn't seen Eleanor or Nancy in weeks, not since Cara had come home, and she had no intention of going to see her daughter without giving her a piece of her mind. It just wasn't *in* her to accept the despicable things she'd done.

'It's not my way,' she told herself. 'She's behaved really badly; sleeping with that RAF feller, hiding out in Parliament Terrace for months, marrying Marcus Allardyce on the sly in one of those heathen Registry Office places, having a baby without telling her mam.' At this last, Brenna suppressed a sob. 'She deserves a good telling off,' she finished with a sniff.

She went into the kitchen and put the kettle on. Was it her own fault that everything had gone so badly wrong? Colm had suggested it more than once. 'You're too rigid, luv. You should learn to bend with the wind.' But Brenna had no intention of bending in a full-blown storm. She had her standards and expected people to live up to them.

The kettle boiled, she made tea and took it into the living room. Time was when a quiet cuppa was a luxury, but now the house was quiet all the time, although that could easily be changed. All she had to do was slip on her coat and go to see Cara, pretend nothing untoward had happened and the old, loving mother-and-daughter relationship would return. Cara would come to see her every day with the baby and that Fielding person she'd met in the Army, or Brenna could go and see her.

No! It wouldn't be right, she thought, her mouth setting in a straight line – rigid, Colm would have called it. It would be too humiliating. She would be condoning a multitude of sins.

She was about to peel a pile of spuds, when she remembered there was an almost full pan left over from the night before that she could slice and fry with bacon when people came home. These days, she never knew how many, apart from Fergus, would turn up for a meal. Sometimes, Maria and the lads ate at her mam's. For pudding, there was half of one of them eggless sponges also left over from yesterday. There'd been a time when it would have vanished within seconds, eggs or no eggs, when the whole family had sat down to tea together.

She returned to the sitting room, feeling bored with nothing to do. The house was scrupulously clean, there was no polishing or dusting to be done, everywhere was tidy – no, not *every*where. What sort of mess had Maria had left in the bedroom? It wouldn't surprise her to learn that the Murphys had never been in the habit of making beds and Maria only made a rough and ready job of it.

'I might have known,' she muttered when she entered the room and found Maria had merely straightened the coverlet and not bothered to tuck in the blankets underneath. Brenna tut-tutted as she made the bed *her* way: the same with the lads' bed in Cara's old room.

Before returning downstairs, she went into her own bedroom to take a look at the sapphire ring. Unknown to Tyrone, his mam looked at the ring quite a few times a day. Only occasionally did she wear it: when she went to meetings of the Townswomen's Guild, for instance, or to Mass on Sundays, or if she was in the house by herself when she would slip it on her finger, twist her hand this way and that, getting enormous pleasure from the way it flashed and sparkled in the light. In fact, she'd wear it now while she still had it, before Cara wanted it back.

But the little velvet box wasn't underneath the hankies, the place it was always kept, the place where she'd put it only last night before getting into bed after admiring it for the umpteenth time. Had one of the lads got hold of it? She felt underneath the hankies, stockings, gloves and scarves, then threw them on to the bed leaving the drawer empty. There was no sign of the ring. Frantic now, she did the same with the other drawers, but the ring wasn't there either, not that she'd expected it to be. It had been put under the hankies last night: she could remember quite distinctly.

Was it possible that Colm had taken it to give back to Cara? Much to Brenna's annoyance, he visited his daughter whenever he had a rare free moment and she might have asked for it. But surely he wouldn't have done that without telling *her*? Unless, she thought uncomfortably, he wanted to avoid a row and was waiting until she found the ring missing and a row became inevitable.

Someone came in the back door and Fergus shouted, 'I'm home, Mam.'

'I won't be a mo, darlin',' Brenna called. She went slowly downstairs. Earlier, she'd been looking forward to the fried potatoes and bacon, but now she couldn't have eaten a thing. It was silly, but she would have liked to have said goodbye to the ring, had a good look at it, knowing it would be the last time it would be in her possession.

'You're on edge tonight, Mam,' Fergus commented, as she flitted in and out of the kitchen, standing up and sitting down for no apparent reason.

'D'you think it'd be all right if I went round to the ARP station to see if your dad's arrived yet? No one'd mind, would they?'

'I'm sure no one'd mind a bit, but seeing as there isn't a raid on, Dad would've come straight home, wouldn't he?'

'I suppose.' Brenna had often wondered how it was that Colm seemed to arrive in Toxteth the minute a raid started so there wasn't even time to drop in for a cup of tea and a snack. She went into the hall for her coat. 'Even so, I'll pop round there now, just in case, like. Tara, son.'

The ARP station was situated in a scout hut in Park Road. Brenna had never been before. The furniture consisted of a long, worm-ridden table with a telephone on top and a dozen or so chairs. There was a map of the area on the wall that two elderly men were studying when she went in, and a clock announcing the time was ten to seven. 'Excuse me,' she said brightly.

The men turned. 'How can we help you, missus?' asked one.

'I'm looking for Colm Caffrey. D'you know what time he'll be here?'

The other man shook his head. 'We haven't seen Colm in a few days. He telephoned to say there was trouble at home or summat like that.'

'I'm his wife and there's no trouble at home.' There would be if she discovered he'd returned the ring to Cara and not said a word.

'In that case, I'm afraid we can't help you, missus. I'm only repeating what Colm told us.'

'Ta.' Brenna tossed her head and marched out. The man was talking rubbish. Colm had probably said there was trouble at work, not home. It made far more sense, even if he'd hadn't said anything to her about it. And what did it mean that Colm hadn't been seen for a few days? Perhaps the man had got him mixed up with someone else. She felt uneasy and a bit confused. She couldn't stand things not being completely straightforward and uncomplicated. It was the way she liked life to be, the way she ran her own. She didn't hold with people who removed rings without telling anyone, or left messages, the meaning of which was unclear.

She was halfway home when the siren went, signalling a raid was about to start – and on such a lovely May evening, too. The sun was a great golden ball in a sky the same colour as the stones in the missing ring. She didn't quicken her pace; the siren usually gave people plenty of time to get to their shelters.

It therefore came as a fearful shock when she heard the drone of aircraft overhead and saw what looked like a good hundred planes appear in the sapphire sky like a flock of evil blackbirds bringing more death and destruction to the city of Liverpool.

She fled home. 'Is there anyone in?' she yelled when she ran into the house. There was no reply, but she noticed Maria's shopping bag on the chair. She must have come back and gone out again to the public shelter when the siren went. Maria couldn't stand being in the house during a raid with only the lads for company. Brenna was sorry they'd missed each other. She preferred having company during a raid herself and the lads hated the shelter, unable to sleep in the racket. Joey was scared of the drunks who came pouring in when the pubs closed. He was a nervous little boy, just like Fergus used to be before he'd started sleeping with married women.

Brenna picked up her handbag and shut herself in the cupboard under the stairs, preoccupied with the missing ring and the odd message Colm had left at the ARP Centre. Irritating though these things were, however, it dawned on her after a while that the raid in progress was a raid like no other she'd known before. The bombs were raining down, there were explosions every few seconds, the earth shook, the house trembled and it was bedlam outside, what with the screams and shouts, the bells and the hooters, the thud of feet along the pavement and the sound of children crying.

At a time like this, a person needed their family around them, hands to hold, shoulders to lean on, lips to kiss. But Brenna had no one. She began to weep.

The Irish men had another think coming if they expected him to turn up on a night like this. Tyrone had no intention of risking his life walking through the streets as far as the Docky to deliver the ring. In the pub he was in now, a few men had left for home when the siren went, but most had stayed and continued supping their beer as if nothing untoward was happening. They might wince if there was an explosion close by and there'd be a slight pause in their conversation, but otherwise they stayed calm. A few were playing cards for matchsticks, but Tyrone had lost all interest in cards. He found it hard not to hope that the Black Horse would receive a direct hit and all his problems would be over: he'd put the ring back in the dressing table drawer and Mam would never know it hadn't been there all the time.

'This is it!' Nancy said grimly as she shielded her head with her hands when there was a bang that nearly burst their eardrums. A cloud of plaster drifted down from the ceiling and two plates fell off the dresser. The bricks of the big house seemed to shift slightly and the beams creaked and groaned, followed seconds later by the loud rumble of collapsing buildings. The rumbling seemed to go on for ever. More dust fell from the ceiling.

Cara almost bent double as she tried to shelter her sleeping child. Kitty opened her eyes, disturbed by the bang, sighed briefly and closed them again. 'It's all right, sweetheart,' she whispered. 'You're quite safe with me.' But it wasn't all right and it wasn't safe. Tonight it was hell on earth and it had been going on for hours. She'd be surprised if there was much of Liverpool left standing by morning.

'It wasn't "it",' Fielding crowed when, suddenly, there was silence and the house had remained intact. 'We're still alive!'

'So we are!' Nancy laid her arms on the table and they grinned at each other. 'But that was close. Would you like some more wine, pet?'

'Wouldn't say no. I'd like to get completely blotto and not be able to hear a thing.'

'Good idea.' Nancy refilled both their glasses. 'Are you sure you wouldn't like some, Cara?'

'No, ta. I'm still breastfeeding Kitty, aren't I?' Cara said shortly. The pair were getting on her nerves. You'd think Fielding was Nancy's long-lost daughter the way they'd taken to each other and she felt a tiny bit jealous, having always considered Nancy belonged to *her*. Between them, they were gradually demolishing the contents of Marcus's cellar. If the raids went on much longer, the cellar would be bare.

'Would you like us to make you a cup of tea, pet?' Nancy asked kindly. 'It's so much worse for you, isn't it? You've got Kitty to worry about as well as yourself.'

'It's horrible for us all, and yes, I'd love some tea. Thank you, Nancy.' Now Cara felt awful. They were just coping with the raids in a way that was far better than getting hysterical and panicking every time a bomb fell. It was how she, Nancy and Marcus had coped when he'd been alive. But now she had Kitty and found it hard to pretend the raids were something to laugh at, particularly this one.

It was a weird feeling, sitting in the kitchen full of familiar objects, talking normally, yet knowing that any second you could be dead. Two years ago, if she'd been told such a thing was going to happen, she would have refused to believe it.

Fielding got up and opened the blackout curtains a crack. 'The world's on fire,' she announced, 'and I think next door's been hit, or it might be next door but one. The road's full of rubble.'

'Bloody hell!' Nancy gasped.

'I hope me dad's all right,' Cara said fearfully. 'He's outside in all that mayhem. And I wish I'd made up with Mam. If she's killed, I'll never forgive meself. She's never even set eyes on Kitty.' Tomorrow morning, first thing, she'd go round to Shaw Street and take Kitty with her. Mam could tear her off a dozen strips, but she didn't care. By the time she'd finished, they'd be friends again.

★

Brenna had already made up her mind that tomorrow she would go and see Cara. Nowadays, life was too short and too precarious to hold grudges against people you loved as much as she loved her daughter. She felt ashamed that she hadn't gone before, ashamed that Cara had been too scared to come home when she discovered she was having a baby, that she'd had to turn to Nancy for help.

'I'm a terrible mother,' she moaned, rocking back and forth on the uncomfortable bench that Colm had constructed in the cupboard under the stairs, hoping there'd soon be a lull in the bombing so she could make a cup of tea because her nerves were in tatters and she kept wanting to cry. Was Fergus safe? Tyrone? Maria and the lads? Cara and the little granddaughter she still hadn't seen? Where was Colm? What was all that nonsense about 'trouble at home'? Most nights when there was a raid, he'd pop in to see her, but he hadn't been tonight when she wanted him more than at any other time.

The cupboard door opened. 'Colm!' she cried, but it was Tyrone, swaying on his feet, as drunk as a lord.

'It's murder out there,' he said. 'I nearly fell down a crater.' He gazed into the cupboard, bleary-eyed. 'Where's Maria, Joey and Mike?'

'Gone to the shelter, son, probably the one in Ferguson Street, it's the nearest. There was no one in when the raid started and you know Maria doesn't like being in the place by herself.'

'I'll go and look for them.'

'But you can't, darlin'!' Brenna protested. 'It's not safe out there.'

But the words were wasted because the cupboard door had closed: a suddenly sober Tyrone had gone in search of his wife and children.

He should have come home hours ago, but his time in the pub had been spent in a pleasant, drunken haze, unable to imagine a bomb disrupting the peaceful scene before him – men drinking, quietly discussing football and other mundane topics, playing darts, dealing cards, as if they believed a good fairy had cast a spell over the pub and they were perfectly safe within its four walls. Perhaps the spell had touched him too, because Tyrone felt convinced he would never see the Irish men again. He might have felt cheerful at the thought, but knew that in a few hours he would be sober and remember how much he loathed being a civilian when there was a war on. His longing to be a soldier, to wear a uniform and fight for his King and country, hadn't abated with time. It was still there, gnawing at him, every hour of every day. His brother had done it, his sister, even little Fielding, who hardly came up to his shoulder, had joined the forces and emerged minus an arm.

Tyrone was slowly coming out of his pleasant haze when he heard someone remark, 'It's just gone midnight,' and he got unsteadily to his feet, surprised. This must be one of the pubs where the landlord continued serving until the all-clear went and he hadn't realized it was so late. He would have preferred to stay, but Maria would be worried about him, not to mention Mam.

He made his way to Shaw Street, wobbling all over the place, holding on to walls, avoiding heaps of smouldering bricks, narrowly missing being mown down by a speeding ambulance. There was a shout, 'Get indoors, you bloody idiot!' and he wondered if they meant him. The cacophony of so many different sounds hurt his ears as he stumbled on and would have fallen head first down a crater had he not tripped over a chimney pot lying in the middle of the street.

Home at last, only to find Maria had taken the lads to the public shelter. Tyrone had no idea why this should fill him with dread. She'd been to the shelter before, but then there'd never been a raid like this before.

'I'll go and look for them,' he said, slamming the cupboard door on Mam.

Outside again, he became conscious of things he hadn't noticed earlier. How red the sky was, for instance, how many fires he could see, the ominous gaps where there used to be houses in streets where he'd played as a child. Instead of a cacophony of sounds, he could distinctly hear the shriek of ambulances, the bells of fire engines, the crackle of fires, the rat-a-tat-tat of ack-ack fire, the roar of planes overhead, the whistle of the bombs as they dropped and the deadly, earth-shattering thud of the bombs exploding. And, somewhere in the middle of this grisly pandemonium, his wife and children were sheltering.

For a moment, Tyrone couldn't remember where Ferguson Street was. The next street, *the next street*, a voice said in his ear. He began to run, sprinting over the rubble like an athlete, around one corner, around another, but stopped when he heard another voice, a real one this time.

'Dad!' the voice said, and Tyrone looked down and saw his son,

Joey, sitting in a doorway, clutching the ancient teddy bear that had once belonged to Cara.

'Joey!' Tyrone lifted the child into his arms. What was he doing here? Where were the others? 'Where's your mam and Mike, son?'

'They were in the shelter, but I ran out. I don't like the shelter, Dad.' Joey buried his head in his father's shoulder and began to cry.

'I know, son.' Tyrone patted Joey's head. 'Never mind, I'll go back there with you. You'll be quite safe with your dad.'

'We can't, Dad,' Joey lisped. 'We can't go back 'cos the shelter got all blown up.'

The all-clear hadn't gone until half past four and it had taken a while before Cara could bring herself to go to bed and even longer before she nodded off. It felt as if she'd only been asleep five minutes when someone shook her shoulder and said, 'Cara, Cara,' in an urgent voice. She pretended not to hear in the hope the person would give up and go away.

'Cara, Cara,' the voice said again, and her sluggish brain recognized the voice as Nancy's. 'Your Tyrone's downstairs, pet. Something terrible's happened.'

Cara's eyes snapped open. 'Is it Mam?' She struggled to sit up. After living through the night in such high spirits, Nancy looked as if all the wind had been knocked out of her.

'No, pet, it's Maria and little Mike. They were in the shelter in Ferguson Street when it got a direct hit. Joey's all right, but Maria and Mike are both dead, God bless their souls.'

'Hello, Cara, luv,' Mam said quietly. She was sitting in the chair under the window, nursing a sleeping Joey in her arms and appeared to have aged ten years since Cara last saw her. 'Has our Tyrone been round yours?'

'Yes, Mam, Nancy and Fielding are looking after him.' When she left, Nancy had been trying to persuade her devastated brother to swallow some whiskey. 'I thought I'd come and see how you were. I've brought Kitty with me. She's asleep at the moment.'

'I'm all right, darlin', although I wish it had been this house that got the direct hit, not the shelter. There were nigh on forty people in there including Maria and Mike.' She sighed wearily. 'I'll put Joey to bed in a minute and take a proper look at Kitty, but the poor little heartbroken lad only went to sleep half an hour ago. What time is it?'

'About half seven.' She'd slept less than an hour. 'Tyrone said some drunk came in the shelter and was sick all over the place. Joey felt frightened and ran out to look for his dad. He'd hardly been gone a minute when the shelter was hit.' Cara eased herself on to a chair. Her head and her entire body throbbed with exhaustion and Kitty felt like a ton weight.

'That's right, and now Tyrone's all for blaming himself, but if it was anyone's fault Maria went to the shelter it was mine.' Mam's face crumpled, as if she was about to cry. 'Running all over the place, I was, trying to find out about that bloody ring. I was only halfway home when the siren went: Maria had already gone when I arrived.'

'What ring, Mam?'

'That one o'yours, darlin', the sapphire one.' Mam gave her a sharp look. 'Did you ask your dad for it back?'

Cara was glad she was able to answer, 'No.' Her mother seemed to be rather quietly overwrought and she had a feeling she only had to say a wrong word and all the resentment would come pouring out. 'To tell the truth, Mam, I'd forgotten all about the ring. So far as I'm concerned, you can keep it.'

'It doesn't matter now,' Mam said listlessly. 'God knows where it's gone.' She waved a limp hand. 'Have you seen the state of this place?' There was a film of dust over everything and the fireplace was full of soot.

'It's the same back home. Outside, the air's thick with it and everywhere smells of burning. Two houses in Parliament Terrace were destroyed last night. The bomb only missed us by a few yards.'

'At least you had company. I had to sit through it all by meself until Tyrone came home with Joey in his arms and told me Maria and Mike were dead.' There was a hint of accusation in her voice, as if to say Cara should have been with her.

Cara ignored the hint. 'Where's Dad?' she asked. Perhaps he was still out there helping to rescue the people buried under the rubble.

'He's disappeared,' Mam said bitterly, 'like that bloody ring. I can't remember when I last saw him. All me family have deserted me.'

Cara changed the subject. 'Would you like me to make a cup of tea, Mam? I'll put Kitty down on the settee in the front room.'

'I would dearly, except there's no water and no gas, and no electricity either. All the mains got damaged last night.'

'I forgot. There's nothing working in Parliament Terrace either, but I'm sure it'll all be fixed soon.' She went into the parlour and laid Kitty down any road, then returned to her mother.

It was a relief when, minutes later, the back door opened and Fergus came in. 'I didn't realize things were so bad until I stepped outside,' he said soberly. 'We . . . I mean, I slept through the whole thing.'

'Well, it's nice of you to show your face,' Mam said acidly. 'If you're wanting your breakfast, there's none to be had, not even a glass of water.' Suddenly, without warning, she burst into hysterical tears. 'This war's really getting me down,' she cried. 'What sort of world is it when people can't sleep in their own beds any more and little children are murdered? It's evil, that's what it is, evil. Last night, I prayed to the Blessed Virgin to keep us all safe, but she mustn't have heard me for the bombs.'

'Shush, Mam,' Cara said gently. 'You'll wake Joey.' Joey had started furiously to suck his thumb. 'Fergus, will you carry Joey upstairs and put him to bed?' She added in a whisper, 'Maria and Mike died last night when the shelter in Ferguson Street got a direct hit.'

'Jaysus!' Fergus went very pale and looked as if he was about to be sick. 'Oh, Jaysus!' He carefully removed his little nephew from Mam's arms and took him upstairs. 'I didn't know,' he said wretchedly when he came back. 'If I had, I'd've come home straight away.'

'I know you would, Ferg.' Cara patted his arm comfortingly.

'Where's our Tyrone?'

'He's with Nancy. What are we going to do about Mam?' she asked quietly. 'She really needs Dad, but he's done a disappearing act.' They glanced at their mother who had stopped crying and was sitting very still, eyes closed, her face creased as if she were in enormous pain. In the parlour, Kitty had woken and was making little chirruping noises.

'I'll stay with Mam,' Fergus said, 'then I'll be here for Tyrone when he comes home, but I'd like you to do something for me – telephone Littlewoods when you get back and tell them what's happened. Ask for Mr Worrall, he's my boss.'

'OK,' Cara promised, guiltily relieved that it seemed all right for her to leave. Mam had hardly glanced at her new grandchild.

'Your dad's just phoned,' Nancy said when she went in carrying a screaming Kitty who was announcing to the world that she was starving. 'He said to phone him back straight away. I left the number on the desk in the study. I told him about Maria and Mike, by the way. He was terribly upset.'

'I'll phone him the minute I've fed this little madam. Did Dad say where he was? And where's our Tyrone?'

'I got the impression your dad was at work and I persuaded Tyrone to lie down for a while. Fielding's gone to tuck him in. Oh, and the water's back on, there's still no gas, but I remembered there was a paraffin stove in the cellar, so I've made a pot of tea. Would you like some.' It was hard to believe Nancy had had so little sleep. She looked calm and capable, as if she was in charge of a minor military operation.

'I wondered what the horrible smell was. I'd love some tea, Nancy, ta.' Cara undid the buttons on the front of her frock and attached the frantic baby to her breast. Kitty seized it like a clam and began to suck audibly. 'Greedy little thing,' Cara murmured affectionately.

'How's your mam taking things?' Nancy asked as she poured two cups of tea, one for Cara, one for her.

'Really bad. Our Fergus is with her.'

'In a minute, I'll make some tea in that little aluminium pot, wrap it in towels, and take it round. I know how much she loves her tea and it's ages since I saw her, what with all the excitement going on here.'

'She'd really appreciate that, Nancy.'

Kitty fed, the tea drunk, Cara went up to the study, the baby in her arms. First, she telephoned Littlewoods on Fergus's behalf, then rang her father. A woman answered and said she'd fetch him. 'He's on the shop floor somewhere.'

'Cara,' Dad said breathlessly when he came. 'How are you, luv?'

'Tired, Dad, but so is everyone. Why haven't you been home?' she asked accusingly. 'Mam's in a terrible state wondering where you are.'

'I'll explain everything soon, luv. I'm dead sorry to hear the news about Maria and Mike, but it's you and Kitty I'm concerned about at the moment,' he said urgently. 'I don't want you staying in Liverpool if there's going to be another raid like last night's. You're to catch a train to Kirkby Station – the trains are running, I checked – and close by you'll find the Westminster Bank, it's only a little branch, no bigger than a shop. Round the back, you'll see a staircase that leads to the flat upstairs. The door isn't locked and you'll find plenty of food. Stay there, Cara, and don't leave until it's safe, d'you hear?'

'Yes, Dad,' Cara said meekly. 'Can I take Fielding with me?'

'If you like. Look, I have to go now, someone wants me. I might see you tonight. Tara, luv.'

'Tara, Dad.'

Kirkby was on the outskirts of Liverpool, yet could have been on another planet, Cara thought when she got off the train and pushed the pram up the slope towards the road. The only sound she could hear was the twittering of birds in the trees. The air smelled fresh with a hint of flowers. There was a pub across the road, the Railway Arms, and half a dozen customers were lounging outside enjoying the sunshine.

A few yards along she found the Westminster Bank – closed for lunch – and the iron staircase at the back her father had described. Washing was pegged to a line in the overgrown garden. Lifting a cooing, smiling Kitty out of her pram, she climbed the staircase and entered a small kitchen with red-and-white gingham curtains, a sink full of dirty dishes, and a door leading to a white-painted sitting room with two large armchairs covered in red linen. The shelves on each side of the fireplace were crammed with books and under the window at the side there was a round table with two chairs and a typewriter on the floor underneath.

'I wonder who lives here?' she asked Kitty when she opened a door at the far end of the room and found a pretty bedroom with an unmade double bed and a dressing table littered with make-up. The room smelled strongly of perfume. 'It's obviously a woman Dad must know who's had to go away somewhere. I must say she's made it look very nice. I wouldn't mind some curtains like that meself.' The frilly lilac drapes hid the ugly blackout tucked behind.

She laid Kitty on the bed and returned to the kitchen to investigate the food. What she had thought was a larder turned out to be a minuscule bathroom and lavatory, and the food was kept in a cupboard on the wall; lots of tins, half a loaf, some funny-coloured butter in a glass dish that, on investigation, turned out to be Spam – tinned meat from America that was delicious fried or cold with salad. After washing the dishes, she made a Spam sandwich and ate it sitting in one of the red chairs, pleased to discover Kitty had gone to sleep. A sheet of paper with writing on had been dropped on the hearth and she wondered what it said. She found the occupant of the flat intriguing and was interested to know who and where she was.

'Darling,' the note said in curly, dramatic letters.
The pains are back, but this time I'm convinced they mean business. I've phoned the hospital to say I'm on my way and will catch the next train. Just think, next time we see each other, I shall probably be a mother!
Yours
Lizzie.

Cara felt even more intrigued. Lizzie obviously lived in the flat and had gone to have a baby. The note had been left for someone, presumably her husband, but where was he? Why wasn't he sleeping there while his wife was away?

Suddenly, tiredness overcame her curiosity and she joined Kitty on the bed where she slept soundly for more than two hours and woke up feeling completely refreshed and ready for a walk in the countryside. She fed Kitty, changed her nappy, washed the old one and hung it outside to dry, as she didn't want to return to Liverpool with a bagful of dirty nappies.

She was putting Kitty in the pram when a smiling young woman formally dressed in white blouse and black skirt appeared. Her hair was coiled, most unattractively, in plaits around her head. 'Hello, I thought I heard footsteps upstairs and wondered if it was Lizzie back after another false alarm – I work in the bank,' she explained. 'It must've been third time lucky – for Lizzie, that is. I might phone the hospital later and see what she had. But perhaps you already know. Are you a friend of Lizzie's?'

'No, we've never met.'

'Then you must know Colm, her husband?'

Cara caught her breath. 'A bit,' she stammered.

'How old is your baby?' The girl came and looked into the pram. 'Oh, isn't she a smasher? What's she called?'

'Kitty, she's three and a half months.'

'Lizzie was hoping for a girl. Oh, well, I'd better get back to work or Mr Miller, me boss, will get a cob on. Tara – I don't know your name. I'm Mary.'

'Cara.'

'Tara, Cara.'

'Tara, Mary.'

The girl disappeared and Cara was left to face the fact that Colm, the husband Mary had mentioned, could only be her father, inconceivable though that may be. It was too much of a coincidence to be otherwise. She felt her blood run cold. Dad had been having an affair with this Lizzie woman and it was *his* baby that was about to be born when the note was written – had almost certainly been born by now.

Kitty looked quite happy in the pram. Cara half raised the hood to shield her from the sun, and went back into the flat, leaving the door open in case she cried. She was glad now that Fielding hadn't come with her.

'I'd sooner stay with Nancy, if you don't mind,' she'd said when Cara had told her about the flat in Kirkby where they'd be safe if there was another heavy raid that night.

'Of course I don't mind,' Cara had said, although she had. Fielding was supposed to be her friend and she would have welcomed her presence in this strange place, but now she far preferred to be alone with her thoughts. What would this do to Mam? As if she hadn't been through enough over the last year – much of it Cara's fault.

She began to search the flat, unsure what she was looking for: clues, confirmation that Lizzie's 'husband' was definitely her dad. The first thing she saw was a head-and-shoulders photo in a silver frame on a little corner table she hadn't noticed before. It showed an attractive young woman with doe eyes, a cupid mouth and a long dark fringe. She studied it carefully. The woman was smiling slightly as she stared into space, not vacuously, but as if she was thinking deeply about something very important.

If this was Lizzie, then Mam, with her middle-aged spread and rapidly greying hair, didn't stand a chance. Yet, in Cara's eyes, her mam and dad belonged together. She couldn't imagine one living without the other until death did them part, but her next discovery merely provided proof of what she was searching for – a photo taken in the untidy garden of the pretty, doe-eyed women in the arms of a tall, exceptionally handsome man, both looking, not at the camera, but at each other, in the same way that Kit and Cara had once done. She sighed. She'd forgotten how good-looking her father was, yet it came as an embarrassment to discover he was in love with another woman.

She decided not to pry any more and take Kitty for a walk, although hardly noticed the snow-white May blossom adorning the hedgerows, and the dandelions, buttercups, daisies and other wild flowers, whose names she didn't know, spurting in their hundreds and thousands from underneath. Even the silvery stream she passed over, only inches deep, which seemed to be playing a tune as the water rushed and bubbled along its bed of white stones, didn't stop her from worrying what would happen when Mam found out Dad had been having an affair. Did he intend leaving her for Lizzie and the new baby? If it hadn't been for Kitty, she would have gone back to Parliament Terrace and tried not to think about it, hang tonight's raid – but if it hadn't been for Kitty, she wouldn't have come in the first place.

Back in the flat, she searched for clean bedding and found sheets and pillowslips in the bottom wardrobe drawer, all professionally laundered. She visualized her mother struggling with mountains of washing every Monday morning in a kitchen full of steam, and wanted to cry. If Mam were as rich as Croesus, she would still insist on doing the washing herself. She felt angry with her father yet, at the same time, was able to understand the appeal Lizzie held for him. Perhaps she, his daughter, was more like him than she'd thought. Not every woman, no matter how much in love she might be, would have agreed to marry a man she hardly knew in a foreign country without telling anyone at home. Dad had taken a risk with Lizzie, as she had intended to do with Kit, and to hell with the consequences.

'I suppose you've guessed,' Dad said when he turned up at about half past five looking so weary that Cara immediately felt sorry for him. Kitty lay on a blanket on the floor examining her toes.

'I didn't have to,' she replied levelly. 'A girl from the bank, Mary, told me someone called Lizzie was having a baby and her husband's name was Colm.'

'I've been meaning to tell your mam for months, luv, but I just couldn't bring meself to hurt her.' He closed his eyes and sighed deeply. 'I couldn't stand the thought of the row that would follow either. I'm too much of a coward.'

'You can't tell her now, Dad. I went to see her this morning and she's really cut up about Maria and Mike.'

'I know, luv.' He sighed again. 'I'll leave it a while until she's stronger.'

'How is Lizzie?' she asked. It was an awkward question to ask. 'Has she had the baby?'

'Yes, it was a boy – Bernard – but Lizzie had a hard time. She's forty-three and it was her first.' Dad's face softened. 'It took all night. I stayed with her in the hospital, holding her hand.' He blushed slightly and Cara did the same.

'Have you known her long?' she enquired, surprised to hear that Lizzie was only three years younger than her mother.

'We first met twenty years ago. She's Cyril Phelan's girl, the chap who owned the building yard where I used to work. We only met up again about a year ago when she applied to stand for Toxteth and Dingle after Ignatius Herlihy died.'

Cara's eyes widened. 'She wanted to be a politician? She must be clever, Dad.'

'It doesn't automatically follow that politicians are clever, luv,' her father said dryly. 'I reckon more than half are as thick as two short planks. They see it as a job where you don't have to work very hard in return for a hefty salary. Lizzie's different, she cares, not that it helped any when she tried for the seat. She was rejected in favour of a man, although she was the best candidate by a mile. Well,' he pushed himself tiredly to his feet, 'I'd better be going. It's time I had a few words with our Tyrone after the poor lad losing his wife and one of his kids, not to mention letting your mother know I'm still alive, if not exactly kicking. And I've been neglecting me ARP duties over the last few days, what with Lizzie due to have the baby any minute and living in this place on her own.' He bent and kissed her. 'Tara, luv. I'll try and call in again tomorrer – that's if you want

322

to see me like. After this, you might not want to have anything to do with your dad again.'

'Don't be silly.' She caught his hand and pressed it against her face. 'You've been a wonderful dad and I'll always love you.'

Cara stayed in Lizzie Phelan's flat for five days while the raids over Liverpool continued unabated. Every morning, she telephoned Parliament Terrace to make sure Nancy and Fielding were all right, and Fergus, who was spending his nights in Shaw Street and neglecting Jessie Clifford, rang from work to report that her mother and Joey were safe, although he was worried about Tyrone, who was insane with grief: 'He seems to blame himself for some reason.' Each evening, her father came to see her and, although they'd always been close, they seemed to grow closer with each visit as he tried to convey to her the reasons why he'd fallen in love with Lizzie Phelan.

'Vanity, I suppose,' he said thoughtfully one night. 'I was flattered that she liked me. She made me feel young, whereas your mam made me feel old. Lizzie manages to convince me there's nothing in the world I can't do. When the war's over, we're going to America.'

After her father had gone, Cara would turn on the wireless for *Band Wagon*, *Garrison Theatre*, or *The Old Town Hall*, listen to the nine o'clock news, then switch to the forces network for the songs that reminded her of Kit and Malta.

At night, with the bombing of Liverpool merely a distant rumble, she and Kitty slept soundly, waking up to the sound of birdsong and the passing of the occasional bus or car. The days passed slowly by and it would have been a simple matter to go to Liverpool for the day and come back to Kirkby at tea-time, but Cara relished the quiet and tranquillity of the little flat, although she knew she would soon get bored with nothing to do but go for walks.

It might have been instinct, or just a sudden longing to be home, that she returned to Parliament Terrace the day the raids stopped, although not for ever. Cara had enjoyed her short holiday, but now it was time for things to return to normal – or whatever what was considered normal when there was a war on.

Brenna's life had also assumed a vestige of normality. Cara and Kitty came to see her a few times a week, and Brenna often took Joey to Parliament Terrace where he'd fallen in love with Nancy. As soon as

Eleanor had heard about Maria and Mike, she'd come rushing round to Shaw Street to sympathize and now they were friends again – she and Oliver Chandler had spent the raids in the shelter at the bottom of the garden with the battery wireless blasting out Radio Luxembourg, singing along at the top of their voices with every familiar song.

Life could hardly be called sweet, but it was the best she could manage under the circumstances, so when Colm confessed he'd been having an affair with Lizzie Phelan and she'd had his child, Brenna decided enough was enough. She had Joey to look after, as well as an inconsolable Tyrone, and she had to stay strong for them. She took Colm's confession, if not calmly, then with a certain amount of resignation. They'd been growing apart for some time – at least, he'd been growing apart from her.

'Ah, well, if that's how you feel, Colm,' she said with a shrug when he told her that from now on he would be living with Lizzie in Kirkby. She had a strong feeling that it was only temporary, that one day he'd be back. Their marriage wasn't over, just put to one side for a while.

It was his fault, *his* fault. If he hadn't pinched that bloody ring, then Mam wouldn't have gone in search of Dad to see if he'd taken it. She'd have been at home when the siren went and there'd have been no need for Maria to take the lads to the shelter. His wife and son would still be alive and well. He would never stop blaming himself if he lived to be a hundred. And now Mam and Dad had split up and, although common sense told him it wasn't anything to do with him, for some reason he felt faintly responsible.

The day after the raid, he'd chucked the ring into the bedroom. It hit the wall and fell to the floor where Mam had found it. 'How on earth did it get there?' she gasped and stuffed it into a drawer. 'I never want to see it again. If it hadn't been for that . . . ' She didn't finish, but Tyrone knew what she'd been about to say.

Out of curiosity, he'd gone round to the Black Horse to see if the Irish men were still around – they could break his legs, break his whole body, and he wouldn't care – but the landlord said they'd been arrested. 'Apparently, they were involved with the IRA and were in Liverpool to raise funds or something. In their spare time, they circulated the pubs with a set of marked cards tricking customers into playing with them and making loads of lolly, although anyone with half a brain would have recognized they were con men from the start. Still,' he shrugged philosophically, 'they say a fool and his money are soon parted.' He frowned at Tyrone. 'Aren't you one of the ones who was taken in, lad?'

Tyrone shook his head. 'I never play cards for money.'

'Smart feller. Stick to that and you'll never go wrong.'

Now he was drinking himself to death, drowning in alcohol, hardly eating, going straight from work to the pub and refusing to let Fergus come with him because he wanted to be alone in his misery. He churlishly ignored anyone who tried to engage him in conversation and only left when they shouted last orders and he went home to his bed and cried himself to sleep.

It was a month since he'd lost his wife and child, and he was in a pub where he'd never been before, where he knew no one, figuring he'd be more likely to be ignored, when the bench he was on creaked and someone sat beside him. 'Can I get you a drink, mate?'

Tyrone groaned inwardly. 'No, ta,' he said rudely.

'You look as if you need bucking up a bit. How about another pint? I need bucking up a bit an' all. Perhaps we can do each other a favour. I'm Kevin, by the way.'

'Oh, all right. I'm Tyrone.' He couldn't be bothered arguing. He watched the man go to the bar and order the drinks. Thirtyish, not very tall, his face was deeply tanned. He looked healthy and fit and was neatly dressed in navy-blue trousers and a snow-white shirt. He returned with two pints of brown ale.

'Me boat only docked this morning,' he said, shoving a glass in front of Tyrone, 'and I went home to find me house had disappeared in the blitz and me ould ma was dead and buried.' He made the sign of the Cross.

'I'm sorry.' It wasn't as awful as Tyrone's own misfortune, but it was awful all the same.

'I'll miss her, Ma,' Kevin said reflectively with a sad smile. 'She's the only one I had left in the world. Me da did a bunk ages ago, tuberculosis took one of me brothers when he was only little and a U-boat caught the other, our Bertie, last year when he was halfway across the Atlantic.'

'Was he in the Navy?' Despite himself, Tyrone was interested.

'The Merchant Navy, same as me. Ma used to worry about me

something rotten, but in the end it was her who hopped the twig first.'

'I'm *really* sorry.' Tyrone felt as if he could easily cry. So many tragedies, so many needless deaths, so many people left to mourn.

'Ta, mate.' Kevin patted the duffel bag on the bench beside him. 'I'd brought some washing home for me ma. I can easily get it done on the ship, but ma missed doing washing so I always fetched her a bit. Look, Tyrone,' he said persuasively, 'if you want to get something off your chest, I'd be a willing listener. I'm already feeling a bit better meself, having talked to you, like.'

But Tyrone's own tragedy was too raw to relate to a stranger. He'd sooner talk about something else. 'Where had you been on the ship?' he asked.

'Haifa,' Kevin replied. 'That's in Palestine, thousands of miles away' he added when Tyrone looked at him blankly. 'We carried a cargo of arms for the troops out there. A Messerschmidt 109 had a go at us when we sailed through the Suez Canal, but,' he chuckled, 'we managed to shoot it down.'

'You mean you were armed?'

'Sure thing. Two Oerliken anti-aircraft guns for'head and a four-incher aft.'

'What sort of ship were you on?'

'Just an old coal-fired tramp steamer, mate,' Kevin explained. 'If you want to know the truth, I was looking forward to spending a few days on shore with Ma, but now I can't wait to get back on board. Takes your mind off things, it does, particularly since the war started and you're taking your life in your hands every time you sign on.'

Tyrone, who never read a paper or listened to anything on the wireless if it wasn't accompanied by music, had no idea that the Merchant Navy was actually involved in fighting the war. He had always imagined rusty boats sailing to and fro between foreign ports transporting spices, tapioca, carpets and other unimportant stuff.

'Could someone like me join the Merchant Navy?' he asked Kevin.

'Well, I don't see any reason why not.'

'Do you get given a medical? I've got summat wrong with me heart, although it doesn't give me any bother.' Tyrone sniffed dejectedly. 'That's why I'm not in the forces.'

Kevin looked him up and down. 'You look fit enough to me, and they don't give you a medical, no. Just go down to the pool and sign on.'

'Without any training?'

'I did me training as an apprentice, but you're too old for that. Have you got a trade, Tyrone?'

'I'm an electrician.'

'Well then, there you go. They'll take you on as an electrician in the boiler room.'

Tyrone's heart began to race. It was that easy! 'Would you like another drink, Kevin? Then you can tell me more about the Merchant Navy.'

Next day, Tyrone didn't go to work, but walked as far as the Dock Road where the 'pool' was situated, in other words the office where the men called in for their pay at the end of a trip and signed on and off their various ships. It turned out to be a dusty building, still intact after the raids. He marvelled at how busy and alive the Docky was despite its recent pounding, the evidence of which was everywhere: heaps of debris all over the place, craters and skeletons of buildings waiting to be demolished because they were unsafe.

In the office, he was given a form to complete. 'That's if you can write,' said the bluff, red-faced man who handed it to him.

'Of course I can write,' Tyrone said indignantly.

'Don't get the hump, lad,' he was severely told. 'Some men can and some men can't and I have to give the buggers a hand.'

'Have you got your papers with you?' the man enquired when the form had been completed and he had admired the writing.

Tyrone produced the papers to prove he'd completed his apprenticeship – Kevin had advised him to bring them.

The man gave them a superficial glance, then said, 'Right, well, the SS *Mimosa*'s due to dock in five days' time – she lost her electrician in Port Said, got murdered for some reason,' he added ghoulishly. 'She'll be sailing in another five days for New York, calling in at Glasgow on the way to pick up a consignment of Scotch whisky.'

'New York!' Tyrone said faintly.

'New York. Does that suit your lordship?'

'Yes.'

'That's a relief,' the man said sarcastically. 'Now you need a uniform. You look a normal shape, so you can probably buy one over the counter rather than have it made. The best place to go is Danny's in Howe Street. Tell him Barney sent you and he'll see you all right. Have you got the money for it?'

'Not a penny, but someone told me you can take it off me pay.'

'Then someone told you right. Five quid should do it. You'll need a couple of sets of whites an' all.' He opened a drawer, produced the notes and gave Tyrone a receipt to sign. 'Oh, and tell Danny you'll be a third officer so he'll know exactly what you want.'

'Is someone upstairs?' Brenna shouted when she came in with Joey and could hear muffled sounds coming from the front bedroom.

'Yes, Mam, it's me,' Tyrone shouted back. 'I'll be down in a minute.'

'All right, lad, take your time. Come and help your gran make the tea,' she said to Joey. 'Then we'll play cards until your Uncle Fergus comes home. I've never known anyone as good at snap as you are, darlin', you beat me every time.'

Joey looked pleased. He was healing much more quickly than his father, although Mrs Murphy, his other gran, didn't help, weeping and wailing and covering the lad with sloppy kisses every time Brenna took him to her house. An amnesty had been called between the two women, although Brenna didn't think it likely it would last long, as she had a burning desire to thump the woman every time she opened her mouth.

'Would you like a biccy, darlin'?'

'Yes, please, Gran.'

'Mam,' Tyrone called from the living room.

'Coming. Oh!' she cried, pausing in the doorway, astonished. 'Oh, son, you look wonderful! Where did that suit come from? It looks dead expensive.'

'But that's not all. Look, Mam.' From behind his back, Tyrone produced a navy-blue peaked cap with a gold badge and put it on. 'What d'you think of your dad now, Joey?'

'You look the gear, dad.' Joey's eyes were like saucers. 'Is that a uniform or something?'

'It's a Merchant Navy uniform, son, and your dad's a third officer.'

'An officer!' Brenna breathed. Eleanor was always complaining

328

about Jonathan not being promoted and now Brenna could boast that Tyrone was a third officer. It sounded desperately grand.

'I'll be sailing to New York in ten days, Mam.'

Brenna opened her mouth to protest, but changed her mind just as quickly. Trying to run her children's lives had already caused enough trouble and it could only be for the best – it was years since she'd seen Tyrone look so full of himself. And Joey didn't protest, just looked proudly at his distinguished dad.

'Will you bring me a present back from New York?' he asked.

'Ten presents,' Tyrone said promptly. 'Come here, son.' Joey ran into his arms and the two hugged as they'd never done before. 'You don't mind me going away, do you, son?' Tyrone asked in a muffled voice. 'You can take care of your gran for us.'

'No, Dad, not if you're going to fight Hitler. And I'll take care of Gran, don't worry.'

Tyrone looked over the child's shoulder at his mother and Brenna didn't think she'd seen so much suffering on a face before. 'I haven't forgotten, you know, Mam,' he whispered. 'I'll never forget until me dying day.'

'I know, darlin',' she said gently. 'I know.'

Cara wasn't sure whether to laugh or cry. She was pregnant again! She must the most fertile woman who ever lived. Making love with Marcus had been the last thing on her mind when she'd gone into his room, alerted by his groans, the night before she went to London. Quite innocently, she'd slipped into bed with him and all of a sudden they were making love, despite the fact he was in pain. It would have been the easiest thing in the world to stop him, yet she hadn't.

Why not? she asked herself.

Because you quite enjoyed it, came the reply. Even though you only married him for Kitty's sake, in a way, you loved Marcus Allardyce, even if you weren't *in* love with him.

That's true, Cara conceded, and she cried for a long time because Marcus was dead, then dried her eyes and began to laugh because she was thrilled to be having another baby – a little brother or sister for Kitty. Mam would go through the roof, Eleanor would be shocked beyond words, Fielding would wink lewdly and say something rude. Only Nancy would take the news calmly because nothing that people did surprised her.

Chapter 14

1942

'We're nearly out of lavatory paper, ma'am, size ten boots, pencils and them ladies' cotton wool thingies,' Corporal Tennant said gloomily.

'Thank you.' Sybil made a note on a pad. The 'cotton wool thingies' were sanitary towels and she wasn't sure if it was because of ignorance or embarrassment that Tennant never gave them their real name. It was more likely embarrassment as he called knickers 'ladies' under thingies'. 'In case I don't see you again before tomorrow, Corporal, I hope you have a Happy New Year.'

'Thank you, ma'am, and the same to you.' He closed the door with a tragic sigh. He was a man who never smiled and deeply resented a woman being in overall charge of the stores. Sybil couldn't imagine him enjoying New Year's Eve, let alone a whole year. She pushed the list to one side: she'd order the things from Central Stores in the morning. It was almost five o'clock and she wasn't in the mood for more work.

Her mother's latest letter was on the desk and she read it again for the fifth time.

Oliver and I had a wonderful Christmas, darling – such a pity you couldn't join us. Jonathan was home for almost a week and Oliver and I took him to the pantomime at the Empire, just as I used to do when he was a little boy. We had a meal afterwards and enjoyed ourselves enormously.

Christmas Day, we had dinner in our old house and what a difference there was compared to dinners of old, the place so full of life and noise. Brenna was there and Joey, who is such a dear little boy. Fergus came with his latest girlfriend; he's become a real Don Juan of late, but the girls are frightfully common. And of course Fielding, whom I adore, she's so funny and brave –

personally, I think she and Fergus are sweet on each other, but neither has realized it yet. Nancy we all love and she kept us in order and fed us well – we all contributed towards the food and ended up with quite a feast.

It seemed odd to see Brenna without Colm, but she seems to have taken the end of their marriage with enormous dignity, although is convinced he will come back one day. If it were me, I wouldn't want him, but then we're all different, aren't we?

I've left the most important news till last. A week before Christmas, Cara gave birth to an adorable little boy whom she's calling Sean – apparently, this is the Irish version of John. (Frankly, I far prefer John.) Just think, Cara has had two babies within a single year! Something of an achievement, but how tragic that both fathers are dead. That old goat, your father, would be thrilled as Sean looks very much like him and has his lovely brown hair, a whole thatch of it. Anyway, mother and child are doing very well and you now have another half-brother.

It seems that Catholics have their babies baptized within a few days of birth – it's something to do with going to heaven if they die, rather than a place called limbo which is terribly tedious. Anyway, Nancy was asked to be godmother – all the children she's helped to raise, yet this is the first time she's been a godmother. Poor old thing, she was in tears throughout the whole service, which that took place the day after Boxing Day.

I do hope this letter doesn't sound too superficial, Sybil, dear, but months have gone by without a single air raid and it's almost as if the war is over for us. Silly, I know, after the terrible thing that happened at Pearl Harbor only a few weeks ago and us losing Malaya and Hong Kong to the Japanese at a stroke. Still, now the Americans have joined the war, thank goodness, and it might be over much quicker than we'd thought.

So, bye, my darling. Oliver sends his love. I hope you have a truly Happy New Year. We are throwing a party and I shall be thinking of you all the time.

Sybil threw the letter on to the desk with a smile. She wondered when the penny would drop and Mummy would realize Oliver was a poofter. She'd be enjoying herself too much at the party to think of her. The smile quickly vanished when she thought that Cara would almost certainly be there. It was the reason she hadn't gone home for Christmas, knowing the Caffreys and the Allardyces would almost certainly spend it together. She had sworn never to enter the house in Parliament Terrace again and she meant it. Now, the two families were actually related! Sybil grimaced at the thought.

The phone went and she picked it up at the first ring. 'Hello, Allardyce speaking.'

'Sybil!' boomed a hearty voice. It was Steve Richardson, the vicar of St Jude's. 'Just wanted to make sure you'll be there tonight, that there's no sudden emergency and a load of new recruits have landed on your doorstep and need kitting out.'

'No emergencies, thank goodness, and no new recruits until the day after tomorrow.'

'Excellent,' the vicar hollered. 'See you later then, at about a quarter to seven, earlier if you can make it.'

'I'll do my best to make it earlier,' she promised.

There was a crash as the telephone at the other end was put back – the Reverend Richardson had played rugby for Cambridge and his abundant energy was extended to everything he did. Sybil went over to the window to check on the weather. Last night it had snowed a little and the day had been too cold for it to melt. British summer time had been extended by an hour, so the sky was still a dusky blue with just a light powdering of stars, and everywhere was covered in a thin layer of white, making the camp look almost pretty. It was similar to the one in Lincolnshire where she'd done her basic training, a collection of single-storey wooden huts, except this one was close to the ancient, but lively village of Melton Purvis.

The ladies of Melton Purvis WVS along with members of St Jude's, the parish church, had accepted the responsibility of having hundreds of servicemen and women – although only a handful were permanent – billeted on their doorstep with all seriousness, seeing it as their job to keep them entertained. There were dances every Saturday night in the village hall, the amateur dramatic society always gave an extra performance free of charge – on Sunday, Sybil was going to see *Puss in Boots* – there'd been a party on Christmas Eve and there was another tonight, along with a concert in the church at which the choir would sing.

If someone had told Sybil that one day she would join a choir, she would have laughed in their face but, six months ago, not long after she'd arrived and had been keeping very much to herself, not wanting to make the mistakes she'd made in Malta, a feeling of utter boredom had set in. She'd made a vow never to accept a date, had refused two invitations to take her out and was left with the choice of spending her evenings in the officers' mess or reading in her billet.

Neither choice particularly appealed and when she'd read the typed notice on the village hall board of the functions on offer during the forthcoming week, none of those appealed either: on Monday, Mrs Winifred Glendenning was giving a talk on roses; Tuesday, there was a whist drive; Wednesday, a debate on local government; Thursday, a meeting of the Conservative Association; and Friday the youth club met. On Saturday, the weekly dance would be held, but it was open to all ranks, often got quite rowdy and was studiously avoided by the female officers.

At the bottom of the notice, as if it had been added as an afterthought, was scrawled, 'Ladies required for St Jude's church choir. Contact Steve Richardson at the vicarage,' followed by a telephone number.

It would be something to do, Sybil thought with a sigh, only faintly interested. She'd been in the choir at school and was considered to have quite a good soprano voice, although she'd like to bet that everyone in St Jude's was as old as the hills.

In fact, this wasn't true. There was a mixture of ages from eighteen to eighty, and it turned out to be one of the best decisions Sybil had ever made. Within a matter of weeks, she'd made loads of friends, men and women alike, and, as the choir sang before and after the well-attended eleven o'clock service on Sundays and on Sunday evenings too, her face became a familiar one in the village and she was greeted warmly on the streets and in the various small shops, as if she'd lived there all her life. She wasn't used to being popular and rather enjoyed it.

It was time she left to have a wash and change into the black dress she wore in the choir: St Jude's was only a short walk away. She opened the door and saw Corporal Tennant had locked the stores and there was a stern CLOSED sign outside. About to lock her own door, she paused when the telephone began to ring and wondered whether or not to answer it. She decided she'd better in case it was something important and was glad she had when she discovered that her brother, Jonathan, had called to wish her a Happy New Year.

'And the same to you!' She grinned at the phone. 'Where are you?'

'At some girl's house, her name's Morag. We're going to a party, you'll never guess where.' He paused dramatically. 'John O'Groats! Morag's taking me in her dad's van.'

'I hope you've not thinking of getting married while you're there or Mummy will have kittens.'

'I wouldn't mind, sis, Morag's gorgeous. She has red hair like Rita Hayworth and an incredible figure.'

'You won't though, will you?' She felt slightly alarmed. He was only nineteen, an overgrown, fresh-faced schoolboy who had only recently started to shave.

'Nah! She's already got a boyfriend in the Army.' He gave a rueful laugh. 'We're just good friends. Why didn't you come home for Christmas, sis?' he asked in a pained voice. 'I really missed you. You didn't come home for your twenty-first, either, and Mummy had to make do with the party for Cara. 'Fact,' he said accusingly, 'I haven't seen you since Marcus's funeral.'

'I was only allowed a few days' leave at Christmas, Jonathan,' she lied, 'and I would hardly have reached Liverpool, when I would have had to come back. As for my birthday, I couldn't get away at all, but they had a lovely party for me at the vicarage.' Had she gone home, she would have had to share a party with Cara – the September girls. What a joke!

'Of course,' he chuckled. 'You're in the choir. I can't imagine you in a choir, sis. I wish I could be there to hear you.' He sounded as if he meant it.

'I wish you could be too.'

'Anyway, sis. I'd better go. I promised to give Morag's dad five pound for using his telephone and I think I might have overspent a bit. Oh, by the way, rumour has it we're being sent to India in the New Year, so this might be the last time we'll talk to each other for ages, let alone meet. But don't tell Mummy, will you?' he said warningly. 'She'll only worry and, you never know, it might not happen, although I'm keeping my fingers crossed.'

'I won't breathe a word.' She knew how desperate he was to see some action. 'Look after yourself, Jonathan – and have a really Happy New Year.'

'You too, sis. I hope the weather's OK where you are, it's really wild up here.'

She put down the phone, feeling incredibly sad. He didn't realize how much she loved him, that she would be just as worried as their mother at the idea of him being sent abroad.

An hour later, marching over the crisp snow towards St Jude's in her fur coat and long black velvet frock, carrying her suede shoes, she felt a little better. There was a war on and all you could do was hope that you and the people you loved got through the next twenty-four hours. If you let yourself worry about the future you could easily go mad.

Tyrone and his mates were touring Manhattan's clubs and bars, sampling a different cocktail in each followed by a beer to wash it down. They had already caused some confusion in one bar by welcoming the British New Year – no one had bothered to change their watches and, so far as they were concerned it was already 1942 – with a great deal of shouting, thumping of backs and shaking of hands. In a few hours they would do it again along with the citizens of New York.

The contrast between New York and their own blacked-out country couldn't have been greater. Here, neon lights dazzled the eyes, blinking on and off, changing colour all the time, sending messages to the stars. The shops were still open, the windows decorated for Christmas, throwing more light on to the crowded pavements where people didn't hesitate to push if someone was in their way – New Yorkers were very rude. Music thundered from every doorway, a mixture of jazz and carols, blues and the big band stuff that was Tyrone's favourite, adding to the sound of the never-ending traffic and the drivers impatiently sounding their horns in a vain attempt to escape the clogged-up streets. He couldn't remember when he'd last seen a car at home with its headlights on.

There was something in the air, an extra zip that he put down to the fact that America was now at war with Japan and Germany. Perhaps everyone thought that this would be the last New Year of its kind for some time and they were making the best of it while they could.

They were gradually making their way towards Times Square where thousands of New Yorkers were reputed to gather to cheer the arrival of another year but, by then, Tyrone would have left his mates for the Zelinda Club, a dance hall, where you paid for girls to dance with you by purchasing a ticket for a quarter. Tyrone would buy a bunch of tickets for Sadie, his girl in New York. Afterwards, she would take him back to her apartment and they would make love, something for which Sadie didn't charge a dime.

Sadie was small, dark, and pretty and reminded him very much of Maria. In fact, if he'd drunk enough by the time they reached the Zelinda Club, which seemed more than likely, it could have been Maria he was dancing with; Maria he was kissing when the clock struck midnight; Maria he was making love to in the shabby apartment. Although when he woke up in the morning, Maria would be gone and he would find himself in bed with Sadie with her smudged make-up and badly painted nails, who only reminded him of the wife he'd lost.

Colm found the noise of revelry coming from the Railway Arms across the road unsettling. Until now, he'd always celebrated the New Year in a pub with people he knew. Although he wasn't a serious drinker, tonight was one of the few nights he got mildly plastered before going home to Shaw Street where there was usually a party going on, even if it was only the family and a couple of friends. It didn't feel natural to spend such a momentous night in the quiet flat in Kirkby with Lizzie and Bernard, now eight months old and fast asleep in the bedroom, despite the noise.

'Why don't you go over and have a drink?' Lizzie suggested, laying down her book, having read his thoughts. 'You look a bit edgy.'

'I'd sooner stay with you and Bernard,' he replied, 'and I can have a drink here.' He picked up the wine and refilled their glasses, although he'd never been much of a wine drinker. The red always tasted like vinegar and the white no different from lemonade. It was a bit late now, but he should have bought himself a few bottles of beer.

'I managed to get a quarter of ham today; make yourself a sandwich if you feel like it.'

'I might later.'

Lizzie gave him a brilliant smile and returned to her book. Across the road they were singing 'We're Gonna Hang out the Washing on the Siegfried Line', finishing with a tremendous cheer. Colm wondered wistfully how the party was going in Eleanor's house – Cara had told him about it when he'd gone to see the new baby, Sean. Eleanor's parties were never as raucous as some he'd been to, but they were fun and a good time was had by all.

It wasn't that Lizzie didn't like parties, but they had a baby son and parties were out until he was old enough to be left with a sitter. If Colm was feeling a bit out of things, then it was his own fault for having fathered a child when he already had grandchildren.

'I'll just go and see if Bernard's all right.' He went into the bedroom, lifted the curtain and looked through the window. If it hadn't been for the noise, the Railway Arms with its blacked-out windows and doors, not a speck of light visible anywhere, could have been deserted. Two men emerged, supporting each other, and singing, 'Run, Rabbit, Run Rabbit, Run, Run, Run'. He watched until they turned a corner, then let the curtain fall, switched on the bedside lamp and looked down at his son asleep in his cot. As soon as Bernard was old enough to have a room of his own they'd have to find somewhere bigger to live.

A quarter of a century ago, Colm remembered looking down at his other sons. Then, they'd lived in Ireland and had been dirt poor, the future holding no promise of better things to come until he'd won ten pounds on that sweepstake, and Liverpool and his brother, Paddy, had beckoned.

More memories came, of his frantic search for a copper on their first night in Liverpool when Cara was born. He'd found Brenna and his kids in a house in Parliament Terrace. Who would have thought that one day Cara would own the desperately grand place in which she'd been born? Life was strange, so strange that sometimes it scared him.

In those days, he'd never dreamt that the time would come when he'd fall out of love with Brenna and in love with someone else. Brenna was always so brave and supportive. He'd actually felt, most unreasonably, a little bit hurt when she took the end of their marriage so coolly, not raising even a word of protest. He wanted to cry again at the idea that she no longer loved him, and nor did Fergus or Tyrone, neither of whom he'd seen since he walked out of the house in May. He hadn't even known Tyrone had joined the Merchant Navy until Cara had told him.

Bernard made a noise, a tiny cry, as if he was having a bad dream. Colm stroked his face and murmured, 'It's all right, son.' He was a bonny little fellow, Bernard, self-contained like his mother, never making much of a fuss about anything.

The door opened, Lizzie came in, took his hand and led him into the living room where she pushed him on to a chair and sat on his knee. 'Are you feeling nostalgic, darling?'

'Yes,' Colm admitted.

'That's all right, perfectly normal. You can't be expected to empty your brain of everything's that happened before, particularly on a night like this. Are you thinking of Brenna and the children?' Colm nodded. 'Tell you what,' Lizzie continued, kissing his nose, 'let's celebrate the New Year in bed, much better than a rowdy pub full of drunks.'

Colm nodded again. If ever he had doubts about having left Brenna for Lizzie, Lizzie only had to do something like this and the doubts would vanish in an instant.

At first, Eleanor thought the ringing was the alarm clock, until she remembered it hadn't been set because by the time everyone had left the party and she'd gone to bed, it was four o'clock and she was looking forward to a long lie-in. According to the clock, silent except for the tick, it was only five to nine, and the ringing was the bell on the front door.

'Damn!' she muttered as she crawled out of bed and reached for her dressing gown, swaying slightly. She'd drunk so much the night before she probably had a slight hangover. The party had gone very well and everyone appeared to enjoy themselves. Oliver had invited some friends from work and all the Caffreys were there, the ones still around, that was. Fergus had turned up with a different girlfriend from the one at Christmas. Cara had left just after midnight to relieve Nancy, who was looking after all the children, so it was late when Nancy arrived.

Downstairs was in a frightful mess, glasses, bottles and plates all over the place. Brenna had wanted to tidy up before she left, but Eleanor had pushed her out and said she'd do it herself in the morning.

'I'll come round and give you a hand,' Brenna had offered.

'There's no need, Bren. Oliver will help.'

Brenna was incapable of sleeping in, and if this was her come to give the promised hand, then Eleanor would go back to bed and let her get on with it.

Instead of Brenna, a tall man in a Fleet Air Arm uniform was standing on the step. Eleanor blinked blearily – the daylight hurt her eyes.

'Mrs Allardyce?' the man enquired courteously, but without a smile.

'Yes,' Eleanor conceded.

'I'm Lieutenant Palfrey. May I please come in? I'm afraid I have some rather bad news.'

'Jonathan!' The hangover disappeared and Eleanor was completely alert. Her heart began to thump like a drum. 'Has something happened to Jonathan? Has he been hurt? Tell me, please tell me.'

'I'd prefer it if you sat down first, Mrs Allardyce.' He stepped into the hall and took her arm. She went into the living room and almost fell on to the settee. The lieutenant released her arm and sat beside her.

'I had a telephone call about an hour ago from our base in Thurso,' he said gently. 'Last night, there was an accident. It seems a girl was taking Jonathan in her father's van to a party, a force ten gale was blowing, and the van must have been crossing a bridge when it was caught in a gust of wind and blown into the water. It wasn't found until the early hours of this morning and Jonathan and the girl were dead, they'd drowned.' He put his hand on Eleanor's and squeezed it. 'I'm so sorry, Mrs Allardyce.'

'But I thought he was safe in Scotland,' Eleanor whispered. She began to scream, a high-pitched keening that made her ears buzz and her eyes water. How could she possibly live without Jonathan?

Oliver came in. 'Eleanor, what on earth's the matter, darling?'

She ran to him, throwing her arms around his neck, 'Jonathan is dead. Oh, Oliver, I want to die.'

Oliver kissed her forehead, but didn't attempt to hold her. 'Christ, what a terrible thing. Look, darling, let me fetch you some whiskey, then I'll make tea.' He walked away, leaving Eleanor's arms to drop to her sides.

'I don't want anything.' Abandoned, Eleanor stood in the middle of the room feeling completely lost and terribly alone. Jonathan, her beloved child, was *dead*.

Lieutenant Palfrey got to his feet. His eyes were desperately sad, as if it was his own child who'd been lost. 'I'll leave you to grieve in peace, Mrs Allardyce. There's just one thing, would you like the funeral to be held in Liverpool or Scotland? I'm sorry to ask so soon, but we need to know.'

'Scotland, please.'

'Are you sure that's wise, darling?' Oliver returned with the whiskey she didn't want, couldn't have drunk to save her life. 'It's a frightfully long way to go.'

'I want to see where he died,' she sobbed. 'I want to talk to the mother of the girl who died with him.' She'd go to the ends of the earth for the sake of her darling son.

The lieutenant took her hand in both of his; it felt warm and comforting. 'I'll arrange transport for you. I have your telephone number and will be in touch this afternoon.'

While Oliver was showing the man out, Eleanor raced up to her bedroom and threw on some clothes. 'Where are you going, darling?' Oliver asked when she came down barely a minute later.

'To see Nancy. I have to see Nancy.' She needed to be held in someone's arms and had only just realized it was no good expecting Oliver to do it. Their relationship had been a hollow one and had meant even less to him than it had to her.

The scenery was as bleak as Eleanor's heart. Everything was grey; the water, the sky, the cottages situated close to the frothy, swirling waves of the North Sea, which beat against the grey, craggy rocks. What must it be like to live there, Eleanor wondered, so cut off from the rest of the world? The staff car turned a bend and the cottages disappeared from sight, although the sea remained, the waves curling angrily, as if it were in a terrible temper. They continued along the winding coast road, the angry sea to the left and the barren countryside on the right, passing the occasional isolated house.

Eleanor was being taken to see Hector Ingram, the father of Morag who'd died with Jonathan on New Year's Eve. He wasn't a local man and had come to live in the area from Glasgow twenty years ago when Morag was a baby. His wife had stuck it out for a few years, before returning to Glasgow. Soon after, they'd got divorced and she'd married someone else: The police had been unable to trace her. There were two sons: one in the Army, the other in the RAF. Both were married and had one child each.

Jenny Waters had told her all this, the pretty WREN who was driving the car and had been designated to look after her during her stay in the lonely wilderness of the north of Scotland. After Hector Ingram, she was being taken to see the bridge where Jonathan had died.

It was Jenny who had booked her a room in a hotel in Thurso. Eleanor had asked for another room to be reserved for her daughter. 'She'll be arriving later today or tomorrow, as soon as she can get here.'

She'd completely forgotten about Sybil, that she might want to come to Jonathan's funeral, and it had taken Nancy to remind her that she must be told.

'Will you tell her, please?' she'd asked Nancy piteously. 'I'm just not up to it.'

'Of course, pet.' As ever, Nancy had provided a strong pair of arms and a shoulder to cry on. Brenna couldn't have been more upset had Jonathan been her own son and Cara had made endless cups of tea and been sympathy itself. Fielding, usually so flippant, had cried at the news. 'He was such a lovely chap,' she wept. 'We got on really well over Christmas. Next time he came home, we were going to the pictures. How can life be so cruel?' She looked at Nancy, as if expecting her to provide an answer, but Nancy just shook her head and looked bewildered. 'I don't know, pet.'

Jonathan was being buried the day after tomorrow in a tiny, unsheltered graveyard that belonged to a church Eleanor had never heard of. The denomination didn't bother her, she told Jenny. 'At home, I never go near a church except for weddings and christenings. And funerals,' she added, remembering it was only nine months since Marcus had died. Would Jonathan still be alive if she had gone to church every week and prayed for his dear soul? No, she decided. It wouldn't have made any difference. Brenna virtually lived in church, but it hadn't saved Maria and Mike.

'What does he do, Hector Ingram?' she asked Jenny. As if she cared, as if it mattered what the man did. She was just making polite conversation for Jenny's sake because nothing mattered any more now that Jonathan was dead.

'He's a sculptor, but not the normal sort. He welds bits of metal together, or something. I'd never heard of him until . . .' Jenny paused. 'Well, until this happened, and I found out as much as I could.'

'Will he mind me turning up like this out of the blue?'

'He's expecting you,' Jenny said surprisingly. 'I thought it best to ring first and make sure you'd be welcome. He lives just around this bend.'

Minutes later, the car turned into a muddy drive and stopped outside a grim, two-storey house covered in shingle. 'I'll stay here,' Jenny said. 'It'd be best if you saw him alone.'

Eleanor shivered as she approached the front door. Even her musquash coat, fur-lined boots and woollen headscarf didn't provide enough protection from the icy wind that felt as if it were penetrating her bones. She was about to knock when the door was opened by a slight man, not very tall, with closely cropped brown hair, and a scar on his lean, brown face. It ran from just below his left eye to his jaw and looked as if it had been done by a razor many years before. He wore thick, corduroy trousers and a black polo-necked jumper. Despite his slim build, he looked immensely powerful. 'Come in, Mrs Allardyce,' he said gruffly. The unfriendliness in his eyes took her aback.

'Thank you.' She entered a long, comfortably furnished, rather shabby room, with a log fire burning in the grate, rushes in a vase on the hearth and numerous pictures on the walls. Through the window, she could see a garden with a few large trees, a neat lawn surrounded by a thick green hedge and a long shed where Hector Ingram no doubt did his sculpting. Beneath one of the trees, there was a mound of black soil and a spade on the grass beside it. She drew in a quick, sharp breath, realizing that this was where his daughter would be buried. Suddenly she felt very hot. The fire was burning her legs and under her arms felt sticky. 'It's lovely and warm in here. Do you mind if I take off my coat?'

'Please yourself.' He shrugged. 'To be frank, Mrs Allardyce, I don't know why you're here. I didn't like to refuse when the girl rang and asked if you could come and see me, but perhaps I should've.' His Scottish accent was so thick, his voice so gruff, that she could barely understand him.

'It's just that this was the last place where Jonathan had been before he died,' she stammered. She didn't remove her coat, just loosened her headscarf a little, wishing he was a bit more welcoming. He hadn't suggested she sit down and was standing by the door, arms folded, as if he were already waiting for her to leave. 'I just wanted to see what it was like, know what he said, what relationship he had with your daughter.'

'They were just friends,' he said shortly. 'Morag was already going steady with a lad who's in the Army. Your son was only here a few minutes and asked if he could use the phone – he offered to pay, but I refused to take his money.'

'Do you know who he called?' She felt hurt that it hadn't been his mother.

'I didn't ask.'

'Is there a photo of Morag I could have?'

All of a sudden, he lost his temper. 'There's plenty, but you won't be getting one,' he rasped, eyes blazing. 'They're dead! Morag's dead, your son's dead and for the bloody life of me I can't understand why you want to know this and want to know that. What does it matter? They're gone and we'll never see them again. *That's* what matters. That's *all* that matters, not this,' he gestured angrily with his hand, ' – this other rubbish.'

'I'm sorry to have bothered you.' Eleanor ran to the door, tears blinding her eyes. She still had on her gloves and had difficulty with the catch. Hector Ingram opened it for her and she'd hardly stepped outside, when the door slammed shut behind her.

'You weren't long,' Jenny remarked as Eleanor climbed into the rear of the car – until now, she'd sat in the front because it had seemed a friendly thing to do, but now she didn't give a damn about being friendly. The engine was switched on, the car moved forward a few feet, then stopped. 'Do you still want to go to the bridge where the accident happened, Eleanor?' Jenny asked quietly without turning around.

'I'd sooner not, not just now. I think I'd prefer to go back to the hotel and have a lie-down. You go back to the base, I won't need taking anywhere else today.' It struck her what a horrible thing the girl had been asked to do: keep company with a woman who'd just lost her son, drive her to such miserable places.

'I'll stay with you, if you like.'

'It's all right, dear. You never know, my daughter might arrive soon.'

'I'll give you my number at the base, just in case you want someone to talk to.'

'Thank you.' Eleanor closed her eyes and they didn't speak again until she was dropped off at the hotel.

She was in a cave and the icy sea was pouring in, wave after wave of it. The cave's walls were smooth, there was nowhere to climb, no escape, and with each wave the water got higher, until it reached her waist, her chest, her neck, and now she was swallowing it. She'd forgotten how to swim and knew that the next wave would be the last and she would drown.

'Help me!' she screamed. 'Someone help me.'

'Mrs Allardyce.' The voice came from very far away, from somewhere outside the cave. 'Mrs Allardyce. You're all right, open your eyes.'

Eleanor obediently opened her eyes and found herself in the hotel room with Hector Ingram bending over her, his hands on her shoulders, pressing her against the bed.

'You were having a nightmare,' he said. 'I could hear you shouting from outside.' He stepped back, his face grim and showing no emotion. He wore a duffel coat and a thick woolly hat that covered his ears, making him look slightly sinister.

'I was drowning,' she gasped as she sat up, still breathless from her struggle with the waves, 'and I shouted for someone to save me. Does that mean I don't want to die? When I heard Jonathan was dead, that's all I wanted to do – die.'

His face clouded over and his eyes glistened with grief. 'I wouldn't know. All I do know is that when they told me about Morag I wanted to die meself – I still do.'

Eleanor sighed. 'But you can't just *die*, neither of us can. You have other children, like me, and you have to go on living for their sakes.'

'That'll be easier said than done.' He nodded wearily. 'Look, I came to say I'm sorry about this morning. I shouldn't have been that rude. To be blunt, I didn't want you there. I didn't want to be reminded of the night Morag died and that's all you wanted to talk about.'

'I'm sorry, too. I shouldn't have come. I suppose everyone responds differently when someone they love dies. I wanted to retrace Jonathan's footsteps and it was silly to think you'd feel the same.' Outside, the sky had turned a sickly green. She reached for the wall light overhead, but Hector Ingram raised a hand, a signal for her to wait, and drew the curtains first.

'I didn't realize it was late enough for the blackout. I must have slept for hours.' She put the light on, swung her legs off the bed. She'd removed her boots before lying down, but still had on her fur coat, although there was no heating in the room and she was freezing. 'It's probably time for dinner.'

'You can eat?' He sounded surprised.

'No, but it's warm in the restaurant and I order a pot of tea, then a second in lieu of a meal. I haven't eaten since . . .' She stopped, not wanting to say the words in case it upset him.

'Neither have I. Do you mind if I have a pot of tea with you, Mrs Allardyce? I don't feel like going back to the house on me own.' For a moment, he looked quite lost: a strong man made weak by the loss of his child. 'It doesn't feel the same any more.'

'Of course I don't mind,' she said. She was glad they'd sorted out their differences and knew how the other felt. It must be the reason why, right now, she'd sooner be with Hector Ingram than anyone else on earth. She looked at him shyly. 'You must call me Eleanor.'

'I'm Hector,' he said.

Sybil arrived the following morning. She'd spent two nights and a day getting there and looked worn out. 'Mummy!' She hugged Eleanor tightly and burst into tears. Eleanor couldn't remember seeing her daughter cry since she was a little girl. 'It's so awful. He phoned on New Year's Eve and said he was going to a party in some girl's van and that the weather was really wild. Perhaps I should have tried to dissuade him, but he wouldn't have taken a blind bit of notice, would he?'

'Of course he wouldn't, darling.' She patted Sybil's back, deeply resenting that Jonathan had chosen to telephone his sister, not her, on New Year's Eve. 'You mustn't blame yourself for anything, not ever. But tell me what he said, every word. Let's go into the lounge and have something to drink – would you like coffee or tea? Oh, it's so nice of you to have come.'

'Coffee, please. Black might help to keep me awake. When's the funeral?'

'Tomorrow.' Tomorrow it would all be over. Eleanor would go

back to Liverpool, leaving Jonathan behind in the little graveyard, knowing that she would never see him again.

Jenny drove Eleanor home. They started off before it was light and it was mid-afternoon by the time they reached Manchester where Jenny stopped to drop Sybil off at the station to find her own way to Suffolk. The London train arrived about an hour later and she was lucky enough to find a seat, but the journey seemed to take for ever, the train stopping frequently to let on more passengers until everyone was so crushed together, they could hardly breathe. The air was thick with cigarette smoke and the smell of sweat, and it was a waste of time even to think of fighting your way through the mass of bodies to the toilet or in search of a hot drink.

When they got to London, it was very late and very dark. She wasn't confident of being able to catch a taxi to Liverpool Street Station and the tube was packed with people who'd been to the theatre or the cinema and, unlike her, appeared to have had a marvellous time. She arrived in Liverpool Street feeling more dead than alive and discovered the last train to Ipswich – the nearest station to Melton Purvis – had already left and she would have to travel to Colchester and get a bus from there.

The train crawled along and it was almost one o'clock by the time it arrived at the blacked-out station. The handful of passengers who'd been on the train disappeared as if by magic, there was no sign of a buffet, she hadn't a clue where to find a bus, or the vaguest notion how to get to Melton Purvis any other way. If only she'd had the wit to stay in London and find a hotel for the night! There was no desperate hurry to get back: she still had a day left of her week's leave. Trouble was, her brain was so clogged with grief that she couldn't think any more.

She managed to find the unlit ladies' waiting room and stretched out on a bench, knowing there wasn't the faintest chance that she'd fall asleep. The last six days had been the worst of her life, much, much worse than Malta where she'd had a perfectly horrible time.

'It's so nice of you to have come,' Mummy had said, as if Sybil hadn't come because she was heartbroken that her brother was dead, but to be 'nice'.

She'd expected her and Mummy to comfort each other, but Mummy had met this thuggish chap dressed like a tramp who turned out to be the father of the girl who'd died, and they were as thick as thieves. 'Each of us knows how the other feels,' she cried tearfully.

What about how *I* feel? Sybil wanted to scream. I'll miss Jonathan for as long as I live, but no one seems to care how much I'm hurting inside.

In the cemetery – Sybil felt as if she was standing at the furthest edge of the world – when the coffin was being lowered into the ground, she'd imagined her little brother inside, with his cherubic face and ever-cheerful smile, and a lump had come to her throat that emerged in a sort of choking groan. She heard her mother make the same noise and turned to put her arm around her, but the thug had got there before her and Mummy was sobbing her heart out on his shoulder.

Next day, Mummy had gone to his daughter's funeral – she was buried in the back garden of his house – but Sybil had remained in the hotel, feeling unwanted, almost wishing she'd stayed in Melton Purvis and mourned her brother there. She could have asked the Reverend Richardson to hold a little service in St Jude's. At least she would have been with friends who cared and the choir could have sung a lullaby for Jonathan as he began his last, long sleep.

Even on the way home, Mummy had got on her nerves, nursing the sculpture the thug had given her: three stick-like figures in a circle holding hands, crudely made. These apparently were his children and the smallest was Morag, the girl who'd died.

'This was the first thing he ever did,' Mummy sniffed. 'I feel terribly honoured that he gave it to me. I shall cherish it all my life.'

As soon as she saw a glimmer of daylight appear beneath the waiting-room door, Sybil went to stand on the platform to wait for the Ipswich train. One came almost straight away and, when she reached the station, a staff car had just dropped off its passengers and the driver took her back to the camp. By half past seven, Sybil was in bed in her billet, dead to the world.

Next morning, after a shower, a hot drink and a slice of toast, she felt much better physically, but her brain was still numb from the shock of Jonathan's sudden death and the awfulness of his funeral. She wondered if she could ever forgive her mother for being so offhand. After all, there were only the two of them left, if you didn't count Anthony who seemed to have deserted his family altogether.

347

She made her way through the weak, lemony sunshine towards the stores, opened the door of her office and found a soldier she'd never seen before sitting behind the desk. He looked about fifty and must be a regular. 'Good morning, Sergeant,' she said, noting the three stripes on his jacket. 'I'll take over now,' she added.

The man leapt to his feet and saluted. 'Good morning, ma'am.' He seemed surprised to see her. 'Haven't you spoken to Major French yet?'

'Do I need to?' She assumed the sergeant had been standing in for her while she'd been away.

'I think he has fresh orders for you, ma'am. I've been put in charge of the stores for now.'

Damn! She'd liked working in the stores. It was a responsible job that she'd done efficiently, the only drawback being Corporal Tennant's permanently unsmiling face.

'How are you, Allardyce?' Major French enquired kindly ten minutes later when she was seated in his office. He was a tall, sporty-looking man who'd been a minor tennis star before the war, as well as a solicitor and a member of the Territorials, the latter being the reason why he'd been called up before the conflict had even started. He was popular and well liked. 'I was sorry to hear about your brother.'

'Thank you, sir. I suppose you could say I'm bearing up, or at least trying to.'

'That's all one can do, isn't it, try? By the way, I was at St Jude's on New Year's Eve. The choir put on a jolly good show, Allardyce.'

Sybil acknowledged this with a slight nod. New Year's Eve had only been seven days ago, but felt like more like seven years.

Major French shuffled the papers on his desk. 'I expect you'll be sadly missed by the choir.'

'Missed!' She was being posted somewhere else where she wouldn't know a soul. Her heart sank. She'd always had difficulty getting to know people, making friends. Melton Purvis had been the exception to the rule and she would miss it dreadfully. For some reason, she thought of Cara and the camp in Lincolnshire. Everyone had liked her and she'd made friends of them all.

'Where am I being sent, sir?' she asked dully.

'Bombay, Allardyce. As you know, the Japanese have just raised their fearful little heads and we are vastly expanding our base in India

– one never knows where they will strike next in that region. Singapore is likely to fall into their hands any minute and they have already entered Burma. Arrangements have been made for you to leave tomorrow.' For a moment, he looked wistful. 'I only wish I was going with you. I didn't join the Army to push pieces of paper around. I'm raring to see some action.'

'That's exactly what my brother used to say, sir.'

She wanted to go into the village and say goodbye to everyone, but there'd been enough sadness lately and she couldn't bear any more. Instead, she wrote a note to the Reverend Richardson telling him about Jonathan, that she was being posted abroad and was sorry she had to leave the choir. Really, she should phone her mother with the news, but she would probably cry and Sybil would know she didn't mean it because Jonathan was the only person she'd ever truly cared for. A letter would just have to do. She would have liked to call Nancy who would be genuinely sympathetic, but Cara or Fielding might answer and they were the last people in the world she wanted to speak to.

'Oh!' Sybil threw down the pen and buried her head in her hands. Why did everything have to go wrong? How much better it would have been for everyone had it been her, not Jonathan, who had drowned!

Chapter 15

July, 1942

The stairs to the attic were hidden behind a door that Fielding had always taken to be a cupboard. She opened it one day by mistake when looking for clean sheets and discovered wooden steps, steep and narrow, leading up to an area of total blackness.

'Let's explore,' she urged Cara when she went downstairs, eyes glowing with excitement. 'I didn't know the house had an attic. There might be all sorts of interesting things up there.'

'I looked once and there's nothing but old luggage and chests and cardboard boxes,' Cara told her.

'Yes, but what's *in* them, that's what I'd like to know. Oh, come on, the kids are asleep and you'll hear if they wake up.'

'Oh, all right, if you must.' Cara rolled her eyes with pretend impatience.

'I couldn't see a switch for the light, so we'll need the torch.'

'We can't take the torch. The batteries have run out and Nancy hasn't been able to buy more for love nor money.' Like so many things, batteries were in extremely short supply. 'We'll take a candle – they're hard to get, too, but I think we've got a few left.'

The candleholder was found, the candle lit and they cautiously climbed the narrow stairs. 'I feel like Wee Willie Winkie.' Cara giggled. 'There must be a draught up here,' she remarked when she reached the top and the flame began to flicker madly. 'Are you all right, Fielding?'

'I'm fine.' Fielding hated being reminded that she only had one arm and might find things more difficult than if she still had two.

The candle was placed on the floor, the flame settled, and began to burn quite steadily, with only the occasional flicker.

'It's creepy up here.' Cara shivered. 'And it smells dead musty.' The loft felt cool, although the weather was hot and humid, threatening a storm to come, and the light wasn't enough to reach the corners of the room that was so large it must have covered the length and breadth of the house. However, it was possible to see the dozens of cobwebs hanging from the rafters and the thick layer of dust that covered everything. The roof peaked like a church and Cara's voice echoed eerily, the words seeming to hang in the air long after she'd finished speaking. 'What's that?' she cried when there was a faint rustling sound. 'I hope it's not rats.'

'It's birds in the eaves,' Fielding said confidently, although she had no idea what the sound had been.

'What if we find a body in one of the chests?'

'It won't be a body by now, it'll be a skeleton.'

Cara snorted. 'That makes me feel much better. What shall we open first?'

'This chest.' Fielding kicked a black lacquered chest with a badly tarnished brass clasp. She pressed it a few times and the clasp sprang open. 'I thought it might need oiling,' she said, lifting the lid. 'Phew!' They both stepped back, overwhelmed by the powerful smell of mothballs.

'It must be clothes.' Cara gingerly peeled away several sheets of yellow tissue paper and lifted out a long, ice-blue velvet dress with thick, ivory lace panels from the shoulders to the hem and long, tight sleeves with lace cuffs. 'It's lovely!' she breathed. 'Is it Edwardian?'

'I wouldn't know. Let's see what else there is. I wonder who this stuff belonged to?'

'Eleanor's mother, I expect. It might even be Victorian.'

The next outfit was a dark-green velvet costume trimmed with white fur around the jacket and the hem of the long flared skirt. Something fell to the floor and Fielding picked it up. It was a little white fur muff. 'Ermine,' she announced, 'to match the costume. See, I told you we might find some interesting things.'

Cara lifted a pink taffeta dress lavishly decorated with bunches of darker pink satin roses. Layers of tissue paper floated to the floor. 'This looks like a ball gown.' She held it against her. 'Imagine going to a dance dressed like this!'

The chest was emptied of more beautiful clothes that looked as new as the day they were bought, if very badly creased and stinking of camphor.

'Nancy can cut these down and make us some dead fashionable outfits,' Fielding said gleefully.

'That would be a shame. Imagine cutting up something like this!' Cara pointed to the last item she'd found, an ankle-length black serge coat with a satin collar and cuffs and giant satin buttons down the front.

'All that needs is the hem taking up and it would fit you perfectly,' Fielding pointed out, smiling at the sudden look of interest on her friend's face at the idea of a new coat. 'This stuff is no use as it is. Now that clothes are rationed, we may as well use it.' Not only were they rationed, they were called 'Utility' and made out of the minimum amount of material. The styles were very uninspiring.

'I should ask Eleanor first if she wants them. After all, they belonged to her mother. As for Nancy, hasn't she already got enough to do without making us clothes?' Nancy had not long left for a meeting of the Friends of Russia Society.

'Eleanor won't want the whole lot.' Fielding grinned. '*She* can make us some clothes. She's a better dressmaker than Nancy.'

'Fielding!' Cara laughed. 'You are a horrible, opportunist bitch. Look. I'd better go and feed Sean.'

'Can I stay and see what else there is?'

'Of course. After he's been fed, I'm taking him and Kitty round to Mam's. She's just finished knitting Kitty a cardigan. I don't know when Nancy will be back and our Fergus is coming to see us on his way home from work, but I should be here by then.' She gave her a worried look. 'Will you be all right on your own?'

'Yes,' Fielding snapped. 'I'll be fine.'

'There's no need to get your knickers in a twist.' Cara began to climb down the ladder. 'Tara for now.'

Fielding didn't answer. You'd think she was an invalid or something, the way everyone watched out for her, wanted to help cut up her food and that sort of thing, when she could manage perfectly well on her own. Well, almost. Very occasionally, a potato or a slice of meat would go shooting across the table, but it didn't happen often these days.

She opened a round cardboard box and found it full of fantastic hats: huge, wavy affairs decorated with feathers, flowers and magnificent bows. They'd be perfect for *Pygmalion* – she'd played Eliza Doolittle years ago when she'd belonged to a repertory company.

The next box she looked in contained books that she didn't

bother with: books were OK, but not nearly as fascinating as clothes. She opened a suitcase and stared at the contents, aghast. They looked like instruments of torture, but they were corsets, a horrible fleshy pink colour, all heavily boned with yards of laces.

Cara shouted, 'I'm off now.'

'See you later,' she shouted back.

The front door slammed at the very same moment as the candle went out and the attic was plunged into darkness so complete that she couldn't see a single thing. 'Cara!' she screamed. '*Cara!*' As expected, there was no answer. Cara had gone.

Maybe the candle was still lit and she'd gone blind. Could you go blind within the space of a single second? It had only taken that long to lose an arm. She closed her eyes and opened them again, but still couldn't see a thing. Gradually, though, objects began to take shape, only dimly: the trunks, the boxes, an ugly standard lamp, a deer's head with enormous antlers and all the other detritus of dead people's lives that had been stored in the attic. She could see a faint area of light where the stairs must be. She could escape!

Fielding stood and screamed again when a cobweb curled around her face and she frantically clawed it away as she stumbled towards the stairs. She sat on the edge of the opening, her feet on the steps, then realized she couldn't climb down that way, she'd have to go backwards. But when she tried to turn around it was impossible: she needed another arm to steady herself and it didn't help that she was shaking so badly. She'd just have to wait until Cara came back and rescued her, although she'd pretend she'd been on the point of coming down and say casually, 'Give us a hand,' as anyone might do even if they had two arms.

There was a strange flash of light down below, as if someone had switched on a light and immediately switched it off again. Seconds later, thunder rumbled in the distance and Fielding froze. The flash had been lightning and the storm that had been threatening all day had started. She'd forgotten all about it. It was the only thing that she was terrified of: thunder. Bombs were one thing, she knew where they came from, but thunder was a mysterious, supernatural freak of nature that she would never understand.

There was another flash, more rumbling, closer this time and louder, and she whimpered in fear. More flashes, but this time the thunder was like the crack of a giant whip, as if the earth was being punished for some monstrous crime. Then the heavens opened and rain began to fall, beating against the roof of the loft so hard that she expected the slates to break open and it to come pouring in.

She gritted her teeth and tried to think of something else, of those wonderful months in Malta she'd spent with Cara, Mac and Kit. It had been the best time of her life, better even than starring in a show. She recalled the night in Gozo when she'd fallen in love with Mac and he with her. He'd said he could never bring himself to leave his wife and kids, but it hadn't bothered them. All that mattered was *now* and the fact their affair wouldn't last for ever had made it even more exhilarating. She would never forget the thrill of making love in all sorts of strange places – dangerous places, where they could have easily been discovered, like the backs of lorries, behind Marzipan Hall, or in the workshop after it had closed for the night. Cara hadn't known. She was such an innocent, Fielding thought fondly. After Gozo, she and Kit hadn't made love again. Apparently, they required a proper room with a proper bed, unlike her and Mac who were prepared to do it anywhere. Now Mac was just a memory, occupying only a tiny portion of her life.

What she would have done if Cara hadn't found her in that flat in Soho, she had no idea: killed herself probably. She'd actually been toying with the idea of suicide for weeks – a bottle of aspirin followed by a bottle of gin would have done it – but then Cara had appeared and brought her back here, to Nancy and all sorts of other people who seemed to love her, making her feel as if she belonged to a proper family, something she hadn't experienced since her mother died.

None of these people guessed how she felt inside, how much she hurt, how devastated she was about losing her arm, being incomplete, only half a woman, who would never sing or act again. She hid her feelings behind a shield of cynicism, making jokes, pretending to be tough. 'You're so brave,' Eleanor kept telling her. 'I do admire you.'

The thunder was getting even louder, making the house shake and, in the deathly silence that followed, she heard a sound behind her. She turned quickly and saw two eyes staring directly at her. Her heart threatened to leave her body and she screamed again and couldn't stop screaming until it came to her that the eyes belonged to the deer that had probably been dead for a hundred years. What the sound was, she had no idea – perhaps there really were birds in the eaves and they were sheltering from the rain. She prayed it wasn't rats.

'Cara,' she groaned. 'Come home.' But Cara wasn't likely to come until the storm finished, and when Nancy came in, it wouldn't enter her head that anyone was in the loft and she wouldn't hear the loudest of screams from the kitchen.

She began to cry wretchedly when there was another thunderclap that threatened to tear the sky apart. It died away and, in the silence that followed, a man's voice said, 'Hello, is someone up there?' A dark form appeared at the bottom of the stairs and she uttered a little frightened moan.

'Is that you, Juliette?'

'Yes, Fergus,' she whispered. Fergus Caffrey was the only person who called her by her first name. She'd started calling Caffrey 'Cara', the same as everyone else did, but 'Fielding' seemed to have stuck, not that she minded.

He climbed towards her, she almost fell into his arms and he carried her down as easily and tenderly as if she'd been a baby. She clung to him, sobbing quietly into his shoulder, while he carried her down more stairs and into the kitchen, where he sat down and she stayed on his knee, unwilling to be let go.

'Have you been up there during the storm?' he asked gently.

She nodded and his hand came up and stroked her hair and she could feel his thumb pressing against her cheek. She turned her face towards his and all of a sudden they were kissing and it felt really good, making her head swim. The events of the afternoon: being stranded in the loft, the thunderstorm, the staring eyes, might never have happened.

The kiss ended, as kisses do, and he said, 'Why are we doing this?' and she said, 'I don't know,' and they began to kiss again. There was another pause and he said in an awed voice, 'I think I love you, Juliette,' and she told him it was quite possible that she loved him. 'But you have so many girlfriends, I didn't think you'd noticed my existence.'

'I noticed all right.' He rubbed his cheek against hers. 'I liked you the minute I set eyes on you, but you never showed the slightest interest in me.'

'It seemed a waste of time in view of the girlfriends.'

They continued to kiss, the girl without an arm and the young man with a limp, who'd come through a cruel, merciless war and found each other.

The pink material sped smoothly under the foot of the sewing machine. Cara had tried on the dress inside out and Eleanor had pinned tucks in the bodice so it would fit her slim figure perfectly. The smell of mothballs had almost gone and it would make a perfect bridesmaid's dress. It was a pity her mother would never know that her lovely clothes were being remodelled for a wartime wedding. The memory of her mother was only vague in her mind – she couldn't even recall her passing away. Perhaps it was because Nancy had immediately taken her place and she'd always been so close to her father.

Eleanor had been the only person who wasn't surprised when Fielding and Fergus had announced they were getting married. 'I always knew they were sweet on each other. I wonder what happened to make them realize it?'

As expected, Brenna wasn't too pleased. She wanted a perfect wife for her son and Fielding didn't meet her idea of perfection. 'How will she manage with only one arm when they have children? It used to take me all my time to change a nappy with two.'

At this, Eleanor had got quite impatient with her. The girl had actually agreed to become a Catholic, was seeing a priest weekly, and Eleanor suspected she was only doing it to please Brenna – she doubted if Fergus gave a damn what religion his wife was. 'For goodness' sake, Bren, knowing Fielding, she'll soon learn to change nappies when the occasion calls for it. If she doesn't, they'll be living in Parliament Terrace, won't they?' The young couple were going to occupy Marcus's old bedroom. 'Nancy and Cara will help.'

'I'll be the baby's grandmother,' Brenna said, bristling with indignation, as Eleanor had known she would. 'If me daughter-in-law needs help, *I'll* give a hand if I'm around. Any road, she's a nice girl and I really like her. I'm sure she and our Fergus will be very happy.'

Since then, she'd accepted the situation and had joined in the preparations for the wedding. Although it wouldn't be until next spring, clothes had to be made, a job Eleanor had taken upon herself to do and had already begun altering the beautiful things that had been found in the attic, starting with the easiest, the pink ball gown for Cara that needed only slight adjustment.

For herself, she had chosen the ice-blue velvet dress with lace panels to turn into a costume. There was nothing to fit Nancy, so Eleanor intended making an outfit out of two afternoon dresses of different shades of cream. Brenna had taken a fancy to an elegant grey silk visiting dress that wouldn't require too much alteration apart from the hem being taken up.

A white crêpe negligee and matching nightdress were to be transformed into a wedding dress for Fielding. She visualized it having a long cape top to disguise the fact that the dear little girl's left arm was missing. It would be one of the best-dressed weddings Liverpool had seen in quite a while − clothes like these were no longer available in the shops.

It was such a pity Sybil would be unable to come. Eleanor would love to have made her something pretty out of her grandmother's clothes, but Bombay was thousands of miles away and she would never be allowed leave even if a close relative was getting married and Fielding and Fergus were neither. Eleanor finished a tuck and started on another. She wished Sybil would write more often, but she'd sent just three letters since New Year when she'd come to Jonathan's funeral.

Jonathan! She paused in her sewing and her eyes misted over. She thought of him virtually all the time. It was nine months, two weeks and three days since he'd died. Everyone thought she'd taken it surprisingly well and she supposed she had, but it was all due to Hector Ingram. He wrote to her every Sunday and the letter usually arrived on Tuesday when she would write back to him. They confided in each other their deepest, saddest thoughts, holding nothing back. They didn't tell each other that time was a great healer or that one day the pain would ease, as other people had tried to convince her. Perhaps the people were right, but Eleanor found it no help at all when all she wanted to do was grieve, not listen to platitudes from those who hadn't lost a child as precious as Jonathan had been − or as precious as Morag had been to Hector.

His last-but-one letter had torn at her heart.

I looked out of my window when I got out of bed this morning, and the sun was shining on Morag's grave. I wondered if I was now bound to this house for ever because Morag is here and I can't desert her. I had always meant to leave here for a city, any city, when she got married, knowing how lonely I would feel without her. But now I feel obliged to stay and feel lonelier than I had ever thought possible.

'Why don't you move Morag to the cemetery and let her lie beside Jonathan?' she had suggested when she answered his letter. 'After all, they died together and they'll be company for each other. Then you can live anywhere you like, knowing she's not alone.'

'I think I will,' he'd written back.

She had invited him to stay for Christmas and New Year, knowing how terrible it would be for him to spend the first anniversary of Morag's death on his own. It was the least she could do for someone who was still suffering as badly as she was over the loss of a child. She was quite looking forward to seeing him again.

It was Nancy who found the Yank and brought him back to Parliament Terrace. He'd been standing outside the cathedral looking lost, so she'd asked if he would like a cup of tea. It was November and the rain hadn't stopped all day. He was a very personable young man, brown-haired and brown-eyed, barely eighteen and very shy, nothing like the Yanks Cara and Fielding had so far come across who'd tried to lure them into bed with nylons and packets of chewing gum, even when they were merely out shopping or at the pictures.

'Over-paid, over-fed, over-sexed and over here,' was how the Yanks were usually described, but Nancy's Yank was different. His name was Eddie Malone, and his father was of Irish descent, his mother Scottish.

When Cara first saw him, he was in the kitchen, nursing Kitty on one knee and Sean on the other, and her mother was beaming at him. Earlier, Mam had taken the children to the park, while Cara had gone to Eleanor's to see Fielding try on her half-finished wedding dress – she had looked like a miniature Greek goddess.

'This is Eddie Malone, he's American,' Nancy announced, then to Eddie, 'Cara is the children's mother.'

'I've got a brother and sister back in Boston only a few years older,' Eddie said bashfully. 'I've got two more brothers, too: one of them's called Sean.' Kitty, only two months away from her second birthday, was looking at him adoringly as he jiggled her up and down, and Sean, only weeks away from his first, was clapping his hands joyfully.

'And he knows a lad called Caffrey,' Mam said. 'I was wondering if one of me sisters ended up in America and it could be her son.'

'If she's had a son, your sister must have got married, Mam, and her name wouldn't be Caffrey any more.'

Mam looked disappointed. 'I didn't think of that, darlin'. Any road, Eddie's just had a jam sarny, and he's coming back for tea on Sunday with one of his mates. Nancy was lucky enough to get a tin of corned beef this avvy, so we can have corned beef hash.'

On Sunday, they didn't have hash for tea because Eddie arrived with a bag full of groceries. Nancy nearly fainted when she saw the contents: a large piece of cooked ham, fresh vegetables and fruit, a tin of pineapple bigger than anyone had ever seen before, three tins of cream, a jar of pickled onions and one of chutney, and, most precious of all, two packets of tea.

'Where did this come from, Eddie?' she gasped. 'Have you been raiding the kitchen, or something?'

'It was given to me when I said I'd been invited to tea with some English folk,' Eddie explained. 'They said you were short of food over here.'

'Well, if that isn't the truth, I don't know what is. Thank you, Eddie. We're all very grateful, but I hope you don't mind if we don't keep it all to ourselves. I'd like to share it with people who aren't so lucky.'

'I'd better telephone Eleanor and invite her to come,' said Brenna. 'We can't let her miss out on a feast like this. Come on, Joey. You can dial the numbers for me. I know how much you like using the phone.' Joey had started school at Easter and could already count up to a hundred with only a little help.

Fielding was rooting through the bag and came up with an orange. 'Do you know what this is, Kitty?'

Kitty shook her head. She'd never seen an orange before.

Eddie's friend, Dexter, was a broad, beefy young man with a good-humoured face, much less shy than Eddie, but with the same innocent young eyes. He was awed, he said, when he'd noticed the houses only a few doors away had been demolished by a bomb.

'It was dark when I came last time and I didn't notice,' Eddie explained.

'Were you in this house when it happened?' Dexter asked.

'Sitting at this very table,' Nancy said dramatically. 'Me, Cara, Fielding and little Kitty – she was only a babe in arms then.'

'Were you frightened?'

'Petrified out of our wits, lad, but there was nothing we could do about it.'

'Boy, you Brits have certainly been up against it.'

'Dexter is a whizz on the piano,' Eddie said proudly.

'There's a piano in the parlour,' Cara said, 'and he can show us what a whizz he is.' Dexter's fingers were short and podgy and she didn't believe he could be all that good.

But Dexter's podgy fingers positively flew over the keys when he was seated in front of the black, satinwood piano. Eleanor had had lessons when she was a little girl but, since then, the lid hadn't been lifted except to be dusted.

'Macnamara's Ragtime Band' was followed by 'Don't Sit Under the Apple Tree', 'We'll Meet Again', 'Chattanooga Choo Choo', 'Deep in the Heart of Texas', and 'A Foggy Day in London Town', the song that Fielding had sung in Gozo, which had given so much pleasure and drawn so much applause.

'Sing, Fielding,' Cara commanded, expecting a refusal, but Fielding had been treading on enchanted ground since she'd got engaged to Fergus and willingly jumped to her feet and joined in the song. When it had finished, Dexter whispered something to her, and she began to sing, 'Yours till the stars lose their glory . . .'

Her voice, unused for so long, was as pure and smooth as it had ever been, but something had been added, a tinge of melancholy, as if she wasn't just singing the words, but feeling them, experiencing the emotions they expressed. An awful lot had happened to Fielding since she'd last sung in public.

Cara noticed Mam's face was sad and drawn. Was she thinking about Dad? She'd expected them to stay together until the stars had lost their glory, yet he'd left her for another woman. She reached for her mother's hand and squeezed it: she responded with a brave smile.

'He'll come back one day, I just know it,' she said in a low voice, as if they'd read each other's thoughts.

Nancy, who'd stayed in the kitchen to prepare the tea, came to say it was ready, and they eagerly trooped downstairs. It was a long time since they'd looked forward to a meal quite so much.

The following Sunday, Eddie and Dexter brought another friend, Nelson, and even more mouth-watering delicacies, including whiskey, two bottles of wine, and sweets and chocolate for the children – they called it candy. Nelson was about six foot four and beanpole thin. Back home, he'd already been the star player in a junior basketball team and had been on the point of taking it up professionally, but the war had intervened. He took Joey into the yard and showed him how it was played.

The Americans were like breaths of fresh air, Cara thought, bringing light into lives that had grown rather dark since the onset of a war that was now in its fourth year. It wasn't just the blackout, but the never-ending struggle to keep warm, feed their families, a shortage of almost everything, and the people you loved being sent to faraway places, making you wonder if you'd ever see them again. And, worst of all, losing the people you loved, as she'd lost Kit, Eleanor had lost Jonathan, and Tyrone had lost his wife and child.

'This is nice,' Brenna remarked, glancing around the crowded restaurant. It was Christmas Eve and an elderly man in a dinner jacket was playing 'God Rest Ye Merry Gentlemen' on a white grand piano. Three giant chandeliers hung from the ceiling, shivering slightly and casting an extra sparkle around the room. 'I've never been here before. I've never seen so many fur coats before, either.'

'I've been coming for years, since I was about fifteen.' Eleanor signalled to a waitress that they were ready to order. 'Frederick and Hughes has always been my favourite shop.'

'When I was fifteen, I was cleaning house for some actress – what was her name now? I remember it was Miss Francesca O'Reilly. She was a bit of a tyrant, used to follow me round searching for places I'd missed with the duster.' She chuckled. 'It wasn't often she found any.'

The waitress tottered over. She was very old and her white cap was askew. 'What can I get you, Mrs Allardyce?'

'We'd like two Christmas dinners, please, Enid, and plum pudding for afters. Would you like a sherry, Brenna?'

'I'd love one,' Brenna said promptly, 'but could I have a cup of tea while we're waiting?'

'Two sweet sherries and a pot of tea, Enid. I need the sherry, it might help steady my nerves,' she said when Enid had gone. That afternoon, she was meeting Hector Ingram at Lime Street Station. His train was scheduled to arrive at four o'clock, but she was fully prepared for a long wait.

'There's no need to feel nervous about anything. Aren't you two the best of friends already?'

'Yes, but I still feel nervous at the idea of meeting him again in the flesh – and I've almost forgotten what he looks like.' The tea arrived and she poured milk into the cups. Brenna furiously stirred the pot to make it stronger.

'Any road, you look lovely. I'm sure he'll be impressed.' Eleanor had made herself a dead smart coat out of a pair of tartan travelling rugs found in the attic, even down to a little matching pork pie hat with a black spotted veil.

'It's not that sort of relationship, Bren. Hector won't give a damn how I look.'

Brenna didn't ask, if that was the case, why she had taken so much trouble with her appearance. Eleanor had had her hair set earlier – it looked smooth and glossy beneath the hat, not a sign of grey – and had been sewing like blazes to have the coat finished for today. Instead, she said, 'It's a pity you'll miss everything tomorrow. Last night, Eddie came all the way from Warrington in one of them jeep things with a turkey as big as an ostrich so Nancy can have it ready in time. He brought a cake an' all, almost as big as the turkey, loads of balloons and paper hats, as well as presents for the children. He, Dexter and Nelson are having Christmas dinner at the base, so we're leaving ours till five o'clock so we can all eat together and have a party afterwards. It means they'll have two dinners, but since they've hardly finished growing it won't do them any harm.'

'I'll see how Hector feels about coming, but I doubt if he'll want to. Have you noticed,' Eleanor said, 'that the Americans haven't shown the faintest bit of interest in Cara or Fielding? It's not girls they're after, but a home-from-home with substitute mothers and children to remind them of the brothers and sisters they left behind.'

'Well, they've found a home in Parliament Terrace. Nancy thinks the world of them.' Brenna's face softened. 'They're hardly out of nappies, poor lads. Imagine how their mams and dads must feel with their sons halfway across the world! Still, at least they're safe while they're in England.'

Eleanor's head drooped and the veil cast a shadow over her face. 'Jonathan was only in Scotland, but *he* wasn't safe, was he, Bren?'

The train was a mere half-hour late. It chugged into the station, disgorging clouds of dirty smoke and hordes of troops coming home on leave for Christmas. She hoped Hector and the other civilian passengers hadn't been ordered off at some isolated station in the middle of nowhere to allow the troops on.

A small crowd had gathered by the ticket barrier waiting for passengers to come through. Every now and then, there would be a little scream of welcome and someone would be seized and showered with kisses. It had been daylight when she entered the station, but now it was almost dark and difficult to see. A man appeared out of the gloom wearing a donkey jacket, a duffel bag slung over his shoulder. She was about to dart forward, but when he got nearer she saw he was too tall and much too young. He was followed by a man in a belted raincoat and soft trilby hat, the right build, but too well dressed for Hector. Eleanor stood on tiptoe, straining to see over the heads of the people in front.

'Hello, there,' said a gruff voice. 'I'm sorry I'm so late.'

She gulped. The man in the raincoat had stopped and raised his hat in greeting. 'I didn't recognize you. I wasn't expecting you to look so smart. Oh, I'm sorry,' she burbled, 'that was a terribly tactless thing to say.' She'd had a second sherry in the restaurant, but the effects had long worn off and now she was acting like a silly schoolgirl.

'It doesn't matter, Eleanor.' He gave the shadow of a smile, while still managing to look terribly grim. She felt embarrassed at having opened her heart to this dour individual who couldn't even smile like a normal person. 'Morag bought me the raincoat last Christmas and I'm wearing it for the first time. I didn't want to make a show of you in front of your friends.'

If he expected to meet her friends, perhaps he would be willing to go to Parliament Terrace tomorrow for tea. She hoped so. Nancy and Brenna were dying to meet him. Nancy referred to him as 'your Scottish penfriend', as if Eleanor had penfriends all over the place.

After all the things they'd written to each other, she couldn't think of a single word to say – and it would seem that neither could he. He walked silently beside her as she led the way towards the exit. Outside, the blackout was upon them and all that could be seen were the headlamps on the crawling traffic showing tiny pin-pricks of light.

She said, 'I think we'd better hold on to each other, Hector. If you get lost, I might never find you again.'

Hector took her arm and tucked it inside his. 'Don't worry about it, Eleanor. I'd soon find you.' And Eleanor knew that everything was going to be all right.

Nancy had come to live in the house before the turn of the century and had lost count of the number of meals over which she'd presided. The first she could remember had been when Eleanor was a tiny girl and had held tea parties for her dolls. Sometimes, Mrs Allardyce, poorly though she was, had come down and joined them. There'd been birthday teas, birthday parties – slightly grander affairs with more guests – and special teas if someone was going away or returning. There was that short period when the Caffrey lads had been in St Hilda's orphanage and the whole family had come to tea on Sunday afternoons. She recalled Sybil's first birthday tea when Marcus had condescended to join them. Daniel Vaizey and Nurse Hutton had been there and Daniel and Eleanor had, unintentionally, made it plain for all to see that they were in love with each other. Not long afterwards, Marcus had thrown Eleanor out of the house, a good thing as it happened, as having to live on her own had done Eleanor a power of good. Then there was Sybil and Cara's seventh birthday party when Sybil had made a terrible show of herself – Marcus had spoilt the child rotten.

She wondered what Sybil was doing now. What would Christmas Day be like in India? There'd been a time when the girl had written to her regularly, but she seemed to think Nancy was partly to blame for Cara marrying Marcus, had sworn never to enter the house again and hadn't written to Nancy since Marcus had died.

But of all the meals she'd served in the basement kitchen over the years, none could beat today's Christmas dinner for such good humour, high spirits and the sheer happiness of all concerned, not to mention the glorious food.

If she could have waved a wand and made a wish, Nancy would have wished the day never to end so that no one in the room would ever be unhappy again, that they would keep on smiling and enjoying themselves until the end of time. She couldn't have been more pleased that Eleanor had come with Hector, her sombre Scottish friend. It was the first occasion in ages she'd seen Eleanor smile and Hector couldn't resist grinning at the antics of the young Americans and Fielding's dry remarks.

A voice, said, 'Has she gone asleep with her eyes open?'

'I think she must be in a trance,' another voice said.

'Nancy!' a third voice said sharply.

Nancy blinked and became aware that a dozen faces were staring at her with a mixture of amusement and concern. Sean was fast asleep in his high chair and Kitty was sitting on Eddie's knee. 'I'm sorry,' she stammered and felt her face flush. 'I was lost in me thoughts.' The truth was that she was drunk, very drunk, having indulged in the occasional sip of whiskey while making the meal. It was a very big meal and had taken a long time to prepare, even though Cara and Brenna had helped while Fielding had looked after the children. By the time it was ready, the sips had amounted to a quarter of the bottle, she'd felt unsteady on her feet and had been glad to sit down.

'Are you sure you're all right?' Brenna asked.

Nancy nodded somewhat dazedly.

'What were you thinking about?' Eddie enquired.

'Nothing much,' Nancy replied, recovering her composure; well, more or less.

'We were just about to drink a toast to our American friends,' Fergus said, waving a bottle of wine. 'Shall I fill up your glass?

'No, ta,' Nancy said quickly, putting her hand over the glass. 'You know me, I don't drink an awful lot. I'll have lemonade.'

The toast drunk, Eddie and Nelson looked quite overwhelmed, but Dexter, the most self-possessed of the trio, said they'd all been dreading Christmas, the first they'd ever spent away from home, 'But you English folk have made us feel truly welcome. I hope we can all be together at the same time next year.' There was a chorus of 'Hear, hear' and Dexter continued, 'And now we've finished eating, can we go up to the parlour? I can't wait to get at that piano.'

There was a rush for the door, but Nancy stayed where she was. She had no intention of washing the dishes, but she needed a couple of strong cups of tea before she dared attempt to climb the stairs.

Sybil carefully drew a black kohl line around her eyes, smoothed brown shadow over the lids and brushed her lashes with mascara. She stood back from the mirror in the ladies' toilet to examine the effect. Her eyes looked enormous above the heavily rouged cheeks and red-painted lips. In fact, she hardly recognized herself. 'I can't believe it's me,' she said.

'It isn't you, and this isn't me,' smiled Anne Purcell, a first lieutenant like herself, whose face was similarly painted. 'You are Yasmin and I am Fatima and we are exotic Indian dancers. It's Christmas Day and we are about to dance in front of a large audience of men and women – mainly men, already drunk out of their minds – and will be met with a chorus of wolf whistles and catcalls.' She looked at herself thoughtfully in the mirror. 'You know, I'd love to stick a sequin on the side of my nose, but I might not get it off.'

'How about a beauty spot? It would easily wash off with the make-up.'

'Good idea!' Anne applied a beauty spot to the side of her mouth. 'You know, Sybil,' she said warmly, 'you've been an enormous sport, taking over from Hettie when she got cold feet. And you're much better than she was. You really let yourself go, whereas Hettie was terribly stiff. And to think I always thought you rather snooty.'

'I don't quite know what got into me,' Sybil confessed, 'offering to dance.' She supposed it was because all the junior officers on the base had been involved in some way with the concert they were giving on Christmas Day and she'd been feeling left out, until a few weeks ago that was, when she'd heard Anne and Hettie Bartholomew having a furious row in the mess. It seemed the women had agreed to dance at the concert if two of the men did a striptease, but Hettie was having second thoughts since she'd seen the costumes, which were very revealing.

'What if my fiancé finds out?' she'd asked nervously.

'He'll only find out if you tell him,' Anne snapped. 'And even if he does, you're not exactly being unfaithful.'

'No, but I shall *feel* unfaithful. I'm not doing it, Anne. My mind is made up.' To avoid further argument, Hettie left the mess, the look on her face suggesting she'd just upheld a strong moral principle.

'Bugger!' Anne said crossly to no one in particular. 'What am I supposed to do now?'

'I'll take her place,' Sybil offered impulsively.

'You! But when we put up the list asking for volunteers to help with the concert, you were virtually the only one who didn't put their name down.'

'That was months ago and I didn't feel like it then.' She was still thinking about Jonathan, still hurt by what had happened at his funeral, fed up getting letters from Mummy going on about the thug, how they wrote to each other every week, what a comfort he was, extolling the virtues of Sean: 'Your new half-brother – at least you have another half-brother in place of Jonathan, darling. I shall never have another son.' Just as if Sean, a child she'd never seen, never wanted to see, could possibly replace Jonathan in her heart. It was such a crass remark that Sybil hadn't written to her mother again for months.

By September, she was beginning to feel better. She quite liked her post as officer-in-charge of Colonel Samson's office. She got on reasonably well with the four female typists, who called her everything behind her back, but that was par for the course and she didn't care. She also realized she loved India. She loved the people who, in the main, were kind and generous and incredibly childlike. Sometimes, the heat was barely tolerable, the insects a pest, the snakes terrifying, the food either delicious or horribly bad.

Her favourite time was evening when it was cool and she would wander around the dimly lit bazaars, like an Aladdin's cave, full of handmade jewellery, pure silk scarves and clothes, loads of tooled leather handbags and beautiful ornaments. She wished she hadn't made an enemy of virtually everyone she knew in Liverpool and could buy them presents – everything was ridiculously cheap.

'Before you commit yourself,' Anne had said, 'I'd better show you the costumes. They're in my billet and they *are* rather revealing.'

Anne's outfit was pink, Sybil's a dusky yellow. They comprised short-sleeved satin tops, which left the midriff bare, and sheer baggy trousers, the legs gathered in a band of tiny bells at the ankle. Everything was liberally sprinkled with jewels, sequins and miniature mirrors, including the headdress and the veils that half covered the face. There were dozens of gold bangles and rings as big as knuckle-dusters.

'What d'you think?' Anne had asked. 'There're no shoes. We dance in our bare feet and we'll have to get pink and yellow knickers to wear underneath.'

'Well, if you're prepared to wear them, so am I.' Anne was a rosy-cheeked, down-to-earth young woman who'd played hockey for her school. Sybil couldn't imagine her doing anything even faintly shameful.

'Shall we try them on, see how they fit? Then I'll explain the dance. It's very simple, just a few steps either way and you have to wave your hands about a lot. The whole thing's supposed to be a joke, like the striptease, but as my grandmother always says,' Anne's lips stretched into a straight line, 'if a thing's worth doing, it's worth doing well, so I'm determined to put on a jolly good show.'

'I'm with you there,' Sybil agreed.

'I bought a book on Indian dancing,' Anne continued, 'but all we can do is look at the pictures because the text isn't in English. All the gestures mean something and we must learn to synchronize them. Oh, and we should practise putting the make-up on. I don't know about you, but I've never used mascara or eye shadow in my life.'

'Neither have I.'

Anne was a hard taskmaster and they'd rehearsed every day in her billet until they had the movements off pat: the shuffling feet, the swaying hips, bent knees, head jerking from side to side while keeping the shoulders absolutely still.

And now it was Christmas Eve and the mess was full, not just of Army officers, but RAF and Navy personnel, too.

There was a knock on the door and a voice shouted, 'Are you girls ready to be introduced?'

'How about you, Yasmin?' Anne asked nervously, looking scared all of a sudden.

'I'm ready if you are, Fatima.' Sybil hooked the veil across her face, covering everything except her eyes. Anne did the same and Sybil gave her a little shove towards the door. Perhaps she should have gone into show business. She'd loved singing in the choir, and now she was really looking forward to dancing in front of an audience. 'Come on, let's go.'

There was the expected rowdy, jubilant welcome when the girls danced on to the floor, an earth-shattering explosion of whoops, whistles and cheers, drowning out the sound of the sitar and the little drums being played by two Indian musicians who'd been hired for the night. When they reached the centre, the girls paused, clasped their hands together as if in prayer and bowed demurely, causing another burst of cheers.

They began to dance, slowly at first, swaying their hips and languorously waving their arms, like slender trees blowing in a gentle wind. Sybil imagined the wind getting stronger: she began to dance faster, the bells on her ankles jingling now, and she could hear the bangles slither up and down her arms, making a dull tinkling noise like scales being played on an out-of-tune piano. She was Yasmin, a native girl, a dancer, whirling around like a top, conscious of Fatima keeping up with her every move, with the thrust of her hips and the slap of her feet on the wooden floor. Behind the veil, her lips curled into an alluring smile and her eyes cast an invitation to the men nearby. One in particular stood out from the rest: tall, dark, slim-hipped, slim-waisted, dressed all in white – a naval officer, watching her appreciatively. Now she was dancing for this man alone, no one else, offering herself to him. 'Take me,' her body was saying. 'Take me. I'm not Sybil Allardyce any more. I can do what I like, be whoever I want to be. I am Yasmin, a dancer.'

The music stopped, taking her by surprise, and the dance ended in a final, dramatic whirl. The girls ran to the door, followed by shouts of appreciation that almost lifted the roof and calls for, 'More. More.'

'I couldn't dance another step,' Anne gasped when they were outside. 'I'm bathed in perspiration. Gosh, Sybil, you danced so fast I had trouble keeping up.'

Sybil blinked. 'Did I? I'm sorry.' The spell had broken and her body felt limp and lifeless. 'I could have danced all night. I never wanted to stop.'

'I'm desperate for a drink. Shall I fetch you something long and cold?' Anne looked herself again, an ex-hockey captain wearing a garish costume and too much make-up.

'No, thanks. I think I'll sit on the veranda for a while.'

While she got used to being Sybil Allardyce again.

As an antidote to the hot, humid days, Indian nights could be surprisingly chilly. Sybil sat on the veranda in a wicker chair and shivered, but wasn't prepared to change her clothes for something warmer. She wanted to be Yasmin for as long as she possibly could.

Coloured lanterns, a candle in each, hung from the veranda roof, the flames burning steadily and giving off a musky scent. The sky was a dark luminous blue, with a sprinkling of over-large stars. She was the only person there, the only one prepared to miss the concert in the mess from where shrieks of laughter came. Perhaps it was the striptease they were laughing at, or Ted Lacey's ventriloquist act – his dummy was a goldfish.

'You'll catch a cold,' a voice said. 'Shall I fetch you something to put round your shoulders?' The tall naval officer had followed her outside, his uniform starkly white against the dark blue of the sky.

'Please.' He was enormously attractive and she was glad he'd come, as well as a bit scared, half hoping he hadn't taken her inviting looks too literally, half hoping that he had.

'I won't be a minute.' He went away and she wondered what he would bring. There was nothing in the mess that belonged to her.

He returned with a gauzy stole that he'd found on the back of a chair. 'Lean forward and I'll put it around you.' Sybil leaned forward and could feel his hands warm on her neck and arms. 'That better?'

'Much better, thank you.'

The chair creaked as he sat beside her. 'Are you Yasmin or Fatima?'

Sybil smiled, pleased to continue the pretence a little longer. 'Yasmin.'

'You're a corking dancer, Yasmin.' There was something very familiar about his accent.

'I do my best,' she said demurely. 'Are you from Liverpool?'

'Indeed I am. What about you? Where do you come from?'

'I was born here, in Bombay. My mother was a dancer and my father an officer in the Army. He was killed in the Indian Mutiny.'

He laughed. 'The Indian Mutiny happened a century ago.'

'Well, some mutiny.' She shrugged and waved a careless hand, enjoying herself. It was a long time since she'd flirted with a man. Now that she could see him properly, she had the strongest feeling that they'd met before, but couldn't think of anyone she'd known in Liverpool who'd joined the Navy. 'What's your name?' she asked.

'Rudolph Valentino,' he replied, joining in the game. 'When you tell me your real name, I'll tell you mine.'

He'd barely finished speaking when she remembered who he was: Tyrone Caffrey, whom she'd last seen when she was about thirteen and he was four years older. His wife and son had been killed in the raids: he'd joined the Merchant Navy and had instantly been made an officer. Mummy had been very cross. 'It hardly seems fair,' she'd written. 'Tyrone has always been a bit of a rogue, not only that, he left school at fourteen, yet Jonathan stayed until he was eighteen and shows no sign of getting promotion. As you can imagine, Brenna is full of herself, telling everyone.'

Tyrone Caffrey! She'd had a bit of a crush on him, if only because he made it obvious he couldn't stand her. He must never find out who she was.

A waiter appeared and Tyrone asked if she would like a drink. She asked for orange juice and he ordered whiskey and soda for himself. The waiter went away.

'Don't you take the veil off your face when you drink?'

'Of course, I do.' She removed the veil and his eyes searched her face, but showed no sign of recognition.

'I can find out who you are quite easily, you know. All I have to do is go inside and ask someone the name of the gorgeous dancer in yellow.' She hadn't thought of that. 'But I won't,' he said, much to her relief. 'I like pretending to be someone else, although, if this were a film, Rudolph Valentino and Yasmin would have a passionate affair in a tent in the middle of the desert. In the end, he'd carry her off on a camel and they'd be happy ever after.' He slid his arm along the back of her chair and she could feel his breath on her face. 'Would you like that, Yasmin?'

'Yes,' she whispered, 'very much.'

He pressed his lips gently against hers. Sybil felt as if a fire had been lit in her chest and, as his lips pressed harder, the flames became hotter and her insides began to melt with desire. She returned his kiss with passion and groaned when his hand caressed the bare skin of her waist. She been touched in far more intimate places before, many times, but it had never felt like this.

Then, all of a sudden, from nowhere, a memory surfaced: Malta, and what had happened there. She pushed him away, struggled to her feet. 'I suppose now you'll tell everyone that Yasmin is an easy lay and it'll be all round the camp by morning,' she said.

He fell back in the chair, his face mystified and hurt. 'That would be a lousy thing to do. I wouldn't dream of it.'

'All men are the same, they like to boast about their conquests.'

'A bit of a rogue' Mummy had called him. She recalled he'd had to get married when he was only eighteen.

'Not all men. You've obviously been out with the wrong sort.' The hurt had given way to indignation. 'You'll have to learn to trust people, Sybil.'

'Sybil!' She felt the blood rush to her head. 'You bastard, Tyrone Caffrey! You've known all the time.'

'Seems I wasn't the only one. I recognized you straight away. There's something about the way you hold your head – arrogant, like.' He burst out laughing, but all Sybil wanted to do was crawl away and die. 'You always were an uppity little madam.'

The waiter came with their drinks and Tyrone invited her to sit down again. 'No!' she said, drawing further away. 'You should have said that you knew me.'

'You didn't say you knew *me*. And what would we have done if we had? Talked about our families? How your mother is, how is mine? What a surprise that our Fergus is getting married to Fielding? Things like that.' He looked at her through lowered lids and she felt her heart turn over at the expression in his eyes. 'We would never have kissed, would we, Sybil? And that's what I wanted to do when I saw you dance – kiss you.' He patted the chair and said coaxingly, 'Sit down and we'll do it again. I promise not to tell a single soul.'

She shook her head. 'I'd like to get changed first.' She was fed up being Yasmin. After all, it was Sybil whom Tyrone had wanted to kiss, not an unknown girl pretending to be someone else.

'That's not a bad idea. I'll wait for you here.'

Sybil walked slowly back to the billet, a whole tide of emotions sweeping over her. What a night! And it still wasn't over – all sorts of other things could happen before it was.

In her room, she took off the yellow costume, folded it neatly on a chair, removed the jewellery, then washed the make-up off – she had to wash twice to get rid of it completely. Her face looked pale and naked without it. She put on a white sleeveless blouse, a pale-blue cotton skirt and slipped her bare feet into Indian sandals with a single strap and a stubby bit that went between the toes. Finally, she combed her hair, tied it back with a white ribbon, and clipped tiny pearl studs on her ears. When she looked in the mirror, the girl who stared back couldn't possibly have been more different than the one she'd been pretending to be all night. The longer she stared, the more she became convinced that she was just a little bit mad. Normal people wouldn't take over a mythical identity as whole-heartedly as she had. She remembered how cold it had been on the veranda, picked up a white cardigan and left.

There wasn't a single soul about when she walked, even more slowly, back to the mess. More stars had appeared in the sky and she could hear music as the concert continued – the three girls impersonating the Andrew Sisters were singing 'The Boogie Woogie Bugle Boy from Company B'.

It was strange to think that in another few minutes she would be sitting on the veranda with Tyrone Caffrey, of all people, and he would kiss her and she would kiss him – more than strange, dead peculiar. They'd known each other in Liverpool, but he'd changed a lot since then, become more sophisticated, a man of the world. And she'd changed, too, although she had no idea what she'd become – more mixed up than ever, with no idea where she belonged. A little bit mad! Was Tyrone over the death of his wife? she wondered. Maria had been her name. Sybil had never met her, but Mummy had said she was very pretty. Perhaps he was just using Sybil to help him forget.

Oh, what did it matter? All that mattered was the next few hours. After that, anything could happen. Or nothing at all.

She arrived at the mess, but to her horror the veranda was empty. He must have got fed up waiting, or perhaps he'd decided she wasn't worth waiting for.

But then the door to the mess opened and he appeared with something in his hand. 'Misteltoe,' he called when he saw her, dangling it in front of her eyes. 'I pinched it in case you refused when I tried to kiss you again.'

As if she would!

Chapter 16

May 1943

Cara woke, remembered what day it was, scrambled out of bed and rushed over to the window to look at the weather. She drew back the curtains and uttered a little cry when all she could see was mist, dense and as white as snow, pressing against the glass.

'Please, God, make it go away,' she prayed aloud.

The door opened and Fielding came in in her pyjamas. 'Nice day for a wedding, isn't it?' she said in a flat voice. 'I won't be able to see in the church and I might marry the wrong man. Or the car might take me to the wrong church and I'll still marry the wrong man.'

'Don't be an idiot. It won't be misty in the church.'

'How do you know?'

'It isn't misty in the house, is it?'

'No,' Fielding acknowledged. 'I think I'm having second thoughts about marrying your Fergus.'

'If you do, I'll kill you. Everyone will kill you. You'll die a thousand deaths. We've been preparing for this day for months. Second thoughts aren't allowed, Fielding.'

'All right.' Fielding nodded obediently. 'I won't have them.'

'Have you had a bath yet?'

'No.'

'Then have it immediately. It's half past seven and we haven't got much time.'

'I'm not getting married until two o'clock this afternoon.'

'Yes, but we have a million things to do before then,' Cara said sternly. 'You're due at the hairdresser's at ten.'

'That gives me two and a half hours to have a bath.' Fielding stuck out her tongue and left the room, just as Nancy came in. 'Kitty and Sean are in the kitchen having their brekky. I thought I'd better tell you 'case you went into their room and thought they'd been kidnapped during the night.'

'Did they come down on their own?'

374

'They did an' all, hand in hand, looking terribly important.'

'Little rascals,' Cara said fondly, although she must tell Kitty not to do it again. Sean was only seventeen months old, the stairs were steep and there should have been a grown-up with him. 'I'll be down in a minute, I'll just throw on some clothes.'

'I'd better get back to the children. Have you seen the mist? Let's hope it clears up soon.'

When Cara went downstairs, her mother had just arrived, her arms full of flowers from the market: red roses, pink carnations, purple pansies, ferns and gypsy grass. She complained about the mist. 'I could hardly see me hand in front of me face. Let's hope it clears up soon.' They both sat at the table to make a start on the bridal bouquet, posies for the bridesmaids – Cara and Kitty – and buttonholes for everyone else. Nancy fetched the bag of silver paper she'd been collecting to wrap around the stems, and Kitty demanded to help. She grabbed a rose and pricked her hand on a thorn.

'What's that, Mammy?' she asked curiously when a tiny trickle of blood ran down her palm.

'Blood, sweetheart. Nancy, would you mind putting something on it? You're not to touch the flowers again, Kitty, until me and Gran have cut the thorns off.'

'She didn't cry,' Brenna marvelled. 'If you'd done something like that at her age, Cara, you'd've screamed your head off.'

'No, I wouldn't.'

'Yes, you would.'

'I wouldn't.'

'She wouldn't have, Brenna,' Nancy interjected. 'She was a very brave little girl.'

'Oh, well, perhaps it was our Fergus. I know one of you used to scream at the sight of blood.'

'Shall we use the roses for the bouquet, the pansies for me and Kitty's posies, and the carnations for buttonholes?' Cara looked questioningly at her mother.

'That's fine with me, darlin'. How many buttonholes will we need?'

'Let's see.' Cara screwed up her eyes and thought. She'd made a note of it somewhere, but couldn't remember where she'd put it. 'Three extra big ones for Fergus, Tyrone and me dad.' Fergus had insisted Dad be invited to his wedding and Mam had agreed it was the proper thing to do. Not only that, she'd promised to speak to him civilly on the day. As Fielding's father and stepmother had refused to come, saying they couldn't face the journey all the way from Devon, Colm had offered to step in and give the bride away. Tyrone had managed to arrange to be best man, so all the Caffreys would be together for the first time in years. 'Two more for you and Nancy,' Cara continued, 'and little ones for Eleanor, Hector, Oliver, the three Americans and the twelve people Fergus has invited from work.'

'How many is that altogether?' Brenna asked.

'I've no idea,' Cara confessed.

'Five big ones and eighteen little ones,' Nancy supplied.

'Eleanor's feelings might be hurt if she doesn't get a big one.'

'All right, Mam. Six big ones and seventeen little. Have we got enough safety pins?'

'They're in the bag with the silver paper,' Nancy said. 'I'd appreciate it if you'd ask for them back before everyone goes home. I'm getting a bit short.'

Fielding came in wearing her dressing gown, having had her bath. 'I washed my hair by accident. I forgot I was having it set. Did you know the sun's come out?'

Brenna and Cara rushed over to the window and looked out – the sun didn't shine through the basement window until midday. 'So it has!' Brenna breathed a sigh of relief. 'It looks as if it's going to be a lovely day.'

'Lovely day,' echoed Sean, banging his spoon on the table. 'Lovely day, lovely day.'

'Won't Sean need a buttonhole?' asked Brenna.

'He'll only eat it, Mam.'

'Will I have a buttonhole?' Kitty piped up.

'No, sweetheart, we're making you something called a posy instead.'

'I promise not to eat it, Mammy.'

'Good girl.'

'Will you two be long with them flowers?' Nancy demanded. 'I'd hoped to have started on the sarnies by now and you're in me way.'

'We'll be ages yet. Shall we take them up to the dining room, Mam?'

'We'd better had.'

'You'd better not be too long there, either,' Nancy said. 'I'll be wanting to set that table soon for the reception.' The reception was being held in Parliament Terrace, just a buffet meal laid out in the dining room that was big enough to hold everyone, so long as they all didn't want to sit down. Once the speeches were over, they could take the food anywhere in the house.

'Stop nagging, Nancy,' Cara muttered.

They were sweeping up the flowers in their arms when there was a knock on the door. Nancy went to answer it and returned with a giant wedding cake, three tiers high, with figures of a bride and groom on top. Unlike Fergus, who would be wearing a new grey suit, the man sported a top hat and tails.

'He looks like Fred Astaire,' Brenna remarked.

Nancy gave the cake a tap and it responded with a hollow sound. It was made of cardboard and would fit over the very much smaller, but real cake she'd made. It was one of the realities of war, that icing sugar was no longer available in the shops, fruit was hard to get, eggs a rarity, nuts unheard of, so cakes for grand occasions like weddings and christenings were no longer available. People made do with imitation cakes, just for show, the one to be eaten merely a pale imitation of the real thing.

The Americans had offered to provide a feast, but Fielding had refused. 'It wouldn't be fair. It's wartime, and I'd sooner have a wartime wedding, with everyone mucking in and bringing what they can. I'm sure they'll enjoy it more that way.'

Cara had been inclined to agree, but Brenna and Nancy thought she was crazy. Brenna told her so, in her own blunt way, but Fielding had stubbornly shaken her head. 'It's *my* wedding and I don't want to feel more advantaged than any other girl getting married on the same day. I'd feel uncomfortable, sitting down to cold ham and chicken and fresh tomatoes and every sort of pickle you can think of, with trifle and cream for afters. I'd sooner have spam sandwiches and stuff like that. The Yanks can bring a contribution like everybody else, but that's all.'

It had proved a challenge, trying to get enough food together to feed twenty-seven people including the bride and groom, but Fergus kept bringing home tins of fruit and meat given to him by people at work, and Brenna, Eleanor and Nancy scoured the shops daily for any luxuries they could find. Between them, they had managed to acquire four tins of pilchards, two of sardines, a box of chocolate biscuits it was suspected were stale, half a pound of mixed fruit, three cracked eggs, two jars of jam, a bag of wholemeal flour and a packet of paper doilies. The fish would go in sandwiches, the eggs and the fruit had gone in the cake, and the jam and flour turned into jam tarts. The biscuits would be arranged decoratively on one of the doilies – at least they would look nice, even if they tasted horrible.

Cara and Brenna took the flowers upstairs. Kitty stayed to help Nancy with the sandwiches, while Sean watched, banging his spoon occasionally to remind people he was there. Fielding wandered around looking lost. Cara told her to dry her hair and get ready for the hairdresser's. 'Would you like me to help you?'

'I can dry my own hair, thanks,' was the curt reply.

'I don't know why she's going to the hairdresser's,' Brenna remarked. 'Her hair looks lovely as it is. Look at the way it's drying into pretty little curls.'

'It was her own idea, Mam.'

Fielding drifted away and Eleanor came in. 'I've brought three loaves and my entire butter and margarine ration,' she said. 'I've got Hector staying and we'll be eating dry bread all weekend, Oliver, too.' She sat down. 'Nancy ordered me to help with the flowers. Apparently, she wants this table soon. That bouquet looks very professional, Brenna, and the roses smell gorgeous. What shall I do?'

'Buttonholes.' Brenna pushed a tangle of carnations in front of her. 'Just a single flower and a bit of fern and gypsy grass, then wrap silver paper around the stems.'

'Why have some got three flowers and loads of fern and gypsy grass?'

'They're for the important people.'

'What sort have I got?' Eleanor asked, looking tense.

'An important one.'

Eleanor relaxed. 'The dining room looks lovely today. I used to think it terribly gloomy, but this house seems to know when the people in it are happy. I could feel it the minute I walked in, the atmosphere seems to tingle.'

Cara agreed. 'I can feel it too. I've always been happy here – well, most of the time – but today feels extra special.'

'It feels exactly the same as usual to me.' Brenna counted the buttonholes. 'We've still got another ten to do. Oh, by the way, El, our Tyrone came home from sea yesterday and brought a wedding present from your Sybil: a carved wooden coffee table, dead fancy. You wouldn't believe the work that's gone into it.'

'How on earth did my Sybil meet your Tyrone?' Eleanor's eyes were round with astonishment.

'I was dead surprised, too, but it seems they came across each other at Christmas in Bombay, then again a month later when his ship called in on the way home. She sent little presents for everyone – Tyrone's bringing them to the reception.'

'There's nothing in it, is there?' Eleanor looked quite agitated. 'I mean they're not romantically involved?'

Brenna looked up so quickly that her neck creaked. 'It never entered me head they were. Your Sybil isn't our Tyrone's type.'

'And Tyrone isn't Sybil's,' Eleanor said tartly.

'He never liked her when they were young.'

'She didn't like *him*!'

'People can change, you know,' Cara said.

Her mother turned on her. 'Are you suggesting they *are* romantically involved?'

'I'm doing no such thing, Mam, just saying that people can change.'

'They don't change *that* much,' Eleanor murmured.

Nancy came in with Sean in her arms. 'He fell asleep at the table, Cara. You'd better put him down for a while. It must be because he got up so early.'

Cara got to her feet with alacrity, only too glad to escape the tension in the room. Mam and Eleanor would be best friends again in no time, but she'd sooner be somewhere else until it happened. She took Sean; she'd been badly neglecting her children all morning.

'What's Kitty doing?' she asked.

'Right now, mashing up the sardines for sarnies. She's not a bit in the way.'

'Has Mam told you,' Cara whispered when they were in the hall, 'that our Tyrone brought back a wedding present from Sybil? They met each other in Bombay.'

'She hasn't told me, no.' Nancy's eyes gleamed with interest. 'I wonder how they got on?'

'I've no idea, but they met again a few weeks later. Now Mam and Eleanor are terrified they're "romantically involved".' They grinned at each other.

'It'll set the cat among the pigeons if they are. Brenna loathes Sybil and Eleanor's never had much time for your Tyrone.'

'They more or less told each other that just now. If I were you, Nancy, I wouldn't go in the dining room for a while. It's very frosty in there.'

Sean stirred in her arms and she took him upstairs and laid him in his cot. He was big enough for a bed but, since he'd started walking, he was inclined to go for a little wander at night and a cot was safer. She spread a sheet over him, then sat on Kitty's bed and watched him sleep, her heart swelling with love.

He was an adorable little boy, placid yet, at the same time, full of beans with an enormous sense of fun. It always amazed her that, at his age, he knew how to make people laugh with his funny faces and his ability to bend down and look at you upside down from between his legs. He was dark, like Marcus, with the same grey eyes and slightly olive skin. She prayed that he would grow up to be a happier person than his father – he seemed happy enough now, but perhaps Marcus had been full of fun when he was a baby.

Kitty tiptoed in and climbed on to her knee. 'Are you tired, sweetheart? Would you like a little lie-down, too?' Cara asked.

'No,' Kitty replied adamantly.

It was a stupid question to have asked. Kitty would never, never admit to feeling tired. For some reason, she considered it a weakness, yet her eyes were blinking drowsily. She badly needed a nap before the wedding.

'I think I'll lie down a minute and you can keep me company.' Cara stretched out on the bed and hoped she wouldn't go to sleep herself.

'Awright, Mammy. Shall I sing you a lullaby?'

'No, luv. Sean's already asleep and it might wake him.'

'Sean sleeps all the time.'

'Not *all* the time.'

'*Nearly* all the time.'

'All right, Kitty, *nearly* all the time.' Cara couldn't be bothered arguing, knowing two-year-old Kitty was determined to have the last word, yet also knowing she shouldn't give in so easily or her sweet little daughter would end up as spoilt as Sybil.

'Caffrey!' a voice said wretchedly. 'Look at my hair!'

Cara sat up, pleased to see that Kitty had dropped off straight away. Fielding was standing in the doorway, her lovely blonde hair set in tight, unnatural waves, making her look very cheap, like a nightclub hostess in a film. 'It looks very nice,' she lied.

'No, it doesn't. Your mother just said it looks as if it's been tortured.'

'It'll be hidden under your veil.'

Fielding sniffed tearfully. 'I can't spend the whole bloody day hidden under my veil. Anyway, it stinks something awful. It must be the setting lotion.'

Cara came out of the children's room and closed the door. 'Then wash it again and leave it to dry on its own.'

'That's a waste of half a crown.'

'Would you rather waste half a crown or get married with tortured, smelly hair? It's up to you.'

'I'll wash it again.' She plodded dolefully into the bathroom. 'That's three bloody times in one morning.'

Cara found Nancy carrying trays of food from the kitchen up to the dining room. 'I'll give you a hand. Where is everyone?'

'Your mam's gone home for her wedding outfit and Eleanor to the hairdresser's. She goes to some dead posh place in town, so she's not likely to come back looking like Fielding. Did you see her?' Nancy asked indignantly. 'The poor little lamb looked a sight.'

'She's washing it again right now.'

'Good thing, too. I've never been near a hairdresser's in me life. Oh, the Americans have been and gone gallivanting off again. Nelson can't come, he's on guard duty, or something, so they've brought someone else along instead. I said no one'd mind. They promised to be in the church by two o'clock. Don't tell Fielding, but they brought all sorts of tinned stuff and two giant pieces of ham, already cooked, I'm pleased to say, not to mention enough beer to drown a cow.' Nancy paused for breath. 'Would you like to give me a hand to slice the ham, pet? It means we'll need knives and forks on the table.'

'Have we got enough?'

'There's a couple of canteens of cutlery around somewhere, still in the cases and hardly ever used. They'll probably need polishing, but they'll just have to do tarnished or not at all. If people don't like it, they can polish it themselves, either that or eat with their fingers.' Nancy paused for breath and Cara insisted she sit down and have a cup of tea while she sliced the ham. 'You've been on your feet since the crack of dawn. It's time you had a rest.'

'I've got to have a bath yet,' Nancy said after a few minutes of quiet.

'And I've got to bath the children, although I can have them in and out in a jiffy, then I'll have a quick one meself. Then we've all got to get dressed and someone will have to help Fielding with her wreath and veil.'

'Eleanor will do that, she knows how these things go. Any road, she's made it her job to look after the bride.'

Cara paused in the process of cutting a slice of ham. 'I'd always imagined having a white wedding.'

'Were you going to marry Kit in white, pet?' Nancy asked softly.

'No, in uniform.' Suddenly, forcefully, Cara wished it was *her* getting married today, that Kit had turned up saying it was all a mistake, he hadn't been killed after all. These things happened in wartime, he wouldn't be the first man to appear from the dead.

But she'd *seen* Kit dead. She'd seen him without a face and there wasn't a chance in a million there'd been a mistake. Tears came to her eyes at the thought that she'd lost him before they'd even got to know each other properly, that he would never know about Kitty, that they would never live together as they'd planned. Her grief felt as fresh and raw as if it was only yesterday she'd lost him and she had the same sensation she'd had on the plane back to England, that she was at the bottom of a deep, dark pit, where she was destined to spend the rest of her life with no chance of escape.

'Are you all right, Cara?' Nancy asked.

'No.' Tears were flowing freely now. 'I'm not sure if I can get through today, Nancy.' The tears choked her voice, making it thick and unsteady.

'You will, pet,' Nancy said roughly, giving her arm a little shake. 'You're a very strong young woman, never making a fuss, chasing after Fielding and bringing her back here, as if you didn't have enough troubles of your own. You had two babies in a single year and there wasn't a father in sight, yet you did it without blinking an eyelid. You stood up to your mam.' Nancy smiled. 'Now *that* takes courage. You'll come through today with your head held high and a smile on your bonny face and no one'll know how much you ache inside.'

'Oh, Nancy!' Cara knelt on the floor and threw her arms around the big, awkward woman, the first person to hold her when she'd come out of her mother's womb, who'd been there for her ever since, and for so many other people. 'I don't know what I'd do without you – what we all would do without you!'

Nancy stroked her hair. 'You'd manage, pet: you especially. Me, I'm just a silly old woman who doesn't know much about anything.'

'You're the wisest person in the whole wide world, Nancy. Somehow, just talking to you makes me feel better.'

'Cara, pet, if you keep on saying things like that, you'll make *me* cry,' Nancy said shakily.

Footsteps could be heard coming down the basement steps. Cara scrambled to her feet just as her mother came in, her eyes extraordinarily bright. 'I found your dad in Shaw Street,' she said in a rush. 'He's brought Bernard with him. He's a dead handsome little fella, just turned two. You'll never believe it,' she went on, 'but that Lizzie Phelan woman was offered some posh job or other with the Red Cross and has only gone to live in America and Colm's been left to look after Bernard on his own.'

Before Cara could respond, there were more footsteps and Eleanor arrived in the blue costume she'd made out of one of her mother's dresses, and a huge wavy straw hat with a blue satin band.

'Why, don't you look a sight for sore eyes,' Nancy said admiringly.

'We all will by the time we're dressed.' Eleanor gave them a dark look. 'I'd have expected you lot to have made a start by now. It's just gone half past twelve.'

'It never has!' Brenna screeched.

'Where's the time gone?' Cara groaned. 'I've still got to get the children washed and I've not nearly finished cutting up this ham.'

'Well, I'm not prepared to help with either,' Eleanor said emphatically, 'not in these clothes. Where's Fielding? Did her hair turn out all right?'

'No,' Brenna snorted. 'That hairdresser wants flogging to death. She turned a perfectly good head of hair into a regular dog's dinner.'

'Oh, my God!' Eleanor wailed.

'It's all right,' Cara said quickly. 'She's washed it again.'

383

'Will it be dry yet?'

Cara confessed she had no idea. 'I've completely lost track of time. I thought it was only about eleven o'clock.'

'Someone should have been keeping an eye on the girl,' Eleanor sniffed. 'She doesn't know whether she's coming or going.'

Nancy ordered everyone to calm down. 'Cara, just give the children a wipe over with the flannel and do the same to yourself. Meanwhile, Eleanor, you see to Fielding, and me and Brenna will get dressed, then I'll sort out Kitty's clothes and Brenna will see to Sean's, leaving Cara to get dressed on her own. Is everyone happy with that?'

'Yes.' Cara fled from the room. Two members of the Townswomen's Guild had offered to help with the food at the reception. Hopefully, they would arrive soon and they could sort out the meat and look for the cutlery. She was past caring.

Fielding looked ethereally lovely in her wedding gown, slim-fitting to make her look taller, her face partially hidden behind Eleanor's own wedding veil secured with a wreath of wax lilies of the valley – the sort Cara had wanted. In the car, she clutched Colm's hand tightly, as if she never wanted to let it go. He was terribly gentle with her, Colm, showing no sign of how he must be feeling after Lizzie had abandoned both him and their little son.

It wasn't normally done for the bridesmaids to travel to the church in the same car as the bride, but the hire company was only able to provide one car with enough petrol for a single journey to the church and back. The other guests had had to walk, Brenna taking Sean in his pushchair. Cara and an unnaturally quiet Kitty, overawed by the occasion, had accompanied the bride and her substitute father for the day.

When they alighted from the car, there was a chorus of 'oohs' and 'aahs' and cries of, 'Doesn't she look lovely!' from a crowd of women who seemed to spend their time on Saturdays waiting outside the church to see the various weddings. Someone waved and shouted, 'Hello, Cara!' and Cara recognized a girl she'd used to work with in Boots. It seemed so long ago that it was hard to believe she was the same person who'd stood behind a counter selling sticking plasters and tins of ointment.

Eleanor was waiting for them in the porch. 'Come quickly,' she urged. 'The organist didn't turned up, so Dexter was persuaded to take his place and he's been playing "Ole Man River" over and over again. It must be the only tune he knows that sounds like a hymn. Some people actually started to sing and the priest is going berserk.'

'Mammy!' Sean cried joyfully when they entered the church, and there was a loud 'Shush, darlin',' from Brenna.

Dexter must have been alerted that they'd arrived and he began to play a syncopated version of 'Here Comes the Bride'. Fielding looked undecided as to whether to tuck her arm in Colm's or hold on to the bouquet. 'Here, luv,' Colm said tenderly, 'let us carry the flowers so I can lead you down the aisle and you can pretend I'm your dad.'

Oh, Lord! Brenna thought sometime later, any minute now I'm going to bawl me head off. It's all so desperately *sad*. Fergus and Fielding had just exchanged vows and he'd had to slip the ring on to the third finger of her right hand because her left one was missing. A sudden bout of coughing and sniffing had overtaken the congregation. Still, the girl was marrying into a good, caring family. The Caffreys would look after her: she could count on that.

And just look at our Cara! Brenna's heart swelled with pride. Tall and slim with a calm smile on her face, she looked a picture in that frock, although it was a bit off the shoulder for Brenna's taste, showed too much flesh. Eleanor should have made a scarf to go around her neck. And Kitty looked dead pretty in that sort of Victorian pinafore thing with a lace blouse underneath – give Eleanor her due, she was handy with a needle.

Brenna doubted if there was a woman in Liverpool who had better-looking children than she had. Was there, for instance, a film star in Hollywood who could wear a uniform with such elegance as Tyrone? If that snooty bitch Sybil Allardyce thought she could get her hands on him, she had another think coming. Fergus, a tiny bit smaller, a tiny bit paler than his brother, nevertheless looked terribly distinguished in his new suit and new glasses. Anyone who didn't know would have sworn he was a doctor or a headmaster, someone very grand and highly educated.

Sean squirmed on her knee and she patted his leg, whispering, 'Stay still, darlin'. It'll soon be over and then you can go to your mammy. Look at Bernard, he's being as good as gold.' Bernard had seemed a bit lost at first among so many strangers, his dad otherwise occupied giving the bride away, but Nancy had taken him under her wing and he looked perfectly content to be cuddled on her knee.

Brenna wasn't sure whether to be glad or sorry that Lizzie Phelan had taken herself off to America. Most probably she was sorry for Colm and glad for herself because now she stood a chance of getting him back. So far as Colm was concerned, she didn't have an ounce of pride – she would take him back tomorrow, today, if he asked.

Eleanor hadn't expected to cry. After all, it was a joyful occasion. She felt sure Fergus and Fielding would be very happy: there was no reason on earth for tears.

Except the bride had no sooner joined the bridegroom at the altar when it dawned on her that she would never see Jonathan get married. It was a privilege than had been lost to her. She held her breath, determined not to cry and make a show of herself, and glanced at Hector. Was he was thinking the same thing about Morag? But she couldn't tell: his face was grim, as it so often was. After a few seconds, she was forced to release the breath and with it came the tears and a muffled sob. She was aware of Hector shuffling closer and his arm went around her shoulders, squeezing them. He whispered something in her ear and she froze, wondering if she'd heard right. She looked at him again and this time he was smiling.

'Yes, Hector,' she whispered back, wiping the tears from her face. 'Yes, I will marry you.'

The music could be heard all over the house, in the kitchen, up in the bedrooms. 'Somewhere Over the Rainbow', 'Whistle While You Work', 'Wanting You' . . . The wedding would be the last time Dexter would play the piano in Parliament Terrace. In a few days, he was being transferred to somewhere on the south coast, along with Eddie and Nelson, their precise destination so far unknown. It was rumoured a vast army was gathering in the south to prepare for the invasion of France and the eventual routing of Hitler.

After three and a half years of fighting, the Allies finally had the enemy on the run. The Japanese had been forced by American might to retreat in the Pacific; in Russia the Germans lost whole armies of men as they were relentlessly driven back; and the British were gradually winning in North Africa. Night after night, day after day, Allied planes flew over Berlin, reducing the city to rubble.

By no means did this mean the war was almost over. People were still dying in their thousands in battle or when their ships were sunk. There was a long way to go before the conflict ended, but at least the journey had begun.

'You look very serious, Cara. Is there something wrong, honey?'

Cara looked up, startled, to find Jack McGarry looking down at her. He was a distant cousin of Eddie's who'd only arrived in Warrington a few days ago. Eddie had brought him to the wedding in place of Nelson. 'No, I just got involved in this long chain of thought about the war, starting with you all being sent to the south coast.'

'I won't be going, not for a while yet.' He was older than his cousin, about twenty-five, with a fine-featured, sensitive face and thick curly hair. His eyes were so dark they were almost black. They'd been introduced earlier and Cara had felt an immediate attraction. It was impossible to miss the look of admiration on his face when they shook hands. 'Why are you sitting out here on your own, honey?'

'Sean and Bernard insist on playing in the hallway. I thought I'd best keep an eye on them in case they get into mischief.' She was sitting at the bottom of the stairs, feeling a bit out of things, as she watched the boys who'd become instant friends. Laughter issued from the dining room, Dexter was playing the piano in the parlour where Fielding had started to sing, and there was an animated discussion taking place in the kitchen: something to do with politics. It sounded as if Nancy and her dad were involved.

'Fancy some company?'

'I wouldn't mind.'

'Are the little guys cousins?' he asked as he sat beside her.

'No, believe it or not, Bernard – he's the biggest – is Sean's uncle. Sean belongs to me, Kitty, too. Me and Kitty were bridesmaids at the wedding,' she explained. He probably had no idea who Kitty was.

He smiled. 'I must admit that at the wedding I didn't take much notice of anyone except the tall bridesmaid in pink. What's that song? – I only had eyes for you.'

Before Cara could think of what to say to such an outrageous compliment, Fielding and Fergus came bursting out of the parlour and announced it was time they went on their honeymoon, but first they had to get changed.

'Where are they going on honeymoon?' Jack asked when the pair had swept past them on the way to the bedroom.

'Blackpool,' Cara told him. 'It's a holiday resort, quite close to Liverpool. I've always wanted to go meself. Unlike the other resorts, it hasn't closed down and is still full of life.'

'Perhaps I could take you one of these days, Cara. I can always borrow a jeep.' His tone was light, but she sensed a note of seriousness behind it and knew he wasn't just asking for a casual date.

'Perhaps,' she said, just as lightly. 'We'll have to see.'

'Cara, darlin',' her mother bellowed, 'are you going to the station with the bride and groom to wave them off? Nancy's offered to look after the children.'

'All right, Mam.' She got to her feet and Jack McGarry did the same.

'I'll come with you,' he said quickly.

She'd been hoping to escape his dark eyes and admiring looks, but it seemed that wasn't going to happen and she wasn't at all surprised that she didn't mind a bit.

'Who looks after Bernard while you're at work, Colm?' Brenna asked at around seven o'clock when things had grown quieter and some people had already gone home. Cara had taken the children out for some fresh air and the remainder of the guests lolled around the house, waiting for the evening's entertainment to begin. Brenna and Colm had the dining room to themselves and could talk freely.

'A woman from the new estate by the station, Mrs Hall. She has a little boy of her own about Bernard's age.' He looked awfully tired, she thought with compunction, holding down a full-time job and having an energetic toddler to look after in his spare time.

'I bet he was upset at first, being dumped on a stranger.' She found it hard to keep the anger out of her voice.

'He was a bit disturbed, yes. In fact, he still misses Lizzie. She was a good mother, Bren.'

She could tell he was warning her not to go too far with her criticism of Lizzie Phelan, but Brenna couldn't resist another barb. 'She couldn't have been all *that* good, shooting off to America just because a good job came up with the Red Cross.'

'It's more than a good job, Bren,' Colm said patiently. 'It comes with enormous responsibility coupled with doing an awful lot of good for mankind. She left two people behind in order to make life better for thousands. That's the way Lizzie is made.'

Brenna was tempted to say a mother should always put her children first and there must be something desperately cock-eyed about the way Lizzie was made, but thought she'd better shut up or they'd end up having a row. She said, 'If you like, I'll look after Bernard. Our Fergus is leaving, so there's only Joey left. Tyrone's only home occasionally and then it's just for a few days. If you like, I'll take the little lad permanent, like, so you wouldn't have to bring him every day. You could even come and stay weekends,' she added casually.

Colm leaned forward in the chair, eyes bright all of a sudden, the tiredness gone. 'Actually, Bren, I was going to ask you much the same thing. Would you take Bernard for me? You see, I'd like to join up. Oh, I know I'm nearly forty-nine,' he said when she looked at him askance, 'but I could pass for less and they've already started calling up men over forty.'

'You're not going to fight, are you, Colm?' she asked faintly.

'I will if they ask me, but I'd probably end up driving an ambulance or working in a hospital. Will you, Bren? Will you look after Bernard for us?' He looked completely rejuvenated.

She nodded. Although sincere in her wish to look after the little boy, she'd rather hoped it would come with Colm's frequent presence in the house in Shaw Street, so she could feed him up, remind him what a good cook she was, how well she did the washing and the ironing, how clean she kept the place. Instead, he was about to disappear out of her life, out of all their lives, and they might never see him again.

'Oh, Colm,' she moaned and, to her intense horror, she began to cry.

'Don't, luv,' he said awkwardly.

The 'luv' only made her cry more, bringing back memories of when they'd been a real man and wife and he'd called her 'luv' all the time. 'I've felt like crying all day,' she wept, thinking that she must have a smidgeon of pride left, as she didn't want him to know he was the reason for her tears. 'I managed to avoid it in the church, but it just came over me all of a sudden, our Fergus getting married an' all.'

'Our Fergus is going to be very happy with Fielding, Bren.'

'I know, Colm, but he's left a big hole in me life. The house will feel dead empty without him.'

'Maybe Bernard will fill the hole, luv.'

'Maybe,' she sniffed.

He must have decided to change the subject. 'That's a lovely frock you're wearing, luv. It suits you.'

'It's not a frock, it's a costume. It belonged to Eleanor's mam and she altered it for me.' She fingered the fine material of the skirt. 'It's silk.'

'Costume, then.' He smiled at her affectionately. 'You're a very handsome woman, Brenna Caffrey.'

Handsome! She didn't want to look handsome. *He* was handsome and so were her lads. Women described as handsome were usually middle-aged and over-large. Nor did she like being smiled at affectionately, as if she were a baby or a pet animal. 'I'd best go down and see if Nancy needs a hand with getting the food ready for tonight,' she said stiffly.

'What's the matter, luv? Are you all right?' He must have noticed her stiff tone and reached for her hand as she was about to brush past him.

'There's nothing wrong with me.' Oh, but there was. The touch of his hand had brought a thrust of desire. She wanted him! She wanted to lie in bed with his arms around her, wanted them to make love, then fall asleep with their bodies touching. A voice came to her from across the years saying words she'd thought were long forgotten: '*I see a woman weeping because she has lost her loved one.*' It was Katie MacBride staring into a cup of tea leaves. '*Who is it?*' Brenna had asked, but hadn't waited for an answer because Cara, next door, had begun to cry. '*One day the loved one will return,*' Katie had called as Brenna rushed from the house. Was *she* the weeping woman? Brenna wondered now. The entire reading had been about her: the fourth baby, the loss of something precious, the cruel betrayal. Everything had come true. The loved one could only be Colm.

'Bren, are you all right?' he asked again.

'Yes.' He *would* come back one day, even if right now it seemed most unlikely. But hadn't Katie predicted it? She made for the door, but before she could open it, Eleanor came in holding Hector Ingram's hand. In all the years they'd known each other, Brenna had never seen her look so blissfully content.

'Guess what?' she cried. 'Hector and I are going to get married and he's coming to Liverpool to live. He actually proposed to me in church and I accepted. I've been meaning to tell you all day, Brenna, but this is the first opportunity.'

'Congratulations, El, and you too, Hector.' She kissed them both, tried to pretend how pleased she was, when secretly she was so eaten up with jealousy she suspected her face had turned bright green.

They sang until they were hoarse and danced until they were exhausted. Now it was past eleven and the Americans would soon have to leave for Central Station to catch the last train to Warrington and the other guests to take buses and trams to destinations all over Liverpool. Dexter played 'Goodnight, Sweetheart', the final tune he would ever play on the Allardyces' piano and Jack McGarry took Cara in his arms for the last waltz. They'd danced with each other all night.

'When can I see you again?' he whispered.

'I don't know.'

'Tomorrow? The next day?' He pressed his hand into the small of her back, as if trying to encourage her to name a date.

'I'm sorry, Jack, but I don't think I can see you again.' Now that she was faced with making a decision, Cara knew she could never go out with Jack McGarry. She liked him, felt attracted to him, but today had been enough. She wasn't in the mood for a romance, she wasn't ready. While they'd danced, she'd kept thinking about Kit, comparing him with Kit. Jack didn't come off worse in the comparison, except that he *wasn't* Kit and it would be a long time before anyone could take his place. That time with Marcus had been an aberration. She'd felt sorry for him and it had happened suddenly, taking her by surprise, although she would never regret it. But Kit would always be the love of her life. It was something she could never escape from and wasn't sure if she would ever want to.

The Americans left, amidst a great deal of kissing and hugging and promising to write, as well as quite a few tears, particularly from Nancy who was devastated.

'What a day this has been!' she sobbed when the boys had gone and there were just three of them, Nancy, Brenna and Cara, left in the kitchen. 'I've never cried so much or laughed so much in all me life. And what about Eleanor getting married again! It's the best news I've heard in a long time.'

'Isn't it?' Brenna said, a touch bitterly.

Cara glanced sharply at her mother: she'd sounded envious. Perhaps she'd been hoping Dad would come home now that Lizzie had gone abroad, but he'd told her earlier he was going to join the forces. How awful to love someone as much as she'd loved Kit, yet the someone was still alive and no longer loved you.

'Would either of you like a cup of cocoa?' Nancy asked.

'I would, but I'll make it, Nancy. Do you want one, Mam?'

'No, ta, darlin'. I'll be off home. Is it all right if Joey stays the night? He was dead to the world in Fielding's bed when I last looked.'

'Of course, Mam. Why don't you stay the night too? You can sleep in Marcus's bed. It's already made up for when Fergus and Fielding come back.'

'But that'll mean you'll have to change the bedding.' Brenna pushed herself wearily to her feet. 'To tell the truth, darlin', I feel like a really good cry and I'd sooner do it in me own house than anywhere else.' She was out of the door before anyone could stop her.

'I'll better go after her.'

'Leave her be, pet,' Nancy said with a sigh. 'If your mam wanted company, she'd have stayed and had the good cry here. There are times when a person would far sooner be on their own. Don't make me any cocoa, I'd prefer a glass of whiskey. It'll help me sleep. Me body's completely worn out, but me brain's still alive and kicking.'

They stayed in the kitchen a while longer, picking over the day, from the mist early that morning, to the party that night, and all the funny things and near disasters that had happened in between.

'All in all, it's been a really good day,' Cara said. She thought of Eleanor's radiant face and her mother's rushed departure a few minutes ago. 'Although it was better for some than it was for others.'

Chapter 17

Wednesday, 8 May 1945
VE Day

The war ended on a day as bright and sunny as the one on which it had begun almost six years before, but on this day, the sun seemed even brighter, the sky a prettier blue, the air intoxicating. In fact, Cara felt a little bit drunk when she woke, knowing that at last the nightmare was over. After an eleven-month struggle, starting on D-Day when the Allies had landed in France, they'd finally taken Berlin and Hitler had killed himself.

Peace had arrived, the lights were on and once again people could sleep easily in their beds. Last night, she'd raced around the house tearing down the blackout curtains. It really was over.

She leapt out of bed and ran downstairs to the kitchen where Nancy was sitting at the table with a cup in her hand. She bestowed a kiss on the older woman's head. 'Isn't it the gear!' she cried.

Nancy nodded, smiling, although she looked tired. 'I've kept meself going for today,' she said. 'Now I feel I'd like to sleep for a hundred years like Rip Van Winkle.'

'Why not go back to bed now? I'll see to everything,' Cara offered. Nancy would be seventy in a few weeks. It was about time she took it easy. She didn't know that a surprise party was planned: Brenna and Eleanor were attempting to track down all her old friends to invite.

'You can see to everything tomorrow, pet,' Nancy promised. 'After such a long wait, I've no intention of missing a single minute of today. Any road, there's sarnies to make for the kids' party in Shaw Street and I've loads of other things to do.'

'Whatever they are, I can do them.'

'Tomorrow,' Nancy said again. 'I'd never sleep for a hundred hours, let alone a hundred years, but I wouldn't mind a nice long rest.'

Kitty burst into the room. 'The war's over,' she announced as if nobody else knew.

Cara agreed that this was so. 'Shall we walk into town later to see all the flags and decorations?'

'Yes, please, Mam.' Kitty gleefully clapped her hands.

'Sit down and I'll make your brekky, then I'll take drinks upstairs for Fielding and Fergus.' The day had been declared a National Holiday so Fergus didn't have to go to work.

'I'll do that, pet.'

'You will do no such thing, Nancy. *I'll* do it. And when I come back, I'll start on the sarnies and you can just sit and watch for a change.'

On her way with the tea on the tray, Cara looked in on Sean. He had dressed himself in a short-sleeved shirt and short trousers, and was struggling to fasten the buckles on his sandals. He was three and a half and determined to keep up with Kitty, who was almost a year older and very forward.

'Clever boy!' she marvelled. 'But don't you think you'd better put socks on first?'

'I forgot,' he said forlornly.

'I'll be back in a minute to give you a hand.'

She knocked on the door of Marcus's old bedroom. 'Are you decent? Can I come in?'

The only response was a groan that she took as permission to enter. Fielding's head was hidden under the clothes and Fergus was sitting on the edge of the bed nursing Harry who was nine months old, a delicate little boy who was sick a lot, although neither the hospital nor the doctor could discover the reason why, or why he cried so much and was seriously underweight.

'I heard him cry during the night,' Cara said. 'Did he keep you awake for long?'

'Long enough.' Fergus grunted. 'He's asleep right now, so keep your voice down a bit, luv.'

'I won't say another word,' Cara whispered as she tiptoed in with the tea, put the tray on top of the dressing table, and tiptoed out again. Fielding was expecting another baby in five months and she prayed Harry would be better by then and he and the new baby would be as fit and healthy as her own had always been.

★

All the shops in town were closed, but must have been hard at work the day before decorating the windows with photographs of the King and Queen draped in the Union Jack. There were flags everywhere and the brilliantly sunny streets were crisscrossed with red, white and blue bunting. Despite the closed shops, the city centre was crowded and there was little traffic, leaving people free to walk in the road. A long line of young women danced the conga, curling like a snake down Ranelagh Street, while an ancient gentlemen marched down the middle of Houghton Street banging a toy drum and singing 'Land of Hope and Glory' at the top of his voice. Everyone looked stupidly happy, almost dazed by the victory that, during the dark times, they'd thought would never come.

Cara was kissed and hugged, had her hand shaken over and over by complete strangers. The children were picked up and petted, and an old lady gave them sixpence each. In the end, the heady atmosphere got through to her and she began to fling her arms around people she'd never seen before in her life and would no doubt never see again.

A genuine sailor danced the hornpipe in Clayton Square, surrounded by a cheering crowd. In another part of the square, people were doing the hokey-cokey. Sean stroked a stray dog, a mangy, ugly-looking thing, and it immediately began to follow them.

'Go away, dog!' Cara said sternly. The dog stopped and gave her a sullen glare, but when she looked around, it was following them again and did so all the way down to the Pier Head and back to Parliament Terrace by which time Sean had fallen in love with the damn thing and the dog appeared to have fallen in love with him. It sat on the pavement outside the house with its head poking through the railings, staring longingly through the window.

'He's hungry,' Sean announced. 'Can I give him something to eat?'

'If you feed it,' Cara said warningly, 'it'll never go away.'

'I don't want him to go away. I want to call him Rover and keep him.' Sean looked mutinously at his mother. 'Why can't I keep him, Mam?'

'Because he probably belongs to someone else, sweetheart,' she said, although this seemed most unlikely. The dog looked half starved, didn't have a collar and was urgently in need of a bath. She wouldn't mind having a dog, but preferred a puppy that would grow up to be more cuddly and attractive than the ugly beast outside. The dog was forgotten when she heard the sound of a baby crying upstairs: Harry!

Nancy had heard it too. 'Fergus phoned the doctor earlier. He should be here in a minute. When Fielding fed the poor little mite, he brought it all up again. He's hardly stopped crying since.'

'I'd better go up and see them.'

Fielding was still in bed, Harry crying pitifully in her curved arm. She looked tearfully at Cara. 'Did Nancy tell you? He'll never put on weight if he's sick every time I feed him. It's actually getting worse. He should have started on solids by now, but he can't even keep down breast milk. Fergus rang for the doctor and he's in the parlour keeping an eye out for him.' She looked down at the baby. 'He sounds so weary. He's probably more tired than we are.'

Cara sat on the bed. 'Would you like me to take him for a minute, luv?'

'If you wouldn't mind, my arm is aching badly.'

The baby felt terribly hot. His tiny face was as red as a beetroot as he continued to wail. 'If only they could find out what's wrong with him,' she said with a sigh.

'I worry all the time that he'll die,' Fielding said in a cracked voice. 'I long for him to stop crying, but when he does I'm terrified he's stopped because he's dead.'

'Juliette!' Fergus called. 'The doctor's just about to ring the bell. Least, I think he's a doctor 'cos he's carrying a bag, but he only looks about sixteen. He's probably just a locum,' he finished in a tone of faint disgust.

Cara passed the doctor as she went downstairs. He did indeed look awfully young, although much more than sixteen and refreshingly eager to help.

In the kitchen, the door was wide open, there was a tin bath at the foot of the steps, and Rover was in the course of being bathed by Nancy and Sean. Both were getting very wet in the process. The dog stood quite placidly, allowing himself to be scrubbed.

She told Nancy sharply to sit down, she'd take over. 'Today, you're supposed to just sit and watch.'

'We've nearly finished, pet. He just wants lifting out and

wrapping in this old towel. There's a nice meal waiting for him when we're done.'

Perhaps Rover had understood. He leapt out of the bath and raced around the kitchen, shaking himself and spraying everyone in sight. Kitty screamed and ran upstairs. Sean laughed and clapped his hands. Nancy managed to catch the dog in the towel and began to rub him vigorously. Cara grumbled it was a waste of time insisting that she rest.

Her mother arrived with Joey and Bernard in tow. 'What on earth's going on?' she asked, stepping over the bath.

'It seems we've got a dog, Mam.'

'His name's Rover,' Sean supplied.

'He's quite a nice-looking creature,' Mam said, and Cara was forced to agree that Rover looked more curly than mangy since he'd been washed. 'Where did you get those hats, boys?' Joey and Bernard wore red, white and blue knitted bobble hats.

'Grannie made them for us,' Joey said proudly – Bernard was too interested in watching Rover gulp down the food. 'She's made ones for Kitty and Sean too.'

'I've been knitting all week. I managed to sew the bobbles on last night,' Mam said breathlessly. 'How's Harry today?'

'Not so well. The doctor's with him right now. You're not to go up there, Mam, until he's gone.' Cara barred the exit from the kitchen when her mother made for the stairs. She was likely to give the doctor an earful, angrily demanding that they find out what was wrong with her grandson.

A few minutes later, the front door closed and Fergus came in, a baby's bottle in his hand. 'Is there any boiled water in the kettle, Nancy?' he asked.

'Yes, pet. Would you like me to heat it up again?'

'No, ta.' He half-filled the bottle with water from the kettle, then lit the gas underneath. 'I just want a little bit of hot to melt the sugar.'

'What's all this about, lad?' Mam demanded with a frown.

'The doctor thinks Harry might be allergic to something or he's got a blockage somewhere. We've got to give him nothing but sugared water for a few days. He's coming back to see us the day after tomorrow.'

'What on this earth does "allergic" mean?' Mam's frown

deepened. She nursed a deep distrust of doctors. 'I've never heard of the word before.'

'It means that something doesn't agree with you, Mam, probably the milk.' Fergus rolled his eyes at Cara in expectation of their mother's reaction.

'Since when did milk disagree with anyone?' Mam snorted. 'It's what makes babies thrive. That doctor needs his bumps feeling.'

'Well, Harry isn't thriving, is he? And Doctor Bennett's the first to suggest something positive, rather than just say he hasn't a clue what's wrong. If this works, we can try Harry with the orange juice Juliette gets from the clinic and a baby tonic.'

'Well, if you're sure, darlin',' Mam said doubtfully.

'I'm not sure, Mam. I'm not sure about anything, but Harry's really sick and me and Juliette are willing to try anything if it'll make him better.' Fergus left the kitchen on the verge of tears.

'Poor lad,' Mam sniffed, close to tears herself. 'I hope that doctor knows what he's up to. Not many of 'em do.'

The street party was due to begin at two o'clock. A row of tables of slightly different heights and a variety of widths wobbled precariously on the cobbles in the middle of the street. About twenty children ranging from aged two to thirteen were already seated on chairs as they waited, tongues hanging out, for the women to serve the food. It was Cara's job to supervise and make sure everyone got their fair share – Kitty would make a grab at everything in sight, whereas Sean would hang back and not eat a mouthful if he wasn't encouraged.

Nearly everyone had been putting little treats aside for this extra-special day: tins of Spam, biscuits and fruit, and evaporated milk to pour over jellies, jam, sweets and chocolate. Precious eggs had been used to make fairy and sponge cakes, used in turn to make trifles. There were jugs of custard, mountains of sandwiches and cream crackers spread with meat paste and Heinz sandwich spread.

Nancy had surprised everyone by producing a catering-sized tin of peaches that the Americans had brought years before. 'I'll write and tell Dexter we ate it on VE Day,' she'd said. 'He'll be thrilled.'

Dexter and Nelson were in Berlin with the triumphant American Army, but Eddie, brown-eyed, brown-haired Eddie with his bashful smile, had been killed within hours of the troops landing on French soil. Brenna had had a Mass said on his birthday ever since. Cara hadn't set eyes on Jack McGarry since the day Fielding and Fergus had got married.

The women emerged from their houses with the sandwiches and crackers, and the children fell upon them. Cara followed with a tray of lemonade in the cardboard cups that Eleanor had found in the attic when she was clearing out the house in Tigh Street. She and Hector were moving to a bungalow in Formby that overlooked the Mersey and also had a big garage where Hector would have more space to do his sculpture.

A group of men, fathers and elder brothers, lounged against the walls, supping beer from the Baker's Arms just around the corner and discussing the finer points of the war, winning it all over again, while the sun beat down, blessing their small part of the earth with its warmth and beauty, making the salty air tingle.

The sandwiches and crackers gone, bowls of trifle appeared, carefully shared out. Cara eyed it wistfully, hoping there'd be some left over, but doubting it very much.

Eleanor arrived. 'I didn't want to miss anything,' she said to Cara. 'It seemed wrong to do housework on VE Day, anyway. Hector's started a new sculpture – he's going to call it *Victory* – but he'll be along later. Where's your mother? D'you think she'd like a glass of wine? I've brought a couple of bottles with me.'

'Well, *I* would, and I'm sure Mam would, too. She's in the house.' As Eleanor was about to go inside, Cara called, 'Tell her if she can grab me some trifle, it'd be much appreciated.'

It was time for the cakes, which disappeared in a jiffy. Cara distributed more lemonade and told everyone they'd behaved very well. 'Now there's going to be games,' she said. The older children, teenagers enjoying a day off work, were organizing the games and, apart from helping to take the tables and chairs back to where they belonged, her own tasks were over and she could go indoors for a well-earned rest. When she did, all the trifle had gone.

Four o'clock and by now the sun had passed over the houses and half the street was in shadow. Some of the beer drinkers had fallen asleep where they lay, others still supped their pints for, against all the laws of licensing, the Baker's Arms had stayed open, reckoning that not many bobbies would be around to check on such a momentous day.

'After all, what the bloody hell did we fight for,' one man, who'd never been near a battlefield, asked loudly, 'if it weren't for the right to drink when and where we liked?'

Sean and Bernard were asleep on their grandmother's bed, while Kitty, who had the stamina of an ox, played football with Joey and a gang of lads twice her size.

At half past four, Tyrone Caffrey appeared, a fine figure of a man in his Merchant Navy uniform. His boat had docked at Harwich the day before and he'd hitchhiked home. 'I was determined to reach Liverpool if I possibly could,' he told his delighted mother. 'There's nowhere else on earth I'd sooner be today.'

After Brenna had finished kissing and petting her son, Eleanor jumped up and did the same, only slightly less effusively. Another wedding was on the cards and as soon as Sybil was demobbed and came home from India, she and Tyrone were getting married. They would live in Eleanor's house in Tigh Street.

Mam had given in to the inevitable, having learned from experience that it was no use trying to stop her children from doing what they wanted. If Tyrone were intent on marrying Sybil, then he would go ahead, no matter how much she protested.

It might have been Hector who had convinced Eleanor that wild young men didn't necessarily stay that way for ever, that with the years they could become quite tame. After all, Hector's face bore a scar that could only have been inflicted by a razor. Cara suspected he hadn't exactly been an angel in his youth spent in Glasgow.

The prospective mothers-in-law seemed quite happy with the situation, Tyrone looked more content than he'd done in years, Sybil had sent Cara some nice letters from Bombay implying she'd been forgiven for marrying her father and Cara was very much looking forward to another Caffrey wedding later in the year.

After a second glass of wine, she left the children with Mam and returned, a little unsteadily, to Parliament Terrace to see how Harry was getting on. The sun was cooler now, but there was still magic in the air and she could hear singing whichever way she turned.

She paused in front of the gap in the terrace where two houses had once stood until they'd been demolished by a bomb. The rubble had been cleared and thick planks of wood supported the properties on either side. Two people had been killed, but Cara hadn't recognized their names. People in the terrace kept very much to themselves. As soon as the war's over, she thought, then corrected herself, *now* that the war's over, I'll sell the house and buy one with a garden for the children to play in. I'll take Nancy with me, naturally, although she'll miss her little basement flat.

There was no sign of Nancy when she went in, but her father was in the throes of putting the kettle on and said she must have gone for a walk. 'Maybe to see the decorations in town.' If so, she must have taken Rover with her, as there was no sign of him either.

Dad had been terribly disappointed when he'd volunteered for war work. He'd been sent to work for the railways, which were desperately short of manpower. He maintained lines, repaired signals and hadn't set foot outside Lancashire in the two years since he'd joined up.

'I'm on the early shift this week, so I came to see how Harry was before going home,' he said. He still lived in Kirkby in the flat above the bank. 'I'm just making our Fergus and Fielding a cup of tea, they've hardly been out the bedroom since they got up this morning. Not much of a way to spend VE day, is it, luv?'

Cara shook her head. 'That's why I came, to see Harry. I'll just pop upstairs a minute.'

Harry lay in his cot and Fielding and Fergus were sitting on the bed watching. The baby's face, so red that morning, was now as white as snow. At first, a horrified Cara thought that he'd passed away, but could just discern the slight movement of the sheet when he breathed in and out.

When she saw Cara, Fielding came out on to the landing, closing the door quietly behind her. 'The doctor's been again,' she whispered. 'He said he couldn't get Harry out of his mind and tomorrow, first thing, he's going to ring Great Ormond Street Hospital in London to ask if they'll take him – it's a special hospital for children, and if they can't find out what's wrong, then no one can.'

'That's marvellous news, luv!'

'Isn't it?' Fielding beamed. 'He said our doctor's an old stick-in-the-mud and he'll probably raise objections, but we're not to take any notice. Anyway, Harry's been peacefully asleep for hours. I think it's the longest sleep he's ever had.'

'Why don't you come round to Shaw Street later?' Cara suggested. 'I know you don't want to leave Harry, but you can come first, then go home and relieve Fergus. Our Tyrone's home, Eleanor's there and Hector's due any minute.'

'No thanks, Cara, I'd sooner stay with Fergus and I'm sure he'll feel the same. We might go downstairs and have something proper to eat in a while, but that's as far as it goes.'

'Ok, Fielding. I'll see you later.' Cara was about to leave when Fielding grabbed her arm.

'Will you do me a favour? Now the war's over, d'you think you could start calling me by my proper name? It's all right for you, but I'm fed up being Fielding to all and sundry.'

Cara kissed her friend on both cheeks. 'OK – Juliette!'

Dad could be heard coming with the tea. 'You're to call her Juliette from now on,' Cara told him when he arrived. Fielding – Juliette – took the tray and returned to the bedroom, and Cara and her father went downstairs together. He'd made them both a drink, he said.

'Are you coming back to Shaw Street with us?' she asked when they were seated at the big table where she'd sat so many times before, although it felt strange without Nancy being present.

'No, luv. I don't think so.'

She thought he looked rather uncomfortable. 'Why not? Bernard's your son, don't you want to see him?'

'Of course, I do.' He squirmed. 'It's just that your mam . . .'

'What about Mam?' He seemed stuck for words.

'Well, I think she wants me to come back, keeps dropping hints, like.' He ran his finger around the collar of his shirt, as if he found it too tight. His time with the railways hadn't done him much good. He looked much older and greyer these days. 'The thing is, luv, I don't want to go back. I'm fond of your mam, I always will be, but I seem to have fallen out of love with her. I can't think why, but I have.'

'She desperately wants you back, Dad,' Cara said soberly. Mam had always hoped it would happen one day. 'Have you heard from Lizzie Phelan lately?'

'Not for a while.' He refused to meet her eyes. 'I wouldn't be surprised if I never heard from her again. Lizzie only sees the big picture: she has no time for the little ones. She's probably forgotten all about me and Bernard.'

'What's going to happen to Bernard?'

'Well, I'd sooner he was with your mam than anyone else on earth, Lizzie included.' He managed a smile. 'Once I've done with the railways, I shall make me way to London. There'll be a big election shortly and Churchill's going to get the surprise of his life when he finds himself chucked out. I've belonged to the Labour Party since I was a young man and I'd like to play a part right at the heart of things – if they'll let me.'

People walked past the house, dragging a stick against the railings and singing, 'When the lights go on again, all over the world . . .'

'When I was little,' Cara mused, 'I used to feel dead lucky I had a mam and dad like you two. Oh, I knew you used to row occasionally, least Mam did, but the house was always full of love and I felt safe there. And it was cosy and snug, not like some other people's houses. I'd imagined it always staying like that.' She sniffed and suppressed a sob. 'I can't stand you and Mam being separated.'

'Do you think I should go back to her, luv?' He looked at her keenly.

'No, of course not.' She violently shook her head. 'You must do as you wish, Dad. *I* did when I came back from Malta. I don't think we should run our lives to suit other people. I'd do it for the children,' she added quickly, 'but that's all.' She put the cup back in the saucer, the tea had gone cold. 'I'd better run. I told Mam I'd only be a few minutes and she'll be worried there's something wrong with Harry if I take too long.'

Dad reluctantly pushed himself to his feet. 'I'd better come with you. I should go and see Bernard, any road, today of all days. I worry that one of these times your Mam'll ask straight out if I'll come back and I'll just have to tell her no.'

Hector had just arrived in Shaw Street bringing the most remarkable news: Anthony had telephoned from America. He'd lived in Canada during the war and had returned to Gaudulet College for some reason and found dozens of letters waiting for him, all from Liverpool and several years old.

'Did he say why he never wrote to his family?' Eleanor demanded angrily, at the same time looking pleased as well as astonished that her long-lost son had at last been in touch.

'No, El, and I didn't ask him either,' Hector said gruffly. 'He's going to ring again tomorrow and you can ask him anything you like.'

'Could he hear you? Remember I told you he's deaf.'

'Well, he seemed to understand when I said you were at a party. Perhaps he's got a hearing aid. I think they can make them very small these days.' Hector clamped his mouth shut and looked unprepared to open it again. He and Eleanor got on exceptionally well and appeared to love each other very much, but he was a most taciturn individual.

'Mam, Dad's outside,' Cara said. 'He's giving Bernard a piggy-back.'

'Is he? Oh, is he now?' Her mother patted her hair and straightened her frock. 'I'll go and have a word with him.' She glanced in the mirror on her way out.

Tyrone invited Hector for a drink and they both left, leaving Eleanor and Cara alone.

'Anthony always said he'd marry you when he grew up,' Eleanor remarked.

Cara was about to shriek with laughter, but realized just in time that it would look rude. 'Once Tyrone and Sybil are wed,' she said, 'I think there'll have been enough marriages between the Caffreys and the Allardyces, don't you?' Had Eleanor forgotten she had married her ex-husband, Anthony's father?

'Probably. Anyway, I suppose Anthony could have a wife and family by now. If only Hector had asked him more questions!'

'He's phoning again tomorrow.'

'I shall make a list. Wouldn't it be lovely if he could come to Sybil's wedding?' Eleanor's face softened. 'It sounds awful, but I'd far prefer it if it had been Jonathan who'd phoned out of the blue. Sometimes, I wonder if it was all a big mistake or that I dreamt it. I'm still not used to him being gone.'

'I used to feel the same about Kit, but I've managed to accept the fact that I'll never see him again, although it took a long time.' She visualized Kit's body with his lovely face blown away.

'You're a beautiful girl, Cara,' Eleanor said softly. 'I really hope that one day you fall in love again and get married.'

'I don't think that's very likely.' She was twenty-five, a widow with two children: falling in love was something she never thought about.

'If I can do it, Cara, then so can you. Oh, listen! There's music outside — it sounds like a harmonium.'

'They're playing "Knees Up Mother Brown". Shall we go and see what's happening?'

Eleanor made a face. 'We'll go and see, but I've no intention of doing "Knees Up, Mother Brown", not in these shoes and this skirt.'

The night wore on. The sun disappeared altogether and dusk fell on the narrow streets. People went indoors and turned on the lights, upstairs and down, so that every window was illuminated, a sight so unusual that everyone just stopped and stared in wonder. The blackout had been one of the hardest things for civilians over the last six years.

The mood became quieter and the harmonium player adjusted his music to the more sombre atmosphere. The war was over and for most it would become just a memory. For others, it meant a lifetime of sorrow as they remembered the loved ones they had lost: the husbands and sons who'd died overseas, the men, women and children killed in the blitz. Eleanor's son, Tyrone's wife and child, and Cara's lover were just a few casualties of the brutal conflict.

Cara sat on the step, watching her mother and father dance together: 'Who's Taking You Home Tonight', a slow dreamy waltz. She'd like to bet Mam had asked Dad up and he hadn't liked to refuse. Poor Mam! She was wasting her time trying to get him back. One of these days the penny would drop and she'd be devastated.

The smaller children had gone to bed. Kitty, the youngest left and a bundle of energy, was playing hopscotch on the pavement. Joey clung to his dad; Tyrone had to return to Harwich in the morning. Joey would stay with Mam when Tyrone married Sybil. The lad had already had two mothers and it didn't seem right to pass him on to a third. His dad would only be a few minutes away in Tigh Street.

A young man in Air Force uniform had entered the street. Her heart turned over because he looked so much like Kit, the same height, the same build, the same age as Kit would have been now. He even had a single stripe on his sleeve, just like Kit.

The stranger was speaking to a woman sitting on the opposite step and she nodded in Cara's direction. Cara stood as he came towards her, removing his hat, smiling. Close up, he was nothing like Kit, but she still felt as if she were seeing a ghost.

'Hello,' he said.

'Hello,' she stammered.

'You don't remember me, do you?'

'No.' Perhaps they'd met in Malta.

'That's not surprising because I don't remember you, at least not what you look like, although we were very close for a while.' His eyes danced, as if he were enjoying her confusion.

'Would you mind putting me out of me misery and telling me who you are?' Cara said tartly, although her own eyes were dancing at the same time. Like Kit, he wasn't the least bit handsome, but he had an appealing manner and a charming smile.

'My name's Charlie Green and you're Cara Caffrey. I gave you a lift home from Lime Street Station once on me motorbike.'

'I remember now! The war hadn't long started. And you actually remembered me name and where I lived after all this time?'

'Never forgot 'em,' he said promptly. 'I was always curious to know what you looked like, the first girl ever to put her arms around me.'

'I bet I wasn't the last.'

'Well, no,' he conceded with a grin, 'but you're the best-looking by a mile. The woman I just spoke to, she said your name isn't Caffrey any more, that you're a widow with two kids.'

'That's true, and I don't live in Shaw Street any more, either, but me mam does and that's why I'm here.'

'So, I was lucky to find you.' He sounded as if he really meant it.

'Seems like it.' She felt pleased that he had.

He held out his arms. 'Would you like to dance, Cara?'

'Why not?'

In Parliament Terrace, Juliette and Fergus were in the kitchen having a snack, the door wide open so they could hear Harry if he cried. Their hearts ached with love and worry for their child who'd been sleeping peacefully for hours.

'I'll go to London with him,' Juliette said.

'Not on your own, you won't,' Fergus said firmly. 'I'm coming with you. Don't forget you're four months pregnant.'

'As if I would! But what about your job?'

'Bugger me job. It'll be coming to an end soon, any road. No one's going to want barrage balloons in peacetime.'

406

Their eyes met and Juliette said huskily, 'I do love you, Fergus Caffrey. I wonder where Nancy is? She's been gone an awful long while.'

'Enjoying herself somewhere, I bet. Perhaps she's gone to the party in Shaw Street and she's having a dead good time.'

'I hope so.' Juliette looked around her uneasily. 'The house doesn't feel the same without Nancy in it. And where's that dog, Rover? I thought he'd come to live here.'

'Perhaps he wasn't a stray, after all, and he's gone back home.'

Nancy hadn't set foot out of the house all day. She'd gone to bed mid-afternoon without saying a word to a soul. People would only worry if she told them how tired she felt, so tired that her bones had difficulty supporting her heavy body. All she wanted to do was collapse. She'd been looking forward to VE Day for so long and was disappointed that she'd taken no part in it, but there was always another day even if it wouldn't be quite like this one.

Rover slept at her feet. Perhaps he was tired too, as he'd hardly moved for ages. She liked having the dog for company, keeping her feet nice and warm, reminding her he was there with a little snore now'n again.

She wondered how the children were getting on. Nancy looked upon them all as her children: Eleanor and Brenna, Cara and Sybil, Kitty and Sean, and all the other people she'd taken under her wing since she'd come to live in Parliament Terrace when she was little more than a child herself, including the lovely young Americans who'd made themselves so much at home.

One thing was for sure, they'd be living in a better world as from now, a world where there'd be no more hunger, no more poverty, where people would come together in friendship, and humanity would flower. The war that had just ended must surely have taught politicians a lesson, whatever country they came from, that women didn't bear sons just to be used as cannon fodder and it was time they gave peace a chance.

By God, she was tired! Even though she'd been sleeping for hours, she still felt bone weary and doubted if she could pick herself up off the bed if the house was on fire. Yet at the same time, there was another body, an inner one, that felt as light as a feather, and this other body was floating along a long, dark tunnel in the direction of a bright golden light. A hand beckoned, a voice said, very gently, 'Come,' and she knew when she reached the light that she would never be tired again and all she would feel was joy.

Seconds later, at the foot of the bed, Rover raised his head and began to howl.

Far away, on another continent, Sybil Allardyce couldn't sleep. She tossed and turned in the bed, the sheets becoming knots as she kicked them around, pulled them this way and that, threw them off when it got too hot, pulled them back on when she felt cold. She had been in India, in Bombay, had slept in this very bed for three long years and now she couldn't wait to get home to Liverpool. It was impatience, a longing to be gone, that was making her so restless.

In a few weeks she would be demobbed – she hoped and prayed it wouldn't be months – and she would marry Tyrone Caffrey and live in Mummy's old house in Tigh Street. Mummy had actually married the loathsome thug and was now Mrs Hector Ingram. Sybil supposed she should start thinking of him in more respectful terms, as they would soon be seeing a lot of each other. Mummy had even suggested he give her away at the wedding. 'After all, darling, he's now your stepfather,' she'd written.

'That's fine with me,' Sybil had replied. So long as the thug gave her away to Tyrone, she really didn't care.

'I'd better get going, luv,' Colm said. 'I'm on the early shift this week and I'll have to be up before the sun rises in the morning.'

Brenna gave him a warm smile. 'Stay the night, darlin'. There's plenty of room.'

'No, there isn't, Bren. Our Tyrone's home.'

'He won't mind sleeping in the parlour for once.' Sleep with me, she wanted to say, wanted to scream. Make love to me in our old bed and let me lie in your arms all night long. But Colm just shook his head.

'That wouldn't be fair on Tyrone, Bren. He's got to find his way back to Harwich tomorrow. And you've got Kitty and Sean an' all: it'd be daft to wake them up and take them back to Parliament Terrace. No, I'll catch the train to Kirkby. I'll see you again sometime, luv. I'm not sure when it'll be.'

Brenna watched him trudge away, wanting to run and throw her arms around him, fetch him back, tell how much she loved him, always had, always would. 'We were made for each other,' she would remind him. 'You used to say that all the time, Colm, darlin'. Why are we living separately when we could live together, happily, for the rest of our lives? You'll come back one day,' she informed the retreating figure. 'Katie MacBride told me you would and everything else she said that day came true.'

Fergus went downstairs to find out why Rover was howling. Sybil fell asleep. Brenna knelt beside the bed and prayed for everyone she knew, particularly Colm. Eleanor and Hector strolled home from the party, arm in arm, thinking about their dead children, marvelling at the fact they'd found each other and that such good could come out of such bad.

Colm sat on the train and wondered if it was all that wise to go to London, a place he'd never been before, where he didn't know a soul and had nowhere to live, just so he could take part in an election, even if it would be the election of the century, breaking all records. Were politics all *that* important, when he could live in the house his brother had won in a card game with his son and the woman he'd used to think he would love for ever? He recalled Brenna's excited face the day they'd seen the house for the first time a quarter of a century ago. 'It's like a palace,' she'd said. He wondered what Lizzie would have thought about the rundown house – and living in that ghastly cellar with a baby for months on end. He'd like to bet she wouldn't have stuck it out with the same fortitude as Brenna.

He stared out of the window, too preoccupied to notice that the street lights and house lights were back on after nigh-on six years, that he passed two bonfires, that the stations the train stopped at were visible again. By the time the train arrived at Kirkby, he still felt confused.

And Cara, she danced with Charlie Green, danced until her feet hurt, until he had to take off his jacket, even though it was nearly midnight and the air had turned cold. They danced under the stars that dazzled in the sky, along with half a dozen other couples unwilling to let the day end, determined to dance the night away.

The harmonium player was still there, strolling up and down the pavement, lulling to sleep the people tucked inside their houses.

'What will happen tomorrow, Cara?' whispered Charlie Green.

'Who knows?' Cara threw back her head and laughed. Tonight, she felt as if her old life had ended and a new one had begun, that she'd shed a heavy cloak that had been weighing her down for years, and now she felt lighter, younger, happier than she'd been in a long while. She vaguely remembered that she had two children, but had no idea where they were, although she knew they were safe. 'Any road, I just heard a clock strike midnight: it's no longer tomorrow, but today.'

'So, Cara, what will happen today?'

'We'll just have to see, Charlie.' She laughed again. 'We'll just have to see.'